Chapter 1

She sat there with tears drying slowly on her tired, forlorn face; little crystals tugging on the skin, pulling it tight around her eyes. She looked ten years older than the ten years older Sam had usually told her she looked. How had it come to this? Why was she sitting there answering these stupid questions? Surrounded by a boundary of crunched-up, soggy, soiled tissues, her greying roots providing an inch-long reservoir leading to her parted brown hair that semi-resembled her natural colour from at least thirty years ago.

Joan could have been one of the ladies chosen to be made-over by the twisted, extra-camp, failed fashion designer who now makes his living preying on needy, weak-minded victims – his duty: to make them feel supremely bad about themselves whilst waltzing around like the emperor and guardian of all things desirable and chic. He invades their home and destroys their wardrobe, looking down his nose at all they hold dear, systematically revealing all its hidden contents, big knickers an' all – no secrets can remain; he will and has to judge them all. The shame of it! Then he'll send them off like a man to his mother-in-law's to see some ultra-beautiful beauticians. These mechanics in white, crisply pressed statutory uniforms – white but made up a brown-orange colour, or black but made up a brown-orange colour, or naturally brown-orange with bright-red lips and black mascara, reeking of perfume – they methodically strip the lady apart, like an old Ford car right down to its bare chassis, before rebuilding it to look like a brand-new hot rod with go-faster stripes on its sides.

This is when he ramps up the embarrassment, and it reaches its ultimate crescendo as a full-length mirror is produced to wishy-washy, plastic piano music, whilst the camera zooms in on the face of the newly bedazzled beauty. As she hyperventilates at her new-found radiance, through clever computer wizardry a photo of the former disgusting wreck of a woman is flashed up on screen as a comparison for the viewers at home, drinking cola and eating iced buns with tears in their eyes as they feast upon the utter ghastliness of the before woman and wonder in awe at the amazing swan now standing before the mirror.

Fat men all around the world agree in unison: 'I'd give her one.' The lucky girl. Here she now stands, rigid yet quivering like a cold Jack Russell, all decked out in a brand-new, sparkling outfit, all ready to go to a fancy West End restaurant or the opera or a musical: hair tugged and pulled, like the rigging on a beautiful yacht, massive pants compressing her belly and bum, boobs hoisted up and eyebrows plucked, beard removed and moustache dyed, toenails chiselled and legs sanded.

With that one new outfit the victim is ready to be thrust amongst her friends and the baying crowd. The token emotional mother figure, who is weeping and tugging on a snotty, lipstick-stained hanky, comforted by the super-bitch failed fashion designer and all his minions. The beauticians, tottering on high heels and weighed down with fake tan, plastic boobs, blood-red lips like trouts, hooped golden earrings big enough to get around your wrist and butterfly eyelashes fluttering in the cheap-perfumed breeze…

'Look what we have created: the perfect polished turd.'

Joan could remember when she was young, playing in the garden with her little sister – those hazy, Instamatic days when they filled glass bottles with water from the garden hose and stuffed in petals from her dad's favourite rose bushes to make perfume for their mummy. Her dress was light and billowed softly in the warm summer effluvium, pollen wafted on the air and bumblebees staggered from stem to stem. Her scuffed blue sandals, a size too small, rubbed her feet slightly where she had been running around all day, getting hot and thirsty in the long summer's light. Her little ankle socks were smudged slightly blue on the toes and slightly red where they'd rubbed the skin away on her Achilles.

Even now, she could almost hear her mummy's musical voice calling to her and her sister. They would come and get fresh glasses of homemade lemonade, cooled with stabbed chunks of ice clunking around in the vessels, grasped by grubby, eager, clammy hands. Palms were thrilled frozen by the chill. The drinks always tasted better drunk quickly, until their teeth hurt and brain ached and top lip glimmered with the hastily supped beverage, leaving a high-water mark or, as they called it, a wet moustache or snail trail. This was usually removed by dragging the back of the hand across the face. Joan would wiggle excitedly, needing a wee but too absorbed in playtime to go.

'Could I use the toilet?' she said, mentally torn between with then and now.

'Please, we need your help. We understand this must be difficult for you, but we need you to help us understand what happened. We're talking about a dead person here. We understand someone has broken into your house. We just need to know what happened next. Please help us to help you. Was it an accident? Was it self-defence? Say it was self-defence and we can work straightaway on getting you out of here. Did he try to hurt you? Please talk to us.'

The police knew they weren't looking at a typical criminal – a murderer. They had seen people like Joan kill before, but equally, people like her got locked away simply because they couldn't defend themselves, out of shock and being unable to comprehend what had happened. At least one of the policewomen didn't want that to happen here. They needed to ascertain the exact details of the evening's occurrence. Perhaps it was a domestic gone wrong, and Joan was the victim here. Only she wasn't, not in the eyes of the law. Was she a murderer? The police couldn't be sure.

The questions just flowed through one ear, barely registering with the other ear on the way out of Joan's head. The policewomen might as well have been quacking like a duck.

'Listen, Joan, you need to cooperate here. We don't know what sort of shit has gone down. You're looking at a seriously long time in prison if you don't start coming up with some answers – you need to cooperate. Can you hear me?'

Joan, Joan, what's going on in your head? You're thick, stupid, useless... Sam's voice spoke to her from the deepest recesses of her mind.

'I'm your sister, Joan,' Janet said now. 'You can trust me...'

The words flowed over Joan but meant nothing. How many times in her life had she been told to trust someone? They always let her down. Now she automatically thought people were untrustworthy as soon as they said 'Trust me'.

The other policewoman simply stared, absorbing her meal like a praying mantis. Patiently waiting for the right moment to strike. She didn't look especially hard or menacing or even unkind, and yet you could imagine her sitting on a train just giving off a vibe, with her long legs crossed and her bag next to her whilst she read a book... She wouldn't intentionally be horrible, and yet there she'd be, taking up the space of three seats, on a busy train just about to get busier when it arrived at the next station. If you wanted her to move, you'd need to ask her or physically move her. You could say she was stubborn, confrontational and single-minded. If you were carrying a baby, or were elderly or pregnant or even on crutches, she wouldn't glance at you, as she'd be totally engrossed in her book. But if somehow you managed to drag her away from her distraction, she'd fix you with a straight-faced stare. She looked intelligent, powerful to a woman and intimidating to a man. Like one of those women who give off an energy saying *don't approach me* – waspish. As a young girl at the school disco she wasn't the type that the boys would approach for a dance. Not that anyone could imagine her ever dancing or being into boys. Perhaps she had been but had been hurt. As an adult maybe, by a Special Forces, fireman, lawyer-type man.

Maybe people should pity her. But that could be one of her strengths: as soon as you pitied her, you let her in – she had won and you were hers. Just a little smile of sympathy at the made-up notion that she might have been unpopular at school and then she'd go on the offensive. That was how she worked. Somehow she lured you into a false sense of security and then you were attacked and devoured by the praying mantis.

She wore a silver brooch with a couple of purple gems, and detective-like clothes: a nondescript skirt, a jacket that neither matched nor clashed with any other items. Her hair was like a flashback to the strange styles Princess Diana would wear. *Bless her,* Joan thought, looking at DCI Burns She could see her sister looked up to her superior, admired her even. Then the woman attacked…

'We've got one dead man, one critically injured and some guy in a kilt claiming responsibility for the lot, but you are the one with blood on your hands.'

'Dad wouldn't have let this happen,' Joan said.

'Dad wouldn't have let what happen? Please tell me what you're thinking. I'm not an expert at mind-reading,' said the policewoman.

'Dad was a good man. He had kind hands; I could look at his hands all day. He wasn't even angry at us for taking the petals off his roses. He never got angry – well, at least not with me.' Joan glanced briefly at her sister. 'Sometimes just thinking of his hands makes me cry.'

'Jesus fucking Christ, Joan, get a fucking grip. We aren't pissing about here... For fuck's sake, did you kill your Sam and try to kill your son? How the hell did it happen?' her sister screamed, totally losing control of herself and the situation.

Joan's eyes glazed over and she again thought back to being a little girl.

She remembered sitting in the back of the car, trying to sleep. She was always tired. She wasn't eating properly and everyone was too sensitive to force her. Life had been turned upside down without Mum at home. It must have been like this for all kids who lost a parent young. Only Joan's mum wasn't dead; she was still alive but in hospital fighting cancer.

'The big C,' her nosy neighbours called it. Joan remembered overhearing them gossip once about her mum whilst she worked a

Saturday shift at Aunt Nellie's bakery. She could still see the pink icing on the iced buns and smell the delicious fragrance of baked dough; she could almost taste it now – her tummy rumbled; she felt hungry.

It was dark by the time they headed home. Dad put Joan in the back of the car, hoping she'd sleep on the way. He thought she was already asleep by the time he started crying. Joan curled up on the back seat, the cold, hard black leather against her face. She scraped her fingernail against the dust, fluff and biscuit crumbs in a bit of detailing on the fabric. This was before booster seats for kids and wearing seatbelts in the back. Every corner meant a little slide around. Sometimes you'd feel the top of your head and neck retract toward your shoulders as you were compressed against the door as your body weight was flipped upside down; other times your weight shifted to your feet and momentarily you were standing up lying down. Roundabouts were the best.

Joan could just about see her father wiping his eyes in the rear-view mirror. She listened to him weep as they drove back towards Aunt Nellie's house to pick up Joan's little sister. Dad was barely coping. He might have told Mum that everything was okay, but Joan didn't believe that. He was scared. She'd never seen or heard him cry before. He was scared Mum was going to die. He quietly sobbed as the windscreen wipers batted away the rain. Joan watched a tear run down his cheek and compared it to the rain on the window being pushed along by the momentum of the car. She wanted to cuddle

Mum; she didn't want to leave her at the hospital. Why couldn't they stay with her and leave Joan's sister with Aunt Nellie until Mum got better?

'Why are you crying, Daddy? Is it 'cos Mummy isn't well?'

He seemed to have forgotten she was there.

'I'm not crying, darling. I just had something in my eye, that's all. Don't worry, sweetheart. I thought you were asleep... You should try to get some rest, you know. It's been a long day for us both and you have school tomorrow.'

'But Dad, I don't want to go to school. I want to stay with you and I want to see Mummy.'

'Come on, darling, try to get some sleep.'

'But Daaaad...'

'Now listen. You have to go to school. You can see Mummy again at the weekend. Now be good and get some sleep. You need to rest and I need to concentrate on driving. Please be good.' His voice sounded angry but not like usual, more like he was asking a question.

'I'm not silly, Daddy. I know you were crying.'

'Please be quiet now and go to sleep, honey bear. I just had something in my eye. I know you're very clever, but please go to sleep and let me think...'

'Daddy, is Mummy going to die?'

'GO TO SLEEP!' he shouted then. He was angry and he made Joan jump. She wanted Mummy.

They both cried then, until Joan's chest shuddered. She did three little intakes and one massive breath out. A shuddering sigh, before falling asleep.

As they traipsed alongside the fields the way they sometimes walked to school, avoiding the main road, Joan and Janet could make out a figure sitting alone up ahead. As they got closer Joan recognised the silhouette, the pale-blue windproof jacket with a white zip and the flat cap. He was staring across the freshly ploughed fields into nothingness, battered by the wind.

'Come on,' Joan said to her sister. 'There's Dad.'

They broke into a trot. *Why is he sitting alone up here?* Joan thought. It was definitely her dad. He must have decided to head off for a walk, perhaps after an argument with Mummy on the phone. That seemed unlikely; they never seemed to row. Maybe it was work or perhaps West Ham had lost. Perhaps he was simply stretching his legs. Joan couldn't help but feel protective and worried about him. She didn't like seeing him alone and miles from anyone or anywhere. Not out here. Joan's childlike dependency and future parental protectiveness were meeting at a crossroads.

He looked strangely at Joan and her sister before flicking the briefest of smiles. 'What on earth are you doing out here?' Dad said.

'Is this a coincidence, Dad?' Janet said.

'I'm just having a sit down. Thought I'd get some fresh air, like,' he said. 'It is a coincidence seeing you, my dears.' He put an arm around both of them.

Joan could feel the wind stirring up a pool of water in her eyes as she noticed a tear roll down her dad's cheek. His nose had a little dew drop as well. *He must be cold,* she thought. He took off his cap and flattened his hair, and somehow when he replaced his hat it was gone. Magic. Joan would have just sniffed if she were him.

Joan thought he looked so handsome when he smiled and she loved his smell. He wrapped his big arms around them, pulling them tight, and said he'd take them to Aunt Nellie's whilst he went to get Mummy.

Joan thought perhaps he was emotional because he was so happy to be bringing Mummy home and that life would be getting back to normal. No more takeaways or terrible Dad cooking or reheated meals from Aunt Nellie, she thought. Maybe she'd still have to help out with her sister now and again, Joan surmised. She had got quite good at a few meals, tidying and doing lots of hairstyles, and she didn't mind helping with the homework. But she was more than happy to hand the role of mother of the house back to Mummy.

She had no idea she'd never see her parents again.

Both Joan's parents died in a car crash on the way home from hospital. There were no other cars involved, no obvious mechanical failure. The car was totally trashed: they left the motorway and careered up a grassy bank, before the car flipped over several times and landed in a wooded field some four hundred metres from where it left the motorway. If the initial crash and spins hadn't killed Joan's parents then the fire that engulfed the wreckage and them shortly after they'd stopped moving surely finished them off. The sodden cows smelt barbecued humans that evening in a strange twist of fate.

The crash left Joan and her sister to be brought up by Aunt Nellie. She was a kind lady who didn't have any children of her own. She was Joan's mum's sister – slightly older, shorter and cuddly, with white hair like cotton wool, rosy cheeks and glassy blue eyes. She worked in the local baker's in the high street, close to where Joan's parents had lived and to their schools. Aunt Nellie was comfortable supporting herself, but the unexpected arrival of two extra mouths to feed caused pressure. She had little option but to use the paltry proceeds from the girls' family home, which still had a fair-sized mortgage attached; there was certainly no will or massive insurance windfall, and the years of hospital treatment had drained the coffers.

From then on after work most of Nellie's time was taken up sorting the estate or inheritance, worrying about the future and looking after Joan's sister Janet, who was just that bit younger.

The difference between coping with Joan the teenager, just coming to terms with her hormones and becoming a grown-up and the quest to become a lady, and dealing with Janet the little girl becoming a big girl, with uncontrollable mood swings, psychotic hormones, blobs, boobs, monthly cycles, spots and boys and more mood swings and a few more boys, filled Nellie with dread, especially as she remembered only just surviving as a child herself.

Janet needed and craved more support and really went into shock when it all happened. She dramatically stopped talking or eating for a week. Joan thought she was going to starve herself to death too. When she finally came out of her room, she was forever looking at the family photos and crying and going through their mum's and dad's clothes. She had a complete meltdown when Aunt Nellie bagged them up to take to the charity shop.

'What on earth do you think you're doing? How could you? I hate you! Leave their stuff alone.'

She didn't speak for another week, and when she did she was really rude to Aunt Nellie and said some words even Joan didn't know the meaning of. She managed to take a shawl of their mum's and a silver brooch of a butterfly with little green jewels encrusted on its wings. Sometimes Joan would see her sister sitting on her bed and crying, just inhaling the essence of their mum from the shawl. Another time, later, Joan remembered her sister sobbing that the shawl had lost their mum's smell. She also kept one of Dad's caps and would sometimes touch the greasy forehead mark on the brow, as if rubbing his head.

On occasion Joan would hear Janet crying in her room, asking the same question that Joan had asked a hundred times before: 'Why?' She never stopped wanting to know and would ask anyone and everyone. When no one could give her an answer, she would inevitably break down, and all over again Joan would hear her sobbing into her pillow, 'Why?'

Of the pair of them, even before the loss of their parents, Janet was the most demanding and difficult and fiery tempered, and their deaths added needy to her personality traits. Undeniably, she took the loss of both parents terribly, and hardly speaking for a year didn't help. She started being vicious and lashing out at school, and this was difficult for Aunt Nellie to deal with, especially as she had had no experience of kids previously and was the least aggressive lady you could ever meet. She was a bit like a lady Father Christmas.

In the end they went to the doctor's, and finally Nellie got Janet some happy pills. All the while, Joan simply muddled on. But a big hole had formed in her heart and she knew it would never mend. She dreamt of her mummy and daddy often. Sometimes she was desperate to go to sleep so she could be with them. She wasn't a big believer in the afterlife. Not now anyway. She often imagined what they would think if she got a good report at school. She considered them watching her when she got angry and said rude words to her sister (which wasn't very often; normally, Janet was angry and shouting at her). She often looked for them in crowded places. She remembered seeing a family waiting for a girl at the Liverpool Street train station once. She watched as the parents followed the girl's every step as she walked along the platform, a grin etched on their faces with an undercurrent of grimace as emotions threatened to overwhelm. She imagined they were her parents and she smiled desperately, empathising. The hole in her heart ached and got a little bigger.

Chapter 2

Joan, Janet and Aunt Nellie sat at the breakfast table – the girls all dressed and ready for school and Aunt Nellie ready for work – idly chitchatting, chewing the cud and passing the time. They all got ready to leave at the same time each day. Joan was eating a slice of toast cooked perfectly under the grill and watching, in a daze, as the butter slowly dripped off the slightly scorched edges.

It was autumn but still warm, and light poured through the kitchen window, illuminating the table and giving the room a bright and sharp focus, even if Joan was still half-asleep. There were very few smells as perfect as the smell of Aunt Nellie's toast. It was a fragrance worth bottling. Janet was chatting away with Aunt Nellie about needing a new bra or something, whilst Joan daydreamed about what lessons she had at school that day. First lesson was English. That was good, Joan thought, more so than the mathematics lesson scheduled after for which she had really struggled to do her homework, although she knew she had a preparation test coming up for her O levels.

Generally, Joan liked school. It was a good distraction and gave her a familiar and comfortable routine. When her parents died and life was turned upside down, school had remained a constant. The same people were always there: the ones she was friends with before, some of whom were slightly awkward and unsure of what to say to her, which she grew to appreciate; and, surprisingly, some of the ones she wasn't so keen on before who had become friends with her in the aftermath. She didn't know whether that was because they felt sorry for her or had been through something similar, and she didn't really care – it would never bring her parents back. She supposed in reality most people were genuinely sorry for Joan and her sister and wouldn't want to go through the same thing.

She also found it quite funny that for a while she was something of a celebrity. Wherever she went people seemed to know who she was and what had happened to her parents. Some kids would whisper in corners and blush, or not want to make eye contact with her. Sometimes she pondered whether what she was experiencing was what those related to terrible people – murderers, rapists and mad dictators – went through. What did people think of Hitler's parents? she wondered.

'English first!' Joan exclaimed.

'What's that?' said Aunt Nellie.

'I've got English first, and I've got to pay for the school trip, and today's the last day, and if I don't pay I won't be able to go, and it's a Shakespeare production, *A Midsummer Night's Dream*, and it's really important for my exam preparation and… and… and… everyone else is going and I've not paid and Mr Hothouse –'

'Calm down, dear,' Aunt Nellie interrupted. 'I'm sure it won't be the end of the world if you pay tomorrow.'

'The trip's tomorrow!' Joan exclaimed, getting worked up.

'How come you're only telling me now?' Aunt Nellie queried, resignation in her tone. It was her fault somehow, she just didn't know how yet.

Janet tutted and murmured, 'Yeah, cuckoo,' as if to suggest that Joan was stupid.

Joan fired her an angry frown across the table, and in retaliation she shoved the arm Janet was leaning on while she ate a big spoonful of milky cornflakes. Joan's push and her sister's attempt at a parry sent the spoonful of soggy cereal speeding towards Joan's face. She recoiled through natural instinct, but somehow managed to pull the tablecloth with her. Two cups spun, spraying a torrent of tea across the table and drenching the remaining slices of perfectly prepared toasted poppy-seed bloomer that had been patiently waiting for their massage with butter and raspberry jam. The sugar pot was witness to a tiny avalanche as its contents sprawled out across the blue-and-yellow-chequered vinyl tablecloth. The table was a disaster area and Joan was covered. Janet laughed, Joan went to smack her arm again and Aunt Nellie shouted:

'Girls, please!'

Aunt Nellie said she didn't have the money for the trip at home but could get it from work, and Joan would have to run to school from there – but first she'd need to change out of her wet clothes so she didn't go to school smelling of old milk.

Joan ran down the corridor, her feet squeaking and clapping. The echoes reverberated off the pastel-painted walls, interspersed by her panting. She held her bag close to her chest, trying to keep everything in order. She couldn't believe she was late – she was never late, and especially not for English lessons; it was very unlike her. Sprinting along the corridor, she suddenly became aware that the bra she'd put on in haste didn't fit very well at all and was, in all probability, one of her sister's… her younger sister's. What was worse was the realisation that Janet had much bigger boobs! Joan's boobs wouldn't stay in the bra. Was that what Janet had been discussing this morning with Aunt Nellie? Had she swapped her bra with one of Joan's?

Joan got to the classroom red-faced and flustered. Through a little window in the door she could see that her fellow pupils were sitting at their desks and the lesson had begun. Joan couldn't see Mr Hothouse but she could hear his voice. She put down her bag and books, determined to rearrange her hair and get her escaped boob back in the bra. No sooner had Joan put her hand inside her top to rescue her missing breast than there was a flash of brown corduroy and the door was flung open by Mr Hothouse. He was halfway through saying 'Nice of you to join us' when the whole class turned to see Joan with her hand inside her shirt, seemingly juggling her boob, and they gasped and gaped and stopped and stared.

Then Joan's wristwatch became inseparable from her shirt button. Again, Mr Hothouse got halfway through a line – 'What on earth are you doing?' – and then the button gave way and went flying across the corridor at meteoric speed. He stepped into the doorway and pulled the door half-shut. Joan's classmates murmured, relatively stunned by what they'd just seen.

Mr Hothouse barked, 'Silence!' and everyone was quiet.

'When you're quite ready, Miss Jones, would you care to join us?' He seemed to smile and understand her embarrassment. But he hadn't taken his eyes off Joan's breasts for the whole incident; it was almost as if he was imagining her naked. There was no saving her blushes.

Joan was never massively popular or unpopular. She was friends with a few girls in her class and occasionally they'd go to the pictures together. She worked on Saturdays with Aunt Nellie at the baker's. In her free time she liked riding her bike and picnics and going to the library and reading Miss Marple novels and murder mysteries and she was just starting to get really into romantic novels. She was harmless and safe and a good girl. It seemed to her, though, that the naughty girls were the ones who had all the fun. Some days she was slightly jealous of their carefree nature; others, especially when she heard stories of the trouble they'd got themselves in, not so much. Things may have been different if Mum and Dad had stayed around, but as it was she'd had to grow up that bit more quickly than normal and now she tried to act more grown-up for her sister and Aunt Nellie. It wasn't forced on her – it seemed the right thing to do and it was what her parents would have expected. Joan almost felt like they were testing her, and that at any minute they would turn up and ask whether she and Janet had been good girls for the babysitter. Joan could never shake the feeling that she was forever being judged.

She was the typical, nice girl-next-door. The local lads might have had liked her, given half a chance, but she probably wouldn't even have noticed. She was certainly not ugly, just plain. She had long, wavy brown hair; she was of average height; she wore normal clothes (her skirts weren't minis); she wasn't Twiggy, stick-thin or trendy; she wasn't big-boned or fat or spotty or sporty. But she did have lovely dark-chocolate eyes and long eyelashes that didn't needed mascara. Her eyes always looked good, no matter whether she was tired or wide awake.

She never had any boyfriends, but she'd had her heart broken by a few crushes – mostly by those she'd seen at the cinema or read about in books. She did, however, especially love her English teacher, Mr Hothouse, more than likely because he'd become an adopted father figure when she lost her own dad. But he also seemed kind, and her young hormones were uncontrollable, unpredictable and unfathomable, and falling in love with your teacher during the grieving period seemed like the most natural and yet also wrong thing to do. Joan was good at English. Mr Hothouse helped her gain better and better marks, and she became the teacher's pet.

English was something Joan enjoyed, and it had made her parents happy when they were alive. They had always wanted to hear Joan's stories and poems for as long as she could remember. One Christmas Dad had even made Joan read aloud to everyone, and although it was terribly embarrassing at the time, it had been Joan's proudest moment. She could still picture the faces of Mum and Dad and Nan and Granddad and Aunt Nellie and Janet and hear the round of applause they gave her when she finished reading a poem. She could picture the smiles fixed on their Christmas-blushed cheeks, tummies full of festive feast and wind-brewed bloatedness punctuated by sherry and port… the aroma of cold meats and the cheese board wafting into the lounge lit by the crackling fire… the tinsel-soaked tree and Christmas cards covering every flat surface and hanging by threads; little robins, snow and holly and nativity scenes everywhere, frozen in paper frames covering pictures, greetings from everyone everywhere in the world… Nellie still wearing her paper crown and Dad in his Christmas jumper… Nan's hand hovering over the olives… the radio playing Nat King Cole and Christmas songs…

Joan tried ever so hard with everything English just for her family… and him. In the end, she did it just to spend more time with Mr Hothouse. He really seemed to understand how much Joan liked English and how much it meant to her. He was her constant. She became obsessed. She fantasised about his corduroy jacket with the elbow pads. She pictured herself in marital bliss. He'd come home, and she'd have been cooking his dinner, and he'd call out, 'I'm home, darling. How was your day?' and then stomp up the stairs before hanging his coat up. She'd have been really busy making the house tidy and putting cut flowers in a vase and playing music on the turntable. Or she could have been out driving in a fabulously red sports car, solving a murder, and then she would rush home, looking wonderful, and reapply her red lipstick, and then he'd come upstairs and say, 'The dinner smells delicious, darling,' before his hands touched her face, her hair, her body. His smell. His handwriting. His hands. She was totally away with the fairies thinking about him. Only to be interrupted, one day, by Roy talking to her at the end of the lesson.

Roy and his mate Stuart were the best of a bad bunch really. They were in the same English and geography classes as Joan. Although Roy was good at sports, he wasn't like the other meat heads. He had kind eyes and a bit of decency about him. He spoke nicely – oh, and he was gorgeous: James Dean and Paul Newman and Elvis good-looking. Most of the girls had fancied him since about the third year, when his hair went from looking like a teddy boy to more sculpted, like a mod. He had had lots and lots of girlfriends. Joan probably would have preferred, or been better suited to, Stuart. He was also keen on English, and was her male nemesis in the eyes of their teacher. She had a begrudging respect for his writing because he always got fantastic grades and he read beautifully, but they always ended up at loggerheads whenever there was a debate and usually the whole class would turn on the pair of them if ever they ended up in a conversation. It became a class joke. Stuart was quieter than Roy and less confident and brash around girls. He always said he wanted to become a journalist.

'Anyway,' said Roy. 'So, like, erm, I was thinking, you know, if, like, no one has already asked you, errr, or anything, like, you know, basically, will you come with me to the summertime ball, like?'

Joan didn't have to think for long. There was no way Mr Hothouse would be her date. She had to get over the infatuation. She was quite happy to ruin his marriage, but also realistic enough to appreciate he was highly unlikely to fall in love with her and leave his wife for a sixteen-year-old girl. She was a lot of things, but unrealistic wasn't one of them. Their relationship could continue in her head, mind you. In her head, Mr Hothouse was a bit of a naughty so-and-so. She didn't think his real self would do half the things she imagined him doing. Naughty Mr Hothouse and his strawberry obsessions… She was daydreaming again.

'Joan, did you hear me? If you're going with someone already, that's fine, you know. Just say…' Roy said.

Joan stared at him blankly, trying to shake out of her mind the vision of a naked Mr Hothouse crawling over a bed of strawberries towards her.

'Well, will you be my date?' Roy asked.

'Yes, of course,' Joan replied.

She watched as he exhaled and then seemed to grow a few inches. Her heart skipped a beat then pounded, and she felt her cheeks flush. She had been asked out by a boy, and not just any boy. In all reality Roy was probably the best boy in her school. Unless you counted Stuart, who was quiet and quirky, but Joan always found him aloof and distant, and she didn't think he liked her at all. Whenever they spoke in English he seemed to contradict her or look at things from a different angle. They always seemed to get to the point in class where they would almost be arguing over each other's points. Although Joan could see his arguments were well thought out, she found herself frustrated to the point of hating Stuart. She was sure if they were in a relationship, they would be constantly arguing. She also couldn't understand why he was vying for her teacher's attention. What was his angle? What was he trying to prove?

Joan didn't realise Stuart secretly felt his heart crushed every time they spoke. All he wanted to do was kiss Joan. Go for a picnic in an English meadow. Drink lemonade and eat sandwiches and roll around in the fields, petting. He really had it bad for her. His dream date would be the pictures with her and then chatting about a silly book they'd both read. He loved her eyes and the way they flashed or sparkled when she smiled. Not that she ever smiled at him, but that was his dream – that one day she would smile for him.

All the other girls, including those Joan thought were her friends, were really surprised, and the sluttier girls really annoyed, that she chose Roy. The fact that Roy had chosen her didn't seem to matter.

'There's just one other thing,' Roy added.

'Yes?' replied Joan, unsure what the added proviso could be.

'Can your sister come too?'

Joan looked at Roy, shocked.

What Joan didn't know was that Stuart had agreed to go along with Roy and Joan on a double date, because he knew Roy also fancied Janet. You could say Roy really wasn't that picky, fussy or loyal, and Stuart didn't like the idea of Roy taking advantage of Joan, especially after all she had been through.

The way Roy saw it, he could have had any girl, but this way Stuart could get involved too and the competition would be fun, and it would be better if his mate was around. Roy knew about how Stuart felt about Joan – it was obvious, written all over his face. In his slightly naive thought process he figured dating one sister was better than none, especially as Roy had a habit of going at relationships like a bull in a china shop, and Stuart invariably ended up picking up the broken pieces and more often than not became the sounding board for the heartbroken girls. It baffled him greatly that his friend, although good-looking, was normally an arsehole, and was so shallow and fickle and only about getting cheap thrills. Stuart hoped the sisters were better than that.

What Stuart didn't know was that Roy was wondering whether perhaps he could manage to persuade the sisters to have a threesome or foursome. He had heard, and believed, this was a distinct possibility. Roy had got the idea from one of the sexy arthouse magazines his cousin had given him, having picked them up somewhere on his travels through Europe.

It wasn't a disastrous prom. The night itself passed by with few catastrophes. In fact, it couldn't have gone much better for Joan and Roy. Well, Roy was blown away... Whilst Joan went to the toilets and Stuart went to get some drinks, Roy made a pass at Janet and suggested a threesome. When Stuart came back and found out, he punched Roy and they ended up having a scuffle.

This upset Janet, who really didn't like all the ridiculous machoism. She wanted to go home immediately, and partly blamed Joan for getting her involved with these stupid boys. She didn't want anything to do with the pair of them anymore, but agreed to let Stuart walk her home, which he did... he was a gentleman. Stuart apologised to Janet for his friend's behaviour and said it was par for the course with him. Then he said goodbye and wished Joan and Janet luck, which struck Janet as slightly odd. Janet was left convinced she could really do without boyfriends entirely.

Stuart decided the best thing to do would be to go back to the prom and explain to Joan what had happened. He fully understood his action would probably cost him his relationship with Roy, but he didn't want Joan getting hurt and Roy really was a bit of an arsehole... All the way back to the village hall, Stuart stewed, thinking perhaps it was partly his fault. All Roy ever saw with girls was green lights; all girls saw with Roy was a good jaw line and babies. *It might prove the end of him one day,* Stuart thought. Perhaps if he had been more of a man and asked Joan out at the beginning, rather than letting Roy get involved, all this would have been avoided. He was doing the right thing, he concluded.

He got to the hall, and Stuart and Joan were nowhere to be seen. He walked around the back, near the old school bike sheds, thinking the worst. A cold chill ran down his spine as he saw a couple making out. It wasn't them. He traipsed along the quiet gravel road, past the damp playing fields alongside the old church, and followed the hedgerow-banked lane that led beside the spooky graveyard. A warm mist hung in the air. Orange globes encircled the streetlights. He looked in at the ancient gravestones. *There's no way they've gone in there,* he thought – hoped.

He got as far as the old stream. Sitting there on the bank under a starry sky was where he'd have liked to have been with Joan. It wasn't a bright, warm, starry evening and they couldn't have looked up at the moon and it wouldn't have been beautiful. Stuart could feel his toes getting wet; his shoes had become drenched as he kicked through the blades of glistening grass. He decided Roy must have walked Joan back via a different route; hence they had missed each other. All this could wait until school next week.

Stuart cut past the school to get home. Then he saw movement in the old wooden bus shelter. As he got closer, he could see a figure sitting with his arm out, looking very comfortable. The old romantic. And then what looked like someone else, perhaps asleep, curled up on his lap. As he got closer, Stuart could just about make out his friend's silhouette. Closer still, and he could make out his smile.

'Roy?' he said.

Then he saw Joan's head rise from between Roy's legs. His heart stopped. He turned and walked away.

Despite the falling-out with Stuart, Roy and Joan started courting. Janet said she didn't like Roy but she didn't really say why, and Joan just thought she was jealous. Roy had said the disagreement with Stuart was over money and she was happy to believe that. Momentarily, Joan didn't have a care in the world.

Roy was knocked off his feet by how full on Joan was. He certainly learnt it wasn't just the easy girls who were lots of fun. He sensed he should give Janet a wide berth.

All in all, life ticked along fairly easily for the blossoming couple. Even Stuart could see that Joan and Roy seemed very happy, though he felt she was slightly misguided. Most of the time they were happy making out and having fun. Occasionally, they would bicker over silly things, but they would enjoy making up – they were love's young dream.

They sat their exams and made ambitious plans: what amazing places they'd like to visit around the world, careers they'd like to try, languages they could learn, universities they could study at... all depending on their O level results, and Joan not being pregnant with twins.

Chapter 3

The O level exam results day soon came around. Roy came to meet Joan at home. She heard his tell-tale *rat-tat-tat* knock at the door and Aunt Nellie asking whether he wanted to come in. He declined. As Joan skipped down the stairs to greet him, Janet moped, heavy footed, the other way, choosing to ignore Roy completely.

'Wish us luck,' Joan chirped excitedly.

'Hmmm, good luck,' Janet murmured, like the effort to use her vocal chords was all too much.

'Good luck, dear, and to you too, Roy,' Nellie said, cupping Joan's cheek affectionately.

And there he stood. Her beautiful boyfriend, her shining knight, her man with an umbrella.

'Oh God, is it raining?' Joan asked, thinking a change of outfit might be necessary. But it wasn't; it was just some sort of fashion statement. He was using the umbrella like a walking stick. He could be so avant-garde, Joan thought.

Off to school they went. Nellie watched as they walked up the road together, holding each other's hands. She thought, *Daft bugger looks like Charlie Chaplin,* and chuckled to herself.

They walked all the way through the school grounds, heading straight for the secretary's office.

'Can we go to the cinema on Saturday night?' Joan asked, thinking they could go out after she finished work.

Roy didn't answer. He remembered one of the lads from his football team had mentioned a party that was happening, but the other lads weren't taking their girlfriends and Roy would need to come up with a decent excuse. He could almost see Joan's disappointed and rejected face, and no matter how fun the party would be, he wasn't sure he could cope with upsetting her and having a row. The constrictor snake, dressed up as responsibility and commitment, tightened her coils around his neck. He felt a cold shiver as he faced the long, dark, lonely tunnel through which a committed man must walk.

They heard distant wails and saw excited groups of kids their age congregating in little covens. Futures and worlds being shaped and shifted, and potential paths being routed and rethought. They watched as brown envelopes were passed out and the pupils desperately scanned the pages, searching for the all-important grades, fingers tracing lines on papers, silent words and curses mouthed. Some wheeled away, whooping and hollering, a torturous summer of pent-up apprehension soon changed to delight, instantly released like a fountain of champagne. Some reread the printed sheet over and over again, colour draining from their ashen cheeks, hoping, praying for some sort of misprint. Peter McCormack collapsed to his knees a few places in front of Joan and Roy and they watched as his shoulders shook on his bony frame; they both clenched each other's hand a little tighter.

Roy hadn't quite understood what all the fuss and bother was about until that very moment. Now, all of a sudden, he wished he'd revised just a little bit harder. He felt like a friend of a friend at someone's party. For once there was no hiding behind the irrelevance of his results. They were final. These were the ones that mattered. He realised he'd either got good grades or failed, and if he'd failed he would have to re-sit or not get grades at all. Those were his choices. Either he would be the older kid re-sitting with the younger lot, or he'd make do with what he'd got.

Just then Stuart walked past, holding his envelope.

'Hi,' said Joan, and she felt Roy immediately tense up and give her hand a little tug. Roy's healed nose and busted lip tingled some kind of self-preservation warning. Joan looked at him to say, *Why the tug?*

Stuart seemed to notice the gesture too. He looked confused and slightly put out by the sudden intrusion into his day.

But Roy changed tack and went with the flow; everything was groovy. 'So how did you get on, mate?' he asked, looking Stuart square in the eye and smiling inanely like a loyal Labrador.

'I've not opened the letter yet,' said Stuart, slightly bemused, looking at the ground between Joan and Roy. He'd been caught on the hop by the sudden resumption of communication and was obviously embarrassed, as he couldn't look at them.

'I'm sure you've done great,' Joan said, and Roy nodded in agreement.

Stuart held the envelope close to his chest. He seemed petrified of what it contained. 'If I don't get good grades, I might as well not go home. I'm dead.'

Joan and Roy watched as the colour in Stuart's cheeks faded until he was a ghostly white. Joan thought she saw tears well up in his eyes. Neither she nor Roy were under anywhere near as much pressure. If they got good grades, they could do A levels at the school or go to a local college and study another course. If the grades were really terrible, they could perhaps re-sit somewhere. There were always options, right? That's what they tried to convince themselves.

Joan got A's in both English literature and language, as she'd expected. Maths was her worst result, but she still got very good grades overall. Aunt Nellie exclaimed, with a proud tear in her eye, 'Your parents would been so happy.' Joan could stay on at school and do A levels if she wanted.

Pulling her close and giving her a full-bosom cuddle, Aunt Nellie noticed Joan felt different. She couldn't put her finger on it; some internal electricity.

She cooked up a feast for them to celebrate, and even suggested Roy's parents, Cathleen and Alec, were welcome to join them. They didn't. They had a bridge night or something already planned. They really didn't want to spend any of their valuable time with those ladies from the baker's. They didn't see Joan as a girlfriend or even as someone from Roy's school, and certainly they wouldn't have believed she had got the better grades – Roy could have done better in everything if he had tried, they assumed. He was unquestionably far better than that girl from the baker's. It was just a fad; his association with Joan was nothing more than biological. Working at the baker's and being with Roy would surely be the pinnacle of Joan's aspirations, they thought.

Cathleen sat at home angrily filing her nails, impatiently waiting for Alec to get ready, all dressed up in her Sunday best, wrapped up warm in her fur coat, not knowing it was fake or that Alec had purchased it out of guilt after he slept with one of the cleaners at his work. She didn't know he had paid more money to that girl to keep her quiet than for any holiday she had had in the last few years. Cathleen was no better, swanning around like she owned the town and flirting with boys not much older than Roy. Mutton, they'd call her as she tottered away like a high-class prostitute, decked out in Marks and Sparks clothes. On Sunday they went to church as a family, but not to pray. Just to be seen. Church was where Roy's parents smiled at their allies and made mental notes about their enemies, appraising those they didn't care for and pitying others who seemed to be wearing cheaper clothes than them. They surely couldn't afford a nice new carpet throughout, but might be interested in the cheap leftovers for a few rooms. Alec scanned the congregation, thinking whose house he'd carpeted, and if he hadn't, which of their friends' houses he had, and Cathleen thought of who lived in the nicer houses and wore the nicer clothes. Roy scanned the aisles for any girls to eye and ponder over.

Roy hadn't done as well as Joan in the exams. He got a few low grades in subjects like music and French, which were very unlikely to become pivotal in his choice of future career. But he was adamant he'd apply for some jobs locally, and if nothing exciting materialised, he always had his dad's carpet-fitting business to fall back on. His laidback nature probably stemmed from always feeling secure in the knowledge that whatever happened, his dad would give him a job and, eventually, a company.

Then they discovered Joan was pregnant. With twins. Aunt Nellie figured it out; she had had her suspicions. Joan had been terribly sick and Aunt Nellie recommended peeing in a plastic pot she'd picked up from Boots the Chemist... then they got the news.

So, without much support or opposition from their immediate families, Joan and Roy decided on a rushed marriage. Mostly because Roy's family couldn't show their faces in church again had the young couple not married. Even Aunt Nellie felt it would be better – she too considered the gossiping in the bakery and wondered whether people would judge her in the community. Aunt Nellie felt she had failed her sister and Joan.

They briefly discussed perhaps terminating the pregnancy or giving the babies up for adoption, but neither was going to happen. It was twins, and Joan imagined them as a boy and girl replacing her parents.

Mini Mummy and Daddy, she told herself. The whole thought seemed ridiculously twisted and absurd – and yet logical, replacing like for like. She even woke up from nightmares in which her parents' faces were on the little babies' bodies. Getting rid of them hadn't even occurred to Joan, until Roy's parents suggested it to him. They said it was the easiest way to end the young relationship and brush it all under the matt. Joan was utterly against the idea. She would take on the responsibility, and she hoped Roy would be a good dad. He seemed a little bit excited about the idea. Privately, he felt the snake constrict a little further.

Aunt Nellie was far more supportive, in her usual fashion. 'What will be will be, love. You'll… we'll just have to deal with it.'

Aunt Nellie had no idea how they would deal with it. She thought there was always a chance nature would intervene and take the problem away. She loved the girls, but she couldn't deny that they had completely taken over her life. Not that she'd had an exciting life or anything to start with, but she couldn't help feeling slightly put out. She was failing them. She didn't want to, but she couldn't help it; she just wasn't cut out for this parental lark. She had no experience. She had never asked for any of this, and now she found herself bringing up two teenage girls who ate her out of house and home, *and* she faced the prospect of two more mouths to feed and entertain. Where would they live? How could they afford it?

Nellie was getting terrible headaches, and she cried herself to sleep pondering all the questions Joan should have been asking but unfortunately seemed incapable of grasping. It was as if she just expected these things to sort themselves out magically. Roy didn't make it any easier, having had everything handed to him all his life on a silver platter. The pair of them were going to learn some very harsh lessons very quickly, and Nellie couldn't shake the feeling she was going to end up picking up the pieces. Joan was still sharing a room with her sister at Nellie's house, so that would never work. They had so much to sort out in so little time and with so little money. Roy's family would have to help, even if they didn't want to.

School was over for the pair. Joan worked all the hours she could at the bakery, saving all the money she could, and it was decided that the young couple should get married as quickly as possible.

The wedding was arranged on a restrictive budget. There was no other way it could be. It was a modest affair, but civil all the same. It was a civil service, all be it in a church. The sentiment was there, at least from Joan; you could see genuine love and emotion in her eyes. It might not have been a fairy-tale wedding, but it felt grown-up, honest and a declaration of love and commitment, and that meant the world to Joan. Roy looked distracted and apprehensive, like he was wearing a giant, invisible, shrinking, reptilian scarf and had another place to be.

It was nothing like Joan had dreamed as a kid or read about in books or seen at the movies: an ancient church; a beautiful, flowing, lacy dress; an old car with white silk ribbons; her dad holding her close, walking by her side, a proud tear in his eye, step-together-step-together up the aisle as the organ blared out the wedding parade; two white dives cooing and flying from the steeple… No, this wedding took place at Roy's family's local church, the only available option at such late notice. It wasn't an especially ugly church, it was just a bit too modern and soulless. It was too wooden and bright and big, it didn't have any stained-glass windows and it wasn't cold, damp or echoey. It felt too hot, stuffy; too carpeted, acoustic and amplified – and worst of all, it had the biggest statue imaginable of a crucified Jesus hanging precariously over the altar. Joan imagined seeing up Jesus' loin cloth and him winking and waving his fingers, and it freaked her out.

The guests included a few friends from school and the other ladies from the bakery, Janet and Stuart, who was Roy's best man, a few random family members and Roy's parents, who looked like they couldn't get away soon enough. Roy's older sister, who lived in the States, had sent a message saying she couldn't make it at such short notice – work commitments or something. Roy didn't care at all as she was always doing her own thing, and he didn't really know her that well or like her much anyway.

Roy's parents were secretly excited about the idea of grandchildren, and although they were embarrassed, they pledged they would be as supportive as possible when the babies arrived. This was slightly worrying from the outset, as their supportiveness was generally overwhelming – they tended to take over, making a simple thing into a jamboree.

They couldn't, however, disguise their displeasure at their wonderful boy having children so young; not even properly out of school and well on his way to being a father before he was married. Disgraceful. It would be seen as outrageous, but all they could do was ride out the storm and front it out. The parish would be looking down their noses. *God knows what effect it will have on the business,* Alec thought. Mrs Legget was sure to be on the phone to Vicar Maginty, wooden spoon in hand, as soon as she heard. These things just didn't happen when they were younger, and naturally it was all Joan's fault. Cathleen chose to forget it was her own relationship with Mrs Leggett's son during the war that had sparked the woman's hostility. It had continued to fester when she married Alec and they opened a carpet shop that rivalled the Leggetts' interiors shop on the high street, which also offering a carpet-fitting service.

Roy's parents also hoped he might yet meet a beautiful girl of substance, one who had a bit more about her than Joan. Sure, she was pleasant enough, but their son was very handsome. Joan was a bit plain. Quiet. Dowdy. Common even.

'She works in the baker's, for goodness' sake,' Cathleen had exclaimed, exasperated.

'And so does Nellie,' Roy reaffirmed, adding more ammunition to his mum's protestations. He had meant it wasn't such a bad thing and that they were nice people, but it fell on deaf ears. The class difference between carpet fitting and baking was something only

Cathleen knew the value of. The truth was, they simply lived on different sides of the same street.

Roy's sister had done modelling in New York, and Cathleen had been quite a looker as a young lady. Not particularly nice as a person, but good-looking nonetheless. She was always a bit of a bitch, to be fair. Spoilt. Not that this guaranteed much in the world, but it certainly helped attract wealthier men with questionable morals. They seemed attracted by the challenge.

Roy's parents could only imagine how difficult it must have been for Aunt Nellie and the girls, as she had received no real inheritance. It would have been easier for Nellie to wash her hands of the pair of them, made them someone else's problem. This prompted Roy's parents to wonder whether Joan had deliberately got pregnant. They thought perhaps she was after their money. They didn't consider that Joan was actually brighter than their son, and that in this time of change and increasing opportunities for woman actually *she* could have been the one to do more with her life – had their son not got her pregnant. No, instead they saw Joan's brightness as the reason she had outsmarted their son. What was done was done, though. She was going to have his children. Their grandchildren. Twins, as it transpired. She would marry their son as quickly as possible, and Roy's parents agreed to give to their son as a wedding present whatever money they needed to get set up – they'd help with the deposit for a mortgage and set them up in a nice little home.

Vicar Maginty took Joan and Roy to one side. He'd asked for a chat, as the wedding had been arranged in such haste and he had a few things on his mind he was eager to discuss. They could tell he'd had a few drinks already, as his cheeks were bright red and he looked in a permanent state of embarrassment. He was a little man with a glint in his eye and smooth, soft, warm hands. He was from somewhere in Ireland. Cotton-wool hair fluffed around on his head like a frothy sea, and spurts squirted from his ears and wormed from his nostrils and strangely unruly dark eyebrows. His eyes were light blue, kind and piercing. Generally, he seemed quite a nice man, albeit slightly all over the place mentally.

'Now then, young Roy and Joan, I wanted to take a few moments to have a little chat, if you don't mind?' Vicar Maginty started. It was like they were about to have their own sermon.

He'd called them for the meeting at the church before a baptism a week before the wedding. The young couple presumed there had been some sort of last-minute hiccup or a problem with dates, or somehow he'd discovered that Joan was pregnant. Maybe a nurse or doctor had given them away...

'I want to talk to you about respect,' the vicar continued.

Joan felt as though she was about to be lectured on how to be a good wife, undoubtedly on instruction from Cathleen. She felt this talk had been orchestrated from the start, and braced herself for a condescending life lesson. Although Joan had never said anything to

Roy, she couldn't help but feel his parents didn't like her and that she wasn't good enough.

'Respect between a man and woman is a very important thing.' The vicar fixed Roy with his godly, icy eyes and blinked and nodded in happy appreciation when he could see he had Roy's entire attention.

Roy fidgeted slightly uncomfortably on the old-school wooden chair. Now it was his turn to wonder where this was heading. He hadn't done anything especially wrong that he could remember, but perhaps God had told the vicar about his thoughts. Maybe the vicar had seen Roy scanning the aisle during the sermons every Sunday since he was a boy and knew all about his wandering eye. Suddenly, Roy was a God-fearing man.

Joan looked at Roy and noticed he was looking nervous. This sparked worry in her. Was she about to learn an unpleasant truth about her future husband? Was the vicar going to reveal a nasty little secret about the future father of her children? For the first time in their relationship she didn't feel totally at ease. Had Roy been lying to her? Doubt kicked open a little paranoid door in her mind.

'Now you see, it's not all about who works the hardest, doing the bits an' bobs, tidying the house or whatnot – you know, out at work or indoors all day…'

Here we go, Joan thought, noticing her place was obviously in at home.

'But you see, the love you share is a very special thing, very special indeed, and the commitment you make on your wedding day is the most important commitment you will ever make. It's more than what you give or do for each other, you see…'

But they didn't see – they had no idea what he was going on about or where this talk was heading.

'Okay now, well then, you see, let me put it this way – you love each other very much, right?'

Roy and Joan nodded like little school kids.

'Right, of course you do, otherwise it would make no sense to get married, no sense at all. But now, you wouldn't want to hurt each other's feelings, would you?'

Joan and Roy looked at each other and then the vicar, before agreeing in unison that they didn't plan on hurting each other's feelings.

'Well now, exactly how well do you two lovely people know each other?' Vicar Maginty said, looking back and forth between them and nodding his head on every word to add a little extra impetus.

Joan replied for both of them: 'Quite well. No, really well.'

Roy carried on his nodding dog impression in agreement.

'Then nothing either of you do or say after you get married will come as a surprise to either of you, as you both know each other inside out, so to speak. Right… that's just grand, so it is.'

Vicar Maginty seemed pleased with himself; he had done the hard bit – there was nothing to worry about with these two.

'There was this couple, you see. They got married very recently, and the respect and understanding weren't there. No sooner were they married than they had an almighty, terrible fight, and I think they're going to end up calling the whole thing off straight away, already. Unbelievable, isn't it? Can you believe it? Do you understand?'

Joan and Roy looked at each other quizzically. They had no idea about this other couple, but as far as they both knew, they respected each other as much as they had ever expected anyone to respect them and they were certainly not expecting another outpouring of respect once they got married.

'It's terribly nice of you, Vicar, to show so much care and thoughtfulness about our future well-being and everything,' Joan managed to say for the pair of them as Roy readjusted himself in the chair whilst nodding supportively. 'But I'm sure we'll both respect each other.'

'Well, that's not it, you see.' A little spit bubble escaped the vicar's mouth. Buffeted by his breath, it burst into a million miniscule droplets. 'It's like this,' he blurted out, like he was getting flustered and having to rush his lines. 'Recently, I married a young couple not too dissimilar to you two, you see? Now then, no sooner had we had the ceremony than all signs of respect went out the window, and it's just not good enough, you know. It can't be happening… it reflects badly on me. Like I'm not doing my job. You know, they want to get divorced now, you see, after only being married for moments. It's a terrible shame and all down to respect…'

Vicar Maginty paused to let his words have maximum impact. Unfortunately, Roy and Joan just stared at him, totally baffled.

'You see, this man didn't respect his wife. As soon as they were married, he suggested they had sex in the back passage. He thought it was his right.'

Roy's attention was grabbed. Firstly, he hadn't known vicars were allowed to talk about sex. What's more, he was interested in the geography of the conversation. For he had been a member of the parish all his life and had run around the church ever since he first sneaked out of Sunday school as a kid. He used to run to the newsagent's, grab a quarter of cough candies and loiter around, waiting for the service to end. Somehow his parents never twigged or cared.

Joan, however, was a little sharper. She sat stiffly in her chair and glanced at Roy, realising he had no idea where this conversation had headed.

'They got married in this church?' Roy asked, confused.

Joan felt a little bit faint and sick.

'You know, it's not fair and right to suddenly expect these sorts of things at the end of the day, you know, once you are married, and especially on the same bleedin' day. God forgive me...' The vicar looked as if he was about to blow as gasket.

'Where's the back passage?' Roy asked, still confused.

'Jesus, Mary and Joseph,' the vicar muttered as he walked out of the little room. 'I'll see you next week, God help us.'

Married life was fine and reasonably uncomplicated at first. Joan wasn't the first girl to get pregnant and married at that age. (It was quite common in those days compared to now, when girls leave it as late as possible, instead building a career. Realistically, Joan going away to further education would have been more unusual. Who did she think she was, Margaret Thatcher?)

Joan did, however, feel very claustrophobic in the strange new house they'd moved to. She gradually became less mobile, and the more pregnant she became, the worse she felt being surrounded by strange pieces of furniture and general tat acquired from second-hand shops to make her feel more like a guest in someone else's home or as if she was staying at a hotel. If it wasn't cast-offs hidden away in Roy's parents' garage or loft, it was knick-knacks presented as moving-in gifts by well-meaning friends or Alec's customers. Joan really didn't need any more storage containers or teapots; they even had two irons.

To make matters worse, Joan and Roy's old friends would occasionally turn up and get really drunk and smoke the house out. It was what she assumed to be the equivalent of student digs for a few days, and then she would be left to tidy up. She was getting tired more and more, and Roy seemed to constantly be celebrating. His freedom, his marriage, his babies' impending arrival, his job – Joan wasn't entirely sure what he was celebrating. He settled into working with his dad and earning a regular wage, and the business did well for having the extra body. At first Joan didn't mind, as she could see Roy was happy at work and he seemed a little bit more mature and that made her happy. But gradually, she grew tired of his going to the pub without her after work, or going to see friends, especially as she didn't feel like doing much but sitting around reading. Roy had felt the coils loosen slightly around his throat.

It seemed to Joan that the closer it came to the babies being born, the less Roy was around. When he was around, he seemed distracted, as if he'd rather be somewhere else. He even made excuses and went out somewhere once when his parents were visiting.

Joan tried to confront him as amicably as possible. She didn't want to cause a scene or argument, but she felt something was the matter. She thought perhaps she'd upset him. She felt huge and ugly. When she finally pinned Roy down, he tried to play it down and suggested she was just being sensitive and that he had been really busy sorting out big things at work, possible massive opportunities. He was sorry, he said; he'd try to spend more time with her. He bought her some flowers, and for a little while things seemed to get back to normal. He also suggested Janet come and stay for a while. He knew he'd probably end up regretting that decision, but Aunt Nellie hadn't been feeling well and it made sense to give her some peace and quiet, plus the extra support for Joan might cheer her up and give him some more free time.

What Joan didn't know was that Roy had met someone else and they had started an affair. Nikki was an older lady by about ten years. He met her when she came into the shop to look at carpet samples, and they were soon flirting outrageously with each other. Nikki asked whether they used outside fitters, and Roy promised to do the fitting himself, to ensure it was a thorough and professional job. He decided extra-marital affairs were a perk of the job. Whilst the husband worked away and phoned home from his office – scratching his stubbly chin, picking his nose, ticking boxes with his pencil and wondering how the carpet fitter was doing, imagining a young lad hammering tacks into a new, quality, handpicked carpet – his wife arched her back in wondrous, carnal, lusty ecstasy, wondering whether she'd imagined hearing the phone ringing.

Roy felt guilty, especially when confronted by Joan, and tried to cool off the second relationship, chiefly as Joan was so pregnant. He knew what he was doing was wrong, but he couldn't help it. He loved Joan, but not like his new girlfriend. Although older, Nikki was young at heart, wild and fun, amazingly good-looking, hot, sexy, naughty, stylish and sharp-witted, pretty much everything Joan wasn't.

Roy really didn't want to hurt Joan. She was his first genuine love, and she truly was going to be a very loving wife. She was a good person. She never really suffered terrible mood swings like other girls or women he had known, and she wasn't bitchy or nasty like the ladies in his family. She was always there for him, she was nice and sincere, she was vulnerable and she doted on him. But Nikki – she was utterly wild. She walked around her house naked. Talked sexy to him. Could drink him under the table and did things he didn't know were legal or possible.

In the last few weeks before the twins were born, Joan went into a cleaning frenzy, turning the house upside down, boxing things up and tidying away. She even found a tin of Pledge polish and a cloth in her dressing-gown pocket. She was forever sending Roy out to get bits and bobs whilst she feathered the nest. Roy didn't mind, as it meant he could pop in and see Nikki just to repeat that things would be different when the babies were born – he was not sure what that meant, but he repeated it until he believed it.

He had no idea how to end the relationship. He had no real burning desire to do so either. It felt right saying he had to cool it off, but then it felt right carrying it on, and it felt right (although it was wrong) suggesting that everything would be different in the future, although he had no idea what that held either! So he was having sex at every opportunity, whilst saying it was going to end and then promising it wouldn't be like this forever. His head was all over the place. But the lies just made it more exciting and more out of control, and the longer it went on, the less chance, or desire, he had to do the right thing.

After staying, Janet had suspicions about Roy's disappearing acts, and one day, whilst on the bus, she was sure she saw Roy entering a pub on the other side of town, hand in hand with a blond lady.

Joan went into labour one evening when Roy was out with Nikki and another couple, getting drunk and having a curry. He had said he had to get home on time, but when he and his friends decided they'd make a night of it, he thought it would be okay if he phoned home with some excuse about work running late and the team doing extra hours on a mega shop installation job. He had to pick up some carpet from a supplier out of town or something. Hopefully, Joan wouldn't kick up a fuss. He was overly confident because he was drunk.

He was slightly fed up with Joan moaning about peculiar food cravings, and her sending him on ridiculous missions to fetch her all sorts of things that she'd forgotten to sort before the babies arrived. Not that he'd said anything to Joan. He wasn't going to be that unkind to her. He felt guilty enough as it was. She must have been uncomfortable and was the size of a house. He was just about coming to terms with the idea that sooner or later he might actually leave her and be with Nikki. He was even trying to tell himself – or fool himself – she wouldn't be devastated. He was so naive, it would be unbelievable to anyone other than a few of his closest friends. A young mum with no direct parents, and he thought she'd be okay looking after two babies whilst he went off with another woman. Something in him, way down in the darkest recesses of his mind, hinted that it might be wise to see how things panned out with the babies first. *But perhaps she could cope,* he thought again.

When he called home to speak to Joan, she wasn't there. Or at least not answering. *Strange,* he thought. *Maybe she's in the bath or has gone to bed early.* He gave it five minutes and then phoned his parents. His dad answered.

'Seven two seven four six two,' he said in his best BBC accent.

'Dad, it's me, Roy. Listen, I tried calling home for Joan and there's no answer.'

'Where are you, boy? Apparently, you're picking up a delivery? What delivery? We aren't expecting any deliveries. Anyway, that doesn't matter right now… Do you understand? It's really not on, you being out and about all the time, it's just not done. Bloody hell, what if there's, you know, bloody lady problems, complications or something, eh?'

Roy could tell his dad was really mad; he never swore. This was the closest he'd ever heard his dad come to being furious. (Other than the one time Mrs Buchanan's black Labrador, Monty, did a shit in the front garden and she refused to believe it was Monty's doing. Roy remembered his dad angrily stirring his cup of tea and pacing back and forth in the kitchen, sweating and proclaiming, 'It's not my bloody poo!')

Alec informed Roy that Joan was on her way to the hospital as her waters had broken, and that Cathleen was following her up there too. Which in itself just wouldn't do. She was supposed to be going to a neighbourhood watch meeting and had bought cakes especially. They understood that Nellie and Janet were racing to get there as well.

This was the closest Roy had ever come to being severely reprimanded or even questioned by his dad. 'He is his own man and can make his own mistakes, dear,' was his father's usual rebuke should his mum ever ask him to have words.

'What's going on, son? Is this work related? You need to be with your wife, boy. Sort it out now.'

It took a while for the words to sink in. It was almost as if the last eight months hadn't really happened and only then did it occur to Roy that he was actually going to be a dad. Then he realised that his whole family were involved and with Joan, and he wasn't. He felt choked. He was on the outside looking in on himself, and he didn't like what he saw.

The chime of the phone's bell echoed in his mind in the moments after he said goodbye to his dad. The chime reminded him of the one at Nikki's house.

His dad also felt the strength and relevance of the phone's bell chime. In his heart of hearts, he hoped this would be the making of his boy, mark the end of him being a lad and the start of him becoming a man. Alec could see Roy had really settled into his job at the company and he had a great way with the customers. He actually muttered, 'Please, God,' and meant it in a prayer-type fashion. All those years at church, not thinking or wanting anything in particular, and there he was wanting something good and right, and not selfish on his part in the least.

He had noticed the lack of interest and warmth his son had showed Joan throughout her pregnancy, and he was getting worried. He had actually grown to like the girl, mostly because his wife didn't. He felt uncomfortable, the way a dad feels when he sees his son acting in a way that's not particularly gentlemanly. He wondered what Joan's dad would have made of Roy had he been around. Alec remembered Roy as a spiteful toddler in the midst of a mighty terrible-twos tantrum, grabbing a toy greedily from his older sister. Those moments had a habit of engraving themselves in the minds of all parents, leaving niggling doubts as to whether the child was actually good or not. Roy was the golden boy as far as his mum was concerned, but she wasn't the best judge of character. Perhaps Alec had allowed these feelings to manifest in his relationship with his son, who had always felt he had something to prove or – worse still – nothing to prove. Perhaps they had spoilt their son. Then it occurred to Alec: perhaps Roy was making the same mistakes *he* had once made.

Roy didn't go back to the table or say goodbye to his friends, he just left and went straight to the hospital, arriving just after the babies were born. Joan had coped on her own with the strange doctors and nurses, and felt better when Janet and Nellie arrived. She was even strangely happy to see Cathleen. Joan had hit the gas and air very hard and made herself quite sick, but her head had cleared in time to see Roy's face when he first set eyes on the babies and knew he would love them. Twins. A boy and a girl. She felt perfect.

Cathleen was an emotional mess; she kept saying how beautiful the babies were and how delicious the cake was, and Joan had no idea where the cake had appeared from.

Janet was initially squeamish and overwhelmed by the whole situation, but then, as she realised Roy had been out and nearly missed the birth and hadn't really been there for her sister, she became angry. She stole her moment whilst away from Joan, in the corridor with an elated, shell-shocked Roy. His mum and Nellie had gone off to get some coffees to wash down the cake and to try to find a payphone.

'I don't know what your game is, mister, but this, or whatever this is, ends right now,' she said.

'I don't know what you're talking about,' he replied gingerly.

'Okay, let me spell it out for you, pal: where the hell were you when your wife was going into labour, eh?' snapped Janet.

'Joan knows I was working, on a delivery, with clients. Nothing's going on, honest, and why are you being like this?' he said.

Janet watched as his eyes flitted about, unable to make contact with hers.

'You're a liar. I can see it written all over your face. Finish it, whatever it is, finish it,' she hissed, bristling with anger and a newfound protective sibling loyalty. She was so mad she wanted to punch his face in.

'I've got your number, Roy, and it stinks. You've always been trouble, ever since the night of the prom, and my sister doesn't deserve this... whatever this is.' She didn't even know what she meant by 'this'; her mouth just seemed to be acting of its own accord.

Roy went to plead his innocence and ignorance, but he could see a genuine threat of violence brewing in Janet's glare. Roy was intimidated and didn't want to have to explain to his mum and Joan or anyone else why his sister-in-law had decided to thump him on the nose.

Janet could feel her fingernails biting into her palms and her heartbeat reverberating in her temple. She was so angry. She felt very different: emotional, but she didn't want to cry. She wasn't sure she would ever calm down, and a part of her never wanted to calm down again. For the first time in ages she felt alive. Roy was an utter, utter prick and she really did hate men.

Roy walked back to the maternity ward, in the direction of Joan and the babies. Looking back over his shoulder, he could see Nellie and his mum battling with a coffee machine behind the bristling Janet. He did a double-take and she was still staring at him with her arms crossed, giving him daggers. He'd never forget her glaring at him in that mustard-coloured, wiry, woolly jumper. She looked like a militant lesbian, he decided.

Janet had always been looked after by Joan. That would change now. She would try to look after Joan. She quite liked that feeling. She felt protective. She decided then that she'd like to be a policewoman or a detective – then she could find out what Roy was up to and what had really happened to her parents.

Janet had first felt the calling not long after her parents died. There were so many unanswered whys. She had never given up hope that someday, perhaps when she was grown up, she'd be able to answer all of life's mysteries. *Why did Mum and Dad die?* Nellie would have been a millionaire had she got a pound for all Janet's unanswerable questions. Janet would have been a wealthy girl too had she been paid to ponder such questions.

When Roy and Joan got home and the dust settled, they seemed just like any other new young parents to twins: sure, they struggled with sleep, and they divided their time between feeds, housework, sleep, baths and shopping and walks. They initiated autopilot.

Roy had a few weeks off work. The first few weeks were the toughest as they tried to get into some sort of routine, probably because Roy wasn't used to spending so much time around the house and Joan wasn't used to having the company. Although hectic, the time seemed to fly by. Somehow Roy seemed to spend most time with Sophie, their daughter, whilst their son, Adam, would settle best with Joan. Whether this was by accident or not, neither of them knew. It just seemed to work that way. Out of the two twins, Roy seemed to get on better with Sophie and Joan with Adam. There was no preplanning or favouritism. Perhaps little hands and feet were easier to handle when each parent grabbed a child each.

Roy found it fascinating to watch Joan mother the two pups. He was enjoying being a dad. He was excellent at changing nappies, and he didn't mind getting up at night and having cuddles and doing feeds. He liked the smell. He laughed at their little squawks and random body movements.

Joan was an emotional, shattered mess. She really loved seeing Roy with the kids. But she had found the last few months of pregnancy really lonely, and at times had worried that Roy was going off her as they were rarely intimate any more – because, Joan presumed, she looked so big and ugly. She looked at herself in the mirror and pinched the soft remains of her recently lost bump. She rubbed her belly, not feeling the same sensation she had felt for almost nine months as her babies developed inside her. It felt different now. Hollow. Not so soothing. Her eyes looked darker than usual and had bags, her hair seemed to be falling out more than usual and was fuzzy and unruly, and she was sure her top-lip hairs looked more prominent. She started to cry again, until she heard one of the babies stir. Then she just stared in the mirror at the tears running down her cheeks.

The twins weren't identical, being a girl and a boy, and they looked different straight away too. Adam had a thick head of dark hair and Sophie was bald. She was also slightly smaller and less plump at first, but this soon changed as she was the better feeder of the two. She also seemed to be the more alert and bright of the babies, whereas Adam was a bit clingy and always wanted to be held by Joan.

Sometimes Roy and Joan had races to see who could change the nappies the quickest. Roy would always win.

It was all going perfectly, until Roy went out to wet the babies' heads with an old school friend. He got drunk. Met up with Nikki, whom he hadn't given a second thought during all the baby commotion. There he found himself, the next day, waking up feeling hungry. The kids would need feeding or changing; it was his turn. He knew it and hadn't even been asked. He would be late for work. He rolled over, expecting to see Joan with the two babies breastfeeding under each arm. But instead he saw Nikki's half-uncovered naked bum, the light from the crack in the curtains illuminating the magnificent curve of her cheeks like a perfect peach. His head pounded as he realised he wasn't at home and that wasn't Joan's buttock…

He saw the photo on the mantelpiece and straight away recognised the grumpy face of Nikki's husband on holiday somewhere like Greece with her. Roy always found himself looking at it after they'd had sex.

Chapter 4

Joan and Janet sat by Nellie's hospital bed, the rasp of her thin breathing slicing through the mundane fuzz filling the pastel-green room. Joan couldn't take her eyes off the lady who had become her rock. She couldn't believe she wasn't going to get any more direction or advice or sympathetic understanding. Again she felt a wave of nausea and emotion bubble up inside her as she fought back the tears. Her chest ached. She noticed Janet switch from her left side to her right on the uncomfortable hospital chair, trying to get some blood back into her buttocks.

It had been like this for days. Just waiting for the inevitable. Occasionally unsticking legs from plastic chairs. Nodding nothingness to nonplussed nurses.

The kids were staying with Roy's parents. They'd barely spoken, but Roy had said Adam was really missing Joan. Not him or Sophie, she noted painfully. She missed him desperately too, and Roy and Sophie, and their old life and Nellie. She just wanted to rewind the clock. When exactly had this nightmare began, she wondered; and then, with angst, when would it end? She looked at Nellie's pale hand lying impassive and motionless on the crisp, starched white sheets and pictured it stirring flour and milk and eggs in a bowl and sprinkling on cinnamon. So many recipes for which she didn't know all the ingredients.

Joan was relieved when Janet fell asleep. It gave her a break from the continual stream of hatred and anger towards Roy she was forever venting, like an angry adolescent spot forever reappearing, angrier and pus-filled. It became so constant that Joan found herself wanting to defend Roy. As much as she wanted to and it was a good idea to do so, she couldn't all of a sudden simply stop loving him. Perhaps he would come back to her; maybe the affair would end. He wasn't that bad. Perhaps it had all been a big mistake. Maybe he still loved her, deep down. Sooner or later he would remember. He could remember. He should remember. Then Joan would think, *Who am I kidding? Look at the state of me. I'm a boring, ugly mess, with frizzy hair and a wobbly belly. Why would Roy want to be with me?* The little paranoid door that Vicar Maginty had accidentally opened was now a sluice gate swamped by a deluge of self-doubt. Perhaps her sister was right.

What Janet didn't realise was that for all the truth behind her damning of Roy, the thing her sister needed more than anything was a cuddle and a cry. For her to get better and move on, first she needed to repair and rebuild. Janet, not having had much life experience, was all hot air and opinions and very little empathy and sympathy. It was all she could do to not actually blame Joan and say, 'I told you so, I warned you,' even if not even Janet could have foreseen Roy dropping Joan from such great height and at such a shitty moment.

Joan tried to close her eyes. It was two in the morning. They'd given up trying to talk to Nellie. It was as if they'd suddenly run out of things to say to her. The words were there, they just couldn't get them out of their mouths. There was so much they would have liked to say, had they had a moment to write down all their thoughts and read them through like a script, but that wasn't to be. They wanted to say thanks for being the nearest thing to a mum they'd known. They wanted to say sorry for taking over Nellie's life. They wanted to tell her they loved her, as they both realised they had never told her. That was the thing they were most sorry about, and they were both so sorry, truly sorry.

They were actors in their own movie, having to ad lib, and they'd arrived at a scene where silence brought power and energy to the storyline. Joan felt a tear well up in her eye and trickle down her cheek. Then she heard the tone and cadence of Aunt Nellie's breathing change, and as she kicked Janet's foot, the lights flickered and Nellie was gone.

Roy hadn't slept much. To say he had a lot on his mind would be an understatement. He'd had to get up in the night because the kids were kicking off. As much as his mum and dad were trying their best to help with the midnight feeds and tantrums, occasionally he had the horrible feeling that they were just as clueless as he was. He knew deep down the kids wanted their mummy, or at least the old routine. Part of him did as well. Then he had his girlfriend to deal with. She had split up with her husband and was pressuring him to move in with her. Pressure wasn't really the right word. She was there, alone, naked and waiting for him – at least that's what his brain was telling him.

He'd choose to forget her dad had said he'd break every bone in Roy's body if he messed his daughter around. Then he'd remember the kids and his parents.

He lit another cigarette off the old Rover's lighter and listened to the crackle of tobacco as the car filled with smoke. He opened the window a crack and the cloud disappeared like a ghost. Here he was, racing halfway up the country with a sales pitch that he had cobbled together following a semi-condescending chat with his dad, a few drunken, sexually charged conversations with his girlfriend and a few phone calls to contacts of her dad's. He had meetings lined up with some of the major retailers all around the country, everyone interested in incorporating a carpet business on a nationwide scale. He had an idea, and all of a sudden everyone wanted to hear about it.

He'd been asked several times if he could play golf, and he thought it might well be worth a try. He was wearing his best suit. He looked amazing. He felt sharp – knackered and stressed, but sharp. For a young man, he had an awful lot on his plate, but this gave him an air of intensity and swagger, of being older than his years. He looked troubled, but sincere. Anyone would be impressed by his aptitude if he knocked on their door. He looked like a young entrepreneur. He looked like a kid going places. He had briefed his dad; most of it seemed like pie in the sky to Alec. Roy would set up these meetings, and if it came to anything he'd bring Alec along at a later stage in the deals, to shake hands and bring a little wisdom, history and formality to proceedings.

Roy flicked the cigarette through the gap in the window and immediately reached for another. It seemed that after the initial talk most of these meetings soon progressed to the pub or a nice restaurant, and then a grotty strip club or curry house somewhere. These made him feel uncomfortable, as he wasn't sure if he was being tested by Nikki's dad or his associates, and he wasn't entirely sure if they were completely legitimate, straight-laced businessmen. Then he tried to fool himself that Nikki wouldn't care in the slightest and neither would her dad; they were very relaxed about that sort of thing. They were from the 'here for a good time, not a long time' school of thinking. He liked that train of thought... he felt his neck and back relax a little.

He remembered meeting her dad for the first time. The cigar in his mouth and his big hands passing the tumbler of brandy on ice. The stiff red-leather chairs, and the heavy arm around his shoulders, leading him into the snooker room. The pictures on the mantelpiece of Nikki's dad as a youngster in a boxing competition – and one of him dressed smartly in a suit with a couple of other blokes Roy recognised at the time but just couldn't place... Then Roy remembered, the memory flooding back like a cold wind on a winter's day: they were the Smith brothers. Gangsters. Why had he only just remembered?

Roy's back and shoulders stiffened up once more. He also wasn't fond of waking up in strange hotel rooms, especially when he couldn't remember getting there. Still, he was even less happy about waking up at home and not remembering how he'd driven home. He figured he was quite a good drunk driver; however, he had woken up once to find he'd parked in the middle of a field. He could only presume he'd gone straight on at a T-junction and smashed through a hedgerow. The thought made him shudder, as he remembered what had happened to Joan's parents and the look on his dad's face when he saw the mechanic's repair bill.

'Seriously, son, it would have been better if you'd written the car off.'

'But, Dad, I could have been dead.'

Alec's face had suggested that outcome wasn't necessarily such a bad thing, faced with that bill. Roy wasn't sure his if his dad didn't love that Rover more than him.

The truth was, however, ever since Roy had got involved in the company, sales had gone through the roof. The business had been doing okay under his dad's watch and could have continued at the same rate for another lifetime, but Roy had somehow transformed it into a serious cash-making machine. The phone wouldn't stop ringing. He'd chatted up someone he knew from school, who'd put an advert in the local paper and also introduced him to a friend in local radio. They'd drunkenly written and then composed an advert one night in the pub and managed to get it played on the radio, and from then on it had been chaos. Somehow the local football team picked up the chant for one of their players, and this in turn led to more business and the shop advertised at the ground, in the fanzine and on the kits. After that they had too much work, but then Roy came up with the idea of putting the company details on the side of the van and on livery, and employing more people – and then more people wanted to get involved. Soon they had opened a second office and they had people answering phones for them. They were looking at other locations when the retail big boys started getting interested.

Alec knew all there was to know about fitting carpet, but this was well out of his comfort zone. It didn't faze Roy at all, though. He revelled in it. The details were mostly written down in black and white in front of them in the accounts. He had the company name and history. They could see how much the turnover had increased. Roy could talk comfortably about every aspect of the job; he'd basically been learning it all his life but had never paid any attention until now. He knew how to fit carpet to stairs, he knew the different manufacturers and the difference in quality, and he could sell carpets to Persians. Anything he didn't know he paid someone to sort out and teach him. He was good at knowing what he needed to know and what to delegate. Roy had streamlined the portfolio. He knew what people wanted in their houses. He could sell everyone in the same street the same carpet. This meant he didn't need such a big portfolio. He bought more of specific carpets, which kept the price keen compared to buying bits of various types. Then he bought cheaper carpets from the Continent that looked like more expensive brands, all the while bringing down costs and pushing up profits. Once he secured the spending power of the retail big boys, he could use his business plan again, just on a much, much bigger scale.

After Joan and Janet buried Nellie, they didn't feel comfortable with the house any more. It felt like she was still there – her presence was imprinted on every room, the smell of her cooking was baked into the paint, her essence was everywhere, and far from it being soothing and homely, it felt burnt and spoilt. So they decided to sell up and divide the profits.

Roy's parents reluctantly agreed to sell the little house completely to Joan and Janet for very little profit, on the condition that Joan would never stop them visiting their grandchildren, and Roy promised to continue to send as much money as possible to help pay for their every need. He felt like he had done the best he possibly could do to ensure they were well set up and looked after, given the circumstances. Janet didn't see it the same way. She saw it as the least he could do, and was still quite happy and willing to physically assault him given half the chance.

Roy moved in with his girlfriend. *It won't last,* thought Joan. She remained as amicable as possible, clinging to the hope that sooner or later he'd realise what he'd done and what he was missing out on and would have a change of heart.

Janet insisted she would live with Joan only until she was old enough to join the armed forces. In the meantime she would be the closest thing Joan had to a husband, mum, dad and Aunt Nellie. It was around that time Janet ceased to be little sisterly.

They fitted shift work in around looking after the kids and, when agreed, dropped them with Roy and Nikki or Roy's parents. Cathleen hardly ever spoke to either of the girls any more, and if she did it was through the children: 'Has your mum remembered to pack a spare set of clothes and your dum-dum? Silly Mummy forgot last time, didn't she?'

Joan didn't usually dislike anyone much, but she thought Cathleen was a wicked-witch-bitch-cow. Alec, on the other hand, would always stand in the doorway and have a chat, asking, 'How are you doing, love?' He was really nice, the sort of man Joan had thought Roy would become. He was slightly shorter, broader and hairier, but he was still quite a charming man and was no doubt quite good-looking when he was Joan's age. Sometimes he even suggest coming in for a cup of tea. It was never awkward or anything, but although merely having a drink and a natter was innocent in itself, it did occasionally come with a slight risk. One time, when she took him up on the offer of hospitality he was wearing a black dressing gown, and whilst he made the cup of tea his robe seemed to accidentally come a little loose. When he pulled up the chair opposite, he left very little to the imagination and she knew exactly where Roy had inherited his good looks from. Unfortunately, Alec seemed totally oblivious to Joan's discomfort, and Joan didn't want to embarrass him by drawing attention to his wardrobe malfunction (she was mostly worried he'd catch a cold). From then on if he was not fully dressed, she would always be slightly hesitant to join him for a cup of tea or coffee.

Alec came to think of Joan like the daughter he never had – or more like the daughter he wished he'd had, unlike the selfish piece of work who lived in the States and was more like her mother than her mother. In a way he felt being kind to Joan was the least he could do, after the way his son had treated her. His relationship with his son was like that between two brothers. He had always struggled to assert his authority, and when he did, he was generally undermined by his wife. He also failed to understand what had happened between Roy and Joan, perhaps due to his advancing years and forgetfulness, or from being henpecked for so long. How to appreciate the inner complexities that make relationships work and fail, the patience needed, the give and take… he'd had that understanding beaten out of him long ago. And unlike family relationships that you are born into, marriages need lots of key spice ingredients added to create the perfect recipe. He had long since forgotten why he and his wife were still together. It certainly wasn't love any more; it was down to convenience. That was it – his life was all about convenience.

Joan decided he was probably only talking to her because it was convenient and she wasn't like his wife.

The badminton game was set up to try to persuade Joan that it was time to finally accept Roy wasn't coming back, that he and Nikki were an unbreakable item and she really should move on. The idea was partly Nikki's and partly Cathleen's. It seemed brutal to Roy, but he did feel it would be beneficial for them all in the long run if Joan could carry on with her life too.

Janet thought it was crazy when Joan said she would accept the invitation. She could see the relationship had remained civil mostly, but it was clear to Janet that Roy had had his cake and eaten it. He had got away with murder, robbing her sister of a life by getting her pregnant and then dumping her.

'I can't believe you! Are you effing mad?' Janet asked in her usual blunt manner.

Joan just stared back at her impassively. She had got into the habit of doing that, much to Janet's frustration. Janet would ask Joan barbed questions, and rather than answer, she'd just stare vacantly for a while as if lost in thought. Broken. The truth was, Joan really was lost in thought. Whenever a horrible thought was provoked into her mind, she'd remember lying on the hospital bed thinking Roy would be there soon, and the pain, the pain like nothing imaginable: burning, ripping, tearing.

She'd pictured her mum and dad burning in a car wreck then, and she was so scared. The nurse – she was Oriental, which Joan thought lovely at the time – had such a wonderful smile and was so caring, and she wiped Joan's head and said, 'He be here soon.' Then Janet and Nellie and Cathleen had arrived, and she was so happy, and yet all she wanted was Roy to be there. She was scared something bad was going to happen to her during the birth, and she was scared something bad was going to happen to the babies. Where was he? She panicked that something bad had happened to Roy. She wanted him there to tell her everything was going to be okay. Then the babies arrived and he turned up and everything was perfect again: she wasn't scared or alone, and he looked happy, and she felt complete.

Then, right then – that was what she wanted. She wanted that feeling back. That's where she went when she couldn't talk. When she was broken. That's what she was thinking about when she looked impassive. Janet would never understand.

Alec decided he'd check on her mental well-being, he would 'broach the subject carefully' to the girl (that was what he called Joan when speaking to Roy or Cathleen or even Nikki). It was the right thing to do, and maybe she'd listen to him, he thought.

'Listen, Joan, how about me and you take the kids to the coast? They could do with running off some steam. You and me could have a little talk perhaps, and you can tell me how it's all going, eh?'

Alec had always liked the coast. He remembered skimming stones there as a youngster, and taking Roy and his sister when they were kids. He had always loved the penny arcades too, and he came prepared with a big bag of coins saved up in a piggy bank ready for the slot machines.

He kept the kids amused by playing the fool, running up and down the beach pretending he was scared of the sea. The kids thought it was hilarious and seemed spellbound by the magic of the seaside. It was a nice day, the best day Joan had had in years, she thought.

Momentarily, all the struggles and sadness were washed away by the sea. If only it was Roy here with her and not his dad, she thought.

Roy had seemed more distant to his dad too. He'd been so preoccupied lately, it was becoming a concern to Alec. Cathleen hadn't noticed. *How could she?* he thought. She was far too self-absorbed. Sometimes Alec couldn't help wonder how someone who doted on a child and professed to love him so much was so oblivious when he was clearly unhappy or out of sorts. Alec could picture Roy as a little boy, obviously unhappy about something, and Cathleen wouldn't know anything was the matter until he was actually crying and pointing to his bump or scrape or burn. No empathy, that was her problem, he decided. That and the fact she was a selfish bitch.

Roy was smoking more than ever and drinking coffee like it was going out of fashion. He wasn't eating. He was caffeine fuelled. He was simmering and always looking stressed. Business was going great, and yet he had so much going on he couldn't relax with the kids or even Nikki. Perhaps he was having another affair, Alec thought. It wouldn't have surprised him. Bollocks for brains. But that didn't seem likely, as he was always at work or off to more meetings with suppliers or setting up exciting new trade deals.

'Did you see that throw?' Alec said, pointing to his granddaughter in an exaggerated fashion and then clapping his hands. 'Speaking of which, I heard our young man here is going to be a fireman when he gets older, aren't you, butch?' he said, roughing up Adam's hair.

Adam looked at his mum and granddad, totally confused, as he had never even thought of becoming a fireman when he grew up. But as his little mind worked it sounded like a great idea, and a huge, toothless grin spread over his grubby, sweaty, little face.

'Roy mentioned inviting you to go out with him and Nikki to the sports club, a game of badminton or something? You sure you want to go through all that, love?'

Janet had called Joan crazy for considering the idea. She wasn't sure what to say to Alec. She decided to be honest.

'I have no idea if it's a good idea or not, to be honest. It's just an evening out, and I rarely go out. We see each other at the weekends anyway, when we drop the kids off, and it's always been okay, so why not? We aren't enemies or anything.'

'But you know Roy and Nikki are going to be there… together, as a couple. You'll see them together – won't it be a little uncomfortable, love, won't it hurt your feelings?'

Alec was right, of course. It was going to be terribly difficult. Joan still loved Roy, and that was plain for all the world to see.

From Roy's point of view, he had been amicable since splitting up. He had few regrets when it came to how he felt about Joan physically, but he did regret the trouble and pain he had caused, not just to Joan but to the kids – he hoped they were young enough to not really have been affected. He had loved Joan and still did love the person he had known and first gone out with at school, but it was a different kind of love, like that for a friend or a pet. He cared for her but didn't really care about her. He loved her for being the mother of his kids, but nothing more.

Joan still loved Roy. How could she not? He was still gorgeous. He had been a boy and now he was a man. He had only made one mistake and that had been Nikki. Perhaps he had got himself in a situation and had no way out. He was still quite young and naive, and all men are stupid, according to Janet at least. Perhaps it was Nikki's father's influence over Roy's business that kept him with her. Joan remembered seeing Nikki's dad around town and even occasionally in the baker's. He had an air of menace about him; he wasn't nice like Alec. Roy had said if it wasn't for Nikki's dad's contacts, the business wouldn't be doing so well. Joan remembered seeing Alec looking a little crestfallen at how little appreciation he seemed to be getting whilst Nikki's dad was gaining all the plaudits. She and Alec also felt it a little odd that Roy didn't think the success was down to his own hard work. Perhaps Roy was using Nikki, Joan thought – hoped and prayed. Then perhaps he'd come back to her and the kids. Maybe he was just doing this to make sure they were all provided for forever. Maybe they would have to run away together as a family. Joan just needed to be patient.

Roy and Nikki had discussed asking Joan for a divorce. Had they tried, Joan would have said no. She knew if she agreed, Roy would be gone forever. She also had nothing to gain from agreeing right then. If he was successful later and still hadn't returned to her then it would have been worth it. Half of nothing is not as good as half of everything, especially when everything is all that they'd have and she had nothing to lose.

'I don't think Roy's happy,' Joan said to Alec.

'What makes you say that, love?' Alec's expression transformed quickly from mock-startled to quizzical; he'd seen that Roy wasn't himself.

'I just don't think he is,' Joan replied.

Alec went quiet, thinking. He wasn't entirely sure why Joan thought it was anything to do with her.

'What about Nikki? Do you think they are... do you even like her?' Alec asked, changing tack.

'She seems quite nice,' said Joan, lying. She hated Nikki, who had stolen her man and messed up her life, and what's more, she was beautiful and sporty and had nice clothes, and seemingly lots of money too.

Joan didn't want to admit it, but she had always felt like Nikki hated her and looked down her nose at her all the time. She thought Nikki may even have stolen Roy partly just to spite Joan, who was just a piece of shit on her shoe.

This was unsubstantiated. Nikki really didn't see Joan as anything at all really. Just Roy's ex. The mother of his kids. And the lady with the key to the divorce and the potential for Nikki's happiness in the future.

Nikki could see the reasons to be nice to Joan. If she and Roy were perceived as being horrible in any way, Joan was more likely to make any future life plans hard for them. She could cost them a fortune. The kids were another matter – she definitely didn't want to test Roy's loyalties to the kids versus her, and she felt Joan knew that too. Basically, Nikki had decided long ago that Joan needed to be handled with kid gloves and Roy agreed. The best-case scenario that Nikki could foresee was Joan meeting someone else, and she thought she might just be able to help orchestrate that. But first she would need to befriend Joan and win her trust. Not easy for someone who had taken Joan's husband, Nikki appreciated, but she felt it might work.

On the day of the game, Roy had a bad stomach ache and couldn't shake the cough he'd had for a while, but against his better judgement he agreed to go along and not cancel the game.

Roy and Janet kind of agreed on something for the first time in years. The badminton game was a bad idea. Joan figured the get together was some sort of an olive branch or a way for her to prove herself as a good, fun person. She was never a bad person, and although never the life and soul of a party, she could have a laugh, she tried to convince herself. What was a laugh? She didn't even know what fun was any more. She would just try to be as happy as possible and laugh at any jokes even if she didn't understand them. Joan was sure Nikki would try to outsmart her and tell tricky jokes with double meanings that would go straight over her head. She felt a little knot tighten in her belly and a thousand butterflies break free from their burning chrysalises.

It had been years since Roy, or anyone, had invited her to do anything as a singleton, couple or group, and she was tickled pink to actually be going out. The kids were old enough now for her to finally be able to leave them for a few hours and the world wouldn't crumble. Perhaps this was the start of her becoming a human again. She had lost track of the number of times she'd believed this was her lot: to be a mum, nothing more, at the beck and call of the two kids. She really felt the signs were positive and that perhaps Roy was starting to make an effort with her again.

Joan hadn't done any exercise for years; in contrast to her sister, who ran daily and ate like a mouse. Joan pleaded with Janet to lend her some gym gear, training clothes, something sporty. But as soon as she held the brightly coloured running shorts up next to herself she knew she'd struggle to get them past her knees, and when she zipped up the hooded tracksuit top it made her look like a sausage and barely covered her boobs.

Joan slumped down on her bed, momentarily bested. She'd tried on pretty much all the clothes she owned before coming to the conclusion she had no clothes to wear to the gym. Undeterred, she decided to cut off a favourite pair of white summer trousers and wear some strappy sandals, as Janet's white plimsolls cut off the circulation in her toes. She opted for a Disney T-shirt too; it was young and fun. She was desperate not to embarrass Roy, but equally desperate to meet some new people and his new friends.

That's how Joan had decided to cope with the presence of Nikki: she would think of Nikki as Roy's new friend. He really didn't know her that well. How could he? They had never been through anything. She thought perhaps she could get on with this new lady. Maybe if she thought hard enough, she could pretend it wasn't Nikki at all. Perhaps they could meet up for coffee and go to the library, or if they ever got to be really good friends, perhaps they could take a trip to London and go to a museum or even a matinée.

Joan scolded herself for getting too excited and carried away. She brushed her hair with the old brush that her mum used to use on her as a kid, not noticing the build-up of static charge that could power a household for a month. Her hair was dry and frizzy, like straw. A week's worth of intensive conditioning might get some moisture back. It might have been easier to shave it off and start again. It was very close to a fully spruced Afro hairstyle. She really had become desperate for new friends.

She practised running on the spot and doing strokes as if playing badminton, looking at herself in the full-length mirror in her bedroom. Twirling a fluorescent hairband, she noticed her boobs bounced around uncontrollably under the T-shirt. Maybe Roy or his friend would find that alluring. Her black woollen tights looked snazzy under her shorts – so Janet told her. Warm? She was sweating just looking in the mirror.

Janet threw some makeup at Joan as she made for the door. She was picking the kids up from their grandparents'. 'I still think you're mad and this is a silly idea,' she said.

Joan fingered the brushes and lipsticks, unsure where to start… some blusher perhaps.

In the end, she'd transformed herself into a clown. If she dyed her hair red, she'd look like Ronald McDonald. She scrubbed it off and, undaunted, tried again. She became a Japanese geisha girl. She scrubbed it off. Her face was starting to get red and her eyes were puffy. She reapplied the red lipstick and decided that would have to do.

It was raining and she put on a big coat, as it was all she had. It was windy too, so she wrestled with the umbrella, trying to dodge puddles, but she could feel the water on her toes before she'd made it to the end of her garden path. Perhaps she should go back and put some wellies on, she thought.

As soon as Joan arrived at the sports hall she realised very quickly she had been set up on a date by Nikki and Roy. What was the point? she wondered – to embarrass her perhaps, or to hook her up so she'd be off their backs. Just the way they looked at her as she approached spoke volumes: there was very little genuine warmth. She had wanted to see kind, welcoming eyes, but instead she saw Nikki's look of disgust, like Joan had walked in carrying a dog turd in the palm of her hand; and Roy's displeased glare, suggesting, 'You see, this is why I'm not with her any more – she is clearly deranged,' instead of a look of kindness saved for a dear friend, lover and the mother of his children; and the new guy just thinking, *What the hell is that? Some sort of bushy-haired swamp donkey?*

She also knew right then that her outfit choice – which could have been perceived in a different light, the fashionistas of Carnaby Street might have approved. It could have been a nice, light-hearted topic of discussion in another circle – was a source of ridicule for her intended partner and those who already knew her.

The urge to turn around and run away overwhelmed her, to the point she physically froze. She felt petrified. Joan thought she heard her date say, 'What the hell is that?' She was looking at her toes, wondering why she felt like she couldn't move. Had she looked up, she would have known she had heard correctly.

Nikki fired an angry growl at their friend, mouthing 'Be nice', which soon shut him up, whilst Roy stood in staggered pity for Joan. She was embarrassing. This situation was embarrassing. He didn't want to put her through this. He felt sorry for her. What could he do now? Events were already transpiring; he was in the lap of destiny. Joan had single-handedly, and without any previous fashion statements, introduced punk fashion to their little leafy village.

As soon as Joan was introduced to the guy, Dave, she knew they'd never get on.

'Wotcha. Nice to meet yous, my love.'

It didn't help that Joan was naturally quite shy, and she wasn't really used to talking with labourers – Roy's carpet-fitting colleagues could be quite coarse.

Roy talked to them in-between coughing fits. Joan presumed he'd been out on a heavy night, as his face looked quite flushed. She watched him closely and thought he really didn't look well; he was a funny colour. She realised she had just been staring at him talking for quite some time and he'd done nothing to include her in the conversation.

After an uncomfortable amount of time Joan stood on the outside of this meeting, feeling like a spare part, Roy finally tried to involve her and Dave in a conversation with Nikki. This didn't go so well; Joan thought he was making some sort of private joke about the whole thing being rather awkward, so she laughed, which made them all stare at her. What Roy had said to Dave was, 'Last time we saw you was just after your mum died.' Joan hadn't heard this bit; all she heard was something about Dave's mum. Presuming Roy was being rude to get the others to cheer up, she laughed a full-belly laugh, which trailed off into an awkward, forced laugh when she realised she was laughing alone.

Dave was a loud brash type of guy, an alpha male, his laugh made other guys laugh. He wouldn't have noticed her usually, had they met at any other social occasion. He was rough and very loud, perhaps slightly deaf, Joan thought, but quite good-looking and obviously a bit of a ladies' man. He had a glint in his eye. Nikki seemed to like him a lot; perhaps they had been an item in the past.

Joan sensed Nikki was trying to read her mind, sussing out what she was thinking about Dave. Joan felt embarrassed. Who was this woman who'd nicked her man and was now reading her mind? Nikki looked her up and down, and the corners of her thin lips raised ever so slightly, as if deep inside she was amused, and yet her eyes showed no clues as to what she was feeling or thinking. The ice witch.

Nikki stood there in her matching designer gear and whispered something inaudible to Dave. Joan felt acutely self-conscious and twirled her hair and crossed her legs, kicking her heels like a schoolgirl. Dave sniggered at whatever Nikki said, then looked at Joan in a strange fashion. Over-friendly, like he was imagining having sex with her, or he was sympathetic. Joan wanted desperately to be liked, so she smiled and blushed when Dave commented that her outfit looked bohemian.

Joan watched as Nikki touched Roy more than she'd seen anyone do so for a very long time. She hadn't got used to seeing them together. She wanted to raise herself above being bothered; she tried to convince herself it should feel quite charming and natural. It wasn't working. She felt her stomach tighten as she watched Nikki's beautifully manicured nails gently and deliberately run along Roy's back. He was actually having a coughing fit and she was patting him on the back. But just watching her hands glide over his body, feeling every crease... Joan felt incredibly jealous and uncomfortable seeing them in close contact. She justified it as being like a masseur or nurse touching a patient.

Joan had forgotten what being in love, or lust, was like. Briefly, she imagined a young couple, maybe her and a handsome stranger, Roy even, walking hand in hand through a meadow on a barmy, hazy summer evening...

'Right then, let's get this going, shall we? How about Dave and Joan together versus me and Nikki to start things off?' Roy said.

Amazingly, it was quite fun. After Dave, Joan was paired up with Nikki, boys versus girls, and much to her surprise they made quite a good team. When she missed the shuttlecock a few times, Nikki and Roy actually said, 'Hard luck.' Dave sneered slightly, though, and was far more competitive. If anything, Roy was the weakest player.

With the game all square, the teams were mixed up again and Joan was finally paired up with Roy. This too was an unexpected triumph for Joan. Although she felt under greater pressure than she had whilst playing with Nikki, she enjoyed the high-fives and pats on the back she got after every point won. It was like they were a couple again and she was helping him – she was really happy.

When they played for the last point, Dave fell over and Joan sent the shuttlecock into the space he'd left as he slid across the floor with his hairy, sweaty belly out. Roy picked Joan up, giving her a big hug and letting out a whoop of delight. Joan looked deep into his eyes and was whisked away, thinking about tropical islands in a far-off part of the world. He'd been on the desert island for far too long, though, she thought, and needed feeding up. He felt really thin...

Roy put her down as Nikki came over to congratulate the winning team and join in the group cuddle. Joan was giddy with happiness and she knew, in that moment, that her sister was wrong. It had been a success, and everything might be all right after all.

Then Joan felt a hand on her bum and a gentle squeeze and her breath was taken away. She pulled herself away, trying to regain some composure and work out whose hand it was. Surely it was Roy meaning to pinch Nikki's bum and somehow pinching hers accidently.

'Oh, cheer up. I'm a loser too,' Nikki mocked Dave, who'd rushed in for the group hug.

Joan backed away from the group, feeling uncomfortable.

'Joan, what is it? What's the matter?' Nikki asked.

Joan looked at them all standing there. Roy, with his confused, vacant stare. Nikki, looking concerned. Dave, with a dirty look on his face…

Nikki followed Joan's gaze. 'What did you do, Dave?' she snapped.

'Er, nothing – honest!' he replied, looking like a guilty schoolkid caught pissing in the school pond.

'Dave, what have you done? Did he hurt you, Joan?'

Joan couldn't take the embarrassment of the situation any longer, and she turned and ran to the ladies' changing room. All of a sudden the whole predicament had caught up with her and she felt hugely frustrated and violated and stupid. She didn't even know why she was crying and running away, only that she felt she had made a fool of herself.

Roy, Nikki and Dave watched as Joan ran out of the gym and then Nikki said:

'That was great. Thanks, Dave.' She gave him an affectionate hug and kiss on the cheek.

'Ahhh, it's no problem. Anything for yous two, eh,' he said, clapping a friendly hand, which had just squeezed Joan's buttock, on Roy's cheek.

'You ought to get that cough checked out, mate,' he said to Roy as he watched his pal root around in his gym bag for a cigarette. 'It's not the cough that carries you off an' all that,' he said, chuckling.

'Right, I won't be long,' Nikki said, reaching up to give Roy a kiss as he exhaled a desperate lungful.

'All right, love, go and do what you need to do and I'll see you in the car,' said Roy.

Nikki made her way into the changing room and walked along the rows of benches. The air was humid and heavy with the smell of sweating bodies and shower mist; the floor was cold, the tiles slimy. After several rows she found Joan sitting and sobbing on a wooden bench beneath clothes hanging on pegs. She looked like a little schoolgirl. Nikki remembered times she had hid in the changing rooms at school when she had fights with other girls, usually about boys.

Her plan had worked. All she needed to do now was apologise for Dave's behaviour, and promise she would never have thought him capable of acting like that, and say how sorry she was. Then Joan would begin to think of Nikki as a friend.

Much to Nikki's frustration, she really did like Joan and admired her naivety and honesty, and she was really unsure how to break the old relationship. The rules seemed different to normal. She half expected Joan to be so angry with Roy that she would want nothing more to do with him and the kids.

Joan, meanwhile, still didn't want a divorce, and she was not convinced Roy's relationship with Nikki would last...

Chapter 5

Alec tightened the precise and perfect knot on his black silk tie.
His white shirt had been impeccably ironed. He'd spent about half an
hour carefully doing it, his mind focused on nothing else.

The house seemed strangely silent, apart from the occasional burst
of aerosol coming from Cathleen's room. She too had been carefully
getting ready, painstakingly applying her makeup and fluffing up her
hair before pinning on her black hat and veil. The house was sombre
in its stupor. They needed the kids' playful shrieks to break the
overwhelming air of melancholy that had engulfed their house and
lives.

Roy's parents were still too upset and broken to bicker. They'd just
realised they'd lost the thing that had kept them together all those
years and made them whole. Amazingly, it had brought them closer
together in some respects. Mostly because they were now scared that
one or the other might mention all the things they could and should
have done differently in the past they faced regret for the rest of their
lives.

'Oh, shit,' Cathleen said as she watched a tear well up in her eye
before running down her cheek, dragging mascara with it and burning
a trench in her heavily brushed blusher. She angrily fingered the top
of her designer black-sequin clutch-bag, which she'd painstakingly
organised with precision: an assortment of lipsticks, brushes,

eyeliners, mascara wands, nail varnishes, tissues and mints. It was all packed so tightly the crack of her fingernail breaking reverberated around her bedroom. 'Shit, shit, shit,' she repeated violently shaking the little bag, spilling its contents out and scattering them all over her bed.

She broke down again and Roy's dad stopped what he was doing, listening to her cry wondering whether to go and see if she was all right. 'It's bloody hopeless,' he heard her sob. She was right, he agreed silently.

Janet called to Joan: 'Are you nearly ready? We need to leave soon.'

Joan was sitting on the edge of her bed, looking out of the window and watching the naked branches on the trees dance in the wind. The spindly sticks were bare, the leaves having long since blown away, but soon there would be sticky new buds. Spring was coming. Life would start again – awoken, reborn. A squirrel hopped around on the grass, buffeted by the wind, looking for a misplaced nut, his tail moving like an undulating snake when he spotted next door's ginger moggy eyeing him hungrily.

It was grey and wet and windy, and Joan just wanted to go back to bed. She really didn't want to go through with today. Everything about it was a nightmare.

They made their way to the church, dodging puddles and wrestling umbrellas. Joan hadn't been there since they were married. She had been so busy, juggling the kids, and so shell-shocked, she hadn't really had time to grieve. She'd spoken briefly to Nikki and Alec, but everything had pretty much been arranged without any input from her, as if everyone had forgotten about her. It was all about the kids now, which Joan could appreciate, but as far as she knew she was still Roy's wife.

As they walked up to the church, Joan could see some familiar faces. She had hoped to perhaps see Alec and have a hug. She didn't know what to expect and hadn't heard from anyone else who was going.

Joan and Janet followed a few people Joan didn't recognise into the church, high heels rattling on concrete and leather soles squashing cigarette butts. She felt relieved as they shielded her entrance briefly, but then they disappeared into an aisle, leaving Joan and Adam and Janet standing opposite the vicar, who looked sheepishly at the congregation in front of him, as if looking for a friendly face or an easy space that he could suggest Joan occupy. None were forthcoming.

An air of steely aggression came from Nikki's family, who had set up camp in the first few rows on the left, and Roy's family and Nikki were on the right. Joan could see Nikki and Cathleen were already crying and comforting each other, while Alec stood impassively staring straight forward. Joan felt like she could read his mind. He knew she'd entered and was now standing there like a spare part. She, in turn, looked like a rejected child. For a second Alec looked like

Roy from behind. She thought he could have been and this was all a dream. She went to call out, but stopped as she noticed a few people turning around and staring at her and whispering, and then more, like a wildfire spreading. Word was getting around that the crazy ex had just arrived. 'I'm just Joan,' she wanted to shout. 'I'm here to bury my husband. And who the hell are you all, and how do you know us?'

Cathleen turned around, twisting like an old, gnarled tree. Her eyes burned into Joan, blaming, cursing, hating, suggesting this was all her fault. Still Alec faced forward. Then Nikki turned and her blond hair looking meticulous, in sharp contrast to her blackened eyes, streaming with muddy tears. A slight smile came to her eyes and mouth as Janet pulled Joan and Adam into the nearest pew.

Vicar Maginty was the clergyman again, as Joan had expected. His eyebrows looked even wilder than she remembered. He thought, as he looked at Joan, that he must ask how that lovely Aunt Mary of hers – or was it Shelly? – was keeping. He was totally unaware she had died.

As Joan sat down, she started thinking about Nikki's family. It was hard not to, as they had taken over the first few rows in the church. Who did they think they were? The men with their sharp suits, fat necks and greased hair, and the ladies, all quaffed, bouffant hairstyles and designer clothes. They weren't daft; they didn't want to miss out on all Roy's hard work and inheritance.

Joan watched as her daughter squeezed out from between Cathleen and Alec, past Nikki, and jinxed over to see Nikki's parents. Nikki's dad pretended to hide something in his hand and then magically found it in her ear. Sophie seemed animated and happy with them. Joan was stunned to see her call them Nan and Grampy, which made no sense as they weren't related at all. She was totally unaware of the relationship her daughter had developed with Nikki's parents. Joan realised how little she knew about Sophie's life independent from her own, Joan had presumed her daughter had spent the vast majority of time with Roy and Nikki and that would have been mostly shared with Roy's parents. All of a sudden she was aware she had another family, Nikki's parents and that Joan and Adam were totally excluded from.

The hums and whispers subsided and the wonky organ screeched through the silence. The old ladies warbled and the men struggled to find the right key and octave.

'How great thou art, how great thou art, then sings my soul.'

Vicar Maginty cleared his throat and began: 'Dearly beloved, we are gathered here today to celebrate the life of Roy Peter Selby, father of Sophie and Adam, son of Cathleen and Alec, partner of Nikki, and friend to many.'

Joan felt her heckles rise even further and a bit of sick came up in her throat. She had been written out of his history, his life, like she had never existed and their love and marriage had never occurred. She'd not asked to split up. She'd at no time wanted their relationship to end. To her it never had. On paper she was still his wife. The marriage was simply put on hold. She felt her knees go to jelly as a chorus of voices in her head started chanting, 'Joan, Joan, Joan, Joan, Joan.'

Vicar Maginty continued: 'It's times like these, when our nearest and dearest are taken all too soon, that we may question our relationship with the good Lord, Jesus Christ.'

Joan switched off; her head was a confused mess of static. She felt Adam nuzzle into her side and looked down to see him holding Janet's hand as she sombrely looked at the priest. What did he make of it all? Joan wondered. They had told him his daddy had gone away; they figured telling him Roy was dead might be too much. It was hard enough for the adults to accept, let alone the kids. The boy's dark eyes stared up at Joan. She could see Roy in him and she missed him so much. He had been her first love. She'd thought they were soul mates. She would have forgiven him, had she been given the opportunity. He had made her feel like a woman when she was a girl. He had loved her and she'd loved him back...

A tear gathered in her eye as Vicar Maginty warbled on in the background. She felt Adam reach up and pull on her coat and he squeezed her hand with a look of genuine concern and love. Janet passed Joan a tissue as the congregation were told to sit. There was a rustle of papers as those gathered checked the order of service to see what was next and who was reading.

Joan felt a strange sense of elation as she watched her and Roy's old school friend, Stuart, rise from his seat and make his way to the pedestal.

He was impeccably dressed, Joan thought, as he walked slowly to the front. A few noises perforated the cadence of his step: coughs and splutters, children being bribed with bits of biscuit and half-crushed orange segments, parents begging toddlers to be quiet. Elderly distant relatives talked slightly too loudly – 'Who is he?' 'I don't know, dear, but he looks important' – scrutinising his character and relevance. The church felt quite cold, but sunlight suddenly broke through the windows. It had been wet and windy when Joan had left in the morning, but then, at that moment, as Stuart made his way to the bull pit, he was illuminated in a saintly fashion. Much of the congregation wondered if he was single, switched on by his godly luminescence.

Stuart stopped and faced the crowd. He took a few breaths to compose himself. He had practised a fair few times at home in front of the mirror. When Nikki called asking him to do a speech he had been slightly taken aback. It felt like only yesterday when he'd visited Roy in the hospital when he heard he was ill. Stuart had bumped into Alec on the high street a few Saturdays earlier. He remembered him saying something about shadows on the lungs and the doctors being very concerned. Stuart hadn't gone out of his way to keep in contact with Roy over the last few years, and he certainly didn't think Roy's treatment of Joan was anything to be proud of, but he'd always known that a breakup was the likely outcome of that relationship. When he'd seen his old friend in the hospital bed, struggling to get air into his skinny, creamy-yellow-looking body, all the barbed comments and 'how could you' sentiments went out the window; all he felt was tragic sympathy. Here was the bloke who was always so full of life and verve. If you looked up 'charismatic womaniser', you'd probably see an illustration or photo of Roy accompanying the definition. You only got one life, and it always seemed to Stuart that Roy tried to live his and take any opportunities that came his way – especially with the girls. The young writer had always been envious of Roy for that; he truly was a ladies' man, and his nemesis to a certain extent. Stuart hadn't been at all jealous when he'd met up with Roy and Nikki after Roy and Joan's separation, and seen the flashy new car and heard the tales of Roy's rapidly expanding business empire. Jealous wasn't the right word; what he felt was sick. He'd tried not to judge how a man could leave a lady so soon after she'd just brought his children into the world. But then he was introduced to Nikki, who had this habit of turning all men in her presence into mush. She caught Stuart with her stare and the sparkle in her eye, and immediately he imagined walking naked and hand in hand with her along a tropical beach and into the sunset. So what if she was Roy's new girlfriend? Perhaps she would fall in love with him. Then he realised Roy had done it again: pulled a cracker. For that he would always be jealous. How did Roy always meet the best girls?

Stuart looked around the room. He noticed Joan. He remembered Roy saying he should keep an eye on her and that she had always liked him. Stuart had thought about this quite a lot. He thought it was a strange thing to say. He understood Nikki wouldn't be short of admirers. Joan, however, was more or less alone, except for her sister and the kids. Stuart knew nothing about kids. Children, to him, were strange, foreign, grubby little creatures, and he wasn't one for pets. But he agreed to all of Roy's requests and said his farewells, not wanting to think for a second this would be the last time he saw his old school friend. He thought it was perhaps just an infection, or a heavy cough. All this talk of cancer was so dramatic, he decided; a few weeks in hospital and Roy would be right as rain again.

'The first time I met Roy was on our first day at Long Meadows School. He was ever so ugly even then…'

This raised a titter from the congregation and then a hush fell over the church. A few stifled coughs and sniffs from those overcome with emotion couldn't halt Stuart's flow. He introduced them to his world, and painted a picture of two young lads who grew up together, sharing memories that would be lost forever once Stuart finished talking.

Roy's parents hung on to every word, desperate to know any last things about their boy that they would never get to know otherwise, picturing him full of life. His dad saw Roy as the man he had become, and his mum as the baby she'd once nursed. The joy in the happy tales twisted the knife through their hearts even more; the hollow sentiment that he would be missed not felt by anyone more than them.

But then you had Nikki and Joan, and they both loved Roy like no other. He truly was Nikki's soul mate; she had known love before, but not like they had shared. Joan, meanwhile, couldn't believe that any other love was imaginable or possible; she had never felt love like it for another man, and doubted she ever would. Joan sat watching Stuart speak, imagining the three of them as kids at school. Her mind switched back to fleeting memories of them talking in classrooms, walking on the playing fields, eating ice creams at the weekend and dancing at a party. In her mind's eye she could picture the three of them laughing, happy and carefree.

At the end of the service they carried the coffin past the congregation, and the first few rows of close family members filed behind the coffin. Joan watched to see if anyone would acknowledge her. Only Roy's dad gave her the faintest of looks as he blinked, but it could have been an attempt to blink away a tear. Roy's mum and Nikki were a tangle of black netting as they snivelled and shuddered back up the aisle.

Janet asked Joan what she wanted to do, and how long they were going to hang about for, and whether she want her to take the kids whilst Joan went to see Roy get put in the ground. Joan didn't want to go and she didn't want the kids to go either. She didn't know what was going on with her daughter. It then struck her that she had no control over her at all. When had that happened? She suddenly felt sick and angry and flustered. When had she given up her child, and how had that happened? She desperately tried to piece together the last few months. The kids had been more or less split up since Joan and Roy separated and Nellie died, but Joan couldn't ever remember agreeing to relinquish Sophie totally. It just seemed the right thing to do at the time, because the pair seemed more comfortable that way.

The kids had never been typical twins who played nicely together and wanted to be friends; no, they always competed and squabbled and fought. All of a sudden Joan was panicking. This issue was of paramount importance. She wanted them all to be together again. Immediately. Before any other harm could come their way. Her kids and Janet, that's what she wanted. She didn't want any more to do with Nikki and her family, and she couldn't care less about Roy's mum. What should she do? Perhaps speaking to Alec would be best…

'I need to see what they are doing with Sophie,' Joan said to Janet.

'What? Why?' Janet said, unsure why all of a sudden Joan needed to rearrange the current living situation.

Janet had also seen how comfortable her niece was with Nikki's family and Roy's parents, without Joan. It hurt her too, as she had built a good relationship with her nephew and felt aggrieved at missing out on the same with her niece. And Sophie was a pretty little poppet with Joan's eyes and incredible long brown hair that went all the way down to her bum. But she had this temper and flew into terrible rages that Joan had never been able to control. Janet had always felt they were down to Joan not being firm enough. The truth was, Adam was never was like that, especially with Joan and Janet. He was quiet and docile, and the only time he was inconsolable was when he hurt himself and Joan or Janet weren't around, and that was usually when he was with Roy's family. A grazed knee for Adam at Roy's house could mean a trip to A&E, but with Joan it meant a plaster. If Sophie was with Joan at the shops and didn't get a toy or sweet she wanted, she would scream and cry until she was sick, whereas Roy would just buy it for her. Roy and Joan sang from different hymn sheets as far as parenting the kids was concerned, and the kids wanted different things from their parents too.

Roy had wanted a closer relationship with his son; he just figured perhaps it would develop later in life. He quite liked the idea of going fishing with him or having a beer in a pub someday – talking about girls and rough-housing. These were the things he told Stuart he was scared he'd never get the chance to do with his boy. He regretted not having played more games with him, always being too busy with work or bouncing between places to kick a football about in the garden for a few hours. This, he presumed, was the reason Adam had ended up spending so much time with Joan and Janet. They gave him their time and were always there for him. This, in turn, was possibly the reason Sophie ended up spending so much time with him and Nikki, and then Nikki's family: they were hers and her brother couldn't compete for their attention. Roy regretted not giving them both his full attention. He wanted Stuart to tell his kids one day, should the opportunity present itself, that he was sorry.

Joan stood up as she noticed Stuart walking over. She wanted to be controlled and calm, but felt really excited at seeing a friendly familiar face. She was suddenly paranoid that her dress was stuck in her knickers and she brushed her bum subtlety, checking her clothes were all in good order. She then had the overwhelming urge to curtsy.

She managed to stop herself mid-bob, but was still acutely embarrassed.

Janet was talking with both the kids after they had weaved their way through the aisles and pews to be together when Stuart and Joan started to talk. Janet said the briefest of hellos, as if standing up and dragging herself away from the children was too much effort and all men were bumbling idiots anyway.

'It's lovely to see you too,' said Stuart in a dry, nonplussed fashion.

Janet fired him a quick filthy look before raising her eyebrows at Joan, who was still bobbing, before turning her attention back to the kids. This left Stuart and Joan facing each other in a slightly awkward silence.

'Your speech was fantastic,' Joan blurted out.

Just as Stuart went to reply, Nikki came up from behind and managed to envelope herself in his arms in a gushing mess, sobbing into his suit lapels. Taken aback by the interruption, Joan was unsure what to think or say.

'What's wrong with Nikki?' asked Janet.

'God only knows,' Joan replied.

Janet gave an eye-roll and shake of the head. 'I think she's auditioning for the amateur dramatics society,' she concluded.

Joan was fairly certain Nikki couldn't hear, but she gave Janet an angry glare anyway. Joan watched as Stuart struggled to regain some personal space. She wanted to laugh at his awkwardness and uncertainty over how to respond to the physical contact. It was like he was holding a live, semi-naked mermaid in the church.

'Are you okay?' Joan found herself saying before she'd even had a chance to work out what she was thinking or going to say.

Nikki turned and reached out a hand to Joan, her skinny protruding wrist struggling to hold up the weight of her jewel-encrusted talons. Joan didn't know whether to laugh, cry, swear, scream or shout. She wanted to smack her hand away. The pathetic wretch.

'It's all just so utterly sad and terrible,' Nikki snivelled through a snotty nose and black-mascara-stained eyes.

Joan took her hand, and the three of them stood linked in the church. Joan looked at Stuart who looked as confused and awkward as she felt, and then back at Nikki, who looked utterly ridiculous with her makeup ruined and her nose snotty and her clothes all over the place like she had just crawled through a hedgerow backwards.

One hundred and one thoughts were racing through Joan's mind. She looked at Nikki, refusing to let go of Stuart's hand, her body pressed to his. Joan hadn't been that close to a man since she was with Roy. The thought entered her head that Nikki was going to make a move on him next. Then she thought perhaps Nikki had already made a move on him. Joan found herself suddenly glaring at Stuart, her head about to pop, feeling let down and used and embarrassed again – set up, taken for a ride, hoodwinked… She realised she was squeezing Nikki's hand very hard and shook her hand free.

'How could you?' she muttered.

'Joan?' Nikki sniffed, confused.

'What's the matter, Joan?' Stuart asked as Joan started to back away, her head pounding, feeling betrayed.

There was a bang and a muffled crescendo as hundreds of hymn books fell from their cupboard near the entrance to the church. Joan saw Janet trying to clamber over handbags and kneeling cushions, and then, out of the corner of her eye, she saw the kids fighting like cat and dog, their silhouettes black against the light streaming in from the outside world. An ancient Chinese puppet show. Animated kids' violence.

Joan raced over and grabbed the pair of them by the arms, oblivious to the crowd growing in the doorway, wondering what was causing the commotion back inside the church.

'Pack it in, the pair of you,' she hissed as both of them continued to try to kick and punch and scratch at each other. Adam was already in tears as Joan asked, 'What on earth has got into you?' looking at both of them quizzically.

Adam spoke first, whimpering, 'She started it.'

Joan looked at Sophie, who fixed her brother with a stare Joan recognized – it was the one Joan usually reserved for her sister.

'Well, what did you say? What's it all about, eh?'

The little girl just stared at Joan with a thunderous look and defiantly squinted her eyes and buttoned her lip, refusing to talk.

'She said it's all your fault that Daddy is dead.'

Joan felt her hands loosen their grip on her children's arms. She felt suddenly faint and stabbed through the heart. How and why would her daughter have thought or heard or said such a thing? Joan went to kneel down so she could speak to Sophie. In her head she was preparing a speech in which she'd calmly point out to Sophie that Mummy had loved Daddy very much. But she didn't get the chance.

'It's all true and I hate you,' Sophie snapped.

Joan felt the knife twist in her heart and a thousand mirrors smash in her mind. She went to reach out to Sophie, who was backing away, but the girl slipped on the pile of books. As she fell she hit her head on the marble plinth holding the small crucible of anointed liquid. A collective gasp from all nearby was audible as the big marble plinth shifted precariously and the little glass bowl holding the holy water toppled free, sending a cascade of tiny droplets spraying out over the floor. As Sophie looked up, everyone could see she'd bumped her head and would have a nasty egg forming. She scrambled to her feet and ran with arms outstretched to Nikki, who crouched down and comforted the little girl like she was her own.

Joan just sat on the floor, gobsmacked, staring as Cathleen joined Nikki in seeing to her little girl – and then Alec and Nikki's parents joined in the gaggle of overprotective relatives, all delicately pawing at Sophie's head and casting blaming, accusing stares at Joan.

Stuart watched as Janet helped Joan to her feet and the crowd converged around Nikki and Roy's parents. Vicar Maginty was in animated conversation with the concerned congregation. Joan, Janet and Adam, meanwhile, exited discreetly at the side of the church, off into the back passage.

Chapter 6

Sometimes Joan thought the whole world had forgotten about her. Even her sister had moved on. It was just her and Adam now. Bumbling along. A few years had passed since the funeral, and Joan's existence and life totally revolved around the two of them. She worked to feed Adam and clothe him and protect him from the wicked world. He was her life now, her only project, her everything. She would drop him at school, go to work at the local library and meet him again after school. They'd have dinner together and chat about their days and what they might do at the weekend, and then she would read a book or watch TV whilst Adam did his homework, and then they would go to bed. This was the routine, and Joan presumed it would be her lot until the time came when Adam too would leave her.

Occasionally, Janet would come and stay, but she had her own life and was travelling the world with the Navy. She often said she would move home sooner or later because she wanted to become policewoman locally, but Joan just took what she said with a pinch of salt. Somewhere along the line Joan had grown slightly resentful that Janet had her own life and had gone off and left them. Whilst Janet was off 'God knows where', Joan was left with Adam. But they got by just fine.

Very occasionally, Sophie would visit, but she was never really happy see Joan and Adam. She was far happier with her life with her other mum, Nikki, doing fabulous things like riding horses and seeing wonderful stuff.

Joan hardly heard from Roy's parents, and often wondered whether they'd moved away. She wasn't bothered personally, but she couldn't work out what her son had done to warrant seeing his grandparents rarely, if at all. Maybe he was too much of a reminder of Roy? Joan couldn't get her head around it. Perhaps it was her? Then, out of the blue, Alec would turn up for a cup of tea, and all he would speak about was the wonderful stuff Sophie and Nikki were out doing. Joan would decide Cathleen had rowed with him, or sent him out, or was poorly, or perhaps had died, so he was now free from her demands and able to visit again. They never spoke about her. But when Alec turned up talking about how wonderful Nikki & Co. were, Joan wished he hadn't bothered.

Adam was now ten years old, and the time had arrived for him to go to secondary school. The school Joan and Roy had gone to seemed the logical choice; it was a good school and local.

On the day of his induction at his new school, Joan walked with Adam and held his hand, and she felt good – youngish, healthy, happy and in love. Of course, it was a different love, but the sun was shining and just for a second she felt like a schoolgirl holding Roy's hand again. It all felt like yesterday…

As the old school building loomed on the horizon, Joan felt Adam's hand tense up just a little in apprehension and his walking pace slowed a bit.

'Oh, don't worry, it's not that bad,' Joan reassured him. 'This is where I first met your daddy. We had some lovely times here.'

Joan pictured herself walking with Roy to get their exam results. Was that the last time she had been here? She wondered.

They walked down the wide gravel driveway leading to the main entrance. Other new kids in a variety of different local uniforms were desperately pulling their parents towards their friends, huddled in familiar colour-coordinated clans. Adam didn't seem too bothered about joining up with the kids from his school, and although they acknowledged each other, Joan noticed Adam didn't do so with the same excited, childish glee as the other kids. Joan was aware that her boy was somewhat aloof. He was calm and controlled. Perhaps shy? But he was definitely more confident than she ever was. Maybe he was hip, cool and trendy, she thought... maybe he was more like his father. Perhaps he'd be a leader of men rather than a follower – Joan hoped so. She always worried she had mollycoddled him too much. She wanted him to grow up to be a man's man and a gentleman. She always worried about everything imaginable when it came to Adam. She had never had anyone tell her she was a good mother. She just did what she could and took each day as it came.

They walked through the big glass doors at the front of the school. The main hall was to the left, a large stairway was in front of them and a marbled corridor led off towards the staffroom on the right; they were caught at the crossroads.

'Miss Jones!' called a familiar male voice.

'Yes, sir,' Joan answered, as quick as a flash, turning in the direction of the voice, a natural smile illuminating her face.

'My goodness, it really is you. How very charming. Well, you certainly haven't changed in the slightest, nope not at all. No doubt you're late again, eh?' Mr Hothouse said in a warm, jovial fashion.

'No, sir, I mean Mr Hothouse, err…' Joan bumbled through her words, caught in a time warp and for the first time in a long time completely tongue-tied and flabbergasted.

Mr Hothouse stood facing her wearing the same style of beige corduroy jacket he'd worn when she was at school. He had one hand on his hip, like a cowboy about to reach for his gun, but his eyes were fixed on her whilst he grinned animatedly. He'd aged quite well. *He's still a tall man,* Joan thought for a second, before getting cross with herself for thinking he might have somehow shrunk in the few years since she'd last seen him. At least he wasn't bent crooked by age. His hair had gone a little grey around his ears, but that made him look a bit more sophisticated. There was still something about him, Joan decided, as all of a sudden she felt a little hot under the collar.

Then a slight yank on her hand slapped her out of the stupid red-faced grin she was currently producing, much to her son's bemusement.

'Mum!' Adam snapped, trying to get Joan to regain her composure.

It was no good. Joan simply giggled and did some over-exaggerated blinks and tittered as if she'd just been told a joke that only she had heard.

'Right, well then, absolutely lovely seeing you again, errrrr, Mrs Ermmm?' Mr Hothouse left the question open-ended and raised his eyebrows, waiting for Joan to fill the gap.

'Mrs... well, Miss really... well, it's kinda complicated, you know. I was, am, Mrs Sweeting... haha ha. My husband, Roy, you know, you remember him, you taught him too – he died, ha ha ha.' Joan was rambling, and then she realised she'd made a joke about her husband being dead and laughed about it in front of her son and old school teacher. 'Oh God, erm....' She swallowed a chortle and in the blink of an eye her mood went from hysterical to just-trod-in-dog-poo. 'I'm just Joan. Call me Joan now, please.'

Mr Hothouse held out his hand, smiling, and looked deep into her eyes and said sincerely, 'How awful. It must have been absolutely horrific for you, my dear girl.'

Joan held his hand. It was quite big and surprisingly warm and soft – slightly papery, with an imperceptible greasy feel, she decided, making her hand at home in his. He didn't let go, just stared deeper still into Joan's being. She stopped breathing.

'Mum, I've got to go,' Adam pleaded, desperate to break his mother's trance.

'He's quite right, Miss Jones, I mean Joan. The young man doesn't want to be late on his first day!' Mr Hothouse said with a cheeky glint in his eyes.

Joan slowly awoke from her mental shutdown. 'Yes, right, erm, okay. Well then, be seeing you, Mr Hothouse.'

'Be seeing you then,' Mr Hothouse said; and he followed up with a barely audible, 'hopefully.'

As Adam led Joan off, Mr Hothouse just stood in the corridor, beaming at Joan. Eventually, he did a slow overhead wave, like he was wiping a high window, continuously watching as Joan was escorted away. She turned twice more whilst being ushered along the corridor, checking he was still watching, before she gave a coy little wave and, for no reason at all that she could justify, a saucy heel lift. Then Adam pulled her into the classroom where his induction was about to begin. Had Mr Hothouse really said 'hopefully'? And did he really seem overly pleased to see her? Joan pondered, excited by the reunion.

Adam hadn't even sat down before he decided he didn't much like that Mr Hothouse. 'God, Mum, you are so embarrassing.'

Joan would have agreed, but she was off already on another steamy Mr Hothouse daydream.

The first day at school soon came around. Joan had been through the lessons thoroughly, making sure Adam had all the right gear in his bag to face any eventuality. He had a rugby kit, PE kit, and every colour of textbook imaginable: green for biology, blue for physics and English, yellow for geography, red for maths and chemistry. Eventually, his bag weighed a ton, but once he knew what lessons were on which day, they could then plan accordingly and remove any unnecessary weight.

Joan had taken Adam to get his hair cut at the weekend, and he looked really neat with his short back and sides. When she saw him standing in his uniform, looking so smart, she spoke to Roy in her head. It wasn't the first time she'd done it, but this time it was to say Adam had turned out all right. She was proud of him and pleased with herself, and she wanted Roy to know his son looked good. She went on to think, *No thanks to you*, but banished that thought quickly. She was slightly alarmed to see just how well Adam's blazer and trousers actually fitted him. She had bought them a little too big on purpose, in the hope he'd grow into them over his first year. He was definitely shooting up, but she hadn't expected to need to buy a uniform more than once a school year. She'd seen kids in the shop whom she thought would take a few years to grow into their uniform, their hands totally covered to their fingers by their sleeves and the blazer shoulders so big they looked like they were dressed up in some sort of Teddy Boy suit.

A few terms passed, and Adam seemed to settle in quite quickly. It was soon his first parents' evening. Joan was really excited, not just for the update on how her son was progressing, but also, sadly, because it was an evening out and something to do. She had managed to get earlier appointment times, so she could go straight from work and meet Adam at the school gates. They shared a packet of chips before Joan inspected his uniform and attempted to lick down some spikey hairs, but was brushed away by an embarrassed Adam.

'God, Mum!' he said, pulling away and ruffling his hair, checking no one was watching or hiding in the bushes in front of his school.

'Are you nervous about seeing any of the teachers?' Joan asked, expecting some level of apprehension,

'No, not really,' Adam replied, totally at ease with the situation. 'Mrs Dimmock is a bit of a cow bag,' he added.

'Hey, don't be rude,' Joan said playfully, pretending to be cross and smacking her boy on the leg, but she made a mental note to take whatever Mrs Dimmock said about Adam with a pinch of salt.

'Then there's your favourite, Mr Hothouse…'

Joan's heart fluttered at the mention of his name. She had been deliberately trying not to think about him, as she'd done so little else since their last meeting. She hoped she wouldn't make as big an idiot of herself again.

'Oh, I'm sure you will be fine,' Joan reassured her son, thinking she wished she could say the same about herself. Then she thought, *I must make sure I don't laugh at anything silly.* Joan was well aware she had a habit of laughing when nervous or when she didn't quite get a joke.

'But I'm not you, Mum,' Adam replied sincerely.

'What on earth does that mean? Why would you say that?' Joan asked, slightly taken aback.

'Mr Hothouse thinks because you were excellent at English I should be too, but I'm not. I'm not you, and I don't want to be because, well, because English is boring…'

'Oh, well, you think so, do you? I'm sure Mr Hothouse is just trying to help you. You know, sometimes teachers are hard on you because they want you to succeed. I'm sure you are very good at English, and could be even better if you wanted to be,' Joan rattled off, oblivious to how boring, patronising and condescending she was starting to sound.

The first few meetings were an overwhelming success. Adam was naturally very good at sport, and he enjoyed metalwork class. Joan felt pleased he was clearly showing no signs of being over-mothered and incapable of holding his own in a male environment.

Next up it was English, and Mr Hothouse. He was sitting on a chair, listening intently, as a large lady with short, blond, permed hair and bright-pink lipstick talked at him. Her husband was a lot smaller, with thinning brown hair swept over in a side parting, a large Roman nose and a thick brush-like moustache on a protruding top lip that overhung a non-existent chin, making him look like some sort of ferret. He seemed quite content to let her do the talking whilst he surveyed the horizon, checking for eagles. She was clearly the boss.

When Mr Hothouse noticed Joan and Adam take their places on the row of grey plastic chairs to wait their turn to see him, he sat up in his seat, suddenly animated, and flicked out his long arm to expose his wrist and check the time on his watch.

'Goodness me,' he said, interrupting the large lady's flow, 'we seem to have run out of time!'

This sparked the rodent-like man into action. He too sat up in his seat and looked around desperately for some sort of clock to check and a referee to adjudicate over whether the allotted time allowance had depleted.

'Mrs Heath, I assure you I will look into all your concerns, including modernising our reading list, but I can most definitely tell you that the reading list will not at any point in the future include anything about Tottenham Hotspur Football Club. Thank you for your time and good night.'

With that Mr Hothouse stood up and ushered the family away. Joan stood up, smiling, as Mrs Heath walked past, saying to her husband in an out-of-breath fashion, 'Well, that was a bit rude.'

Her son, Toby, looked nonplussed. As he passed, Adam gave him a slight eyebrow raise. A mutual understanding between boys that they would far rather be outside playing football than stuck with the embarrassment of being with family in a public situation. It was by far the most excruciating thing ever to happen in their young lives; right up there with clothes shopping, or going to the cinema or McDonald's, or any other pastime that was equally humiliating if witnessed by any peers… a bit like wearing your sister's knickers or wetting/shitting yourself in public around friends or potential girlfriends for any lad.

The Heath clan scowled as Mr Hothouse smiled warmly and shook Joan's hand and ruffled Adam's hair. Adam looked at Mr Hothouse like he'd taken leave of his senses, and watched as he sat back down with his long arms and long hands virtually halfway across the table. His body language and demeanour couldn't have been more in contrast with his previous meeting. He was sitting there smiling like *he* was the child being praised for good performance at a parents' evening. In fact, he looked more like a dog sitting opposite a butcher with a handful of minced meat…

'Well, I'll start off by saying it's all coming along nicely with Adam's English. He's quite the chip off the old block, if I may say so.'

This was all news to Adam, who had been sure Mr Shithouse was going to give him a hard time because he certainly didn't seem to think Adam was a good or favoured pupil during the day.

Joan was delighted, and gave her son a gentle elbow in the arm and said quietly, 'I told you so.'

Joan wiggled her back straight on the plastic chair, sitting up intently, expecting to hear more praise for her wonderful academic, sporting son.

'Now, Miss Jones, I wanted to mention the upcoming English trip the school are organising. We're going to visit Chaucer's home and then take in a play in the evening before heading back to school – quite late in the evening, I'm afraid. Well, you see we need a couple of parent helpers. We already have Mrs Blackett, George Blackett's mum, who is also a dinner lady and part-time cleaner and, in extreme situations, a stand-in supply teacher.'

As Mr Hothouse sold the idea to Joan, he turned his palms upwards, as if offering to take Joan away. She was already listening attentively and saying, 'Right, right, well, I'll have to check with work, but the trip sounds fascinating,' as Mr Hothouse nudged his foot forward to see where Joan's feet were situated. She had her legs crossed and was jiggling her hanging foot up and down, so when Mr Hothouse made contact with her foot, she presumed she'd kicked him and she apologised, sat up in her seat and put both her feet firmly on the floor.

As Joan reaffirmed that she would definitely like to come on the trip if she could take the time off work, Mr Hothouse leant back in his seat, quickly scanning the room for any unwanted attention, and then crossed his long legs and glanced under the table, judging the distance from the foot of his crossed leg to Joan's feet. Mr Hothouse glanced at Adam. He had switched off as his mum wittered on and seemed focused on playing with the cotton thread attached to a black button on his blazer sleeve that had started to unravel. Mr Hothouse tried again with the tip of his toe, gradually moving towards Joan's legs. The angle was all wrong for him to tap her feet, so with the tip of his leather shoe he tried to gently run his foot down Joan's leg.

Joan was startled and said 'sorry' again, thinking somehow she'd got her legs in the way of Mr Hothouse's feet.

'Sorry, my fault,' said Mr Hothouse, blinking purposefully, as Joan tried to sit comfortably in her chair and Adam looked at her, unsure what was occurring under the table but thinking it was probably Mr Shithouse's ridiculously long legs and feet getting in a tangle.

'So when did you say this trip was happening?' Joan asked, slightly flustered and unsure whether the second contact was entirely accidental. Surely Mr Hothouse couldn't have meant to kick her? Perhaps he was trying to get her attention. But not in front of all these people and her son, surely. Joan looked at Adam, who was now scanning the room, bored out of his brain. Just checking out what the other kids were doing in their similarly boring situations. Joan noticed him smile as he watched one lad who was obviously getting told off by his parents, whilst the teacher sat smugly, revelling in the turmoil created.

'Oh, yes, quite right, next Wednesday, if you can make it. That would be absolutely superb.' Mr Hothouse gave Joan a suggestive look and a cheeky grin that hinted at far more than just a school outing.

Joan was slightly puzzled by his meaningful stare, but then she felt his foot tap on her shoe three times and she stopped what she was going to say and just stared at him, gobsmacked. He raised his eyebrows suggestively and slight furrows appeared on his sweaty brow. Then Mr Hothouse ran the toe of his shoe deliberately up Joan's leg, causing her to take a sharp inhale of air. The leather detail on Mr Hothouse's brogue got caught on Joan's tights, and as he tugged his foot away it scratched Joan's leg and pulled a ladder and hole in her new tights; there was a slight cracking noise as the nylon gave way.

'Jesus Christ – ouch!' Joan yelped, skidding back a metre in a millisecond in her chair.

Adam looked at her, confused, as she shot behind him on the plastic seat, the plastic studs at the end of its thin black-metal legs roaring their displeasure at being pushed roughly against the old hall's heavily varnished floor.

Mr Hothouse looked quickly around the room at the other parents and teachers – including the headmaster, a small but immensely powerful man who, attracted by the noise, spun around on the spot, mid-conversation with the PE teacher. The headmaster did that thing that spectacle-wearers do: he looked through his glasses on the tip of his nose, trying to see what was going on. But because he was a small man, he needed to put his head quite far back to be able to get the sight lines correct. He also went up on tiptoes to try to work out who was causing the kerfuffle. The head watched, scrutinising the situation and his staff member's reaction, and was slightly alarmed by the parent's expression. But then other parents, alerted by the sound of screeching furniture, thought an opening might have arisen in the appointment game with the English teacher, and they blocked the headmaster's view as they gathered around the scholar's desk. The head momentarily forgot his conversation with the PE teacher as he struggled to see as Mr Hothouse apologised profusely and blamed his 'stupid, ugly long limbs'.

'I'm just not at all suited to sitting on these ridiculous chairs at these desks, not at all. Please forgive me. Whatever must you think…? They are better suited to hobbits and dwarves.' Mr Hothouse grinned at Adam.

Mr Shithouse's shit long arms and shit long legs, more like, Adam thought.

Joan licked her finger and ran it down the scratch on her leg. She was unsure what had just happened. She wasn't sure whether she was angry, alarmed or allured. She looked up at Mr Hothouse, who said:

'Miss Jones, I really am terribly sorry. Please allow me to replace your tights.' But even as he said this a brazen glint came into his eyes, like he was suggesting taking her tights off and putting on some new ones.

'Erm, it's quite all right, Mr Hothouse. I mean, I am sure I can cope. I mean, it's nothing really. Accidents happen. It really is reassuring to know Adam is doing well in his English class. I'm really very pleased, and I'm sure he's in very capable hands with you. I think we have taken up enough of your time for now, so we will be seeing you, Mr Hothouse...'

'Right then, okay, you will let me know about your availability for the school trip, Miss Jones? Won't you?'

The rest of the parents' evening was a formality, and generally Joan was pleased with how everything went. But she couldn't get what had happened with Mr Hothouse out of her head. What on earth was he playing at? Joan was sure he was still married, but he had almost one hundred per cent certainly tried it on with her. She wanted to laugh, but she also felt quite sick. What would have happened if someone had seen? It was crazy. She'd had a crush on him for as long as she could remember, but he was her teacher. Still, that was a long time ago and things had changed, things were different now. She was married – *was* married; she was single now, she corrected herself. A little devil appeared in her mind, allowing her a second's thought of being free and single. Theoretically, she was free and single; she could do what she liked… or whom. But, but… well, this sort of thing just shouldn't happen, and especially not to her. She felt a little bit guilty, but then the thrill of someone wanting her, especially Mr Hothouse, whom she had lusted after for so long, started to cloud her mind.

Joan pulled off her tights and ran her finger over the red scratch again. She looked at herself in the mirror of the bathroom cabinet as it started to steam and blur around the edges from the hot bath she was running. Looking at her face she struggled to see the young girl hiding within the lady staring back. She thought about Roy for a second, and then she thought about Nikki, and then Stuart, and then Roy's dad, and then the guy from the badminton game… Joan laughed and then cried as she poured bubble mixture into the torrent of boiling water.

Nearly a week passed, and Joan avoided making any decision about the school trip. She thought if she didn't say anything, the whole event might come and go, and if she was lucky, it would all be forgotten. She booked the day off work just in case, though. Every now and then she imagined going and played out the different likely outcomes. Would it pass without any further situations developing?

Joan couldn't be sure. She imagined Mr Hothouse acting the gentleman and them both laughing whilst dealing with the kids. Perhaps even Joan and Mrs Blackett would get on and nothing would happen with Mr Hothouse. Adam came home a few times with messages from Mr Hothouse asking if she was coming on the trip, and Joan replied that she was still trying to get the time off work, even though she had already booked it off. Joan wasn't sure what she wanted to do, or even what she was waiting for; she just needed the extra encouragement or discouragement or simply the courage to make a decision – preferably the right decision. She was sure that whatever she did, though, it would be wrong. No one would have entertained the notion of her getting involved with a married school teacher anyway. Joan knew it was wrong, and she knew everyone would tell her it was wrong too – everyone except the bad girls at school, perhaps. The ones who had all the fun.

Then the phone rang. It was late, about half ten.

'Hello?'

'Miss Jones?'

'Erm, yes.'

'Hi, Miss Jones, it's me, Sam Hothouse… Mr Hothouse. Erm, I'm just calling about tomorrow's school trip. I haven't heard from you, but I saved your space just in case and well, I've just heard that Mrs Blackett has let us down. I mean, sorry, goodness this is all a bit of a mess actually… I should say that Mrs Blackett can't come now as she's had something come up, a bereavement or something, and the whole trip will be cancelled if I can't find an assistant to accompany me, and at such late notice you really are mine and all the pupils' only hope.'

Joan was slightly taken aback, firstly by Mr Hothouse referring to himself by his first name, which sounded strange to the schoolgirl side of her, and secondly by how he had now presented the trip – far more formal and above board. It didn't seem quite as risqué, which made Joan feel a little less apprehensive.

'Well, Miss Jones, will you save our English trip? Will you be our Lady Godiva?'

Joan quickly tried to think how her joining the trip could possibly be anything like a naked lady riding a horse through town. Stumped, she agreed. 'I think I should be able to accompany you, yes, that will be fine.'

'Oh, wonderful. I knew you wouldn't let us down. Terrific. Now I'll be driving the school bus, so I'll possibly need you to help with some directions, if that's okay? Fun, eh! An adventure. It should all be quite straightforward really, and I reckon we'll be able to do it with one toilet stop on the way... The parents have been told to pick the kids up at ten thirty p.m., and I'll be able to drop you and Adam home after too. How does all that sound?'

The kids clambered on board the minibus. It was a white van with the school emblem, tattered and faded, printed on the side. It smelt of stale cigarettes, and the material covering the seats had greasy hand-marks where hundreds of sweaty pupils had levered themselves on board following organised forays, often into enemy territory. The floor was grimy and sticky from congealed orange slices, Deep Heat, Vaseline, blood, sweat and Savlon.

'Don't hang about, Miss Jones, climb aboard,' Mr Hothouse suggested in a seaman-like fashion.

Joan resisted the urge to say, 'Yes, sir.' She was eager to establish how exactly she should speak to Mr Hothouse going forward. Perhaps they could discuss how she should address him en route. She couldn't get past him being her teacher... She had to remind herself she was an adult too.

Joan took her place at the front, next to the driver's seat, and watched as Adam clambered on board and took a window seat towards the middle of the bus. He looked thoroughly pissed off already. He gave his mum a bemused look and scowled out of the window. Joan considered this his usual attitude towards everything at the moment; he was no doubt thinking, *This is all so stuuuupid.*

The bus doors slid, groaned and thudded shut, and the van had a final wobble as Mr Hothouse clambered aboard.

'All set, Miss Jones?' he asked whilst looking in the mirror, checking all the kids were more or less seated, before he turned the ignition and the old van cleared its throat and spluttered to life.

'All set, skipper,' Joan said cheerily, deciding to test the boundaries.

Mr Hothouse laughed ardently and smacked Joan high on the lap, saying, 'That's the spirit.'

Joan looked at where his hand had just made contact; she felt the warm glow of his hand's impression heating the surface of her leg. She looked at an imaginary handprint approximately where he'd playfully smacked her. It was closer to her crotch than her knee. She felt her insides tighten. She looked at him, then swivelled in her seat to see if any of the kids could have seen, checking the windows and mirrors for angles. The only mirror she could see was the rear-view one, which was pointing at his eyes, and the seats were shoulder-height so all the kids could possibly have seen from behind was part of Mr Hothouse's face in the reflection and the back of their heads.

Joan was temporarily stunned that he had brazenly smacked her. She could see his lips moving, forming a mischievous smile, as he drove the bus out of the school gates, acutely aware that his actions had affected Joan. He joined the main road leading out of town towards the motorway. Joan was conscious that somewhere nestled within the childish din coming from the seats behind her was her son.

Before she realised what she was doing, Joan smacked Mr Hothouse back, high on the lap. She looked dead ahead, poker faced... *Two can play at that game,* Joan thought. She noticed Mr Hothouse seemed to go rigid in his seat. She watched out of the corner of her eye as he kept his attention fixed on the road ahead, only occasionally taking the briefest of looks at the kids in the rear of the car.

Joan suddenly had a pang of regret and paranoia, thinking perhaps she'd grossly misread the situation and signs. But gradually and purposefully a contemptuous grin spread over his entire face. He looked like he was perspiring slightly. As he went to change gear, he made a clumsy effort to touch Joan's knee again. This time she moved a little further away from the gear stick, and this too prompted a little smirk to come over his face. Joan found herself smiling too. She was enjoying the flirting naughtiness.

'Mr Hothouse, it seems to be getting a little hot in here. Would you mind if I opened the window ever so slightly?'

'Absolutely, of course, no problem at all,' he replied.

Mr Hothouse opened a conversation about the play: 'Do you remember a boy called Miles… Miles Crawford? Tubby chap, blond curls? His uncle, William, works on this production. William and I go way, way back and have been good friends since our amateur dramatics days.'

Joan thought for a second, trying to remember Miles. Was he the horrible bully in her year who was a total creep? She couldn't be sure, but she had vague memories of him kicking cats, thinking he was funny, until one of Roy's friends punched him in the face, and then he went complaining to a teacher – probably Mr Hothouse – who got Roy's friend chucked out of school. It couldn't be the same kid, surely; Joan hoped not.

'Runner Miles,' Joan said, thinking aloud.

'What was that?' Mr Hothouse asked.

'Oh, nothing. No, I'm not sure I remember him,' Joan lied. He was called 'Runner Miles' because all the girls would run for miles rather than get stuck with him… yes, Joan was sure that was him.

Joan waited for Mr Hothouse to leave his hand on the gear stick and considered trying to pin his fingers to the stick using her knees… Joan watched as Mr Hothouse's eyes seemed to linger on her knee and her tights and the hem of her knee-length dress.

They got to the picturesque theatre town and visited places of inspiration and other famous sites connected to Chaucer's life and works. Mr Hothouse was mostly in full-on teacher mode. Joan decided he had relaxed a little from when she was a student. She felt like she was his assistant, or supervisor of sorts; somewhere between a parent and a glorified prefect. Adam was mortified, and his friends ribbed him mercilessly that his mum was Mr Hothouse's assistant. 'Yes, Mr Hothouse, no, Mr Hothouse, certainly, Mr Hothouse… what would you like for your breakfast, Mr Hothouse?' they joked.

During the play, Joan and Mr Hothouse sat next to each other in a row behind the kids, who took up two entire tiers in a block in the dress circle. They sat with their legs resting against one another, gently exerting pressure on each other and occasionally rubbing up and down, feeling the warmth of their legs exude heat into themselves. Joan barely noticed the play. She was only vaguely aware of a spotlight some way in the distance and some shadowy figures moving around and mumbling on the stage. She was also oblivious to the columns of kids in front of her. At that moment in her head she was in bed, making wild, sweaty, lip-biting, passionate love and making up for lost time.

At the interval Mr Hothouse dashed off, as he wanted to see his old friend quickly, but he told Joan to meet him by the bar and suggested they had a glass of wine.

'Cheers,' Mr Hothouse said when they met, clinking his wine glass against Joan's. 'Listen, my friend William has said we can go down and watch the play by the side of the stage, if you'd like? Best seats or stands in the house, eh?!'

Joan thought it sounded very exciting, but a part of her was more than happy with the seats they already had.

'Shall we go?' Mr Hothouse looked excited and eager to get moving, but Joan still had half a glass of wine to drink. 'Oh, go on, down the hatch, Miss Jones.'

Joan rushed her drink and immediately felt a bit giddy.

'Follow me,' Mr Hothouse said and he reached round, offering Joan his hand.

She trotted after him as he weaved around the melee of people shuffling towards the toilets, bar, cloakroom and wherever else people were shuffling to. They seemed to follow a maze of corridors down into the depths of the building.

Joan asked, 'Will the kids be okay?'

Mr Hothouse said, 'They will be fine, otherwise it's a week's worth of detentions. I'll doubt they'll even notice we're gone, and we can head back before the end.'

Joan was struggling to keep pace, her heels working twice as hard to match Mr Hothouse's long strides, whose scarf was flailing behind him as he bounded purposefully into the recesses of the theatre.

En route to the stage door Mr Hothouse passed a young man who gave him a grin and thumbs-up. Joan presumed he was another actor friend of Mr Hothouse or his friend William. Mr Hothouse stopped abruptly outside a dressing room door – old, red and battered – which was marked, unsurprisingly, with three gold stars.

'This is the star's room. Shall we have a look? William said it would be okay,' Mr Hothouse suggested, his face lit up with breathless fervour.

'Erm, okay then,' said Joan, wondering whether anyone would still be in there or whether they would already be upstairs on the stage, performing.

They entered the little room. It wasn't quite what Joan had expected. She'd imagined a big mirror, and a black-silk-covered table for applying makeup, and costumes and photos of famous and glamorous people drinking champagne and smoking in plush bars, looking sophisticated. Nope, this looked and smelt more like a boy's bedroom or, closer still, the school PE changing room. Joan was just beginning to feel a bit disappointed and unsure why they were even in the dressing room when Mr Hothouse turned to Joan, whilst also surveying the scene, and then pulled her close to him, saying, 'Miss Jones, you've been a very naughty girl.'

Before Joan had a chance to think of a witty comeback, or react in any way, she realised she was involved in a full-on French kiss. She had been caught off guard and was trying to react, but all she could do was try to keep her balance as Mr Hothouse, who was quite a bit taller, leaned down on her whilst wiggling his tongue around energetically in her mouth and making excited groaning noises. Joan tried to reciprocate and attempted a few moans too, but her back felt most uncomfortable at that angle, and she really wasn't sure how long the kiss was going to last and how long she could handle standing like that, and she wasn't at all sure what to do with her arms, which were hanging down by her sides. She tried to relax, bent double like a dancer at the end of the tango, struggling not to straighten her back. The more she tried to get on a level footing, the noisier and more excited Mr Hothouse seemed to get. He held her close, with one hand on her jaw and the other in the pit of her back and one leg between hers. He then started fumbling around at the back of her skirt, trying to slide his hand down the back of her knickers and grab her bottom cheeks with his long fingers. Joan put both hands on his chest to try to get into a more comfortable position, but ended up holding on to his lapels, her weight pulling him down seemingly acting as a cue for Mr Hothouse to lower Joan to the floor...

'Mr Hothouse,' Joan said, not sure what to say but taken aback by how quickly the whole situation was developing.

'Call me sir,' Mr Hothouse demanded as he leant in again for another kiss.

'Sir, the door! What if someone comes in?' Joan asked, really feeling like a schoolgirl.

Mr Hothouse seemed caught in a vacuum for a second, unsure what to do next.

'Quite right, good point, Miss Jones,' Mr Hothouse said with a wicked glint in his eyes. He stood up, walked to the door and slid the lock closed, and then he turned, undoing the first button on his corduroy trousers.

'Now, Miss Jones… have you done all your homework?'

Chapter 7

After the school trip, Joan became a regular fixture at every school show, rehearsal, event, fête and activity imaginable. She was virtually a teacher's assistant volunteering to lend a hand out all over the place. You could quite easily have bumped into her during lunch, helping out in the school bookshop, or during the morning or afternoon breaks in the library. Pretty much every place the English department seemed to hold any derestriction, she could be found pottering about, and she sporadically helped with drama classes and any after-school group imaginable (even the chess club). The headmaster joked, 'Haven't you got a home to go to? Or somewhere else you'd rather be?' Joan wasn't sure that she had...

Mostly, she was there because Sam (as she now called Mr Hothouse) pleaded with her to be around, but also because she was enjoying the attention. He wasn't being particularly nice to her in any way in particular; it was more or less just sex. Quick and quite rough, and stolen at any opportunity. But surprisingly uncomplicated. It took place mostly in the school bookshop. Whilst the door was locked, the kids were oblivious to the knocking on the other side whilst Joan was pressed against the wooden divide, or sometimes on the table or even sprawled out on the floor. Sam was insatiable, almost desperate. He'd clumsily go about his business, often regardless of whether Joan thought it was a good idea or not. He'd huff and puff for a bit, regaining his strength, and wheeze a lusty compliment whilst his coffee breath warmed her neck and ear. Then he'd push himself away like he'd just completed ten out-of-shape press-ups, tucking himself in and switching back to teacher mode like the previous few minutes had never occurred. Every time Joan became less and less sure why she'd just engaged in the prior activity, and felt a little more dirty and used. But at least she was being used, she told herself.

If Joan was beginning to not enjoy the sex as much, she enjoyed even less the fallout when they were caught in the act – dressed in theatrical costumes – by another teacher after school. For Sam it meant instant dismissal, which in a roundabout sort of way he blamed on Joan.

'If you hadn't been such a damned beautiful distraction, none of this would have happened… You knew I couldn't resist you, and still you didn't stay away, you wild harlot… I am/was a married man, you crazy temptress…'

Joan wasn't sure, but she felt he might actually have meant a few of his colourful backhanded compliments. Maybe she was slightly to blame, she concluded. Maybe she had partially led him astray. She was aware he was married. Sam's wife was on the board of governors at the school, and a dry, old, wooden witch, according to him. Cobwebs in her knickers, closet lesbian, pillow princess, black heart – those were Sam's usual comments about her. When Mrs Hothouse found out about the affair, she insisted he hand in his notice rather than being sacked, which would have ruined his career; but in return she divorced him and kept their house, and he was left without a pot to piss in.

During the repercussions, Joan was aware of the heightened playground gossip, whispers and stares. Adam got into fights, and it all blew up to such an extent that it was decided they couldn't, in light of the extracurricular activity, continue his education at the school.

When Joan bumped into Sam's ex-wife one day in the high street, Joan was scared stiff she was going to get told off. The timid schoolgirl in her came out and she contemplated apologising. As they walked towards each other from some way off, Joan recognised the woman by her rigid gait, as if her high heels were connected straight to her cankles. She noticed the moment that she too was recognised by the ex-wife, who did a double-take and stopped window-shopping and walked purposely towards her, her eyes locked on Joan... Joan remembered how angry she had felt with Nikki when she'd finally accepted she had taken her man, and her adrenaline started to pump as she prepared herself for some sort of dressing-down. She considered ducking into a shop or crossing the street in a last-minute panic. Maybe she should pretend to see someone on the other side of the road. She thought about waving, and looked to cross, but was unable to as all of a sudden her path was blocked by a stream of traffic held up by a sodding learner driver.

As they drew closer to each other, like two cowboys in a western, instead of shouting Sam's witch of a wife merely smiled and said, 'Silly girl, you really have no idea, do you?'

Joan looked at her smiling face and glassy eyes, trying to decipher whether she was being sincere, jealous or spiteful.

'Excuse me?' Joan replied, preparing for a confrontation, her heckles rising.

'Tell that vile man there's a bin liner full of his old clothes in the garage, and he'd better collect them by the weekend or I'll give them to a sodding charity shop.'

Joan was a little taken aback. 'Oh, okay,' she muttered.

And with that Sam's ex-wife walked away, mouthing what looked like 'silly girl'.

The more Joan thought about it, the more she felt that despite the woman's smile, her eyes told another story. She couldn't forget the fleeting meeting; it ate away at her all the time. What had the ex-wife meant? Had she actually been pleased or relieved to be rid of her husband? Joan was sure she'd never felt the same way about Roy when they separated, and she would never have given Nikki that impression; she had been devastated and heartbroken.

It all moved so quickly: before Joan realised what was happening, Sam had moved in with her. Now she had to get both Adam and Sam ready for a new day at a new school at the start of a new term. They would now go to the same school as Sophie.

Adam hated having Sam around the house. *His* house. He hated being told what to do. He hated seeing Sam touch his mum, which he seemed to do whenever she was within reach of his long, bony limbs and probing fingers. He'd reach out even with his feet and pull her onto him, and they would start kissing disgustingly loudly. He was like a hairy octopus/orangutan hybrid when he ate his meals, and Adam hated seeing him parked on the settee watching boring TV. He hated everything about Sam. He smelt. Adam hated having to go through the whole mess of starting a new school and making friends again. None of it was his fault. He hated the way his old friends had turned on him, and the fights he'd had with them before he left the school as they joked that creepy Mr Shithouse was his new dad. He hated that when he started at his new school everyone knew what had happened at his last school; the past had travelled with him. Luckily or unluckily, it soon became quite apparent to all the other kids that Adam wasn't by any stretch of the imagination the teacher's pet.

Meanwhile, Janet returned from her travels to find Joan had moved on and there was now no room at the inn for her. She remembered Sam from school, but had never been as keen on him as her sister was. She thought he was a creep. There were rumours he'd give better marks to the girls in her class who undid their shirt an extra button or flashed their knickers or bra. Like most men, she hated him; but especially because he had taken her home away from her.

Their first meeting was frosty. Joan was cooking. Adam was sheepish around Sam, who ruled the roost, like it had always been his home. It seemed to Janet that Joan had changed: she was acting super-subservient, as if she had recently read a book on the lady's place, or etiquette, or how to keep your man happy, or some other silly, outdated way of thinking. Janet didn't like Sam's demeanour either, so much so that she didn't even make it to lunchtime before making an excuse, apologising to Adam and leaving.

Sam was happy, saying, 'More food for me.' However, he didn't eat it all and threw half away, even though Adam and Joan could have managed a little more. He left Adam and Joan at the table, got a drink and planted himself in front of the TV. Joan thought he was secretly upset that the day with Janet hadn't gone well, and was acting hurt.

'Nikki darrrling, it's me, Victoria…'

Victoria was one of Nikki's oldest school friends. She had somehow become posher with age. The girl from the council house had well and truly swallowed the plum.

'How are you, baby cakes? And how's Phiphi?' she added – Sophie's pet name.

'We're okay, thanks, sweetheart. Actually, we're just about to go to the stables. Is everything okay? Mum and Dad all right?' Nikki replied. She had always loved Victoria's parents; they were like her second family.

'Listen, darling, it's not a problem – we'll do lunch…' Victoria started, but she wasn't going to wait till lunch, and she wasn't bothered if Nikki had plans either. 'You know all this stuff that's been going on up at the school with your ex's wife and that teacher? Well, I don't want to alarm you or anything… I mean, it was long time ago now and everything… but wasn't he involved with that horrible teacher from our school and Katie Scotland?'

Nikki thought back to when they were kids and their friend Katie. She really was wild – she went the furthest with boys at the youngest age, wore the craziest clothes, and drank and smoked before anyone else. She came from the poorer side of town too. She didn't have a dad, and her mum was always falling off the wagon. But she was a great friend when they first started 'big school', because she wasn't scared of anyone, even the teachers. Then she really went off the rails, though: got in big trouble at school, left, got into drugs and then prostitution, the last Nikki heard. She always felt slightly guilty about not being able to help Katie when they were younger, but at the same time she was just so wild and in trouble all the time. Nikki's family had told her to steer well clear, and that she didn't want to associate with that sort of girl. In time, Nikki just figured Katie was mentally ill and a drug addict, the same opinion that all her friends' families had. When Katie Scotland most needed her friends' support, they all turned their backs. They believed the rumours coming out of school, peddled by the corrupt, twisted teachers' influence, degrading and ruining the poor girl's life to satisfy their own sick desires. Katie was fed to the wolves to save the other babies.

'Yeah, right, erm, thanks for reminding me,' Nikki said to Victoria.

'Listen, it was all just rumours. He's probably totally fine. Just might be worth keeping an eye on him with your Phiphi.'

'Mr Hothouse gave you an A?' Adam asked his sister, surprised.

They had actually got on quite well since spending more time together at school, partly because Sophie's friends had swooned when they met him, and as soon as all the girls liked him, she instantly became more popular.

'That's really nice. Thanks, Adam,' Sophie said, giving him a half-hearted daggered stare.

'Are you sure Shithouse gave you the right papers back?' said Adam sincerely.

'What can I say if I have natural talent?' Sophie laughed at her own truculence. 'I basically copied an episode of *Black Beauty* I'd seen on TV.'

They both laughed.

'Mr Shithouse is a weirdo,' Adam said, desperate to tell his sister how much he hated Sam and how much he wanted their mum to leave him.

'Joan loves him,' Sophie said, bursting his bubble.

Adam always found it slightly strange that Sophie called their mum by her first name. She had done it since they were young. He guessed it was her way of dealing with having two mother figures. Joan was his mum, and he loved her more than anything in the world. Nikki was his dad's girlfriend and nothing more to him, but she had become far more to Sophie.

'He's not that bad,' Sophie said.

Sam continued to give Sophie good marks in English, whilst continuing to give Adam a hard time both in and out of school. Adam mentioned it to Aunt Janet, who it turn mentioned it to Joan, who repeated what Sam had told her: that quite simply Sophie was actually better than Adam. Janet thought this was absurd.

When Nikki heard Sophie bragging that she got better marks than her brother again even she was surprised. Sophie was good at a few things; perhaps it was fair to say she was more creative and materialistic than academic, sporting even. She liked fashion, horses, shopping, art and spending money...

Sam suggested the kids might benefit from extra English lessons together. That way Joan could see more of her daughter; Sophie could sleep over. Sam was already imagining the young lady in her pyjamas... He dressed the plan up, saying that it would be nice for them all to spend some family time together, that he wanted to be a bigger part of the kids' life, the father they didn't have. Joan thought it sounded marvellous. They could be a proper family.

When Nikki started to make excuses on behalf of Sophie, breaking arrangements and blatantly causing as many obstacles as possible to stop Sophie spending time with Sam, he suggested to Joan it was because she was scared of losing control of 'your' daughter, and that Nikki wanted to keep Sophie away from Joan.

Joan at first defended Nikki, saying she had always been quite fair – but perhaps she was a bit controlling, especially where money was concerned. This was a revelation to Sam. 'Money is involved?' he queried. He then found out about the kids' inheritance money. Monthly payments and a lump sum when they reached eighteen. Nikki was in charge of it and the monthly payments Joan received for the kids or half after Nikki had taken her share for looking after Sophie. Sam figured if he could get the kids away from Nikki, she would no longer have any right to control the money, and perhaps somehow it would go into his and Joan's pot if they ever went to court. Maybe they could demand a lump sum. He planted that idea in Joan's head and they discussed potentially threatening Nikki with it. Sam's eyes dilated as he imagined the payout they could receive via a kids' custody appeal…

Sam started flirting with Sophie at school, giving her friendly little blinks whilst handing over her homework or tests with overly generous grades. He'd joke with her during school, saying, 'You can call me Sam, but if anyone else is around, it's back to Mr Hothouse or sir, okay?' A cheeky grin, and he'd offer her one of his lemon sherbet sweets, which he knew she liked, then pretend to catch her finger in the paper bag.

It's only playing, harmless fun, Sophie figured. *He's really quite nice and witty.* She started copying his little eye blinks; it was their little thing to do. She started to enjoy getting the high marks and attention too, believing she could do really well. He would softly hold her shoulders or place a gentle hand on her hair… all harmless, breaking down natural barriers and gaining trust in her personal space.

Joan didn't pay much attention and was just pleased one of the kids was enjoying English, but Nikki got very suspicious, especially as it seemed to be Sam taking all the interest in pushing Sophie's English development and doing all the dinner invitations, whilst Joan had little input. This became apparent when it emerged Joan knew nothing of a Wednesday evening arrangement. Joan said it was unlikely it would have been organised for then as she was working late that evening, like she did every Wednesday, and besides, Adam would also be out, as he had football on Wednesday evenings too. So Sam would have been alone with Sophie. Sam said Joan and Adam not being home had slipped his mind, and he was only thinking of getting them all together for homework and fish and chips. He said to Joan:

'It's nice to get all the family together, and why not? After all she is *your* daughter, not that stuck-up Nikki's girl.'

Nikki was convinced he was grooming Sophie, though. She could imagine Sam twisting and worming his way out of it.

One evening, Nikki phoned Joan to voice her concerns, but Sam answered. He said Joan was busy, in the bath, cooking, anything rather than pass the phone to Joan. Nikki thought he sounded drunk. There was a little menace in the way he said, 'Do you want to leave a message?' He left unnaturally long pauses in the conversation, as if he were enjoying listening to her breathing down the phone. Nikki asked him to pass the message on for Joan to call her back, but he didn't pass on the message.

Nikki called again a few days later, asking why Joan never called her back. Joan said she hadn't received the message, and suggested perhaps Nikki had never asked for a message to be passed on. Joan was sure Sam wouldn't have neglected to pass on the message on purpose. It was a bit strange, though, that Nikki was claiming he did so. With the conversation already frosty, Joan didn't want to listen to what Nikki had to say. Sam has already laid the foundations for his scheme in Joan's mind, and she quickly regurgitated his thinking, almost subconsciously. She suggested that Nikki was jealous that Sophie actually wanted to be in her real mother's life. That Nikki couldn't handle Joan having a man now too. That she was only interested in messing up Joan's life once again.

Perhaps a part of Nikki was very slightly jealous that Joan was getting her life together, but all she was ultimately worried about was her daughter, Joan's daughter, getting involved with Sam. Nikki was sick with worry.

Joan felt strong at first for having scolded and been nasty to Nikki. She justified it to herself as giving Nikki some of her own medicine, or at least a little of what she should have said long ago. But then a part of her thought she had been a bit unkind and Nikki hadn't deserved that at all. Had she really meant those things, or had she voiced Sam's opinions? She couldn't be sure.

Although Joan was happy with the way Sam's relationship was developing with her kids and the effort he was putting in, she was slightly aware Adam wasn't exactly enamoured with the whole setup. Joan felt perhaps if Sam cut Adam some slack, or maybe just eased off a bit at home, it might help. But it seemed Sam had only one speed with kids, and that was somewhere between teacher mode and full-on.

Joan tried to reason with Sam to go easy on her son. 'You know it's not easy for him either. We all need to get along. You must understand he's not used to having another man around the house,' she would say.

Sam would reply, 'The boy needs discipline. He won't get away with such petulance in the real world. He's been spoilt, Joan, spoilt.'

Joan had put any sulky, spoilt attitude from Adam down to his being a teenager. But because it was suggested, she then worried that conceivably Sam was right and Adam had developed a bit of a moody demeanour. She decided she would have a word with Adam and tell him to buck his ideas up. She had always been paranoid he would be a little different, having been brought up largely by her and Janet with little in the way of a father figure. Maybe she had spoilt him… She felt bad for siding with Sam over Adam, but hoped in the long run it might do him some good to respect a father figure and conceivably learn a little about authority.

Unfortunately, Joan was unaware that when she wasn't around, Sam would bully Adam. It started with silly things, like telling Adam to move from whatever seat he was sitting in and go to his room. Sam would tell Adam not to go whinging or telling tales to his mum about anything. 'You're not a tattletale tit, are you, Adam? A tattletale and a cry baby?' Sam would threaten to punch or clip Adam around the ear. He would feint like a boxer and laugh if Adam flinched. He'd kick Adam's legs out of the way or tread on his feet if he was sitting down on the sofa. One of his favourite things to do was squeeze Adam's legs just behind his knees, bear-hugging him and refusing to let go, no matter how much he wriggled.

As Adam saw it, Sam seemed to enjoy the physical power advantage he had over him more than any actual pain he inflicted. It was almost as if he got a kick out of restraining Adam, who was half his size.

Sam even said Joan didn't care about Adam any more, as she'd had to look after him for so long as it was; that he really was a stupid, ungrateful boy; that it was much, much more fun for Joan to look after Sam now, and that she, in turn, loved it when Sam looked after her. Saying this, Sam would raise his eyebrows suggestively and menacingly at Adam, who didn't fully understand the context, and would finish the conversation by saying, 'she needs a man and not some silly little boy to satisfy her needs'.

Adam got so frustrated he'd sit in his room and cry. He'd then be angry with himself for getting emotional and crying. Perhaps he was a silly little boy, he'd think, a cry baby. He couldn't become a tattletale too. From then on, he would try to bottle up his emotions. He wanted his mum back, but more than anything Adam wanted to get bigger so he could punch Sam, really punch him, and then... and then he didn't know what he wanted to do, but it would be disgusting and painful and humiliating. . But Sam was quite a lot bigger and he threatened to use his belt on Adam. So Adam didn't and couldn't do anything, apart from hope that somehow his mum and Shithouse went their separate ways. Or that Sam died in terrible circumstances.

Joan was going to invite Janet over for tea again. Adam had suggested seeing her, as they hadn't for ages. Janet too was feeling distant Ever since she had come over last time, things just seemed difficult. Communicating was difficult. Everything seemed different, disjointed and confused.

Sam had already labelled Janet 'the lesbian' and a man-hater. He had voiced his opinion that Janet didn't like him and protested she hadn't even given him a chance. He said he couldn't remember her much from school, but she was probably jealous Joan was so good at English; if she had been any good, he would have remembered her.

Joan was oblivious to the notion her sister might have been gay until Sam suggested it. She loved her sister no matter what, and had just figured she hadn't met the right man. It simply hadn't occurred to her that perhaps Janet preferred ladies. She was unsure either way; not that she cared really. It just all seemed such a foreign fancy to her; but at the same time, Joan had always had a thing for Aubrey Hepburn.

Nikki picked up the phone receiver and put it down again. Her heart was pumping and her adrenaline flowing. 'It is the right thing to do,' she told herself before dialling the number. She got halfway and hung up again. Perhaps she should just let it go. She couldn't. She dialled again, feeling a bit sick.

'Oh, hi, erm, is that Janet, Joan's sister?' Nikki said, slightly nervously.

She had always been a little intimidated by Janet. Not that Janet had ever done or said anything to her in particular; she just remembered Roy being absolutely petrified of her. 'Seriously, Nikki, she looked like she was going to tear my arms off and use them to beat me over the head!' Nikki remembered Roy saying after one meeting following the breakup from Joan. Nikki thought Janet looked tough, like a female PE teacher or some equestrian lady – she knew a few who were quite big woman, horsey types with deep voices, who liked rugby and drinking lager pints.

'Nikki? What do you want? Are the kids okay?'

Janet was often blunt, but it was always very clear where her priorities lay. There was never any doubting her love for the twins. Even though she had spent more time with Adam, she loved them both dearly, almost to the point of them being like her own kids, a sentiment she shared with Nikki.

'The kids are fine. Well, Sophie is… well, for the moment. I mean… shit, sorry, this is all coming out wrong,' Nikki said, getting her words in a muddle.

'For God's sake, Nikki, I'm at work. Spit it out, for heaven's sake.' Janet's patience was already wearing thin.

Nikki composed herself. 'The kids are fine. I just don't trust that Sam around them.'

Janet went quiet on the line for a second, hoping the silence would encourage Nikki to elaborate further, and at the same time wondering why Nikki was calling. She had previous with her sister. Did she just have it in for her?

Janet actually quite liked Nikki. She could see what Roy saw in her, as she was undeniably everything Joan and Janet weren't. Janet had lots of guilty moments when she'd pictured herself in Roy's shoes...

'Why, what has he done?' Janet said finally.

'Nothing. Well, nothing that I know of. Well, little things. Firstly, there's Sophie grades in English. And he keeps inviting her over to theirs for dinner, and I know that's not strange, or shouldn't be, but last week he invited her over when Joan and Adam were going to be out.'

Nikki told Janet about her last conversation with Joan and her worries, pleading with Janet not to think she was just scared of losing Sophie or trying to take Sam away from Joan like she suggested. Janet actually found this notion quite funny. Part of her could see Roy's attraction to Nikki, but why Nikki would be attracted to Sam, God only knew. Janet certainly couldn't understand what her sister saw in him. Perhaps it was a father-figure thing. Janet didn't understand this... all men were useless.

Nikki then went on to explain that in the past a schoolgirl had talked about Sam. A local druggy girl who was from the wrong side of town, Katie had been friends with Nikki when they were younger. She was a wild child, into everything. There was a story about her once giving an Adventure Scout on crutches fellatio so he would help erect a tent on a Girl Guide weekend away. Anyway, Nikki explained, Katie got into drugs after being used by Sam and his teacher friends at parties. They plied her with drink and drugs, and she became hooked. She was so degraded that she went off the rails after Sam and his paedophile friends had their feel and once she lost her appeal they ruined her school life. Nikki asked if Janet could help, as she had just joined the police force. She asked Janet to check out this girl's story

'Katie Scotland… just look her up.'

Janet didn't do anything straight away, but then, whilst driving through the local red-light area and seeing some desperate-looking girls, she stopped and felt compelled to ask a few questions. It didn't take long to find out that Katie Scotland had died recently. Janet went back to the station with the horrible feeling that she should have acted sooner.

She asked for Katie's file. It was heavy. She didn't want to see how this Katie girl had ended up; her imagination and the girls she had just spoken to had given her enough of an idea. But she flicked straight to the beginning of her file. Janet could see that whilst Katie was at school, about the same age as Sophie, the file suddenly became littered with incidents – and right there, pretty much at the beginning, just before her life spiralled out of control, was an alleged sexual assault against her at a party, and Sam Hothouse was a key witness.

The court case had fallen through because there wasn't enough evidence against the man, and Sam had given evidence against the girl, saying he'd not seen her at the party, so ruining any chance of a conviction.

Now, because the girl was dead, it was too late to follow up, but Janet's blood turned to ice as she looked at a girl's life ruined and Sam Hothouse's name connected at the very start. He had then moved schools, joining Joan's school a few years before she and Janet had attended.

All of this was enough to scare Janet into action.

'Joan,' she said when she called her sister, 'I think you should end the relationship.'

'Why? What on earth has it got to do with you anyway? You know he's right… you really do just hate all men.'

'Don't be ridiculous. Listen, I have my reasons, Joan. Please just trust me.'

'What reasons?'

'Reasons. Look, nothing concrete, but I've been talking with Nikki —'

'Nikki? My Nikki? Roy's Nikki? What the hell? Why are you listening to and siding with that bitch after all she's put me through?'

'It's not like that, Joan… Joan? Are you there?'

Joan had hung up.

Joan couldn't see that Sam was using their relationship as a front. Although he wasn't particularly nice to Joan, she never actually saw him doing anything nasty to either of the kids, and she was never invited to any of his secret seedy parties. He had a second life with a select group of friends who targeted vulnerable kids, usually girls, at school. Most of Sam's friends had previous warnings and questionable past demeanours, but due to having friends in very high places, somehow they led a charmed life and got away with everything. They remained under the radar by being clever and discreet, mostly by not drawing too much attention to themselves; they avoided the media and didn't get caught up in anything untoward. They avoided accountability and denied everything, trusting no one, telling no one and inviting into their group no one new and unchecked. They lived life as normally as possible – except behind closed doors.

Sam had successfully remained under the radar until getting involved with Joan, but now Janet was sniffing around his files and his past. Janet had made sure all her colleagues knew about her suspicions. It could be said this was down to her naivety; being fairly new to the job, she never considered that her colleagues could also be in Sam's club. Her brief investigation served as a double-edged sword, both sides bad and splattered with blood: Sam's friends were now well aware that she was on the case, and they in turn warned Sam. So whilst his circle of friends withdrew from him, keeping a safe distance, Sam being left under no illusions that the policewoman was digging into his past, and the longer she continued to do so, the more his resentment towards Janet grew.

Whatever Janet said to Joan, meanwhile, she remained blinkered and stubborn and refused to leave Sam. Joan thought Janet was acting on unsubstantiated rumours. But to Janet, the truth was clear: Sam Hothouse kept some very bad company for a teacher, and she was going to get him out of the lives of her sister, her niece and her nephew.

Sam suggested to Joan that Nikki and Janet were colluding, and he successfully twisted Joan's mind to believe that Nikki was jealous of them and in love with him, and that if she had her way, she would probably take Adam away and cut Joan out of the picture altogether.

Nikki was scared. She knew exactly what Sam's motives were towards Sophie and could see the damage being done to Adam's education. She couldn't stand by and do nothing any longer. So she threatened to stop Roy's support money, which she had been sending to Joan (Nikki controlled the monthly payments that came out of Roy's estate, but not the final big payment the kids would receive when they turned eighteen).

Joan just thought this was a hollow threat and that Nikki was being horrible to her because she was jealous of her and Sam.

Nikki and Janet then came up with the idea that they could use the money to pay for a private school education – get the kids as far away from Sam as possible. They could see he was already controlling Joan's existing money – pissing it up the wall. He, of course, protested that he was the man of the house and was bringing in an income, albeit only slightly more than Joan's when you added up all the overtime she was working.

Sam then started to plot ways to fiddle the exam results and destroy Adam's results (despite the grades Sam was giving Adam, he was actually very good at English). Sam was jealous and worried Adam would end up doing really well and getting a place at an expensive university, and that would end up taking more money and prestige away from him. If Sam could keep the kids close, like dogs in a kennel, that would be ideal. He was the author and the only wordsmith of the house.

Occasionally, Sam got quite aggressive and hurt Joan when they were having sex. Joan put this down to Sam being in a hurry or frustrated about work or the relationship with the kids or Janet and Nikki, or simply just tiredness – anything but admit there might be something untoward going on. She didn't have many other experiences with other men to compare sex with Sam to. He was very different to Roy. Roy had always been sensitive to her, and they'd both explored each other at the time with youthful exuberance. She was as likely to hurt Roy as Roy was to hurt her in their throes of eager passion. That all seemed so long ago, Joan reflected fondly. But Sam was different; he actually seemed to enjoy being rough and even hurting Joan, especially if she made any sounds. She didn't feel like they ever really made love. She wasn't sure if he was deliberately rough or clumsy. He certainly was nothing like the leads in her books or the classic movies she occasionally watched…

She briefly imagined getting kissed delicately on the neck in a tender moment, a warm, passionate, heartfelt embrace where her lover would hold her arms firmly, without causing pain. She imagined a black-and-white film of herself kissing Marlon Brando to an orchestra of strings… Then she imagined Sam, drunk and reciting loudly some old, obscure English verse or play he'd studied, with curry-sauce stains splattered all down his corduroy jacket and checked shirt with its grimy, tired, worn collar and sleeves, the cigarette-browned fingers on the ends of his long, hairy, bony hands gesticulating madly, like a deranged orchestral conductor wafting his foul stench, accentuating his beats, twirling and littered with spittle – and the moment was gone. But Sam loved her, or so he said, and that was all that mattered.

Joan also found she started drinking more and more, as Sam would be also be drunk every night. He would take a hip flask to school with him, and have a splash with his coffee first thing in the morning and a bit more with his coffee at first break. He'd go for a beer or two at lunchtime, and then he'd finish off his hip flask during afternoon break. On the way home, he'd grab four tins of strong lager and tell Joan to grab a bottle of wine or two for dinner. He would also never be far from an extra-strong mint. His staple diet consisted of alcohol, tobacco, takeaways and extra-strong mints. He seemed to have been drinking a lot more lately, and hadn't been out to see his friends very much.

Joan found it a little easier to deal with Sam if she was on the same wavelength as him. They seemed to get on better. She could speak a little more quickly and less guardedly when she too was drunk. Sam appeared to appreciate a partner in crime. He savoured Joan's drink-induced state of relaxed inebriation; she spoke her mind a little more freely, with a certain fire in her belly.

Joan wasn't aware, however, that as soon as they started drinking every night, Adam would take himself away, as he didn't like seeing his mum getting drunk all the time. Adam could only see Joan and Sam arguing, normally about some English play or poem that was utter nonsense and boring as hell, and then they'd noisily make up.

It got to the point where Joan was sitting in the staff canteen having her morning coffee, thinking she'd actually prefer a glass of wine. Her face felt flushed, and yet it was quite cold outside. Her head was banging. She tried to remember going to bed the night before... she couldn't. She tried to remember the last conversation she'd had with Adam, her boy, her lovely boy... she couldn't remember that either.

She then felt sick as the memories came back like shattered pieces of glass, each containing a fragment of a recollection. Had they argued? Joan desperately tried to fit the pieces of her mind back together. She could see Adam's face. He looked upset. He was trying to tell her something, but then Sam – noisy, plastered, animated – muddled her memory and took over her concentration. What was he so happy about – why was he celebrating? She tried to ignore Sam's face and think about Adam. Where was Adam? Had he gone out last night? Then Sam was back, laughing and dancing around the lounge like he'd won a prize. 'Hooray, hooray, we've got the house to ourselves,' he sang as he danced a ridiculous jig, trying to get Joan to spin around. She remembered feeling queasy. She must have passed out shortly after. But where was Adam?

Joan scratched her head then buried her face in her hands in the staff canteen, suddenly very worried about her son. Where would he have gone – a friend's perhaps? Joan thought for a second, but her mind was blank; she didn't know any of Adam's new friends.

Her sister... that suddenly rang a bell in the deepest recesses of her ethanol-drenched mind and made some sense. She stood up, apparently looking like she had seen a ghost.

'Are you okay, Joan? Whatever's the matter, dear? You look like someone has crossed your grave...' old Mrs Orsett said, looking up from her nearly finished crossword. They usually had breaks at the same time every morning, and Joan would give Mrs Orsett her paper from the bus ride.

Joan was oblivious to the question, and made her way straight to the public call box along the hall, her worn-out left heel click-clacking on the shiny mould-green polished-tiled floor. She thought she really must remember to get those shoes re-heeled. She snatched up the receiver, briefly forgetting her sister's telephone number. The vacant line tone purred angrily in her ear as she waited for the first number to point her call in the right direction. Her fingers sprang to life as if they remembered Janet's number more quickly than her brain. She hastily fingered the digits, waiting impatiently for the line to connect.

Joan stopped listening to the ringing after the third ring and hung up. It was mid-week. Janet would be at work.

Joan rang the police station.

'Janet, it's me, Joan. Your sister.'

'I know who you are. Well, I think I do.'

'Listen, is Adam there, at yours?'

'What do you mean, is Adam there. You know he is… don't you?'

'Well, look, I wasn't sure. I've been, you know…'

'This is unbelievable, you are unbelievable. He should be taken into care.' Janet's voice went from scolding to a hiss.

'Look, it's not like that. It's not that bad. We just got a little drunk. We've got a lot on.'

'It clearly is. I thought Adam was exaggerating, but obviously not. You really are a mess. He is your son, your priority, right? Or have you given up on him too?'

'Too? What do you mean, too? I've never given up on anyone. Listen…'

'No, Joan, you listen to me. Adam is here. He is unhappy. You are making him unhappy. This is not on. What's happened to you? Have you thought any more about letting the kids go to the boarding school, like we suggested?'

'Erm.'

'Is that it? Is that all you've got to say? This is all because of him, that bloody man. You know, you weren't like this before he turned up. He's not good for you, Joan. He's never been any good. He's not good for any of us. Listen, let the kids go away and you can get yourself together again. You'll see them at half-term breaks and some weekends… Joan. Joan, are you still there?'

Joan thought for a moment. She could still hear Sam panting, wheezing. She traced the outline of one of his ear hairs, illuminated by a sharp shard of light piercing in through the window, cutting a segment of the bed with its radiance. She looked at a large hairy mole on his uncovered thigh; his sweaty brow; his greying, bouncy, curly mop of hair. How could this foul wretch of a man have wormed his way into her heart? She had been lonely, that was it. Her heart had ached for some loving. It had felt exciting to be alive for a while. She had idolized Sam for so long.

She ran her fingertips down the flushed, olive, broken-veined flesh on his face, skating over the large, hairy wart on the side of his cheek, letting her fingernails briefly graze his stubble. She hoisted her legs over him and felt him drip out of her, onto his midriff. She lingered for a moment longer, straddling him weightlessly. In his naval a messy puddle of his own doing collected. She imagined head-butting him with all her might clean on the nose, or biting his cheek until a lump came off in her mouth, or sticking her thumbs deep into his eyes as far as they could go, or straddling his face and mouth and suffocating him. The only worry was, he'd wake up and enjoy it.

So she got off him and went to the loo and tidied herself up. She wrapped herself up in her favourite pyjamas and dressing gown and fluffy rabbit slippers. She fancied a nice cup of tea and a packet of chocolate biscuits – that would be dinner – and then putting her feet up and watching TV for a bit whilst Sam slept off his drunken stupor. Adam had locked himself away in his room and would have his headphones on full blast. That was a present from Aunt Janet, the best gift he'd ever had.

She felt the lump in her boob again… Yep, there was definitely a lump.

Joan told Janet she had cancer. The doctors were unable to confidently say whether they had caught the disease early enough to hope for a positive outcome. Joan wasn't sure if she would die or not. She was also unsure if she wanted Adam and Sophie to see her dying or in pain.

Janet offered to look after Joan and Adam if she could move home, but said she wouldn't do so if Sam was still around. But Sam turned the tables, saying obviously he'd look after the kids, as that was what any father figure would do, and besides, there wouldn't be enough room for Janet too. He added that they hadn't needed her help before and wouldn't now. Adam, though, wanted to be with Janet and not in the house with Sam.

This all got too much for Joan, who was super-stressed worrying about whether she would survive, let alone who was going to look after the kids, bring money in, do her job and tidy the house. Finally, she got upset that no one seemed to be getting on. It felt clear to her that everyone was trying to be careful walking on egg shells and just doing and saying whatever was best to appease her, but they weren't actually being honest about how they felt. She just wanted to get drunk and forget it all.

But Sam turned on the charm and managed to get Joan to think the family were all just being selfish. He hinted they were being a little unkind to him and doing him an injustice, because he could definitely cope, given the chance. Ultimately, though, it had to be Joan's decision as to how they should all proceed. Sam was careful to portray himself as the one who was trying to be caring and considerate, whereas Nikki and Janet and the kids had their own agendas.

Sam suggested that Nikki was pleased Joan had cancer, as it increased the chances she might have a chance of getting control of the kids and him – not that he was interested in her at all; even if she was quite good-looking, she was intellectually very stupid.

Sam was considering what he could grab should Joan eventually lose the health battle. There was property, life insurance and inheritance money at stake. Not only was he calculating what he could gain he was also trying to figure out what he could do to help the cancer do battle with Joan.

Then Nikki suggested again that the kids be sent to a boarding school with the inheritance money, she had the money to cover the costs now and they could pay her back later. It was still a few years until their exams; there was a good chance of a decent education, and they could get good results. The kids being taken care of would take a weight off Joan and Janet, and even Sam. Janet was as sensitive as she could be whilst saying to Joan that she felt this option was the best one in the circumstances.

Both Nikki and Janet felt that it might be better for the kids to spend the money now, before Sam managed to worm his way further into Joan's heart and wallet, and that it would be for the best if they were away from their mum whilst she battled against the cancer, especially as there were no guarantees she would win.

Joan felt they didn't really understand what it meant to be a mother. She couldn't bear the kids, or anyone, seeing her really ill. She was torn. She wanted Adam and Sophie there, but she also wanted to be alone. She was almost ready to give up before the surgery and treatments had even started.

When it came down to it, Nikki and Janet won. Joan started the treatment and the kids left. Sam got on with his own life; he dressed up his role maintaining that he intended to keep the house going for Joan. Joan more or less just dealt with herself.

'You are all heart, Sam.' Nikki and Janet would comment to each other.

The kids wrote to Joan, and seemed to settle into the school okay. Nikki and Janet visited them at weekends and on holidays. Somehow Janet and Nikki had built some sort of bond through having a mutual enemy in Sam, and through their love for the kids and sympathy for Joan.

Whilst Joan was in remission, Sam got sacked for being involved in a dodgy porn video. It was a video made in the geography department, in the sixth-form block, a small classroom tucked up at the top of the building... the video room. It was the favourite room of the sixth-formers – those men in boys' uniforms and women squeezed into schoolgirls. The difference between them and the eleven year olds at the other part of school couldn't have been greater. There were children in the junior building who were still naive as to where they had come from – biology lessons would be a real eye-opener. Then you had some sixth-formers who already had a reputation for being anything from a well-endowed ladies' man to a slapper to frigid, et cetera. But all, if not most, were actively and busily forgetting their education in pursuit of more physical studies. These had a tendency to become psychological lessons too, and all but a select few pupils spectacularly failed these early-life assignments with startling aplomb.

So it was of little surprise that those students who were perhaps not yet partaking in the full physical coursework with a girlfriend or boyfriend sought out other means to learn how best to proceed in the real world when the time came to put into practice all their physical urges.

They all wanted to do something; it was just not entirely clear how best to go about it.

It was surely connected to putting stuff in the right boxes, the more analytical of them decided. Others were more concerned with the amount of boxes you ticked. Others, how many boxes you stacked up. It was all about the boxes for the girls too. The most expensive box versus the biggest box. The funniest box versus the best-looking box. In time, the ugly boxes learnt that if they became expensive boxes, they too would become ticked.

These lessons weren't always best learnt in school, but this changed when the sixth-form geography video room was discovered. At lunchtimes and study periods there would quite often be secret meetings, where fastidious scholars meticulously studied, inspected and absorbed every detail about sex that was dramatically, graphically and animatedly illustrated on the TV in front of them.

These videos came from a variety of places. From the secret collections of dads. Older brothers. Other kids from different schools. Bin liners found in local parks. Stolen from corner shops. Rented out from video stores. Acquired secretly by someone at a seedy sex shop in town and used as a sweetener or trading tool or means to groom another naive youngster…

This last was usually Sam's style. He watched the young couples flirting. He noticed those on the outside, looking on enviously. He felt empathy. Deep within him, an interest stirred. He was so fascinated that had it been an examination, he would have studied meticulously and devoted every waking hour.

However the videos got into school, it happened, and in the geography room there was a large collection of well-worn videos, fuzzy in certain places, where the tape had been stopped, started, rewound, fast-forwarded and paused again. These videos were stored in a ceiling roof panel that was easily lifted up and removed by a kid standing on a table. There would also usually be a kid standing guard, looking out of the window and along the corridor. This kid was more interested in impressing the ring leaders and gaining favour than studying the film necessarily. Another would be in charge of buffering and eject button, should the need to hide the video in a hurry arise. This kid was normally the most depraved. A genuine old film about a group of scientists on a field trip to Walton-on-the-Naze to study coastal erosion sat on top of the video, ready for the alibi.

Sophie and Adam first noticed stares and giggles, but these soon turned to disgusted faces, which then became spiteful glares and taunts. The kids had arranged to meet up with their friends at the weekend following a break from their new school and they were excited to be catching up. Unfortunately, the old friends had been distancing themselves from the twins.

Sam wouldn't have been entirely surprised that his cover had been finally blown. He'd had a good innings. It was only a matter of time before he got caught, he supposed. He hadn't been the most discreet of perverts. Part of him had thought it would have happened when he split from his wife. That, perhaps, was part of the thrill.

Before Janet had started sniffing around his affairs, Sam had been a registered and active member of every secret dating agency imaginable. He was a fully-fledged member of a secret sex club. He often checked the newspapers, looking for desperate ladies who wanted a no-string relationship. He collected cards in phone boxes from call girls offering their services. He went to wild orgies. He had been to some of the most sexually depraved parties imaginable. He had been in no fit state to remember the vast majority. Some of these parties may well have been recorded, he conceded.

This behaviour had carried on for years before he met Joan, whilst he was with his wife, and then with Joan. She simply presumed he was at the pub or in the bookies. He had lots of holiday time, like all teachers, and she was never entirely sure how he spent his time. He could have been studying, Joan hoped. He wasn't, though; he was having sex with whatever desperate and lonely lady he could find, or couple of ladies, or groups of young or old ladies, any ethnicity that would have him. He was the opposite of fussy.

'Your dad's a pervert, pervert, pervert, your dad's a pervert.'

It was just blurted out like that to Joan from Adam explaining the black eye and ripped shirt.

There was also a letter from the headmaster of the kid's previous school, requesting a meeting with Joan and Sam.

Joan sat at the dinner table, staring at Adam and Sophie, waiting for a knock on the door that would signal Nikki had arrived to take the kids back to boarding school. They had tears in their eyes at the indignity of the whole situation. They had only come home to see their old friends. Instead, they had been humiliated again because of that man. Right then, neither of them wanted to be at home ever again.

'Well, who said it?' asked Joan.

'Everyone, Mum. All the kids. They were all saying it and laughing, and we didn't know what to say, and I said, "Shut up," but they just wouldn't…'

'But I don't understand. Why would they say such things? What, why? It doesn't make any sense.'

'They said they've seen him. Kim, Rob, Dave, Sarah – all of them. They said he's a pervert and we're all perverts too. He was on a film and the whole school has been watching it.'

'Come on now, surely they're just being silly. Was it just a game or something that got out of hand?'

Sophie stormed out.

'Mum, she said you'd be like this, that you wouldn't listen and you'd take his side again. Mum, they're all laughing at us. You're not a pervert too, are you, Mum?' asked Adam, like it was the last genuine question he'd ever ask his mum again.

'Of course I'm not, love. It's all nonsense, I'm sure. Probably just a silly misunderstanding.'

'You don't believe us, do you, Mum?!' said Adam. 'But they have him on film.'

At the meeting at school, Sam was fired and the video was given to Joan. The headmaster's words rang in her ears: 'And take this filth with you…'

It was the last time the video room was left unlocked and anything other than the Walton-on-the-Naze costal erosion video was watched by the sixth-formers.

Joan wasn't sure what to do with the video. She was sure she didn't want to watch it. In the end, she binned it. Sam was secretly distraught about it being thrown away, like an alcoholic watching a bottle of vodka getting poured down the sink, but he put on a brave face, wondering what party it had been filmed at and how long ago and whether he had put in a good performance on film. At least with Joan not watching it he could make up whatever story he needed.

Janet hoped this would mean Joan would finally leave Sam. But she didn't. Somehow, she felt because he hadn't left her whilst she was ill – though everyone else abandoned her – he deserved a second chance. Sam even suggested that because she had neglected his physical needs, he'd gone looking elsewhere, just like when Roy went off with Nikki. Joan began thinking this was normal behaviour for men.

Sam said it was the intense physical relationship between himself and Joan that had pushed them together originally and he appearing in the video was a by-product of the loss of that partnership. He made out it was marvellous, painting a picture in Joan's mind that was different to her memories – a very special and passionate affair; he had never known anything like it. Joan was slightly flattered, but also confused. Sam also lied, saying he had never been involved in anything dodgy in the past and that the video was due to the stress of the treatment and the kids going away and the whole new school business. It was certainly the first and last time, he said; all he cared about now was getting Joan fit and healthy again (so she could go back to work and support him whilst he drank and gambled all their money away).

Then he lost their car. Absolutely drunk, crashing through a fence and leaving it dumped in a ditch in a field. He woke up the next day in bed, covered in mud and unsure how he'd got home. Janet informed him they had found his and Joan's car in a field, and he lied, saying it must have been stolen during the night. Janet suspected that he had crashed the car and made it home and then fabricated the theft story, but she couldn't prove anything. The car wasn't written off, but they couldn't afford the repairs.

Joan didn't want to hear all the sordid details of what Sam had supposedly been getting up to anyway, so she just took his word for it – much to the frustration of Nikki and Janet.

Sam managed to twist Joan's mind into thinking that everything that happened to her somehow also had a catastrophic effect on him too, and so it was *her* fault that he had been led astray. Joan had led him to stray from his wife, and her illness resulted in him being caught up in whatever happened at this party, of which he had no memory, as he was terribly drunk. Without the video they had no proof it was him either. He agreed he was pathetic and useless, but he was all she had, so she had to take pity on him, just like he had pitied her.

Sam thrived on Joan's vulnerability. He had found a lonely lady struggling to cope with the sorrow people felt when they have lost someone and a void is left in their life, either through breaking up or bereavement. So desperate had she become to lean on that person that she carelessly sought alternatives. She had confided in Sam that there had been times she'd talked to Roy in her head and out loud, imagining his responses. Joan had forgotten she might not like the replies or Roy all the time; it had just become a habit, like two birds in a cage chirping away to each other because they have no choice. They had filled each other's silences. It was what being a partner was all about. This was what Joan yearned for, she thought she found it before meeting Sam and again when they first got together. She had lost her partner's communications until Sam filled that void. It was true, Adam hadn't been able to satisfy the adult verbal and mental stimulation that Joan craved.

Sam: a knight in shining armour who became a nightmare with a sweaty odour. And here was Joan, broken and partially boobless, sitting half-naked on the edge of her bed, a damp towel draped over her lap. Her reflection in the mirror was a sad reminder of what she looked like when she was a little girl, but now with a scar burnt across her chest. Depending on which way she sat, she could look like she had either one boob or no boobs. She felt lopsided. Incomplete. Her hair was wet from the bath, but her cheeks were wet from her tears. Who would love her now?

This was what Sam fed off. He was all she had now. He replaced the compliments with negativity. His kind words became strings of spite, a relentless torrent of verbal stings. Perhaps if he was nasty enough, she would be ill again. Eventually, in time Joan learnt to cherish even these digs. 'Do you want a cup of tea?' *Cup of gnat's piss more like,* she'd reply automatically in her head, pulling a sarcastic, pained face. This soon filled the silent gaps in her head. The black monotony. She became used to the put-downs and the nastiness. At least it was a conversation.

This was the damage her first relationship had done. When Roy went off with Nikki, Joan was left with two kids (actually, one and a half kids) and no one to talk to. Janet didn't understand. Her life was forgotten. Her previous existence forgotten. She went from being a happy, normal girl to being a forgotten, cast-aside wretch. Talking to herself through tears. Depressed mother of two. Even her daughter went and lived with Nikki and became a precocious brat, and Adam only stayed with Joan until Sam came along. He was jealous of the competition, so Sam said; he wanted his mum all to himself; he wanted to control her life too. Then, when the opportunity came along, Adam left her, like his sister, under the influence of Nikki and the man-hater Janet. Why did they hate Sam and Joan's relationship so much? Joan was mixed up by Sam and didn't trust anyone – but Sam didn't leave her. He became her carer. Her solid. She should be grateful, she decided. Not many men would stick by a one-boobed lady. She was lucky really. At least she had him. Although he was far from sensitive, complimentary, understanding...

Sam told Joan some people had probably kept away from her because they thought cancer was somehow contagious. 'If it was out of sight, it was out of mind, Joan. If you don't think about it, you can't catch it.' He was successful in creating a 'them and us' way of thinking, almost like a siege mentality: the two of them versus the world. No one loved them, and they didn't need anyone because they had each other. Really all Sam did was isolate Joan from everyone. She couldn't wait to get back to work, anything to have a bit more in her life other than just them.

Chapter 8

Joan kept a rusty, old chocolate tin hidden away under the sink amongst the cleaning stuff. In it, she kept letters and postcards from Adam, who wrote to her from wherever he was around the world, just like his aunt had done nearly twenty years earlier he went off travelling. The tin was safe there. Sam had never ventured into the cleaning stuff; it was beneath him. The letters meant the world to Joan. They were really her only connection to any life outside her little bubble.

She occasionally chatted to old Mrs Orsett at work, who was kind but, Joan felt, pitied her; even though she was way past retirement age, Mrs Orsett had a busier social life. Joan no longer heard from her daughter very much at all, except perhaps a joint Christmas card from Nikki and her. A bit part effort. It was debatable whether Sophie would have even known Joan's name was to be added. Joan always felt her heckles rise slightly whenever she read anything written by Nikki. She could hear her voice. She remembered imagining Nikki and Roy laughing about her when they were having the affair. That paranoia continued to this day, flamed through Sophie's involvement with Nikki. The lady who stole her husband and daughter, Sam reminded Joan almost daily, continuously pouring fuel on the flames of fear and resentment.

Adam sent the letters to Joan's work. They always said roughly the same thing: he was having a great time, he was fit and well, he'd not found Mrs Right as yet, and Joan mustn't worry about him. But he made it quite clear on several occasions that he wouldn't return whilst 'that man' lived in the same house as Joan. So unless Joan left Sam, Adam would stay away. Joan just figured he was still finding himself, that he was just like his aunt, a traveller, a pig-headed traveller. He probably needed to get out and see the world anyway; it would do him some good, Joan hoped.

Joan didn't know that Adam had contemplated killing himself, or Sam, before leaving. He hated Sam so much, he felt driven away. In a way, he hated his mum too, for getting involved with such a vile man. Hate and love were very close; this was one of the first lessons he learnt whilst in a particularly far-out state of mind after drinking a curious mushroom-flavoured milkshake on a small island near Bali.

Joan would always be torn between Sam and her son. She just hoped one day Adam would understand how she'd found herself in this situation, even if she didn't really know herself.

In the evenings, Sam went to open-mic nights at pubs. He recited poems, usually drunk, that bored the regulars senseless. He'd then get booed off stage, and barred, and after returning home to Joan, he'd berate her for the audience's lack of appreciation, throwing a kebab in frustration before falling asleep on the settee. *At least he didn't hit me tonight,* Joan would think. That would come soon enough, though.

Years passed in an unhappy existence. Joan survived just by running around after Sam. Her daily routine barely left the house habitable until the weekend, when she had more time to pick up his shit between having to scrub, cook and do the washing.

She woke up, scooped up his clothes and put them in the laundry bin. She opened the window to diffuse the arse musty, beer-fart smell in the room, and then wiped the golden-urine-splattered floor of the bathroom and the congealing pools around the toilet seat. She felt quite bilious looking at the pubes in the sink, wondering from what part of his anatomy they were plucked, tugged or dislodged. She looked at the dark, grimy ring around the bath; no amount of elbow grease could shift that.

Joan fell over his shoes on the stairs; carpet-burnt and winded, she lay prostrate on the floor, just thinking, for ten minutes, too fed up to move. She could stay there all day; no one would know or care. She picked up the overflowing ashtray in the lounge and the empty value cans of lager littered around his seat. She picked up the half-eaten cheese-and-ham slice purchased from the local petrol station at some point in the early hours, whenever he had been kicked out of whatever hellhole he had found himself no longer welcome in. She left the plate with the other cups by the sink that she'd wash up in the evening. She put on the kettle and pulled her dressing gown tightly around herself, like she was giving herself a cuddle. She felt the sticky scab sores bite from her fall. Then she pulled the cord until it nearly chopped her in half, like an eel on a fishing line. Not for the first time, she contemplated it: 'Little Jimmy eel, do you feel ill, all sliced up, hanging from the reel.'

Joan let her mind go, imagining a fisherman… a fisherman on a train… not just any train, a train she was on… a handsome, tall, friendly-looking fisherman with kind eyes and big hands, dressed in country tweed and a green body-warmer, with happy red cheeks and a flat cap. But why was he on her train, all dressed up and ready for fishing? What was he looking for? Her, of course… he was hoping to catch Joan… she was his beautiful mermaid… he was going to get his tackle out for her… his maggot…

Joan chuckled, realising it was an absurd daydream, but it made her happy. It made her smile inside. It might have been silly, but it was her thought, and it made her feel better, and no one could take it away from her.

Her only highlight in her miserable life was a brief daydream pondering a rush hour crush, these were free, little snippets from strangers lives supplied without recompense apart from publication to a newspaper column in the hope of telling a complete unknown person how much they found that person attractive.. Joan loved to read the section every day. It didn't matter to Joan that they were her own infatuations or some unknown person writing into the daily newspaper. She found the whole notion that someone out there, anywhere in the world, at any given moment might be attracted enough to write a letter to her favourite column describing the person of their crush. It was a romantic notion in a heartless time. Joan would become fully absorbed no matter if she was sitting, oblivious, on a bus or train, or in the staff room at work, or sitting on the loo until her bum went numb. On her way to work, she would study the little section fastidiously, and after a while start scrutinising the people on her train carriage or bus; she found herself looking out the window or searching crowded places with the descriptions of people running through her mind. How many times had these total strangers wandered past each other or even her and noticed one and other. She often thought, when walking around somewhere new, that strangers walking past could be distant relatives or perhaps people she'd met as a child. She pondered how many people's paths she had crossed during her lifetime. It was surely far more for those living in the Western world compared to those living in remote civilisations on the edge of the world's greatest human outposts. Was she really related to the Amazon River people, or Maasai warriors from Africa, or Inuits from Greenland?

Was that the tall man with the red scarf? Perhaps not… not tall enough. She found herself imagining the people from the rush hour crush segment, or trying to identify the place where the brief liaison had happened – even whilst Sam was having drunken sex with her, or beating her up, or maybe just berating her for something ridiculously trivial. He would shout at her and she would drift off, imagining the scene. It was a self-preservation device, designed by Joan to stop her losing the plot. *Sticks and stones may break my bones, but Sam's words will never hurt me.* But they did; she didn't really realise how much.

Joan only just seemed sane to strangers on the street. She had become quite dotty, almost continuously giddy. If you saw her not in deep thought or aware she was being watched, she looked broken. She continuously pondered what might have been, and was always on the verge of talking to herself, or letting a tear roll down her cheek, or breaking into a giggle as a thought ran through her mind. Joan's daydreams usually ended with something mildly funny happening. This was how she envisaged her life; she wanted it to have been one continual anecdotal comedy, not the neglected, heartbroken, bitter pill that got stuck in her throat each day and that she struggled forever to swallow without the aid of any water.

So she read the daily newspaper, *The Metro*, religiously, searching for rush hour crushes. The section started:

Love (well, lust) is all around us, as is proven by the messages left by our commuter cupids. Are they talking about you?

Joan would freely admit to being somewhat obsessed. The habit became her daily fix. Her drug. A pointless and harmless infatuation that only she really knew about.

On her way to work Joan hustled along the train carriage, scanning for a seat, annoyed with the people protecting a second seat with a strategically placed designer bag or rucksack or newspaper or briefcase.

Damn you to hell, she said in her head – in Sam's voice. 'Where's dinner, woman?' he'd say, followed by, 'Curses! Damn you to hell, woman.'

She found two empty seats towards the rear of the carriage and slumped down, shifting up against the window with her bag placed on her lap. As she leant against the armrest, her arm felt bruised where Sam had grabbed her and pushed her over. She edged onto the other side, nestling her head against the cool glass of the window as the train doors further along the carriage swung shut with a clattering bang.

She was bitterly disappointed not to have picked up her newspaper from outside the station; the delivery must have been late, she thought, fuming. Then she worried that the lovely man who provided a copy every day might have been in an accident. Perhaps he was dead. Oh, the poor driver. How wicked of her to be so demanding. Maybe he wouldn't deliver ever again. She imagined him in his work van, smoking a cigarette whilst driving along a leafy country road. Perhaps he was singing along to the radio, she thought, making herself feel a little more guilty as she imagined a deer leaping from the bushes and startling the driver, who then careered through the hedgerows and ended up stuck in a ditch. She pleaded with her imagination to allow him to be all right. He must continue to deliver her newspaper every day...

As the train started moving and the roads she recognised faded into a greyish-green-brown blur, she noticed, in the glass reflection underneath the luggage racks above her head, that the man in the seat in front of her was reading the paper, her paper! She edged forward, her bum cheeks acting like little feet, trying to peep through the gap, checking the reflection, desperate to get a better view. She could just about make out the newsprint as her nose edged further into the space, closing the distance to the unsuspecting reader's head. Joan's face was less than a hand's width away… The guy in front sensed Joan's breathing close to his ears and turned around. She quickly sat back and checked the window reflection; he seemed unsettled.

When he went back to reading, she gradually butt-shuffled forward again, cheek by cheek, inch by inch. She had virtually got her face in the divide between the chairs when the train driver applied the brakes to slow the train, which was coming into a platform. Joan, sitting right on the precipice of the seat, lost her balance and fell forward, ramming her face into the opening between the chairs. She felt the manmade fibres of fabric, contrasting curiously with the cold plastic frame, momentarily rub up against her forehead and cheeks, nose and lips. The skin either side of her eyes became tight and felt the strain, like an adult being born from the train seat's blue, furry vagina. Joan momentarily appeared through the rupture like Jack Nicolson in the door wielding an axe during the film *The Shining*. She tried to push herself back into her seat, but accidentally managed to get a handful of the man in front's hair, and Joan recoiled as she felt her fingernails grate against his scalp.

'Jesus Christ!' the man shrieked, obviously startled. He actually thought an eagle had dug its talons into his head or he was suffering a stroke.

'Sorry, sorry, I'm terribly sorry,' Joan said, trying to pull herself back onto the seat, squatting. Without thinking, she reached out to try to pat his head better, forgetting he was a total stranger and that he was equally uncomfortable with her patting him on the head as he was her clawing at his brain.

'It's quite all right. Just leave it now, please?' the sweaty, bespectacled, middle-aged man in the suit said as he edged away, looking cross and bemused but trying his damnedest to keep a stiff upper lip. He pulled a handkerchief from his top pocket and dabbed at his head, looking for signs of drawn blood, looking at Joan's nails, thinking, *I'll bloody need a sodding tetanus jab now...*

'I'm truly soo sorry,' Joan said, sitting back in her seat and feeling the eyes of her fellow passengers burning into her as she faded out of view. Strangers looked at each other, exchanging unspoken dialogue, eyes, squints and barely noticeable head movements signalling a collective understanding: Joan was some sort of nutter. She tried to hide from the world as she stared out of the window, her face burning red with embarrassment.

At the very next stop someone sat down next to Joan, unaware that the seat next to hers was marked. Other passengers waited, poker-faced but smirking inside, as the unaware passenger took his seat next to the entertainment. But *they* all knew, so they discreetly watched.

He may even have picked up on the strange atmosphere, the funny looks, been paranoid that his flies were undone or he had toothpaste or some other strange mark on his face that he was unaware of.

Joan didn't move or turn around, as she was still too flustered to face the commuters. She heard whoever it was rustle a newspaper a couple of times. She was desperate to ignore it; she hoped he was perhaps reading a broadsheet or another tabloid, anything but *The Metro*. Then she caught sight of its reflection, and immediately recognised the front page. Automatically, she glanced sideways, confirming it was the paper she'd hoped it would/wouldn't be.

Her head seemed to settle facing forward, her neck relieved not to be twisted whilst looking out of the window, but her brain and eyes had found a new lease of life and a target for her curiosity. Like a child innocently staring at someone who was disfigured, she couldn't resist. She was oblivious to the man's first distracted rustles of the newspaper, like someone getting harassed by a fly. He tried to fold the paper in half, in an attempt to break Joan's stare and concentration, but she was focused on him finding her section. She was truly addicted, wanting her fix. But instead he turned to the sports section, figuring she wouldn't be interested in those articles. He slowly digested every letter of every word written about West Ham United's new schoolboy prodigy, who was already attracting the interest of the world's biggest clubs. He tutted, absorbed in the masses of pounds quoted in relation to a lad who had no qualifications or life skills but was good at kicking around a bag of air. The man daydreamed momentarily, imagining himself transferred to Barcelona, one of the biggest clubs in the world; he pictured himself climbing out of a Ferrari and walking into a fancy tapas bar with a beautiful *señorita*, a Spanish rose.

Undeterred, Joan read an article about this year's disappointing weather at Wimbledon and how injury had robbed the nation's top hope of making it through the first round. All riveting stuff. The man looked at her twice, aware she was still looking over his shoulder, but she didn't blink. She watched as he left the sports section, and flicked past the travel news, adverts, crosswords, food and drink section – all the while her anticipation growing – and paused on 'What to do at the weekend'. Joan liked this section. She often liked to imagine she had a social life and sometimes fancied going to a flamboyant salsa night in the West End to dance the night away and drink cocktails. She even contemplated going to festivals like her kids had done. She could put on some wellies, and she wouldn't mind sleeping in a tent. He flicked onward to the television guide – that was all Sam would be interested in – and then art exhibitions, present ideas, clothes. Joan was positively excited now. Any second and he'd come to her section, and he'd be sure to read it…

Then he stopped, and turned straight to the front page and started reading the main article. Joan couldn't breathe. She was incredulous. Furious, she looked at him and back at the paper twice. What the hell was happening? He seemed to have known exactly what she was thinking, and had deliberately ignored her and changed the logical order in which a man would usually read a paper, from back to front, starting with the sport. He surely decided to read the paper this way simply to spite her. Joan must have stopped breathing sometime earlier, as she gasped now with annoyance.

'What's your problem?' he snapped. 'Here, have the blasted newspaper.' He stood up and flung the paper, spinning it so all the pages fanned out like a giant stunned moth.

Joan didn't say a word as the man jumped off the train. She rearranged the pages and triumphantly flicked towards the centre pages. As the train departed, the rude man looked at Joan through the window and tapped his fingers against his head, but she was too absorbed to notice; and even if she had, it was less abusive than she was accustomed to. The other passengers all sniggered to themselves.

Originally, when Joan first started reading the rush hour crushes, she wanted to see a message about herself from some stranger who happened to fancy her from afar. Then she became convinced they were made up. She became a cynic. As Sam would often point out, 'Who the hell would want *that*?' He said 'that' as if Joan were a thing below anything human, animal or vegetable, anything living. His 'that' was like the sort of thing you would scrape off your shoe, or squeeze from a spot. Then she found out who had created the section in the paper, and she believed in it again and would become its leading disciple, its most devoted apostle. She was Matthew, Mark, Luke and John, and Jesus and Mary, all rolled into one divine being.

Her mission now was to somehow spread the word of her old friend the writer from school, the good-lord-god Stuart Maskell.

Somehow, in the time since she had last seen Stuart at Roy's funeral, he had magically gained some sort of mythical god-like presence in Joan's mind, as if absence had made the heart grow fonder. He was a lovely man, she imagined, based on nothing but a hunch. She was sad they'd lost contact, but in a way relieved too, as she would have hated him to judge her the way Nikki, Janet and her kids had come to. So she imagined they were still friends, even though she would be too ashamed to be friends with him now.

To the gorgeous guy in the long black coat with a coffee: You picked up my ticket when I dropped it at Euston on the way to Platform 8. Coffee with me sometime? – Blue-Scarfed Girl

Blue-scarfed girl, blue-scarfed girl… Joan had walked through Euston Station many times, under the big arrival and departure boards; she might have even passed him or her by on Platform 8. *I wonder what he looked like in his long black coat.* Joan pictured Roy.

To the boy with the bike who travels from Saltaire to Leeds: You bring a smile to my mornings. – Sleepy Girl with Glasses

Joan sighed; in her heart, a mixture of jealousy and empathy.

To the guy with big brown eyes and beautiful eyelashes on the 8.10 Central Line: It was raining but you still made me smile. I've been thinking about you. – Girl in Mickey Mouse Top

Joan remembered she used to have a Mickey Mouse top. She had no idea what had happened to it. Maybe she had given it to a charity shop and it was living a new life with this girl on the 8.10. Joan hoped it brought her more luck than she had had, and lots of cuddles too.

She never went on holiday with Sam. She never took any holiday full stop. Her time would get converted into money that she'd plan on spending at Christmas, but most years Sam managed to dwindle it away before she had a chance, or they were late with some bills, or something expensive needed replacing.

As Joan sat on the train, she thought she didn't have to not take any holiday time; if she was careful, Sam might never know. Joan had more time available than she knew what to do with, so theoretically, she could take a day or two, or even a week off. She could catch the Central Line every morning in the hope of seeing the guy with the beautiful brown eyes. Or conceivably if she found the girl in the Mickey Mouse top first, she could perhaps then get them together that way... oh, wouldn't that be lovely? Joan's heart sped up at the thought; adrenaline started pumping. Then Joan worried that what she thought of as nice eyes might not be the Mickey Mouse girl's idea of nice eyes. *Beauty is in the eye of the beholder and all that,* she reminded herself. Would the girl wear the Mickey Mouse top every day? That seemed highly unlikely. Joan mused on how she could search the Central Line. Perhaps she would need a placard that read: *Are you the girl with the Mickey Mouse top from the rush hour crush?* Maybe if she just stood on an Oxford Circus platform all day with a placard, that might do the job. People would be sure to notice. Perhaps she could print up some leaflets or cards.

She became obsessed with her self-appointed mission to get two strangers together. She wanted to become a cupid. What harm could it do?

Joan started writing notes and making plans. She would need to get to a specific location, like a station or bus stop, half an hour earlier than mentioned in the crushes and scope it out, assess the situation: volume of commuters, where to stand for best exposure. She would need to be able to see and be seen, and do it every morning for a week or so if necessary, in the hope of finding those mentioned with a crush. Some places might be quite scary and dodgy. She might need to stay in a hotel or book an early taxi, depending on where the crush was. Surely Sam would think it strange, her suddenly staying at a hotel or disappearing; he'd get very suspicious. She would need to target the most precise crushes and locations; it would be no use her racing halfway up the country. She felt sick with excitement.

Joan knew she really didn't want to mention any of this to Sam, as he was bound to act in his usual resentful, vindictive fashion, because his brain was a shrivelled-up, useless prune, incapable of generating one solitary creative thought. All he did was regurgitate some boring Prose that no one bar him found vaguely interesting. He liked English poets no one else had heard of, who warbled on in fancy, egotistical verse about nothing that anyone with an ounce of soul would be vaguely interested in. Sam would think that until this mad project or fad of hers came to an end, Joan was certifiably mad. Because he wouldn't be into it. Because it served no purpose. Because it didn't appeal to him. Because it wasn't his idea. He would deem it a stupid idea, and say she was equally stupid and useless and that no money would come out of this hare-brained scheme. It was a waste of time, he'd think. He would be bitter, having been out of work, and uncomfortable about her not focusing on their drab existence or having any sort of project for himself. It was selfish. Why should she take a break from the monotony? So he would be negative and destructive towards her plans and her confidence, and he would only be happy when her plans failed and she forgot the project and came back to her miserable life at home, doing nothing but serving him, doting on him while he suppressed her. 'I told you so,' he would say...

So she decided not to tell him. It would be her own little secret, just like the ones he had.

Perhaps he would be jealous, thinking something was going on with Joan. Maybe he would think she was having an affair. Maybe he would now realise how unhappy Joan was. Maybe he'd see how miserable he made her, and perhaps he'd change. Perhaps thinking someone else would give her attention would spark a reflection in Sam, Joan thought.

The next station was her stop.

Chapter 9

Joan stepped off the train and started her solo pilgrimage. At the florist's at the station entrance, she stooped down to inspect the flowers sitting waist-deep in gloomy, murky water. She spent all her lunch money on the least-droopy-looking bunch in the bucket. She paid the cheery man, who threw her money into a money-belt partly concealed under his flabby midriff.

''Ere you go, my love,' he said, passing Joan back a penny change.

Joan was tempted to ask, 'What am I supposed to do with that?', but felt that wasn't very nice. The chirpy chap was only doing his job, and she couldn't remember the last time anyone had said the word 'love' to her in any context. She also liked the fact he seemed to wear shorts whatever the weather. It wasn't short-wearing weather by any stretch of the imagination, and yet he was wearing shorts and he didn't seem bothered at all. He had very solid legs – probably three times as thick as Sam's spindly stilts.

She gave him a smile and walked off, holding the flowers in one hand and the penny in the other. Maybe this could be a lucky penny, she thought, rolling it around in the palm of her hand.

There was something magical about walking along with flowers, Joan thought. People who saw you automatically jumped to conclusions, both good and bad, but you definitely stood out – you became important. You could be going on a date, or you could have been given them by a lover or a boyfriend or even a girlfriend. You may be going to visit someone who was unwell, in the hospital. That could be sad. And lastly, some people took flowers to graveyards, probably an old tradition to mask the smell of death. That was certainly her, she thought, always trying to disguise the reek of death that followed her about.

Joan smirked to herself. She could even amaze herself sometimes with her depressing and miserable thoughts. Whatever she thought, 'people with flowers just looked special'.

As Joan followed the path, she ignored the freshly dug graves and new flowers. Her eyes followed the path and rested on the back of a figure standing in the rough vicinity of Roy's grave. Immediately, Joan thought it might be his dad, Alec, but from behind it didn't look like him; the man looked taller. As Joan strained her eyes, she thought the chances were if Alec wasn't already dead, he soon would be. She wouldn't have been that surprised if he was dead already and no one had bothered to tell her. Her kids probably went to the funeral and kept it secret.

As Joan drew closer, she couldn't help but feel like she recognised the person, and the nearer she got, the more sure she was that she knew the person standing over Roy's grave. Then she had the strangest feeling that left her cold. She thought the man might actually be Roy. Her heart skipped a beat. Perhaps it had all been an elaborate ruse. She would forgive him, right there and then, and maybe he would come back to her. They were still married; she had never married Sam. Roy could get rid of him, and then her kids might come back.

Joan felt weak, like her knees were going to buckle as her head swam. Perhaps it was Roy's ghost. Joan went to call out 'Roy', but then she felt really giddy.

As Joan opened her eyes, she could hear her name being called.

'Joan, Joan, can you hear me? Joan, it's me.'

Joan blinked a few times, unsure whether she was still dreaming or had died and was in heaven. She could just about make out the silhouette of a person and see the blue sky behind him, but he was upside down. She couldn't make out what he was saying, but she could hear the birds singing.

'Roy?' she said.

The person laughed and said, 'I'm afraid not. However, if I was, that would certainly be a good enough reason for you to faint, I suppose. But no, it's me, Stuart.'

As Joan blinked and her blurred vision sharpened, she could see the outline of her old school friend. He looked a lot older. In her memories of him he was as a young man, but time hadn't been particularly kind to him either.

'Here, take this,' he said, passing Joan his top-pocket handkerchief, which he had been using to fan Joan's face. 'You have a bit of dribble beside your mouth.'

Joan thought about trying to get up, as it was strange looking up at Stuart from down on the ground and he was upside down looking at her. As Joan dabbed the corner of her mouth with the beautiful paisley silk handkerchief, which smelt slightly of cologne, she said:

'I don't know what happened. One minute I saw you standing by the grave, and then…'

'You fainted, Joan. Have you eaten at all today?'

Joan tried to think. 'Yes, of course,' she said, lying. Her belly rumbled.

'Oh dear, Joan. You have to look after yourself.'

Joan wasn't sure whether this was a question, a statement or a demand. It was said in a condescending manner, totally different to what she was accustomed to.

Then came the most curious thing. Stuart tenderly brushed Joan's hair out of her face and gently ran the outside of his hand along the side of her face. It was the first time she'd felt any affection since she came out of hospital, and even then her son had given her an awkward hug, like he was afraid he'd break her, before heading off on his travels. (She didn't know that at the time Adam had been conscious that Sam was watching their every move and that if Sam had known how much they were both hurting and desperate to hug and cry it all out, he would have used it as a weapon against them both.)

Joan became aware they were on the path in the cemetery where she had fainted. Stuart was sitting cross-legged with her head cradled on his lap. Joan suddenly felt wrong, as if being cared for meant she was cheating on Sam. For a second she felt like a young girl courting with Roy, carefree and happy, canoodling in a field and watching the clouds, just wishing the world away.

'I've got to get up,' Joan said, harried.

'Okay, easy does it,' Stuart said, thinking his legs had gone numb and he had pins and needles in his feet, and he was also worried he might need some help getting up. His coat had acted as a blanket, but his trousers were cold and damp from the grass and tarmac pathway. He guessed they had been sitting like that in the cemetery for ten minutes.

Gradually and gingerly, they both got up; Joan still feeling a little light-headed, and Stuart stiff and achy. Anybody passing would have thought they were either a lot older than they really were or very drunk indeed. Joan then became conscious of Stuart's coat tail, all damp and muddy and covered in leaves, and set about trying to wipe the bits off with the silk hanky he'd given her whilst they were on the ground.

Stuart turned around, trying to brush Joan off, saying, 'Please, Joan, honestly, it doesn't matter.'

But as he twizzled, his numb leg gave way, and he and Joan fell over together onto the cut grass by an ancient tombstone whose inscription was barely visible. In the split-seconds as they fell, Stuart managed to twist himself towards the ground, trying to protect Joan. They thumped onto the ground. Joan banged her head into Stuart's midriff, causing him to exhale and gasp as he was winded.

Joan scrambled to her knees as she watched her old friend turn a frightening shade of purple. 'Oh God, oh God,' she whimpered, thinking she might have accidentally killed him. 'Shall I go and get help?' she asked, having the same panicked thoughts that Stuart had had a little while earlier. She started blowing on his face, and panting, and rubbing his hair as she knelt up and fidgeted closer to his face. 'Oh God, oh God,' she kept saying, all the while puffing in his face.

Stuart tried to speak but couldn't. He wanted to laugh, but was paralysed as his body fought to regain control of his breathing. Finally, he managed an, 'Owwwwwch.'

Joan was kneeling on his arm, pinching the skin, as she leant over him, huffing. He moved his arm and Joan realised.

'Oh my God, I'm sooo sorry,' she said.

Stuart started to laugh. 'Joan, I'm not having a bloody baby!'

Joan realised what she was doing and stopped automatically, feeling stupid and ridiculed. 'I'm sorry,' she said, suddenly serious

'It's okay, honestly. No harm done,' Stuart said, noticing her change in mood.

They got to their feet again, brushing themselves down for a second time and shaking limbs, but this time more subdued and sombre, as if they had only just remembered where they were, a place of peace and mourning. They both bent down to pick up the flowers at the same time, but Stuart was quicker, and Joan let him continue.

Stuart then noticed her staring at a penny wedged into the mud, caught in a trance. He deviated in his route to pick it up, and passed it to Joan, saying, 'Find a penny, pick it up, all day long it'll bring you luck,' with the childish grin she remembered from school. He held it out for her and then planted it in the palm of her hand.

Joan stared at Stuart. There was so much she wanted to say, but where to begin?

Stuart also felt bad. Where had the time gone? Was it really at the funeral that they'd last seen and properly spoken to each other?

They shared a moment, just looking at each other. So much to say and so little time. *It's really good to see you,* they said in their heads in unison.

Stuart also felt bad because he had been keeping tabs on Joan via Nikki, but he wouldn't tell her that, because he was aware of the animosity Joan harboured – and somewhat understandably too, he thought.

They moved over to Roy's grave. They were both mindful of each other's presence, and it seemed to distract them from the usual sombreness and the internal dialogue that a visit to Roy's resting place inspired. Joan would have wittered on about how she never seemed to be able to do the right thing (as per usual in total denial that she was in an abusive relationship). And Stuart would have expressed regret that perhaps he wasn't more of a father figure to the children, but they had their own lives and he was never any good at all that stuff, and had Roy not died, he could have looked after them, and it was unfair to pass any responsibility on to Stuart as he had nothing to do with them – but as far as he knew, they were fine and enjoying life.

They placed the flowers. Joan dabbed a tear from the corner of her eye with Stuart's silk hanky and went to pass it back to him.

'No, you keep it,' he said with a smile. He then offered his arm and said, 'Where are you heading?'

Joan said, 'Back to the station, but I have a while before the train leaves.'

'Well, will allow me to escort you, madam?' said Stuart theatrically, acting the perfect gentleman.

Joan held his arm and it felt comfortable and strong. She held him tight, and he her. They walked, arm in arm, in silence, their feet moving and clicking in perfect unison through the cemetery. The sun, breaking through gaps in the foliage, lit up the occasional tombstone. Were those illuminated the righteous people? Joan wondered.

As they left the still, cool surroundings of the cemetery, the sun was no longer dappled by the trees, but shone brightly in her face. Normally, Joan would have put her head down and shielded her face, but instead she felt the rays warm her cheeks. She felt good and safe and comfortable and proud – proud to be walking along with a gentleman, and not some giant, spindly pervert who made her skin crawl. She tried desperately to forget Sam and enjoy the moment. She couldn't remember the last time she'd felt this happy, and she wasn't sure she would again in her life. It really was the little things… She started to laugh.

'What's so funny?' asked Stuart, smiling, not in the least bit bothered by her laughing about something randomly that he didn't know about nor understand. Sam would have thought she was laughing at him and hit her, or said something nasty.

'Oh, erm, well, you see, I have a bit of a confession,' said Joan, as if she was about to reveal some utterly spectacular revelation.

'Go on,' said Stuart, intrigued.

'Well, please don't laugh, but I have something of an obsession.'

Stuart really was interested, and he stopped walking and uncoupled his arm so he could look Joan in the face and give her his full attention.

'Hey, don't stop walking,' said Joan, grabbing his arm and pulling him along. 'You see, the thing is…' Joan was really dragging it out, and trying (and failing miserably) not to sound like a silly, love-struck teenager.

Stuart, in turn, played along, honestly having no idea where the conversation was heading.

It all came out like an avalanche: 'Your newspaper – well, your rush hour crush section, you know… I'm literally your biggest fan! I love it. I read it every day, and am obsessed, I can't begin to tell you how much. Every day I read it, and every day I look for the people who wrote in or were written about.'

Joan sat on a platform, chatting away, emptying her mind of how she was infatuated with the rush hour crush section. Stuart felt a strange sense of elation that his old school friend got such a buzz from a concept he'd thought up whilst being a lonely commuter looking for love, and even sometimes wondering about her.

Joan sat cross-legged, talking at Stuart, whilst he nodded, listened, laughed and added his two-penneth. Joan hadn't had a conversation like this for ages, and she was enigmatic and animated. Her enthusiasm charmed Stuart, and his eyes glistened and shone with empathy and warmth. He could happily have sat there all day.

Joan let a few trains come and go, so engrossed was she in the conversation. Time flew, to the point that Joan was now going to be late. The conversation ground to a halt as the spectre of her normal life suddenly shaded the light that had illuminated their meeting and conversation.

Stuart noticed the change in atmosphere and Joan's mood. He stopped talking as he realised Joan had changed and started worrying about the time and looked panicked.

Joan said, 'I have to leave to meet Sam.'

Ah, there it was, thought Stuart, the little dagger to the heart he remembered from being a child. Every time she mentioned Roy's name, he'd felt the blade twist a little. This was the first time she'd mentioned Sam, or anything about her life outside the afternoon's accidental rendezvous, and Stuart thought that seemed a little strange. She suddenly seemed torn about leaving him, and he sensed that if he asked her to stay with him, she possibly would. Right then and there. Drop everything and be with him. This in itself was a bit strange to Stuart. Was he treading on someone's toes? Was he reliving his youth with Roy again? Was it just something about Joan? He had let her slip through his fingers before and regretted it every day for a very long time…

But he was over her now. He'd banished those thoughts. They were silly. He'd grown up – and anyway, she wouldn't be interested in him now. He was being a fool. Worst still an old fool with high blood pressure. He hadn't been good enough when he was a young man, so why would he be now? She had broken his heart when they were kids, and he wouldn't let that happen again. He'd read the signs incorrectly in the past. He'd happily make do with being friends from now on. If that was what she wanted to do. Whatever went on in her personal life was up to her to deal with, it had nothing to do with him. Or was it?

He wanted to ask her what was going on and if anything was the matter, but realised this meeting had happened completely by accident. Joan had her own life. Surely she would say if anything was the matter? And besides, it was none of his bloody business.

It didn't matter. Joan had formulated a plan. A flicker had been ignited, inspired by their conversation. Filled with ideas about her mission, for the first time in years she felt a sense of purpose. A fire in her belly. For this reason, she didn't want to leave Stuart.

As the train approached the platform, Joan leant across the seat to embrace Stuart and thank him for his time. He, being a gent, said he'd gladly spend time again with her again, that he hoped they wouldn't be strangers from now on and that it was his pleasure being with her. They both could have exchanged compliments and platitudes all day.

Joan felt giddy in his company. He was so charming, and a pleasure to talk to.

Standing up and straightening her clothes as the train approached the platform, Joan realised her leg had gone completely numb from the hard bench and sitting cross-legged for so long. She tried to stamp her feet as the train slowed to a stop, but it was no good.

'Shit, I've got really bad pins and needles, like you had earlier on.'

They both started to laugh. The pins and needles were rampant throughout her leg. The worst she could remember. Had she not been with Stuart, she might have cried. Her leg felt like a numb, dead weight.

Stuart, ever the gentleman, offered his arm as the train's brakes screeched, signalling its approach into the platform. They hobbled towards the train together as the doors opened and a passenger jumped off.

'See you later, Joan. Please don't be a stranger,' Stuart said, looking sincere.

'You look after yourself too, and don't be accosting any ladies in cemeteries,' said Joan, immediately regretting her words. What on earth had she meant? She didn't know herself. She was rambling carried away with the whole situation. She wasn't used to being talked to nicely in public. She was embarrassed and excited and proud, but most of all, in terrible agony and trying to put a brave face on their goodbye.

Simultaneously they leant in to give each other a quick peck goodbye. Mirroring each other they both went in the same direction and performed a strange sort of robotic meltdown as neither of their brains seemed capable of continuing the simple task of coordinating a little kiss. Then, more determined, they held each other's arms, smiling, and tried again, realising they needed to hurry up because the train would soon leave. This time they bonked noses awkwardly. They started laughing.

Stuart said, mock-angrily, 'Oh, forget it. Be off with you.'

Joan was trying not to laugh as she boarded the train, but her leg ached and her nose felt quite sore too.

As Joan got on, almost immediately a guy jumped up, so she hobbled forward towards his seat, thinking how lucky she was that the bloke had got up and she had got his spot. As the train started moving, she waved a heartfelt goodbye to Stuart. Then she noticed the chap whose seat she'd taken standing by the door. Why hadn't he got off? Joan caught his eye for a millisecond before he looked away. Then Joan realised he had given up his seat for her. In her palm, she felt the penny Stuart had picked up in the cemetery. These things never happened to her. Was it the lucky penny? Was he another gentleman? Was it because she was a woman? Was it because she looked old?

Then self-doubt started to kick in. It occurred to her that he could have thought she was disabled. She had limped onto the train. He thought she needed the seat because she'd have difficulty standing! The fellow was obviously aware he had done a good deed, hence his acting coy now. Joan noticed other passengers nodding and shooting approving glances at her good-deed-doer, and sending sympathetic half-smiles towards her – the poor, disabled, possibly mental Joan. Wasn't she brave, facing the world and taking a train all by herself? Poor, crippled Joan.

Joan realised her station was approaching and shortly she would need to disembark the train. The pins and needles had now gone. Her leg felt fine. What should she do? Limp off or walk naturally? Surely pretending she was disabled now would be far worse than people mistakenly thinking she was disabled when she got on. Who was this a crime against anyway? The thought police, perhaps? Would disabled people be offended if they weren't there? Was that even possible? Only if someone uncovered Joan's lie. Only if someone knew she was able-bodied but now impersonating a disabled person. Surely there would be people on the train who would know people who were disabled. She'd certainly have offended them if they were ever to find out?

What about the person who stood up? Would he still be regarded as some kind of hero, or would his new gentlemanly status be revoked and, in turn, would he be reduced to a joke victim, a figure of Joan's ridicule? She'd taken him in and fooled him. Was she now a cold, heartless mickey-taker, poking fun at those who were unable to walk properly and those sensitive enough to recognise an awkward gait?

She couldn't even remember which leg had had the pins and needles. Whilst stretching her useless legs again, she received sympathetic looks from the other passengers. *Oh, the poor disabled old lady,* Joan imagined them thinking. She tried to picture herself ambling hideously onto the train. She could only picture herself lurching about like Quasimodo; she then thought, *If the cap fits…*

She caught the Good Samaritan's eye again. He gave her a coy, boyish grin. A grin that said, 'Yes, I'm the good guy who helped you. I'm a hero, and today it was my pleasure being there for you.' *Oh god, this is utterly hopeless,* Joan thought. Should she just hold her head high and walk off normally? After all, it was an honest mistake. She'd shatter the illusion otherwise. She would upset everyone taken in by her entrance. Perhaps they'd all find it funny.

When the train pulled into the platform, Joan left it as late as possible before getting up and heading for the door. She tried to limp towards the exit as quickly as possible, but her shoe nearly fell off. She dragged it along by her toes, suddenly worried that it would fall on the track, as it teetered on the edge of control by her big toe. As she got to the door, the worry of losing her shoe overwhelmed her, so she kicked her foot forward, making sure the shoe flew off the train and skidded across the platform.

As she jumped off the train, she dropped her penny, and it rolled back into the carriage. Her shoe went one way, and her new lucky penny the other. Torn, she hopped across the platform, one shoe on and one shoe off, over-emphasising her every move. She retrieved her shoe and waited on the platform for a few seconds, trying to wiggle her foot back into her footwear. Her face was burning red with embarrassment.

She set off doing a silly walk just as the train departed. She could feel the eyes of those in the carriage scrutinising her every move. The poor, unfortunate lady. Teenagers tittered at the recollection of her shoe flying off, whilst a girl wearing a Mickey Mouse t-shirt picked up the penny that had rolled across the floor.

Then an alcohol-drenched, tobacco-burnt voice groaned out from behind her: 'Where've you been, woman, and why the bloody hell are you walking like that?'

'Oh, hello, Sam,' said Joan.

Chapter 10

Stuart sat at his desk remembering his last conversation with Joan on the station platform.

'So, what are you waiting for?' he'd asked her, trying to inspire her into action.

'Erm, well, you know, I just don't know if I've got the time,' said Joan.

'Nonsense, you have all the time in the world, my dear,' he said, sounding like an old-fashioned record.

Joan had made some excuse about Sam not understanding and also not having the money. She was thinking about Stuart's grand scheme and considering selling her lovely old pen so she could raise the funds to buy a computer or something. It sounded ridiculous. Stuart remembered smirking at the time, until he noticed her face turn deadly serious and then he felt utterly ashamed – he had become so removed from watching every penny that he couldn't really imagine everything having a value. It was an old pen that had belonged to Joan's granddad, who'd given it to her dad, possibly her only heirloom of consequence – a beautiful sentiment, Stuart thought. It was a pen that had written thousands upon thousands of letters and notes; it had been warmed by the hands of people who would have loved Joan dearly and been used, no doubt, during times of conflict and love… what a fitting instrument, and in the hand of a gifted writer, no less.

If only Joan had had a break like his all those years ago, he pondered. His break was being forced to re-sit his exams at school. Being held back somehow pushed him forward; he'd striven to prove his dad and his fellow pupils wrong… he would have the last laugh. Only when his dad passed away did Stuart finally become brave enough to admit his dad had only wanted his son to do the best he could. But Joan was different; she could have been a well-known writer, of that he had little doubt. If he could, she could. Only she met Roy.

Stuart phoned Joan again to check on the progress of her ideas to follow up the Rush Hour Crushes, and Joan backtracked, saying the plans were on hold.

'On hold? What on earth do you mean?'

'I mean, I haven't got the money any more.'

'Why? What? What do you mean? I'm confused.'

Joan revealed she had placed the pen in a cash converter store on the high street to raise the necessary money, but unfortunately their TV was on the blink and Sam was insisting they needed a newer, bigger flat-screen TV before any computer. They had computers at her work, he said, so why couldn't she just use one of those?

Stuart leapt into action. First he demanded she didn't buy a computer with the money she'd gained from selling the pen; that would just cause arguments and confrontations, and he didn't like the idea of that. He would sort her a computer; his paper had room's jam-packed-full of unused technology. Then Stuart called his friend William, who was a keen collector of all things one found in places like pawnbrokers' and antique shops, and sent him on a secret mission to go and collect the pen and keep it safe. 'God willing it's still there…'

Stuart had told Joan that he felt her idea to start a blog was definitely the right way to go. 'All the kids and big companies are doing it.' It was a brilliant plan. He could see what it meant to her, and he wanted to encourage her to pursue whatever it was she envisaged and to see where this project might go.

It was becoming pretty apparent to Stuart that even if Joan had said she was interested in knitting the world's biggest blanket, he would have told her it was the greatest idea ever and would have supported her. However, he couldn't help feeling something wasn't right with Joan at home with Sam, he was unsure how she could go from being so enthusiastic to deflated in such a short space of time, so he'd need to tread with caution.

To Stuart, the blog really was quite a good idea, not just because it stemmed from his creation, or because the thought of their combined minds somehow reproducing and spawning spontaneously similar to something magical like creating a baby or a seedling sprouting skywards and somehow reaching out like tree branches becoming entwined over time, but also because from a business perspective it could be a great bolt-on to the digital paper and generate interest and feedback. That is, if there actually was any interest in his Rush Hour Crushes… In the past, the paper used to get bucket-loads of fan mail and letters. One of the first jobs assigned to the work-experience kids and new employees and those working a notice period was rifling through the bags of mail and looking for any interesting stories or crushes. Stuart and the editor had discussed the changes and implications for the traditional printed paper for the best part of twenty years, and agreed that the online section of the newspaper was definitely the future.

To the experienced journalists at the newspaper with no real fear of deadlines or pressure at home or one hundred places to be or a million household chores to do, the organisation of such projects would have all seemed quite straightforward and simply an afternoon's work. But to Joan, it was a whole new world, completely daunting and unfathomable – until she stumbled across the *Starting a Blog For Dummies* book in the library. She set about preparing, juggling time to allow her enough hours in the day to research and start her blog. Initially, she wrote everything in her notepad in beautiful italic handwriting. She had used the lovely old pen, the last of her father's belongings, but had now switched to a broken and chewed biro. The thought of somehow switching to a computer felt slightly surreal, but Stuart explained that sooner or later the blog would need to be in an electronic format anyway, so why waste time writing and then rewriting? (Although he also admitted it was lovely seeing her handwriting, and the extra stage might help her write in greater depth and help with editing.)

Stuart leant back in his old leather office chair, looked at the computer screen, typed in www.rushourcrush.com/.co.uk/.net and bought the available website address. He then googled successful blogs and looked for a simple format. Inspired, he called the work-experience kid (who had an unusual sense of fashion, tattoos and facial piercings) and said he had a project for him.

Joan met Stuart and the work-experience kid in a noisy coffee shop. She showed off her scribbled notes on how she envisaged her website. 'Rush Hour Crush' at the top, and a picture of a cherub or Cupid. It only needed to be simple, she thought, no flashing lights or fancy graphics. She choose a fairly simple format. A basic picture of Cupid firing an arrow. She decided she'd start it off with a little introduction about who she was and what her mission was.

My name is Joan. I went to school with Stuart Maskell, the award-winning journalist and original mastermind behind the idea of Rush Hour Crush. I have become something of a fan in recent years and would openly admit to being somewhat obsessed. I have made it my mission in life to try to get together some Rush Hour Crushes…

Joan considered mentioning that she was a mother of two, a spinster and a librarian, but Stuart said not to divulge too much personal information.

'There are plenty of crackpots out there. You can only be honest and open to an extent. Also, how about adding a chat forum or just a contact form that sends you an email or text message every time anyone enters any info?'

'I can do that,' said the work-experience kid. 'I could try to animate the baby – you know, get the arrow to fire out of the bow. It would look well sick,' he suggested excitedly, whilst fiddling with the metal stud between his mouth and chin.

Stuart and the kid both suggested Joan would benefit from having her own mobile phone if she was to regularly update and check proceedings. This would be another expense she had no idea how to afford or conceal from Sam. Maybe she would need to spend the pen money on that instead of the TV and get as many top-ups as possible. But what about the TV and Sam? How could she explain losing or spending the money?

Stuart asked the work-experience kid to write up Joan's notes and help create the blog based on the template Joan envisaged. He sent the kid to Joan's library to meet her one lunchtime and go through the progress on his computer. The other staff thought he was her son. Joan loved it. She felt really important having a meeting and sitting in a park around the corner from her work (it was more of a little square than a park, a tiny bit of green with a bench, somewhere to sit and get some fresh air when the weather was good). Today was a sunny day. Joan shared her peanut butter sandwich and crisps with the kid, and as always she couldn't help staring at the holes in his earlobes and metal studs in his face.

'Did they hurt?' asked Joan.

'Yeah, a bit,' said the kid, suddenly aware Joan was studying him.

He also had tattoos on his arms. He was actually quite quiet and a little bit pretty, Joan thought, for a punk anyway. Or was he a Goth? Either way, he looked like he needed a good wash, a decent meal and a few lighter-coloured clothes, and then perhaps he wouldn't look like a mixture of David Bowie and Edward Scissorhands. But he was a nice kid and he set about the project like it was no problem, and although Joan felt slightly stupid and out of her depth and clueless as to whatever they were trying to create, he sat and listened patiently and diligently tapped codes that disappeared into the computer, saying 'yes' and 'cool, man', which Joan took to mean 'no problem'. She figured perhaps he had done those things, mutilations, as a cry for help. Why else would he be scarring his body and face if not to draw attention to himself? Joan wanted to give him a hug and felt overcome with emotion. She really missed her boy and wanted to talk this project through with him. She dreamt perhaps Adam could help her too – or, even better, she could help him find a Rush Hour Crush.

'I'll be in touch as soon as it looks ready to go live,' said the lad.

'Thank you, James,' said Joan, noticing his name flash up on the computer screen.

Stuart hoped this project would usher in a new, fruitful chapter in their lives in which plans would come together. Ultimately, he wanted what was best for Joan. With her love of writing and enthusiasm for her Rush Hour Crush blog, and now armed with the new computer bolstered by his wealth of experience, perhaps now they could work out a successful plan of action. Something to break the monotony of her life. And a good deed by him, a present to the one he'd once loved, his childhood sweetheart, his personal Rush Hour Crush whom he felt he'd let down.

They wrote notes and sent letters the old-fashioned way, back and forth, like war correspondents, discussing the crushes in their entirety and the history of the newspaper's Rush Hour Crush section. Stuart shared everything except the inspiration, of which Joan was utterly oblivious.

Joan then began trying to formulate a plan to find out as much as possible about the journeys mentioned in the crushes. This, she decided, would be done by interviewing the people who wrote in, either face to face or over the phone (face to face would be better), and then she should start a database. Joan would have two lines of enquiry to follow from the outset. One: the description of the two crushes in the post. Two: any description or any details provided of where the crush had occurred. And a possible third line too, if either party actually contacted Joan and explained the journey up to the moment they laid eyes on each other.

Ultimately, Joan needed to find the people who had written into the newspaper.

The editor sat leaning against the desk, rather than sitting behind it, facing his employee. His relationship with Stuart wasn't formal; they went way back. He liked Stuart's visits, as he never usually had an agenda or went in for arse-licking, brown-nosing, back-stabbing or all the other usual reasons people visited the boss in his office during the working day. No one other than Stuart ever popped by for a social visit or to chew the cud; they always came for a selfish reason, and the majority of time he was too busy to listen. Such was the problem of being the boss: never enough hours in the day.

'You old dog, you really like this lady, huh?' the editor said, looking at Stuart over the rims of his crescent-shaped glasses.

'Don't be so absurd,' said Stuart, unimpressed.

The editor raised his eyebrows and gave a sly smirk and said, 'No offence, old chap.'

'None taken,' said Stuart, bristling. 'You won't mind me adding the web address of her blog for the next few weeks, eh?'

'Excuse me?' said the editor, suddenly aware he might be giving away free advertising.

'What the hell is in it for me, or should I start calling this a bloody charity?'

'Hey, listen, it's not like that. I reckon I could write a little piece in conjunction with it. I think perhaps we could say it's the twentieth anniversary of the Rush Hour Crushes or something. It'll be good. You remember the last time I did an article on the section?'

The editor smiled, remembering meeting William Wallace for the first time. 'Do you still see that funny old sod?' he said warmly.

'Actually, yes I do. I only spoke to him the other day, funnily enough. I'm also taking a computer, okay?'

'For fuck's sake, Stuart, do you want the keys to my car too?' said the editor, trying to look cross.

Stuart got up from the comfy black office chair he was sitting on and gave his boss a friendly smack on the arm. Then he walked towards the door, saying, 'I couldn't afford the petrol... You can put it down as an expense, if you like, or take it out of my wages.'

'Hey, whatever. Listen, if it takes off at all, maybe we can advertise on her site. Hey, that's not a bad idea. Maybe we should...' the editor said as Stuart started walking away, back towards his desk.

'Whoa, hold your horses there, boss. Don't take this the wrong way, but she's not really ready for all that yet. Small steps; it's just an idea at the moment,' Stuart said, trying to get the situation back under his control.

Stuart didn't really have a desk anymore; he had a laptop and was supposed to hot-desk – all part of the push to create a paperless office. 'That's just great, the perfect oxymoron ...A paperless paper...' Stuart and his boss had laughed till they cried once at a late-night drinking session. The editor had said he always collected flyers, leaflets, promos, anything printed and given away, even if it meant putting it in the very next bin he saw somewhere in the street. As far as he was concerned, it was keeping a printer in business somewhere.

Joan hoped that once people contacted her this would lead to further investigations and more concentrated leads she could then open up a case file. Initially, she hoped talking to the Rush Hour Crush contributors would be based on an interview format – question and answer. If she still had nothing to go on, perhaps she would need to just try a good old-fashioned stalking method and stake out the usual daily journeys mentioned in the crushes in a bid to track down her quarry.

Stuart added a strap line to the Rush Hour Crush section in the newspaper asking regular readers to check out Joan's blog (later, when she actually got out and about, he considered mentioning keeping an eye out for the slightly eccentric-looking lady on the train platforms, holding a placard and handing out cards and flyers).

On the third floor was the old tabloid stalwart Stuart, nestled somewhere deep in an enclosed cul-de-sac of corridors in the bustling offices of the newspaper company.

The paper had been founded well over two hundred and fifty years ago, at a time when the British Empire still ruled the world. Writers then busily penned articles about tragic defeats at the hands of the upstarts in American. News came in hot via carrier pigeons, the results of far-flung battles tied to the legs of feathered avian postmen. Reports of problems in the spice isles and plans to abolish slavery were both embraced and ignored. Long-gone rulers and dynasties and strange-sounding empires and countries like Ceylon, Rhodesia and ottomans came and went. Islands were still being discovered and dodos were just dying out, and other advances like the telephone, the television and the telegrams were just being invented. Technology seemed to be moving faster and faster, and Jack the Ripper was still to walk the streets of East London not far from those very same offices, that one man who single-handedly would keep hundreds of journalists busy and terrify millions of readers…

Most of the floors had now been cleared, and the old wooden desks had been upgraded several times. Disparate styles of furniture and decor had come and gone, Victorian to Edwardian to the Twentieth century. Art Deco to industrial, flower power to shabby chic. The old façade of the building remained, but inside it had been redeveloped hundreds of times, constantly evolving. Like the face of a person between the ages of twenty to forty, the outside looked the same but inside a wealth of knowledge and change was blossoming and being forgotten. Writing pens and inks were replaced by typesetting, plates and inks replaced by Apple Macs. Typewriters came and went in the blink of an eye. In Stuart's time alone, mobile phones had been created, originally the size of a modern-day mega-computer but then getting smaller and smaller, to the point that Stuart's big fingers were useless on the keypad unless he wanted to type two letters for every one intended. Keyboards gave way to touchscreens. Tapes, CDs, floppy disks, USBs, file transfers, uploads, downloads, You Send It, We Transfer, DropBox... it was endless. Wi-Fi and the cloud; who owned the cloud? There was a time he'd purposely go out of his way to know the answers to such questions, but now every day there was a new riddle.

Once his job had been to witness a truly remarkable event and then use his brain to regurgitate what had happened, bringing the reader into the very essence of what had occurred. If he saw it, you'd see it; if he smelt it, you'd virtually taste it. Now everything was there for you to see live. Everything. The written word in articles was an afterthought; it would be captured somewhere in real time... newspapers peddled old news for the masses. Old news really was old news now. The papers were obituaries. Some younger writers wrote up what they had gleamed from several eye-witness accounts! Who needed to be on the scene when you had YouTube, TV and Facebook? Journalism had changed. More often than not it was sensationalist rubbish based on nothing more than conjecture with the sole purpose of creating a stir.

To Stuart, all that was left was eloquent reminiscing. This hurt him to a certain extent. The world had sped up and overtaken itself. We were all just too stupid to realise. What if something catastrophic happened? Who would we turn to in order to get information off a CD? How did mobile phones work? Was the World Wide Web backed up anywhere? Where had all the Encyclopaedias Britannica gone? We were all too stupid to know.

There was a massive old cupboard. It smelt ancient, of a time forgotten. Old air. It was mainly used to file backups of all the previous editions of newspapers. These were now stored on computers. At one time no doubt there'd have been numerous chronological cupboards, and rooms and floors dedicated to old newspaper editions. But now years and years' worth had been scanned and were backed up on little more than giant memory sticks and whirring black hard-drives somewhere, just a click or two away. This was where Stuart's old computers came to rest in peace.

He was quite proud of the fact he'd managed to keep them all – over thirty years' worth. It had taken quite some nagging, whining and whinging, but he had got his way in the end. And now they were part of the furniture. Stuart's computer collection had become something of a talking point within the building, and it was a popular stop-off on the show-rounds when new members of staff joined or the kids on work experience were given a tour. The computers were as alien and interesting to the youngsters as he was.

'Seriously, man, these are well mint, bro'. You could get proper loaded if you cashed these in at a museum or something, bruv.'

Stuart wasn't entirely sure if this, from the work-experience kid with ridiculous facial piercings, was a compliment. For starters, given the kid's age, he was more likely to be a son than a brother, but Stuart accepted this was some sort of friendly expression.

'Yeah, cool, man,' Stuart replied, trying to do some trendy finger-pointing hand gesture, but struggling to see past the thin air flowing freely through the black hoops that made the lad's earlobes see-through and the mental bits protruding from his nose and mouth. Some sort of gothic punk madness, Stuart thought.

Stuart had managed to keep his original phone collection at home too. He remembered that originally the paper owners and journalists alike had been excited by the possibilities of mobiles. Journalists could report on events much more quickly, and get directed to somewhere a story was unravelling much faster if already out on the road... Of course, the owners and chief of the newspaper also liked the idea of keeping tabs on their wayward young writers, and the mobile phone seemed a good tool to track their every wandering movement. The days of phoning the most popular haunts and getting the barman or landlady to call around the pub were coming to an end. And so it was that in a relatively short space of time the humble mobile phone became the most essential bit of kit, and all top journos had the very best, well-connected, most powerful phones available. Sooner or later they too would become just another dispensable tool, like the notepad, pen, typewriter and camera before they were integrated and upgraded. When someone worked out how to merge the phone with another item used daily that would be it: all change once again.

The more Stuart thought about it, the more he actually quite liked the idea of giving his old tech collection to the Science Museum one day. He was fairly certain his was a unique chronological collection – a glimpse into the hours he had spent tapping away and looking at different-sized screens, wondering: would anyone actually read and enjoy anything he had written? He'd often thought about adding subtly in a paragraph of an article he'd written: 'Are you actually reading this? And is it any good?' He thought perhaps someone might phone him up, having read that in the newspaper, or he'd get a knock on the door and someone standing there would say, 'Yes, I read it and thought it was very good actually.' Stuart thought this was probably why people settled down with a wife or husband: that's what they would be good for, answering such stupid questions that no one else would bother answering.

Looking at his computers, he admitted the fact that they were his was of very little consequence, and he doubted many, if any, would miss him when he was gone. Scrutinising a grimy keyboard, he remembered seeing kids hammering away at the keys, playing ridiculous games, while poor parents tried to write basic notes and learn simple programming skills, unable to write full sentences without certain words being a problem. He looked at one keyboard that had always had a problematic 'z' key; no doubt at some point it had been over-enthusiastically bashed. He also remembered a time one of the guys from the obituaries column had a complete meltdown one afternoon after a joker switched a few keys around... how they'd all laughed. That felt like yesterday to Stuart, but it was probably before the work-experience kid was even conceived.

It was graffiti to art. Colouring books to photography. Rap music to BB King. Dixie Fried Chicken to Café des Amis in Covent Garden… He must book a table, he thought, as his stomach rumbled. Perhaps he could invite Joan. They could catch up on each other's progress and he could give her the laptop.

Fleet Street, the home of the press. The wobbly trolley. Vapes. Drones and hover-boards. Kids with all-different-sized tablets, iPads, iPhones with little white cables disappearing into every orifice. Hustle and bustle. Big colourful headphones. Noise-reducing grey and black headphones. Cableless and Bluetooth. Handheld devices and large, crystal-clear, HD, flat or curved, 3D, 4K, plasma and LCD screens with sound bars booming. News channels permanently on in every corner on every floor every second of every day. The old writer pondered a generation of protein-rich, sugar-free, brain-shaken adults all blasted senseless by high-powered headphones and 3D glasses and Google specs in driverless cars.

Stuart liked a smoke – the occasional cheeky rollup. He had never been a really heavy smoker, a couple a day at the most, usually after a nice lunch. A lovely bottle of red, a Montepulciano perhaps, a plate of cheeses and a few grapes at his favourite little hideaway in Covent Garden, nestled secretly behind the Royal Opera House, and then a smoke. He had felt a little cross at being shamed into hiding his paltry vice. He remembered fondly sitting at his desk as a young writer having completed an article. He'd take out his small tin of tobacco, Golden Virginia, roll a thin smoke in a matter of moments and pause for a minute to admire its perfect spherical form. A wave of self-appreciation for a job well done – two jobs, in fact, a fine article and a perfectly rolled smoke.

The office switched to silly season on a Friday afternoon nowadays, the wobbly trolley used as an excuse by the other, young, journos to oil the gears before heading out and getting properly trolleyed. Perhaps that had always been the case; Stuart wasn't sure. They seemed to partake in the use of cocaine and alcohol like it was going out of fashion. Almost like life revolved around it. It seemed to the old writer that indulging heavily in life's excesses had been in and out of fashion several times during his career, and he was sure it would continue long after he was gone. He had always felt it made the people who were prats even bigger prats and those who were quiet even quieter – that was his general impression, and he doubted that would ever change. He didn't much care for any of the new bars or any of that recreational drug business either. Nor much for the repetitive loud music – what did they call it? Banging house. He chuckled: it was certainly banging. He loved his music and was more of an old-school blues man, maybe country, bluegrass. Transatlantic folk sessions. The most these kids knew of proper music was a spotty teenager singing like a mosquito while burning his fingertips thrashing an amplified acoustic guitar. They probably wouldn't know Bob Dylan from Adam... Ryan or Bryan Adams even.

He also didn't like the way the younger lot would go to a bar, pub or restaurant and the louder the music, the louder they'd get and the more excitable they'd become. Stuart felt sure when he was younger he'd go for a drink and the more he had, the more it would lead towards an inevitable early night. Nowadays the kids seemed to run on high-octane fuel, caffeine, alcohol and sugar-packed, every shot making them more wired and every trip to the toilet more wide-eyed and loud and runny-nosed. Damn Columbians to blame all the time, apparently.

He was gradually losing touch. He felt it coming faster and faster… every new fad, every blitzed vegetable smoothie, the distance getting further and further from what he was familiar with. Had it not been for the editor, he'd have been totally disenfranchised, chewed up and spat out a while ago. So thanks to his old friend, Stuart muddled on, confused but often intrigued. Perhaps had he another boss he would have been moved aside or given a payoff, but it was obvious he had little else to do… he lived to work. That's not to say he wasn't tempted to ease off a little. He did find it hard keeping his eyes open in the morning and afternoon. The doctor had told him perhaps he should take it a little easier. Perhaps change his diet, go for some long walks, try swimming, stop smoking altogether or something. His doctor was another geeky new kid on the block who knew everything already. More inane twaddle from the younger generation – blab blah blah, healthy diet, blah blah blah, high cholesterol, blah blah blah, high blood pressure, blah blah blah, thickening arteries – leaving him feeling more alienated by the day.

Stuart quite liked being a sounding post or a shoulder to cry on occasionally, but more and more he found himself amazed at the sheer stupidity of some of his younger and higher-educated colleagues. Naturally, some were well mannered, but he couldn't help thinking they were kind to him because he reminded them of their parents. He chuckled at the thought – who was he kidding? They probably thought he was more like a grandparent. Then he mused: to be honest, they were closer to the truth.

Perhaps he should find a nice little local newspaper or village magazine somewhere nearby to see out his final few working years. He didn't really need to commute to work anymore; it was just he didn't feel his creative juices had totally dried up. Moreover he could still pen a decent article. Stuart felt more than capable of looking at things in detail. It wasn't as if he had suddenly lost the power to articulate what he perceived perfectly.

He sneaked into the old cupboard and pulled up a chair amongst the battered metal filing cabinets and stacked, dusty, debilitated computers. With his back to the wall, he heard the mechanical mumble of generator fans and the whirring of backup disks and servers. Little green LEDs flashed their eminence. Through the closed door, he heard the exaggerated laugh of one of the female journalists, Sarah from the sports team. Lovely girl; hopelessly in lust with Simon from the travel team. He wouldn't commit to any of the girls, though were rumours he had slept with virtually all of them. Stuart felt the green-eyed twang of the younger man stirring within him, remembering the jealousy he'd felt towards Roy and his God-given gift with women. *Bastard,* Stuart thought. He could picture Sarah leaning forward, tossing her hair suggestively and curling it around her fingers, kicking a leg up behind her as she leant over his desk, revealing her cleavage. Simon would be laughing and non-committal, scanning the room for fresh adventures, Sarah's twin peaks not challenging enough. Tragic. The similarities between Sarah and Joan were suddenly apparent.

Stuart rolled a cigarette and then ran his fingers along the boxes of computers until he came to a recent laptop, about five years old. Perfect, he thought. He'd hardly used it before they were upgraded; all the cables were still in the box. He pulled it down from the shelf and lit his rollup – and then the lights went out, the sprinklers came on and the fire alarm went off.

'Shit,' a soggy Stuart said.

Rush Hour Crush

To the boy who kept smiling at me on the Northern Line on Wednesday: We both got off at Hendon Central. You made my day with your cheeky smile. – Blonde with Bowler Hat

To the tall, dark, distinguished gentleman in the paisley shirt on the 321 this morning: Fancy going my way? Would love to bake you a cake. – Short Guy in Cheap Suit

To the cute guy next to me on the 8.20 a.m. train to Oxford on Wednesday, wearing a grey coat and with a big leather bag: Coffee? – Not-So-Secret Admirer

To the tall, not-so-dark and handsome businessman wearing headphones at St James's Park at 7.45 a.m. yesterday: You are really fit. – Your Male Admirer

Chapter 11

Joan began targeting selected hubs that were busy crossover points featured in crushes. London Bridge, King's Cross, Liverpool Street and Paddington were her favourite choices. They also roughly covered those travelling in from the north, east, south and west of London.

She aimed to be one of the four locations between seven and nine a.m., and then she'd go straight to work and write up her notes during the day. Joan started becoming a character on many ordinary folks' daily commute, initially as a peripheral figure but gradually as a regular. As the pedestrians made their way through the station, they saw a strange lady with unruly hair and an inane smile (complete with bright-pink/red lipstick-smudged teeth), holding a placard and bobbing up and down like she needed a wee. Generally, she stood to the left of the queue, not quite in the way but definitely adding to the kettling effect. At first, most people tried not to make eye contact with her for fear she was a lunatic; some sort of religious nut was a common misconception. But before long, she started to get recognised and some people were actually quite civil and nice to her ('nice' as in they didn't simply look away like she had an affliction). They accepted the leaflet she was handing out before chucking it in the bin or scrunching it up in a pocket or bag (out of sight, out of mind). Some actually read the placard she was holding; not real reading, more like running their eyes over the words, like tired eyes fed up with a boring book. They didn't stop to talk, not yet anyway, not unless they were old, lost and confused and were hoping for help buying a train ticket. Joan didn't feel embarrassed, though – she felt like she had an important job to do. Every time she saw a person walking past holding their newspaper, she thought perhaps they were one of her crushes, someone she'd been looking for, so she tried extra-hard to be noticed. She hopped from one foot to the other, smiling like a maniac, holding her placard just that little bit higher, her excitement growing.

He looks like my target, the man on the 7.02…

'Have a good day, sir,' she said as cheerily as could be.

He was walking fast and was on the wrong side of three people, so she couldn't hand him a flyer unless she joined the tide of people. His sideways anxious smile gave off the feeling that he didn't really want to talk. If anything, he looked a little afraid of Joan. If she suddenly started after him, along the station corridors, Joan was afraid he might panic and run away, and then he might avoid her in the future. Perhaps she could see him tomorrow, she thought; maybe then he'd be a little less nervous. *Slowly, slowly catchy monkey,* Joan told herself.

She had a real sense of purpose, and for once in her life she didn't felt stupid or ashamed or worthless, because she knew her friend Stuart supported her. She felt good, warm inside and – dare she think it? – not alone.

Joan's blog had gone live shortly before Stuart's remembrance article. Following the guidance of the editor, Stuart's piece was closely related to Joan's infatuation with Rush Hour Crushes (carefully painting a picture of someone who was obsessed, but not a crackpot). The editor liked the idea that it was loosely connected with a made-up anniversary: ten years of Rush Hour Crushes, one million submitted crushes, the history of how Rush Hour Crushes started, some of the strangest crushes they had featured. Stuart started the article with some facts from when Rush Hour Crushes first started: who was at number one in the pop charts, who was the prime minister and what the most popular car in the United Kingdom was (the mini?). He, like Joan, was always curious – did anyone ever get together with their Rush Hour Crush? Now this lady was determined to find out once and for all...

Straight after the article and the blog going live, the blog seemed amazingly popular and gained followers at an incredible rate. Joan, Stuart and the editor were blown away by the feedback and interest. After a month, the blog and Joan's tweets attracted an unprecedented number of followers and Joan surged up the polls of the most popular/new bloggers. The editor and Stuart got the work-experience kid, James, to go to the IT and marketing departments and work on an app that could be downloaded and used in conjunction with Joan's blog and the newspaper website.

Someone even started a spin-off site with pictures of Joan and a 'Where's Joan today?' section. This was the point when an online troll first start rearing its ugly head and targeting Joan. James and the IT department tried as hard as possible to keep a lid on most posts on her site and to delete negative comments from the main pages as soon as they were posted. But unfortunately the troll then migrated to the spin-off site, and whoever ran that soon lost interest in continually moderating it, so it became awash with horrible comments and photos of Joan. The editor and Stuart managed to get the site taken down, but others popped up on Facebook and under different web addresses, always with someone adding nasty comments and photos of Joan. Unlike the photos originally featured on her fan site, these were spiteful and vindictive and designed to make her look as ugly and as demented as possible. Whoever started the spin-off site liked Joan's slightly eccentric fashion sense, but the troll didn't like Joan and just posted really ugly pictures.

Joan wondered whether the troll could be her Sam or one of his friends. Her daughter or Nikki even… Stuart wondered if it was someone at the paper, a fellow journalist or someone else unknown – but why Joan? Then Stuart thought it could be the work-experience guy, James. Maybe he was slightly angry over not receiving any plaudits or recognition or dosh for his creation, which had become an award-nominated blog.

At around this time James's older sister, Rebecca, joined the paper as a journalist (with very little experience or skill; she seemed shoehorned into the organisation). She resented the whispered accusations about her brother and, fuelled by irritation that her brother hadn't got the recognition he deserved, she laid the blame squarely at Stuart and the editor's door. James and Rebecca were the kids of a close confidant and advisor of the newspaper's owner, a mythical Russian figure who lurked, far removed, in the background. Even the editor had very little dealings with him.

"They are a pair of spoilt rich kids and what's more having family connections to the Russian suggests they come from a family not worth trifling with' −the editor's words, not Stuart's.

Joan won a Best New Blog prize, and her Twitter page, App and Facebook pages were amongst the most popular downloaded and liked media pages in the UK. She was officially hotter news than 'Barry Smiles' leaving the boy band One Dimension. This resulted in her becoming inundated with leads and ideas and things to do and places to go and people to see. She even had requests to appear on local radio shows.

Upset to hear of the negativity, but greatly shielded by Stuart, Joan ploughed on, but could only afford to go searching at weekends and days off and holidays. All the while, though, no one came forward to say they had actually met a Rush Hour Crush. Of those that contacted Joan it's always one, the writer… the person that had the crush rather than those that were the recipient. They seemed generally oblivious − or possibly figments of the imagination, Joan started to wonder.

While she was getting ready for work, Joan heard a knock at the door and trudged downstairs. Sam was signing for something – from the postman, she assumed, as she noticed his red van parked outside the front of their house. She heard Sam grunt as the postman said 'Sign here' and 'Thanks, pal, have a nice day'. Sam didn't respond, just swung the door shut in the postman's face, cutting off the rays of light beaming in from outside, as Joan tried to smile and mouth a 'thank you' discreetly behind Sam's back while being plunged back into darkness.

'What shit have you been buying now, woman?' Sam barked accusingly.

'I haven't bought a thing, honestly,' Joan said.

'Well, it's got your bloody name on it – look,' said Sam, jabbing his long, knobbly finger at Joan's name to suggest he thought she was lying.

He tossed the medium-sized brown box at her like a Frisbee and it hit her quite hard in the midriff. Joan just managed to keep hold of the parcel, which was quite light for its size, hoping she wouldn't drop it and damage whatever was inside, before worrying what harm had come to her. Probably another scratch and bruise on her belly. No one would notice.

Suddenly, Joan felt sick as a horrible thought ran through her mind. A horrible, lovely thought. What if Stuart had sent her a gift? He was so generous at times. Sam would be furious and jealous. Joan felt a little bile pearl in her throat. Maybe it was a present from her son. She hadn't heard from him in a while. Sam would be horrible about that too, but not mad. She noticed the postmark was from the UK; that meant it was not likely to be from her son. Another wave of nausea rushed over her as she half-anticipated a punch. She really didn't want another beating. She had so much to do; she didn't want to have to keep out of the public eye whilst her bruises faded.

Sam hovered like he sensed the box might contain something he could use against Joan. Puffing himself up, balling his fists. Joan thought, *Oh, Stuart, what have you done?*

'Well, what is it, woman?' sniped Sam, circling like a vulture.

She opened the box to reveal another new package with dashing, soft-touch laminate and sleek, raised black print and a swish of bright, metallic gold wrapped with a red ribbon. It could have passed for a jewellery box had it not been for the tell-tale mobile phone manufacturer's logo emblazoned on the side, and the matching compliments slip printed on thick, uncoated, watermarked matt paper. Scrawled on the slip were the words:

Congratulations from the Modaphone winner – Best New Blog category. Here, for your use, is a free top-of-the-range handset…

Rush Hour Crush

To the gorgeous brunette who got on at Putney on Wednesday: When the train swerved, you fell on me and I fell for you. Coffee? – Guy in Dark-Brown Coat

You were the guy on the Victoria Line around 5.30 p.m., engrossed in the Justin Bieber article. Believe we could meet? – Girl in Red Coat

To the dark-haired girl with glasses, normally dressed in black: We cross paths every morning just after 8.15 a.m. at Farringdon station. You make my morning brighter. – Shy Guy

To the beautiful builder girl with black hair and a hoodie on the District Line: You make every morning journey more pleasant. Would love to tell you how gorgeous you are over a candlelit dinner. – Builder Guy

To the immaculately dressed guy with the shaved head and diamond earring at Bingley station: You picked up my glove and handed it back to me with a lovely smile. Drink sometime? – Blonde Girl with Long Scarf and Two Gloves

To the Aussie girl with auburn hair on the 8 a.m. Clapham Junction to Waterloo train: You're a work of art. Care to doodle? – Art Lover

To the blonde in the grey suit on the 5.30 p.m. Chester to Liverpool train. I was sitting opposite you and got off at Birkenhead Central. Coffee sometime? – Guy in Black Suit

To the good-looking gent at Potters Bar who always looks dapper with his brolly: Thanks for putting a spring in my step. – Anonymous

To the builder guy on the district line on 8 March: I would love you to say hello. – Builder Girl

To the beautiful young lady who got on the 6.01 at Purley and got off at Clapham Junction: You are so beautiful. I hope I see you again soon and have the courage to say hello. – Shy Boy

To the beautiful brunette girl on the 17.52 train from Edmonton Green to Liverpool Street on Thursday: I sat opposite you. We smiled at each other, but I wasn't brave enough to ask you for a drink. I'll be on the 17.52 from Edmonton Green. – Guy Who Went into Boots

To the tall girl in glasses who catches the Northern Line from Colliers Wood: I'm the total Harry Styles (older) lookalike you couldn't stop staring at. Drink? – Anonymous

To the lady with brown eyes on the no. 17 from Canton to St Mary Street in Cardiff: You make me late for work, but it's worth it. – Stare Bear

That SA woman: Catch you at 4.30 p.m. Central. – Specky Guy

To the Goth girl who catches the 8.36 train from New Cross: You're too pretty to look so sad. – Admirer

To the woman with the lovely smile who gets off the first carriage of the Metro at Seaburn at 8.30: Where have you gone? – Admirer

Dave checked himself out in the mirror in the lounge. His new tweed-style Paul Smith jacket had purple stripes that matched his jumper; his jumper in turn matched his tie, knotted full Windsor today. His white shirt with top button undone looked relaxed and yet business-like, with new collar stiffeners ensuring the edges looked sharp and crisp. His old-fashioned-style flat-cap covered his bald head; he'd have another shave on Saturday perhaps. His pocket handkerchief screamed 'Have a look', but at the same time continued his smart and yet casual look. Then he turned the whole outfit on its head with a pair of very dark-blue turned-up jeans finished off with light-tan brogues and pink socks.

What on earth do you look like? Fabulous, Dave thought. He revelled in the fact he was wearing a tie again, just as the soppy City boys had finally got their heads around not needing to wear a tie any more. Those City boys – always a year or so behind what actually looked good. What a dandy rogue he'd become. He had always maintained no one wore suits as bad as the suits in the City – suits like school uniforms, fucking ugly, thick, pin-striped wool numbers you saw in poxy second-hand fancy-dress boxes, often worn as wannabe gangster outfits. In the middle of summer too. Standing there in bars talking loudly, red cheeks, sweat beading on the brow, whilst the checked shirt with the moth-eaten collar gradually got more saturated and burnt away. Either that or cheap, thin, lightweight summer numbers you saw on shivering young lads, smoking cigarettes outside happy-hour-themed bars, talking football, bonuses, anal sex and cocaine. Fucking arses, all of them.

Yes, Dave comforted himself with the knowledge that his style, however mixed up, certainly suited him – and he congratulated himself on not having worn a pair of trainers at all for years, except for when exercising, as was their correct and intended use. He briefly imagined himself wearing grey flannel jogging bottoms sitting halfway up his Calvin Klein white pants, and a brightly coloured hoodie over a plain white t-shirt. He pictured a pair of nearly pristine white Adidas or Reebok trainers with a solitary mud scuff on the front. The daydream started blurring and Dave laughed as he imagined adding an earring, a neck chain and a cap with his initials emblazoned across the front. It wouldn't be long before the beat from the bass kicked in and he'd start rapping, whilst some disgusting girl called something like Talisa gyrated and wailed next to him, seductively rubbing herself against his chiselled abs and designer stubble. In another hellish lifetime perhaps. He wondered how he'd feel going out in public dressed like that. He supposed he'd have to go to shopping centres or cinemas or quick-fit tyre establishments and chat up young girls in such public places whilst drinking cheap lager or cider, and drive a small car with a loud stereo and an even louder exhaust pipe.

Jesus! He snapped himself out of his daydream and straightened his tie. Just considering being common was turning him on.

Robert crept out of the house just as his wife was going back to bed with their nine-month-old baby. It was a rule of the house that whilst he was working she would get up with the baby at five a.m. and do breakfast until the baby was ready to go back to sleep, usually just as Robert finished getting ready. He didn't mind it, as it afforded him a few precious moments with his little one. A few cuddles and playful kisses and squawks were enough to see him through till the weekend. He felt sad most nights, though, knowing his wife would be fast asleep by the time he got home. Still, this would all change when she went back to work and they had the joy of working out a whole new routine. For now, he tried his best each day to sneak out of the house without waking the baby or the wife.

Every day he scanned the car park opposite, looking for stranger danger. He wasn't comfortable leaving his precious baby at home, alone and vulnerable, even if his wife was still there. She was so tired and still suffering from baby brain – could she be trusted to keep them both safe? So he checked the car park for suspicious vehicles. It had become a habit after his mother-in-law suggested it was a dogging car park. Also, he liked to check no one was plotting to burgle his house. Not that he imagined such things happened that early in the morning. He really wouldn't know.

He passed some school kids on their way to school. Thankfully, he didn't see the group of young girls he thought might have photographed him a few weeks ago. He'd told his wife as it had bothered him – why would young girls want to photograph him? He hoped it was a paranoid moment, but the next time he saw them they giggled and his sleep-deprived mind went into overdrive. Was it that they were doing a fashion project on what old men like their dads wore to work? He thought that was the most logical, and harmless, reason. The worst possibility was that they thought he looked like some sort of paedophile. He thought he looked quite good, but he didn't expect very young schoolgirls to appreciate his fashion. Was it that he had left his flies undone (a terrifying reason but highly probable)? Was it that they were trying out a new camera on their phone and he happened to turn around at that specific moment? He guessed he'd never really know, unless he confronted one of them one day if he ever saw them again and they continued with the giggling business. But if he confronted them and they were already wary of him, that could make the whole situation worse. It was all a little too weird.

He could have left a little bit earlier in the hope of avoiding the girls, but then he'd run the risk of clashing with Mark, the next-door neighbour, leaving to walk his dogs. It was a wonder *he* didn't wake up the baby, to be honest. Mark had two collies and they went crazy about eight a.m. every morning, just before their walk. Robert didn't mind them really; it was just that it was hard to leave the house quietly whilst Mark was leaving – his dogs barking; Mark slamming his door and calling out, 'Hello, Robert, how's it all going then?' It wasn't that Mark was especially loud or would mean to wake the baby up on purpose; he was just accidently loud and very likely to wake the baby. Actually, given the chance all of Robert's neighbours could be really noisy. That's probably why he liked to sneak out so quietly. Like an inverse burglar.

Another problem with Mark was that he didn't seem to know when to shut up or fuck off. If Robert was on his way to work and Mark's dogs were barking because they were excited about going for a walk and desperate for a shit and a wee, Mark would stand there in his big red puffer jacket, wellie boots, tweed flat-cap and fluffy earmuffs, fiddling with his empty plastic dog-poo bags and ask great big open questions like 'How's it all going then?' and 'Do you reckon it might rain today?'

Shit, sorry, Mark, love to stay and chat, but I've got to get to work… and I'm not a poxy weather forecaster.

Mark would be completely oblivious to the fact Robert was in a rush, though. 'Who's your boys got then this weekend?' he'd ask (talking about Watford's upcoming fixture, not two sons that Robert didn't have). He'd tut and add, 'Hope they have better luck than our lot. Meaning Reading. *Who the hell comes from Reading and who the hell even supports them?* Robert would wonder. Then Mark would continue like he'd been answered, but he hadn't. *Mark, shut up! Just fuck off and shut up!*

If Robert tried to wrap things up, Mark would sort of raise an eyebrow, as if about to sneeze or say something else, kind of prompting Robert to say some more. But it wouldn't come. *He'll just have to ponder my reaction whilst throwing his balls to the dogs.* Still Mark would wait, though, with his mouth semi-open, almost aghast – and the silence, the painful, dead silence… eyebrows raised… waiting.

'I'll see you later then,' Robert would say finally, desperate to break the spell and get on his way. Obviously, he wouldn't plan on seeing Mark later.

'Yeah, of course. I'll be there, with bells on…'

There would have had to have been some sort of disaster for Robert to plan willingly to see Mark later. Even if Reading were playing Watford, Mark would be one of the last people Robert would want to go with. If ever there was a knock at the door, Mark was the sort of person who a) banged so loudly on the door it loosened the cement in the brickwork throughout the house, and b) would stand in the doorway not allowing anyone to get a word in edgeways and sucking all the heat from the house out into the environment, thus killing the planet. He didn't mean to do these things; it was just an accidental flaw in his character. Yet he was a natural at it. Robert could imagine Mark going bad and becoming an axe murderer. Instead of smashing down the bathroom door with an axe, he'd see Mark pop up at the side of his garden, looking over the fence with a crazed look in his eyes: *here's Mark, wielding a pair of bloody secateurs he's just used to cut up his wife and dogs after a row over ruined scrambled eggs and Reading's abysmal pre-season form, having just lost to Wycombe Wanderers.*

There was a lovely garden en route to the station, and occasionally Robert saw the old lady who must have spent much of her day tending to its upkeep. She didn't usually say anything, just gave him a half-smile as she bent over to dead-head her flowers, back achingly crooked. She must have been a widow, but she dressed like a lady who was over the mourning and yet not interested in companionship; she had her garden. She preened and snipped, and a little robin shadowed her every move, hoping for an uncovered worm. Robert presumed that was all the company she needed (the robin, not the worm).

Robert usually had to weave past the local schoolboys, so engrossed in their conversation they forgot that walking four abreast left little or no room for ordinary pedestrians like Robert. He tried to run down two steps at a time, to make himself look more urgent and busy, and in doing so take away the need to make eye contact and ask to be excused. The last thing he needed in the morning was banter with spotty pubescent oinks.

He came to a grinding halt on the pathway as the daily game of frogger began. The station was directly opposite, but to get to it he had to cross the road. That meant dodging the distracted mum who was driving whilst eating toast, grinding to a halt whilst talking animatedly in the rear-view mirror to her darling Rupert. He, no doubt, had just remembered he'd forgotten his gym kit and was whining about the probability of having to root around in the lost-property bin at school. The shorts would probably have skid marks, and Mr Percy the Pervert would no doubt take great joy in seeing the boy bend over the old, sweaty, grubby mislaid-kit crate. The mum became momentarily distracted by a handsome City boy getting out of a Porsche, as her conscience wrestled with whether to turn around to pick up the gym gear, because not doing so could put her beloved, wretched son in a potentially damaging situation. She decided the chances were Rupert was laying it on thick, and she'd drop him off to fight his own battles that day whilst she headed to the gym, still fantasising about the city slicker.

A relentless stream of SUV's power down towards the station entrance from both directions. Robert took two steps forward but then –quickly – three steps back as another lady racing driver powered in. He couldn't fathom for the life of him why they had to drive past him before stopping. Why did he need to wait until they'd picked a suitable drop-off point, rather than them using a little care and attention? He knew the answer. Bloody women drivers! It was all about the female brain functioning on the bare essentials. He could quite believe they were more capable than men at multi-tasking, because they didn't pay full attention to anything – except possibly their favourite TV programme, but even then they could take a phone call and easily understand the plot whilst chatting away.

Jesus Christ! He'd nearly got run over again. *That'll be God's punishment,* he decided. *God's probably a woman.*

He made another break for it, but only noticed the puddle before the kerb at the very last moment. He leapt like a gazelle, flying through the air like Billy bloody Elliott. But he had built up too much momentum, too much speed, and the slippery tiled floor wasn't going to help. He bumped into the poisonous elf who got the same train as him every morning but stood at the other end of the platform. Robert didn't trust her. She gave him funny looks. He'd heard rumours, via neighbours, that she'd been seen snogging strangers in cabs who weren't her other half. He'd seen her coming home late after work and she was drunk and she made him feel uneasy. Like she was about to accuse him of something he'd not even considered doing.

In bumping into the elf – for which he received a sullen look – he'd also managed to overshoot the free daily newspapers. Normally, he collected one to help with the monotony of his daily grind. Even if the news in the morning was usually just a rehashed version of the news the night before, at least he got to catch up on the Rush Hour Crush section at the start of the day. It always made him smirk. What sort of nutters wrote in? But the thought crossed his mind almost daily: *I wonder if I've ever been featured in there?*

He stopped and dithered for a moment, feet unsteady, slipping and sliding on the grimy, wet floor. Someone else in a hurry also skidded to a flapping halt behind him, in a mêlée of messy newspapers and hands wedged down soggy suit trousers, desperately looking for wallets. Skating in sodden leather-soled shoes. More tutting and huffing and unforeseen momentarily delays conjured deathly thoughts in all those concerned. So caught up in the rush to spend more time at work, people hated and wished ill health upon those who temporarily delayed any access to the train platform.

An older man had himself organised. He had his contactless card ready, his free newspaper under control, placed neatly under his arm. His boxy black briefcase meant business, with its yellow metal edges. He'd had years of experience passing through this station. He could only see Robert as an obstacle, not the poisonous elf in front of him.

Robert dithered for a millisecond longer, deciding whether it was worth forfeiting the newspaper or his place in the three-person queue. He could feel the huffing and puffing of the rotund, bespectacled, more experienced man building. Shortly, their relationship would evolve. No longer would they be strangers, but future nemeses, foes for another day. Someone to stare at and wish ill health upon. *That cursed man who meddled with my daily timetable.*

'After you,' the man said, completely against the run of play. This wasn't in the script. What was he doing? He was outmanoeuvring Robert that was what.

'No, no, you go. I'm not with it at all this morning,' Robert blithered, trying to regain the upper hand in the English etiquette game.

What have I done? Robert thought. *I didn't mean to say that.* As he let the man pass, he heard the train coming into the platform. He was committed now: a split-second change of mind sent Robert dashing back to get the free newspaper. As he dodged someone else, a lady entering the station, like a meteorite entering earth's atmosphere he realised the gravity of his mistake. Firstly, all the newspapers on the top were wet from the drizzle and were in a right old mishmash. He had to rifle through at least twelve copies before he found a pristine paper. As he yanked it out, like a cheap magician pulling a fully laden tablecloth, at least six more fell onto the ground. He bent over to scoop them up from the wet puddle in which they were now dwelling and instantly decomposing, and as he did so his phone fell out of his jacket pocket. The screen cracked. The phone got wet.

'Fucking fuck-sticks!' Robert shouted, very cross indeed.

The train continued its ascent into the station. Its progress wouldn't be halted by Robert's faffing. As he picked up his shattered, wet phone, his arse in the air, his courier bag flew off his shoulder and landed in the muddy puddle recently vacated by the free newspapers and his phone.

'Arrrrggghhh! Thunder-cunt-sticks!' Robert declared, utterly exasperated. A vein throbbed in his head so hard he might have fainted. The urge to tumble forward and head-butt the ground into oblivion was quite overwhelming.

As he scooped up his bag, he noticed the lady who had briefly crossed paths with him a moment earlier. She had finished topping up her card and, inevitably, decided that she too wanted to race to catch the train he was so desperately trying to reach. Once again he met a foe in 'no-man's-land' just before the gates. The lady could see Robert was clearly in a rush to catch the train and she heard him curse rather loudly, but noted curiously that he was now caught in something of a quandary: ladies always go first, so the rule dictates, and no matter how frustrated and flustered Robert was, he was absolutely incapable of doing anything but letting her go first. Even when she suddenly seemed nonchalant about boarding the train – there was a chance she might be slightly unfamiliar with Robert's gentlemanly conduct. Judging by her comfortable cross-country trainers and gore tex all-weather jacket, Robert was quick to assume she might be some sort of exchange student or, considering her Mediterranean looks, quite possibly on holiday, or perhaps a trip to the glorious capital city for a spot of sightseeing. Either way, he decided this 'ladies first' malarkey was possibly a concept that was entirely foreign to her... and by God she was gorgeous.

'After you,' he conceded, and this time he added a little hand gesture somewhat similar to pushing a small child on the head. His tone was teetering on exasperated and desperate as the train doors opened and other passengers boarded. In his head he screamed, *Just get a fucking move on, you daft but incredibly beautiful bitch!*

But then she smiled a girlish smile. An innocent smile. A smile that said, *Hello, Mr English, I'd like to go on a country walk and get naked in the woods with you.* And with that, Robert froze, the look temporarily binding him to the spot. Dumbfounded. His wife and child but a rapidly disintegrating memory of another lifetime.

'Excuse me, are you getting this train or not?' Another late commuter had entered the fray as Robert dillydallied.

'Yes, yes, I am,' Robert said with as much authority as he could muster. In his head, little baby lambs frolicked around a field with baby-blue ribbons tied delicately around their necks, and beautiful little songbirds chirped melodies pure and sweet, and the sun shone down – until Mr Wolf turned up, listening to heavy metal and drinking beer with a massive throbbing appendage...

Robert snapped out of it, still watching the foreign goddess make her way through the turnstile. Finally, he remembered what he was doing, and he quickly pulled out his wallet, ready to present his card and follow his not-so-fair foreign beauty on their outward journey.

Shimmying behind her, he watched her neat brown hands with perfectly lacquered red nails lay her plastic travel-card precisely on the reader. He held his debit card ready to slot in behind her. She held her hand on the reader for a millisecond too long, though, and just as she eased through the gate and as Robert presented his card, the system went to pot.

Robert didn't know whether she'd double-presented due to her hand lingering a few milliseconds longer than the allotted time. The miniature internal artificially intelligent computer ticket men decided the amount of time required to present a ticket for travel on the Underground network in London, and obviously they hadn't taken into consideration the delicate, beautiful, frighteningly slow touch of the foreign goddess.

The allotted time was somewhere between a quarter of a second and one second. One-point-one second and beyond and the computer would presume you were a terrorist with a gun or knife, determined to kill people and travel illegally. Also, if you placed your Oyster or credit or debit card on the reader and moved it, even by a miniscule amount, the computer would deem you a psychopathic paedophile rapist and would stop your journey. When the Oyster card machines and pay-as-you-go tickets were first introduced, such confusion was commonplace, due to the high number of grave dodgers who use the Underground. Everywhere one went, there would be blue-rinsers busily shining their newly acquired travel-card or debit card or credit card on the reader, giving it a good old polish or sandpaper action, not understanding that the gate had opened and closed and they'd missed the opportunity to progress without human intervention. They'd failed a simple test and were certifiably old, as was anyone who found themselves unable to continue their journey without the good old-fashioned human ticket inspector's help and pity. Just as Robert now found himself.

'For fuck's sake!' he screamed as the man behind him – eagerly presenting his ticket – came crashing in behind Robert, momentarily dry-humping him against the ticket barrier as the machine angrily denied them both entry.

'Oh, do come on,' said the randy little man behind Robert, not realising or caring that it was the foreign beauty's fault. She'd dawdled, not Robert, he wanted to protest. But instead he opted to try to reverse – while the short person behind tried to clamber over him.

'What on earth's the problem, man? I'm going to be late! Do you need money or something?' the short bugger said, implying Robert was somehow stalling for cash and maybe unable to afford the fare.

Robert managed to get him to retreat a few steps and then he tried again. At which point he realised he'd been holding his supermarket card and not his travel-card all along. Bested, he stood rooted to the spot for a moment.

The short man took in the situation and was quick to react, pushing Robert out of the way, holding his travel-card aloft like Charlie and his golden ticket or an old lady winning a school fête raffle. His path unhindered by Robert's uselessness, he breezed through with much less hassle, but the dirty look he shot at Robert sparked him into action. His hand dived into his pocket and wrenched out his wallet like Excalibur. He fingered through it like Dodger under Fagin's watchful stare, searching through his old, unused bank and loyalty cards, until he found his travel-card nestled in an unfamiliar pocket. 'Fuck you,' he cursed the inanimate object.

Composing himself, he proceeded as he watched the short, rotund man bundle onto the train, barely able to get his stumpy, fat legs up the gap between the doors and the floor. He could still make this train, Robert told himself as the gate granted access to the Promised Land. The platform. The gateway to work. Just one explosive burst of energy would see him to the doors. Be a salmon. His brain sent urgent messages to his muscles to prepare for imminent excessive use. Take flight…

Then the doors shut.

Just as he leapt forward to approach the button to open the door, he heard the diesel engines fire up and the button gradually inched further away. Robert watched as the short, portly man squeezed through the carriage; he followed his silhouette through the slightly tinted glass. As he pushed further inside the carriage, Robert noticed a familiar face move into the vacuum the porky man had just created. It was his foreign beauty. She seemed to smile with her eyes, but her mouth didn't move. She blinked as he blinked, and their eyes locked on each other.

The train gathered speed. Robert kept staring even when he couldn't see her face any more. He stayed still on the platform, rooted to the spot, until the next train came.

Chapter 12

Anastasia worked nights in a little village on the outskirts of an old RAF town called Southwood and travelled home the same way as the regular commuters, only her day was ending as most were beginning. She worked all night doing her 'cleaning' job. She wet-wiped away the remains of last night's grime, laced up her trainers and put on a plain outdoorsy coat. It was warm, inconspicuous and practical. She had worked in a few clubs and bars 'cleaning', or so she called it. She was a very good-looking and extremely well-paid cleaner, never short of clients willing to give her glowing references in the hope she'd polish certain body parts: proposals, jewellery, promises of houses, cars, animals. She was actually a very talented stripper. The cleaning story went along these lines:

'I clean the club mostly when it's shut. Whilst it's open, I work in the kitchen or toilets. It's a very posh, sophisticated club, not really for the likes of you and me. It's more for the aristocracy and well-connected foreigners. It's out of town and very expensive and exclusive – you have to be a member to get in.'

So Anastasia said to 'Majiek', her boyfriend, who suggested on occasion that he might like to come down to her club to see her once in a while. She said he wouldn't be welcome, as he wasn't a member, and besides, he couldn't afford it.

She looked quite young and innocent fully clothed and without makeup, but unbeknownst to many, she had a piercing in her nipple and her tongue and somewhere much more delicate, but you'd have to pay to see that, as well as her tattoos. She had something of a thirst for pleasurable pain. It was her creative form of self-abuse.

Anastasia was Bulgarian. She worked every evening in the club, and worked out and studied economics during the day. She certainly had very little time off to see Majiek or anyone else, but that was how she liked it – a relationship of convenience. She was, however, desperate to go home and see her twin sister, who had recently had another baby girl, and split whatever money she could save between her sister in Bulgaria and her own studies and life in the UK.

Anastasia certainly wouldn't let her imbecile of a boyfriend near her money. He had other uses, though. Mostly protection. He was a part-time labourer, but fast on his way to becoming a small-time drug dealer. He sat about at home most days, smoking all his profits, playing computer games and drinking strong, cheap booze with his equally career-confused mates. Some aspired to be top DJs, promoters, gamblers or big-time moneymen, gangsters even, but they hadn't quite got a lucky break yet. All remained hopeful, however, that it would come. They had only been in the UK a short while, and it was about settling in at the moment. If all the other foreign rich boys could do it then eventually so could they. In the meantime, they lived under Anastasia's roof in between jobs. And she, in turn, had twenty-four-hour security on tap. No creeps from the club would ever follow her home and no weirdos from her past could turn up uninvited.

She hadn't said much to her boyfriend. He was happy to believe she was a cleaner in the club, even if his mates now and again questioned the truth. Occasionally, Anastasia and Majiek got together physically – not very often, though, and always on her terms, but he didn't mind. He might be a few things, but possessive wasn't one of them. He knew that she had to leave her home because something bad happened and that she didn't want someone to find her, so him being around with his Polish pals provided some sort of reassurance for her. As long as he was in control of his mates and her past never caught up with her, things would be okay as they were.

Anastasia found British men quite intriguing. She thought their general daft awkwardness was rather charming. She didn't, however, like the sweaty, leering types she met in her club, as they were the same as the lecherous types she met from all around the world. Her favourite Brits were the ones who would get flustered if she caught them looking at her boobs (which she found quite ironic, given her day job), and the ones who got tongue-tied and struggled to keep eye contact when she stared at them. She found the regional accents fun too, but would never say the northern dialect drove her wild like television programs sometimes portrayed other soppy foreign, usually American ladies, playing up to the quaint English accent. How could an accent be cute? Unfortunately, the only British men she got to speak to most evenings were usually fat, unfit, hairy alcoholics who regularly fell asleep within moments of her starting a hypnotic special dance for them. The conversation was limited to a few grumbled foul and abusive suggestions before their eyes glassed over and started to roll. Either that, or the two- or three-word conversations she had with the doormen, mostly grunts before they went back to checking themselves out in the reflection of the window.

Anastasia decided she'd quite like to date Prince Harry, if only to decide whether being rich and famous was all it was cracked up to be. She felt she would probably be just as comfortable with an ordinary Englishman. She could perhaps become a mum and start an ordinary life, baking cakes and keeping the house tidy and going for country walks with a dog and family meals and a log fire and cuddles whilst drinking hot chocolate and watching rubbish TV. Perhaps that's what she was striving for, an ordinary life. Safe and secure and out of the limelight. A million miles from where she and her sister had grown up, in the national care institutions of neglect and abuse, with no family, just dodgy teachers and priests and nuns. She had escaped, but her sister couldn't. She was now trapped. Perhaps one day Anastasia could help save her and her children. They too could run away.

Anastasia yearned for nothing more than a decent conversation to start off with. With an adult. Already she found herself earwigging strangers' conversations, wanting to join in, and then recollecting with anger at the weird language her boyfriend and his mates used to communicate and called English. They sounded like a hybrid mix of television cockneys, Australians and the holiday reps and bar staff who'd been working in the English-dominated resorts in Spain, Greece and Turkey. 'Fackin' fanks, geezer'... 'no fackin' problem, innit'... 'okay-fackin'-dokey, mate' – she couldn't believe any English people really spoke like this.

None of these guys wanted to walk in the countryside. Eat apples. See deer. She wanted to see the great outdoors that was featured in the TV nature documentaries. She wanted a nice dog, like a Labrador, a sheep dog or a golden retriever. She looked at the angry but dopey terrier-mix mutt sitting in the corner of her sitting room, happily licking its balls, whilst the guys played some sort of solider war game on the computer and ate Pot Noodles. This was certainly a little way off how she'd pictured her new life in the UK. She would wait. She still had time, and good money coming in, and plenty of exciting cities and opportunities to explore if this one didn't work out. But deep down, she dreamed of being treated like an English princess, even just for five minutes.

She had read with great interest about the English Victorian lady's roll within the house, and also new feminist books on the modern lady's part to play in the modern world. She had learnt all about the changes that happened during the World Wars that had led to ladies taking men's jobs in factories to help with the war effort whilst the men were away fighting. She had learnt all about changing women's rights, through to winning the right to vote and equal opportunities. She had looked at the differences between ladies in the Western world and where she had come from. She had even imagined what sort of mother hers would have been. She struggled to imagine. Her sister was the one with the mind for such things. Anastasia's was more practical, strategic and unsentimental, more economic and dynamic.

Everything Anastasia did usually came down to money – it was the only thing she understood as being able to change desperate situations. 'If in doubt, spend your way out.' She had never had parents to fall back on, but money had always opened doors and bought protection and altered outcomes. She sometimes looked at her ability to generate income over the space of a week and wondered how much a male equivalent would get if he were blessed with the equivalent tools of the trade. Was there such a thing? Her boobs were perfectly average, and yet a male with an average penis would not stand out in a crowd. How many men would considering selling their body? But in every town there was probably some type of stripper or female sex worker or masseur. Most wouldn't be the best looking or biggest breasted or blessed with any other outstanding attributes men used to measure sexability. Competition was rife. Was it the same for a man? Had she been a man, she thought, she would have started a pole-dancing strip club for gays. The dancers wouldn't be especially butch or camp, but average looking. Plain. Straight, even. She then imagined she was a straight male strip-tease artist working the gay clubs. That wouldn't happen. Men and women were so different, she mused, thinking of the many gay girl dancers she had known who took money from men – yet had the roles been reversed, it couldn't and wouldn't happen! *Equal rights,* she smirked. *Men are just stupid or frigid, or woman are just too clever or fickle.*

As part of her Victorian studies, Anastasia really enjoyed studying books on gentlemanly conduct and etiquette and what used to be expected of them during and after Queen Victoria's reign. Sometimes she'd look around her lounge when she entered the room, hoping someone might offer her a seat or smile and acknowledge her. She wanted a man to hold the door open for her. She wanted someone to order her meal in a restaurant or pour her a glass of wine at home and say cheers whilst looking her in the eye. She wanted to be ushered to the safe side of the path, just in case she got splashed by puddles. She wanted a man to offer his arm. To stand up when she went to the loo or when she came back to the table at a fancy restaurant. She wanted a man to buy her flowers. To offer his coat if the cool evening air chilled her bones. She wanted to hold hands.

She'd had many experiences with men from all around the world but she had yet to meet a true English gent. She wondered if they were as mythical as the English rose girls who were so often featured in the glossy fashion mags. She laughed at the thought of the English football team's girlfriends and wives. Wags. Probably, she thought, because they wagged their tails when given a bone.

The phone rang and Joan looked up from the computer. She'd been updating her blog and scanning through the long and ever-increasing list of responses. She didn't recognise the number. She'd half-expected the display to scream *SAM* in tiny, angry, pixilated black squares.

'Hi, is that Joan? The rush hour crush lady?' said the caller in a mildly familiar chirpy voice.

'Yes, yes, it's me. How can I help?' said Joan, trying to place the voice. He sounded a little bit like Roy's dad. That was it. Joan's heart skipped a beat as she waited for him to say something else, his familiarity bringing a slight comforting air to the conversation. But it couldn't be him.

There was an audible exhalation – like a youth asking for a box of cigarettes whilst the shopkeeper failed to notice the barely pubescent lad standing in front of him, preferring instead to keep an eye on the bloke at the back of the shop checking out the top-shelf magazines, both voyeurs in their own right.

'Well, I think I might have featured in one of those rush hour crushes. I'm not entirely sure, but I think it was me. But, you know, the whole thing is kinda ambiguous and vague, so I could be one of many, I suppose. Oh… I don't know… you know what I mean? Ha ha ha!'

Okay, Joan thought, laughing along but not sure she appreciated joking about what was proving to be her life's mission. The guy sounded more like a buffoon character after all and not like Roy's dad, as it turned out. He sounded about half his age for starters, and Joan felt like he was taking the mickey out of her. She was starting to get fed up with the people who just seemed to like to waste her time by having a chat. Perhaps she had become impatient in her old age. Had she really got to the point in her life when she would regret stopping what she was doing just to devote some time to listen to someone she didn't know prattle on?

'Well,' said Joan, deciding to take control of the conversation, 'can I ask you a couple of questions to start off with, please? Erm, what did you say your name was?'

This fell on deaf ears, as her caller was off and running.

'I like to leave my house at approximately seven fifty-two a.m. each morning. I get dressed after checking the weather by peeping through the blinds and watching the kids on their way to school and the golfers unpacking their kit before hitting the course – and bar, I suppose. Ha ha ha. Using them as a gauge, I'm usually meteorologically prepared enough by then to know what the weather is likely to be that day. If they're wrapped up nice and snug, I follow suit. If they aren't, I leave the coat hanging under the stairs on the multi-coloured coat hook. I grab my wallet and phone, put on my favourite hat, pick up my bag and leave the house for the station.'

'Right, great, that's brilliant. Can I have your name, please?' asked Joan.

'Well, it's all quite important to you, isn't it?' he said, pausing for a second. 'The station's name?'

'No, not the station name, your name, please,' said Joan.

'Well, you need to know what I was wearing and where I was heading, right? For the description to fit, eh?'

'I guess so,' said Joan.

'Okay, King's Cross is the name of the station I'm heading to. But before I leave, I double-check I've got my keys – on both sides of the front door. Pat down my pockets and recite: "Spectacles, testicles, wallet and watch." Ha ha ha, and off I go. Checking I've shut the gate and windows as I go. En route most days I pass the grass-keeper from the local golf club crossing the road in front of me on his little green Jeep lawnmower thing. He has a white Jack Russell with a brown patch over one eye that goes everywhere with him. Delightful, isn't it?'

'What is?' said Joan, unsure of the question. 'Do you travel far?' she asked, trying to get proceedings back on track.

'Well, a lot further than the green, that's for sure. The old green-keeper waves politely every day, and his little dog just sits there. Doesn't bark or anything, just sits there, as good as gold. He he he. He does this every day, come what may – it's amazing, isn't it, really?'

'What is?' said Joan, worrying she had missed a crucial bit of information again.

'It's amazing that I see him every day with his dog.'

'Totally,' Joan said, wondering if the green-keeper might be this guy's crush.

'Occasionally, I see him chatting with the regular dog-walkers. Standing there with his breath clouding in the cool early-morning mist, while the dog-walkers cling to warm plastic bags filled with…

with… well, you know. Ha ha ha. The early-morning joggers are racing back to shower, in an attempt to get ready for their working day, as the dog walkers put the poo bags into the bin.

'When I get to the old memorial hall, I always check the board and wonder what will be going on in there later in the day. Zumba, indoor bowls or dance lessons, perhaps – tap, ballet – or even drama classes, judging by the theatrical hand gestures I've often seen when passing by some evenings.'

'Can I have your name, please?' said Joan, who was losing the will to live.

'I see the same local schoolchildren each morning, gradually getting bigger as the years go by. There's a surly-looking teenage girl who's always fuming, presumably about whatever her parents haven't let her do or boyfriend issues and how it's sooo not fair. And there's a polite young Asian boy who always says 'good morning' every day. What a nice young man. Then there are two other younger boys I always see, dragging their feet, usually caught up in their childish chitter-chatter or looking at rude movies on their phones and chuckling mischievously. They don't notice me rushing for my train. They'll always be late for school, those two. Ha ha ha.'

Joan had started feeling uncomfortable as she listened to all the talk of children. Who was this bloke and where was this conversation heading? She felt a bit creeped out and wanted to hang up the phone, but something made her incapable. Like she was locked in and frozen, petrified – waiting to hear something truly horrific. She carried on listening, no longer desperate to get a word in edgeways.

'I have to wait for the line of expensive, big SUVs to break before I get to cross the road for the train station. Audis, BMWs, Mercedes, Nissans, Range Rovers and Land Rovers evoking the idea we live in farmland, not a mere stone's throw from the M25.'

Joan wrote down 'M25' on a notepad, just in case it led to the discovery of a dead body.

'These drivers seem to practise how quickly they can decelerate from sixty to zero miles per hour, before chucking out their kids or partners and then setting off for the day with a splashed puddle and the roar of a strained engine.'

Perhaps it's big car drivers he hates, Joan thought.

'There are always two men smoking at the station. One sits in his car, fumigating his clothes, keeping warm and waiting for the train to arrive before hustling through the barriers. I've seen him do it when he's late. He tutts and huffs, looking frantic, when people get in his way. The cheek of it! The other man paces back and forth about five metres from the exit, regularly getting in people's way. He sucks too hard on his cigarette. I feel sorry for the people trying to post letters and exit the station, having to walk through his death gas. Can't be pleasant, can it?'

He paused for the briefest of seconds and Joan said, 'No.' Then he was off and wittering on again.

'I've never seen him go through the barriers, mind you, but I imagine he'd smell quite strongly of stale tobacco. Presuming he actually gets on a train. Fancy sitting next to him all the way into town? Pheeeewey.'

He doesn't like smokers, Joan wrote on her pad.

'I walk up the platform to wait for the eight a.m. Metropolitan Line train that takes me to work via King's Cross for roughly a nine a.m. start. On the platform, I see Belinda, an ex-landlord. She's a kind-hearted, stocky woman who dresses in fancy leather boots and a warm coat. She's trying to find something buried at the bottom of her cavernous leather handbag, so she doesn't see me. I skulk by without needing to say hello. She must work in town too, but I have no idea doing what.'

Joan wondered why he wouldn't want to talk to his ex-landlady and whether he saw her looking in her bag every day. Maybe she was hiding from him.

'I also see the two lesbian ladies who wear heavy-duty outdoorsy coats even during the summer. They talk quite loudly and are unmistakably butch. One is slightly taller, with a manlier stride and a harsh undercut blond hairstyle, and her mate is slightly shorter and stockier, brunette with plain, zero-maintenance hair she tucks behind both ears. She has to walk just that little bit too quickly because of her slightly shorter legs and stocky build, which makes her look like a small child struggling to keep up with an adult. They always walk quickly and barely give me a second look. I suppose they see little point in men like me. They probably just see a useless, unattractive penis flump with a mouth.'

Joan struggled not to laugh.

'They seem a little rugged and uncared for, and they have weathered faces and suntanned, brownish-red, blotchy skin. I imagine they like walking to secluded spots in the countryside and enjoying lots of lesbian business in the outdoors.'

'Sorry, what? Excuse me?' Joan couldn't believe what she was hearing.

'I went a little bit off piste there, didn't I, Joan? Oopsy daisy. Ha ha ha ha.'

Joan felt uncomfortable with the way this guy was calling her by her first name with familiarity and yet she still didn't know who he was. She was also uneasy with all the lesbian talk – she thought about her sister and how he would view her.

'What did you say your name was?' said Joan, like she'd finally heard enough and she was drawing the conversation to a close.

'Joan, I'm just Dave! Call me Dave,' he said, like Joan should have known who he was.

'But first let me tell you about the annoying couple. Normally, just before the train arrives – after I've been standing in my spot on the platform – along they come. *You can't stand here,* I think, *right here, because I stand here. Why? Because. It's my blimming spot – I've stood here for years.* Him with his handsome Jeremy Guscott face and the attitude of a man with a really big penis and a suitcase on wheels, and her with her toast squirrelled away in her pocket and her white drawn-on face on her moony, horsey head. They have no regard at all for my personal space. None whatsoever.

'I'd been waiting in the same spot on the platform for years and years and with no competition, until one day *he* decided to roll up. With a flamboyant flick of the wrist, he planted his trolley case immediately beside me on the platform, under the security camera, right in line with where the train doors always open, and that was that. Who invited him into my space? Not me – no way. I'd never dream of walking along a fairly empty platform first thing in the morning and then parking myself right next to someone in the knowledge he must have chosen that spot after years of fine-tuning to give him easy access to the train doors. It's like fishing – you wouldn't plot up right next to someone, uninvited. It's plain rude.

'Then, to make matters even worse, Old Sulky Knickers – his wife – catches him up. The annoying cow makes things doubly bad as she's a loud talker. You know the type: nothing to say and says it all too ruddy loudly. I pray she won't talk all the way to London, but she does. Without fail, every day. She's a flaming twit! She pushes in front of me and takes the seat I'd have opted for, and then takes ages arranging her coat and her handbag and nibbling on her toast, before squatting her bony bum down on what should have been my chuffing seat. Then she huffs and puffs through partly baked bread and looks at her watch every two seconds, thinking this will somehow speed up her journey. She looks like a nervous breakdown is inevitable if ever the train driver announces any snippet of information, automatically relaying how important she is and how desperately she needs to get to work as she has a meeting that could possibly change the world and Tania – or Saskia – is totally incapable of dealing with anything without her being there to hold her hand. She then goes rooting around in her long black coat for her second slice of toast, wrapped up in a piece of tissue, before gnawing away whilst dreaming of burying acorns. Unabashed she proceeds to subject everyone within earshot who's unable to escape to her wretched telephone conversation: "You know, I really don't care how yesterday's meeting went for her… and then I said… and then she said… and I said… and she said… and I said… and she said… then would you believe it…?" And she sniffs. Rather than blowing her massive red hooter of a nose, she sniffs and sniffs, and occasionally I've seen her trying to pinch the snot away between her finger and thumb.

'They make me want to move. Emigrate, even! He always seems keen to catch my eye. I half-expect him to look at me in an apologetic fashion, but instead he looks at me like he's some sort of higher being and the words "smug prick" threaten to fall out of my mouth. He'd only hear the word "prick", though, and see this as a green light to go about unleashing his foot-long python-like appendage. I'm sure he could walk before he could crawl, talk before he was one and drive at the age of seven – and his shit smells of roses! What has he got to be so smug about? Is it the bucket of a wife? His long black cashmere coat? His poxy wheeled suitcase? Nope, it undoubtedly stems from being super-confident of his tall, dark and – regrettably –handsome looks. It has to be.'

Joan wrote down: *dark man in black coat?* She listened whilst Dave struggled to find his train of thought and catch his breath.

'Which begs the question,' he went on, 'why did he end up with her?'

'No idea,' said Joan. 'Why do any of us end up with who we end up with?' she added, suddenly appreciating the question.

'No doubt she was grateful at some stage. Perhaps his ego makes him an unimaginable bore behind closed doors. I console myself with the thought that he's totally stupid. Thick as two short planks. Perhaps even on a mental scale of some sort. A touch autistic? He strikes me as someone who likes little more in life than standing naked in front of a mirror – maybe holding his suitcase with wheels and with some kind of flower stuck up his arse.'

Dark-skinned man, handsome but stupid? Joan mused. He could be Dave's crush.

'The rest of the journey usually affords me the time to get my head down and have a read. I also see pregnant ladies times two, sometimes with partners. The big, ugly couple. Some pretty young ladies. The loved-up girl with the harelip and her bemused-looking partner, and the big, blond, curly-haired lady. Oh, and the guy with the terrible toupee and old blue raincoat who looks like some sort of Bond villain. And there's the Jewish American-Israeli man.'

'Is that it?' Joan asked, ready to try to decipher the crush somewhere between Dave's house and his journey into town. But as soon as she had spoken, she knew she had added a fresh gust of wind to his sails, and he was off again.

'Well, actually there's also the little Jimmy Krankie. She reminds me of a cross between the lady dressed up as a schoolboy and Michael J. Fox in a fat costume. She wears her hair in a short, manly hairstyle and dresses in the kind of clothes active granddads might put on for walking along a canal at the weekend or washing the car. I was quite sure she was a dyke. But she seems to like me. Every day she asks how I am, and in kind I go and sit next to her and chat. This is the sort of travel companion I like to establish over the years, not the silent pushy types. I think the first time we struck up a conversation, I'd asked her to wake me up before King's Cross. It was after a particularly heavy night on the old sauce – a work do, most probably. I remember she took off her headphones and chatted the whole time, not allowing me to fall asleep at all. Charming really, though not the outcome I'd hoped for. I guess she didn't want to be my alarm clock, and decided if I was expecting her attention, the least I could do was have a conversation. I remember once hearing her phone a partner with an idea for a new soap made from different petals and fragrances. I was slightly confused, as I'd imagined her working for the police in some sort of admin position or as a librarian or something, judging by her choice of sensible footwear.'

Bloody cheek, Joan thought, feeling slightly shoe-conscious and looking at her shoes. She wrote down: *Jimmy Krankie lady?* It was not entirely inconceivable that he could mean her. Stranger relationships had happened, Joan thought.

'I leave the train at King's Cross every day and endure the usual melee or scrum simply to disembark. First I have to decide whether I'm going to tread on toes or bash knees with those not inclined to move their legs an inch to aid my departure. I've learnt now that if I stand before the train has reached the platform, I've usually given my fellow passengers ample warning that I'm planning on leaving. Better than the last-minute dash, which usually results in the most tuts and huffs as knees are knocked and toes trampled. I also find if I carry my bag aloft like a rugby ball, rather than flung over my shoulder, it helps minimise casualties and curses from the other passengers. There's nothing quite as annoying first thing in the morning as your feet being trodden on and a bag wrapped around your head. It always seems like someone farts as well, as we get into King's Cross platform in the morning. A lungful of someone's intestinal gas. I sometimes wonder if there really is a more disgusting station to travel through every morning.'

Joan wrote down *King's Cross Station* and underlined it. She now had another focal point on Dave's journey.

'Each morning, as I make my way to the barriers the number of available gates seems to diminish. But the number of staff increases. They stand around chatting amongst themselves and ignoring people

– like the poor, bemused foreign traveller desperately trying to squeeze through the narrow barriers like a refugee at a border, with four massive suitcases, an empty pushchair, a crying baby, a snotty-nosed toddler, an angry-looking wife with a tatty piece of paper, and an elderly relative who's just had a frontal lobotomy. Behind this you'll find me and countless others jockeying left and right, hoping to see a glimpse of clear space through which to whistle in the flash of a contactless card.

'Whenever you see someone politely let someone else go in front of them, straight away you just know they'll regret it. It's a schoolboy error, a terribly English mistake. The person afforded the favour then pulls out a battered bit of plastic, still sticky and smouldering from a toxic spillage and burnt from a meteorite strike, and starts searching for the right place to stick it. Unfortunately, nowhere else in the world is it more important and necessary to throw away all the good manners you might have been taught through life. Make no mistake: the ticket barriers are a place of battle. Mortal combat. Single-minded determination is absolutely necessary if you don't want to stand there all day, just letting people dart in front of you, and then get stuck and hold everyone up whilst you wait for the chatting ticket inspectors to stop whatever it is that they're meant to be doing and come to your assistance. If this isn't pressure enough, all the time new trains are arriving, which means more and more eager passengers are turning up at the unbreachable obstacle with no care in the world for how long you've been there, and loads of them are foreign travellers with masses of luggage and grizzly kids and demented relations trundling up to add to your woe.

'I wouldn't actually be surprised if way back when the train lines first opened, a few kind-hearted people turned up at the gates and ended up stuck there all day and night, unable to leave due to all the determined and pushy (Victorian or Edwardian?) people. So in the end they got chatting, and the next thing you know, someone had given them a uniform and they became ticket inspectors, and then so did their kids, and their kids kids', and their kids' kids' kids, like some sort of family tradition. The reason they don't move or help is because they're hoping you get stuck there too and in the end you'll become one of the clan – a new posse of ticket collectors. Maybe that's the only way they can be released or breed.'

Joan was starting to lose the plot. She knew she should try to wrap things up. She looked at her watch; she had no idea how long she had been listening to this guy rabbit on – maybe twenty minutes? She wrote down: *Dave = timewaster?*

'Once the ticket barriers have been beaten, it's a question of falling in line with the rat race flow. Walking on the wrong side is a guaranteed way to get yourself into a fight. It's the left, stay on the left. You can't beat the flow of people. Walk on the left and get into the flow. I once tried to walk up the right after a bad night's sleep with a stinking cold, having overdone it on the Night Nurse. I managed about ten metres before I was shoulder-barged by an angry-looking suit and then set upon by a Jack Russell of a lady with pointy red shoes and a sharp, vicious face.'

Shame she didn't finish you off, thought Joan.

'Once you're in the flow and have regulated your feet into a marching formation, perfectly in sequence with whoever's in front of you, you must then be prepared for the side-swipe from the executive travellers and enervated, bemused wheeled-suitcase brigade on business trips from Europe. These people have no regard for station etiquette. Strutting cockerel Nazis. They walk hard and fast, like German BMW or Audi drivers on the motorway, and cut you up, and they don't take too kindly to having their cases kicked or you falling over their belongings.

'You also need to try to manoeuvre to the right of the flow, as you don't want to get stuck in the queue for the holes in the wall. This zombie mob really are the most obtuse on the Underground. Who needs cash so badly in the morning that they want to stand in the way of the flow? The undead, that's who! Get out of the station and go to a bank! It's not natural, and they don't even care about the wheeled-suitcase brigade, so desperate are they to get their mitts on their money!'

'Listen,' said Joan, 'I'm really not sure you understand. I'm looking for people who see someone each day and think perhaps there's some sort of crush, and it's featured in the paper, in the rush hour crush section. But you don't seem to see anyone. I think – I'm sorry to say it – you might be wasting my time...?'

'Well, perhaps if you hold your horses just a minute and are a little bit more patient, you might hear what I'm about to say next.'

Joan wasn't sure she cared any more – she was almost at the point of hanging up. If she did, she half-expected Dave to carry on regardless, waffling on about a shoe shiner or a beggar he saw every day, or a *Big Issue* seller, or a ticket officer having a sneaky smoke.

'That's when I see her. Pocahontas. She's always reading the *Metro* at King's Cross every morning, on her way to work or something, I suppose. I believe she wrote in the 12th of September edition: "Shy English prince, I see you at King's Cross and you see me and we smile together. Coffee sometime? – Pocahontas." It's her, I'd bet my life on it; and what's more, I am the English prince!'

Pocahontas. Joan had heard that name before. She scanned through her archived rush hour crushes until she reached the 12th of September, and there she was, Pocahontas. A lead. A real lead.

Chapter 13

Joan came out of a meeting with a stony-faced Mrs Johnson. 'No holidays left' were the words ringing in her ears. Any time taken off work from now on would have to be out of her own pocket. She was to be under no illusions whatsoever: she had expended any goodwill from her full-time employer and was now totally out of money and out of time. She had already started deliberately missing calls from Stuart and the paper, asking for updates on how she was getting on. She was feeling harassed, and the buzz following the Pocahontas lead had heightened the pressure. Now she was unable to devote any more time to the project – which would be much to Sam's delight but was to her frustration. She was caught between a rock and a hard place, and the longer she delayed talking to Stuart, the harder it became.

Then the letters started appearing on her doormat. They were the usual generic junk mail and bill-style correspondence, which would be ignored at first and binned out of hand, but if they reappeared, they'd be placed in Joan's handbag to open at a more opportune moment or dumped, depending on her mood. Junk mail usually offered her a new bargain that she couldn't afford, but if Sam happened to see it, he would often react like a spoilt child wanting a new toy. The worst possible outcome was that Sam would open the mail and discover an unpaid bill, as inevitably it would become another stick for him to hit Joan with. So when he opened a letter revealing that Joan owed hundreds of pounds for a mobile he thought was a free gift (as did Joan) and that it was due to be cut off, he said:

'I told you, woman, you get nothing for nothing in this world. No doubt this is all your fancy friend from the paper's doing, right?'

Joan hoped that would be the end of it. She'd never asked for the phone in the first place. If she was honest, the continuous stream of leads and questions and letters was doing nothing for her self-esteem but bringing her down, and now it transpired she was also being charged to read them: even more reason to quit. What with the missed calls from the paper and Stuart, she was relieved to put an end to it all. She felt set up and used.

To top it off, when Sam found out the bill was definitely hers and had to be paid, he – predictably – went mad. Joan suggested she could ask the paper or Stuart to help with the final demand, but this led to Sam accusing Joan of having an affair, or at least wanting one. He blamed her and her stupid ideas and projects, and took away the phone. She should have no more to do with any of them again, Sam said – this was why the project had to end, because it was ruining their life. Where were Stuart and the paper years ago when she was ill? All they wanted was for her to do all the hard work and they would take all the credit. Where was her pay for all her input?

Sam also said, 'Do you really think anyone apart from me would be interested in you anyway? And is this what I deserve for sticking by you? You're broken. And only I really love you.'

That's when he beat her, and when he finished he made out it was all her fault – she caused all the problems and made him react like this. When she whimpered and cried she was sorry, curled up like a beaten dog on the settee, he pretended to comfort her, and then he made her wipe away the tears and snot and the blood from her mouth before demanding she give him oral satisfaction as a way of recompense.

Joan disappeared into her work for the next week or so. She could hide there fairly easily and people rarely got suspicious. Her busted lip could easily have been a cold sore, and her black eyes could be concealed with makeup and glasses. All she needed to do was keep her head down, and the lumps and bumps and bruises would go in time.

Joan had plenty of practice in the art of concealment. When she was drinking heavily, her bags under her eyes regularly looked like black eyes, and it was only caffeine keeping her awake during the day. She couldn't remember the last time she had been really drunk since the rush hour crush project properly took off, but now she found herself craving a drink on a Monday morning at work after drinking since the previous Friday. Just thinking about going home again was enough to make her want a large gin and tonic or a bottle of wine or several large glasses of sherry. Getting drunk helped clear her head of the project and Stuart and the paper and everything else that was muddying the waters. She had a life. Her life. All this new confusion just led to her having no money and bruises. Sam wouldn't have been like this had she not started this ridiculous project. He said so. It was all her fault. Sam was right. Stuart didn't really care.

Stuart became increasingly worried. He tried Joan relentlessly on the mobile, but just received an automated message. Then he tried her work number, but Joan never returned his calls. Phoning home was useless, as Sam would either just hang up or not answer at all. In the end, he went to her house and confronted Sam.

'Mr Maskell. To what do we owe the pleasure of such a distinguished visit?' Sam said, holding the door half-shut whilst his ungainly frame and sprouts of body hair partly filled the gap.

Stuart wanted to grab the door and smash it in Sam's face, crushing his bony ribcage against the corner of the door.

'Believe me, Mr Hothouse, I'm not here to see you. I just want to see Joan. I want to check she's okay. She's not returning my calls,' said Stuart, mirroring Sam's formality and tone.

'Well, isn't that enough of a message for you, Mr Maskell? I'd have thought a man of your intelligence would understand she doesn't want to speak to you.'

'Why would she not want to speak to me? Is she okay? I haven't done anything to upset Joan. In fact, we've been getting on very well. So the only person who may not want us to talk is you, Mr Hothouse.'

'And why do you think that is?' snapped Sam, getting riled quite quickly.

Stuart looked at the little balls of white spittle forming on Sam's lips. His greasy moustache and mouth looked dirty from whatever meal he'd eaten last. His long, fore and middle smoking fingers wrapped around the door were tobacco-coloured and his fingernails were black with grime. He really was a foul, odious man.

'I have no idea,' said Stuart. 'Perhaps you're getting paranoid about our relationship?'

'Paranoid! Don't make me laugh, boy. You wouldn't know where to start with a woman like Joan. Your mate had the right idea, but you were always clueless. Still, I presumed you perhaps preferred the boys. Never remember you ever having any girlfriends. Are you sure that's not the case now? Perhaps you fancy me, Mr Maskell?' Sam pursed his lips and blew a kiss at Stuart.

Stuart felt his heckles rise and he balled his fists.

'You know she's only got one boob? Get the other off and she might just suit you,' Sam snarled.

Stuart stepped up to the door, ready to grab Sam, but he ducked inside and Stuart heard him latch the door. Regaining his composure, Stuart took a step back.

'You really are a foul wretch. How on earth did Joan ever become involved with a disgusting person like you?'

Sam's fingers appeared like spiders in a gap in the doorway, and gradually his face re-emerged. Stuart still liked the idea of lunging forward and planting a fist in Sam's face.

'I'm more of a man than you'll ever be,' said Sam, appearing to grab at his tackle from what Stuart could make out through the marbled glass.

'Stop hiding behind the door then and come out here and face me,' suggested Stuart, finally reaching forward and grabbing the door.

'Don't be silly, boy. I'm neither dressed nor inclined to get involved in some homoerotic wrestling match with you. For all I know you'd get a kick out of it,' said Sam, struggling to hold the door shut as Stuart threatened to pull it off its hinges.

'You're right, I most certainly would,' barked Stuart.

Sam lashed out at Stuart's fingers and there was a dull thud of impact as the sharp edges of the door hammered into Stuart's flesh. He yelped and cursed as the door slammed shut, leaving him red-faced and worked up.

'If you don't sling your hook, Mr Maskell, I'll call the bloody police. You aren't welcome around here,' said Sam from inside, his voice slightly muffled.

Stuart stood on the doorstep staring at the peeling red paint on the doorframe where his fingers had gripped it moments earlier. His head was swimming and pounding; he felt a little giddy but still too furious to move. He wanted to kick the door down and drag Mr Hothouse out. Perhaps he could punch through the door and still get to him.

'I don't think I'll go. I think I'll just wait here for Joan, actually. I think she'll want to see me. Because I think we're friends. And I think you're being like this because you're jealous and hiding something.

Because you're a sad, jealous old man. And you're scared Joan might actually like me more than you.'

Stuart's heart was really racing and his arm tingled as he bashed his fist against the door. He felt sick. He actually considered passing out as he finished his statement, but he wanted Sam to know he wasn't scared of him and he wanted him to know how much he cared for Joan.

'Ha ha ha. Don't make me laugh, Mr Maskell. Why would Joan want to see you after all you've done? You set her up. She's working right now just to pay off the bloody big bill you lumbered her with. Bet you were probably on commission or something from that sodding phone supplier. Big advertising deal with the newspaper or something, no doubt. Yeah, some great friend you are.'

Stuart had no idea what Sam was talking about.

'What big bill?' he asked, but he didn't bother waiting for a reply. He'd ask Joan instead.

Stuart set off, slamming the gate at the end of Joan and Sam's front garden. The reverberation sent a mini shockwave running along the overgrown hedgerow, all the way around the border, like a floral tidal wave ending at the front of their house. Its slight seismic energy bounced off Sam's back and the palms of his hands, resting against their front door, and triggered a twisted smile of elation that crept across his face. The smile of a person who takes great pleasure in causing unhappiness. A child who pulled the wings off butterflies.

Stuart got to the library and asked a harassed-looking young lady if she knew where he could find Joan. Joan wasn't a book she'd ever heard of. Moments later, the graduate looked relieved to not have been given a task that involved fetching random, unheard-of books. She hadn't studied for four years to do this. Stuart could almost feel her frustration. She suggested he take a seat whilst she traipsed off like a heat-seeking missile to find Joan. Stuart slumped on one of the uncomfy-looking lounge chairs. They were designed to make readers feel at ease and comfortable in a home-from-home environment, but it didn't work on Stuart. His chair was too low for starters, and covered in rough, glass-fibre-like lime-green fabric that was vicious and unforgiving. Any bare skin that came into contact with the material was immediately burnt and needed urgent medical attention.

Stuart closed his eyes and flexed his hand, which had been aching. He couldn't pinpoint the pain. Probably a pulled muscle, he thought. He closed his eyes and focused on the far-off noise of high heels clicking on tiled flooring. Distant, muffled talking. A siren outside, somewhere far away. A child crying. Silence. Darkness. His breathing and heart rate calmed.

'Jesus, Stuart, are you okay?'

Joan looked down at a pale-faced Stuart slumped on the chair, his arm hanging down beside him, his head back and his mouth wide open.

'Stuart, what on earth are you doing here?'

Stuart spluttered and was snapped out of his slumber by Joan's slightly alarmed voice. He must have nodded off while enjoying the peaceful ambiance of the library. Maybe he had done the chair an injustice. He tried to stand up, but a mixture of the seat being too low and him standing up too quickly after being asleep sent him stumbling back onto the chair.

'Oh my God, is he all right?' said the young girl, about to run to Stuart's aid as Joan stooped down and put a hand on Stuart's arm.

'I'm quite all right, thank you. I just stood up too quickly,' said Stuart, chuckling, slightly embarrassed.

'Thank you, Melanie,' said Joan assertively, as if dismissing the young girl from further duties.

Melanie hovered for a second before giving Stuart and Joan an awkward-looking smile whilst trying to remember exactly what it was she was supposed to be doing.

'Stuart, why are you here?' said Joan, looking quite stern and pissed-off.

'I've been so worried. You didn't return any of my calls. I thought perhaps something was the matter,' Stuart said, slightly turning in his chair and placing a hand on Joan's hand and looking her in the face, studying every contour, eyelash and freckle.

'I'm fine, just really busy. In fact, I'm too busy for any of the paper business, so I think it's probably just best if someone else takes over from now on, okay? I quit. I simply don't have the time.'

'What? Why? Joan, I can't believe this. I thought it was something you were into as much as I am,' said Stuart, feeling confused and upset.

Joan looked at Stuart. She was angry. The phone bill had been the final straw. It had cost her financially, and physically – the beating from Sam. She had no time left to devote to the project. Plus, her feelings for Stuart were changing and complicating things. She looked into his eyes. Felt his warm hand gently protecting hers. He looked so smart and genuinely concerned for her. But if Sam found out she was feeling this way, he would kill her. She could virtually feel the heat from Stuart's face on hers, an invisible electric charge building between them.

'Look, I just can't do this anymore. I'm fine, but you shouldn't have come here. I simply can't afford to do any more with the paper.' Joan pulled her hand away. She couldn't cope with the comfort it provided and the connotations it was beginning to conjure.

'I'm really sorry if I've upset you or done something wrong,' said Stuart, conscious of the space left in the palm of his hand as Joan backed away. What he really meant was, *I love you, Joan, and I would do anything to make this right.* For a moment earlier, when they were more or less holding hands and he was looking into her eyes, the beautiful eyes he had known since childhood, he'd realised he loved her. He loved her so much. She looked as beautiful as he could ever remember seeing her, and he realised nothing would ever change that. They had been close enough to kiss. He could have leant forward and felt his lips on hers. But now she was heading away and that moment was gone. He wanted it back; he wanted to replay this scene. But it was too late, and he felt the familiar crush of missed opportunity collapsing down on him.

Joan stood up and walked away, saying, 'You shouldn't have come here, Stuart.'

'Joan, wait,' Stuart said, gingerly getting to his feet.

But she was already walking away and it was obvious that calling after her would attract unwanted attention. They were in a library, and he wasn't about to start breaking the rules and embarrassing her any further.

Stuart let her go, but he knew she hadn't told him the whole truth. He was right to go there. Joan wasn't being straight with him. Things weren't all right, and he was not going to let her down again.

First he needed to call the phone company that had given Joan the prize, and then he needed to speak to the editor.

If he got the phone bill paid and somehow gave Joan some money to take the pressure off, perhaps things would be different, he thought. He needed to find a way to make things better, to get her away from the whole situation she was in, at work and at home. Perhaps it could be discussed over a beer somewhere nice and relaxed.

Stuart went to see the editor and they agreed to pay the bill for Joan. Stuart had another funny turn while with the editor. His head was swimming. He blamed his pills and blood pressure. He explained getting so cross with Sam.

Meanwhile, Joan returned to Sam, who was violent towards her once again. This time Joan had little choice but to blame Stuart for meddling another time.

Joan still wouldn't answer any calls to her work, so Stuart sent James, the work experience boy, to hand-deliver a letter written with the approval of the editor. James told Stuart that Joan's hand was bandaged and her eye looked bruised, which Joan had said was a result of falling down the stairs. Stuart had a bad feeling about the whole plan he'd concocted with the editor, but it was done now and they just had to hope she would listen.

Dear Joan,

Please accept this letter as an expression of our gratitude for all your hard work and devotion to the 'rush hour crush' project, and also our combined utter embarrassment over having put you in an awful situation, both timewise and financially. For this we hope you'll accept our sincere apology. As a token of our appreciation, please find attached the following offer:

1. Your phone bill resulting from the prize provided by Whatphone.com has been paid in full, and all future bills will be covered by the Metro Papers Group Inc.

2. A consultancy fee of £2,000 pounds for your continual invaluable input will be paid monthly for the duration of the rush hour crush project, in which you have invested so much time and effort, diligently working on the development of the crush column and digital spin-offs.

3. A backdated payment of £6,500 will be made for work done to date.

4. An all-zones travel-card will be provided for the duration of the project.

We hope you will accept this offer, and we look forward to an exciting future working together for the duration of the rush hour crush project.

Kind regards,

Stuart Maskell, for and on behalf of the Metro Papers Group Inc.

PS: Joan, we hope this might help change your mind. If you are interested in accepting this offer or wish to discuss them any further, please meet me for an informal lunch at The Lamb and Flag in Covent Garden at 1.30 p.m. on Tuesday 22nd October. I have a friend I'd like you to meet.

Joan sat on the loo in the bathroom and read the letter twice. Then turned it over to see a receipt for the phone bill, a brand-new one-year travel-card and a couple of cheques. She couldn't believe her eyes, but that was partly due to the tears that had welled up uncontrollably. Theoretically, she didn't need to work anymore. But if she did work, she would be making a fortune.

Joan went to check her phone, but it was missing – either she had left it at home or Sam had it. She would need to get it back, if for no other reason than she needed it to know the date!

Suddenly, she had options. But if she went ahead with any of them, Sam would kill her. Perhaps she didn't have to tell him. Maybe she could hide it from him. She could take days off now and the paper money would cover that. She really wanted to see Stuart, partly to say thank you. She felt like a massive weight had been lifted, a bit like winning the lottery but then being tragically told she only had weeks left to live. Stuart kind of did and didn't deserve her gratitude and anger. Then she felt the panic again. The cold chill of betrayal and fear and anger – and Sam's fists. She was scared. Stuart was leading her astray, and she wanted to be led, but she was afraid of what Sam would do.

It felt like the first really cold day of winter and yet it was still October. Already a fire crackled in the corner of the pub, and the smoky ambiance reminded all that winter was edging closer, after Halloween and Bonfire Night.

Stuart checked his watch for the umpteenth time. He realised he was starting to look a little obsessive-convulsive. The time hadn't changed since he'd last checked, only his beer had gone down slightly and a few more nuts had been consumed. Would Joan come? That was the million-pound question. Perhaps after careful consideration she'd decided the offer was vulgar, Stuart thought. He took a sip of beer before checking his watch, and then shook another couple of peanuts from their packet and shuffled them in the palm of his hand like he was about to roll some dice.

Stuart's routine was broken by the sound of the door being flung open and a rather short man stumbling theatrically across the threshold. Stuart chuckled at the comedy entrance and stood up to greet his friend warmly.

'William, you sure know how to arrive on the scene.'

All around the pub, people were either smiling or wide-eyed as William strode over to Stuart and shook his hand enthusiastically.

'My God, have you shrunk, old man?' said William, smiling and looking up at the taller Stuart.

'Oh, only as much as you've grown around the middle,' said Stuart, laughing and patting William's waist.

William relaxed his belly and tenderly rubbed it, saying proudly to Stuart, 'It's all paid for, old man, it's all paid for.'

William was dressed in full Highland getup: dark-green Montrose kilt, sporran at his waist and little dagger tucked in his sock, along with smart polished brogues, black waistcoat with shiny silver buttons and even a jacket, white shirt and tie. He looked very smart, like he was going to a wedding.

This was usual for William, and Stuart would have been surprised to see him in anything else. But by the time Joan arrived, William was sitting down and had taken off his jacket, so she only noticed a happy-looking man, roughly the same age as her and Stuart, wearing a shirt and tie.

When Joan walked in, Stuart stood up, saying, 'Excellent, here she is.'

William just sat and stared as Stuart walked a step and held out his arms, as if hoping for a cuddle. Joan slowed her approach, looking a little coy and slightly self-conscious, and Stuart reacted by offering a more formal welcome. He held out a hand and shook Joan's, saying, 'You have no idea how happy I am to see you.'

Joan replied, 'You have no idea how difficult this is for me.'

Stuart was still fighting the urge to give her a cuddle when he realised they were holding hands and looking at each other and had forgotten poor William, who was sitting at the table like a gooseberry and watching the proceedings.

'Ahem,' said William, feeling slightly excluded.

'My God, sorry, how rude of me. Joan, this is William. William, this is Joan,' said Stuart finally.

William stood up, beaming, and held out a hand for Joan, saying, 'Delighted to meet you.'

Joan noticed the kilt first as he stood up and then how surprisingly short he was. He seemed much taller sitting down, if that was possible, like he had very little legs. With his shirt, tie and smart jacket hanging on the chair, he looked a very happy, dapper, Scottish cheeky chappie and she couldn't help but immediately like him.

'Lovely to meet you too,' said Joan, offering William her hand. She thought her arm might fall off as he firmly shook her hand, but was immediately enthralled by William and his infectious personality. Just holding his hand was like connecting to the National Grid and receiving one hundred thousand volts. They sat down and talked for a while and Joan couldn't help but notice William always seemed to be smiling or chuckling, and the warmth between him and Stuart was clear.

William took his moment whilst Joan went to the loo. 'Good grief, man, what a fine woman you've had hidden away there.'

Roy smiled at his friend, looking at the excited, genuine sincerity spread across his face. His eyes were glittering like a kid at Christmas. He looked like he was sitting with royalty.

'She's a fine rose, and sharp like a razor, yet gentle. I feel like I've known her all my life,' said William.

Joan, too, took the opportunity to speak to Stuart whilst William made it clear – theatrically – he would be going to the bar and demanded they let him buy the drinks.

'Oh, Stuart, isn't he the most fun?' said Joan, equally charmed.

Stuart basked in that warm feeling you get when surrounded by family or friends and the conversation is free and easy, full of joy and no negativity.

'Joan, I'm so sorry we put you under so much pressure. Will you forgive us. Me?' Stuart said, taking a moment whilst William was placing his order at the bar.

'I guess so. Well, I want to, but it's really difficult,' said Joan. Going to the pub had been an easy decision, but that morning, as she was leaving the house, pretending to go to work as normal, she'd had second thoughts. Her carrying on with the project meant accepting the money and hiding it from Sam. It also meant the continuation of her relationship with Stuart, which would need to be hidden from Sam. Whichever way she looked at it, she would be lying to Sam.

'I'm sorry, Joan, the last thing I wanted to do was make your life more complicated. If you don't mind me asking, what would be so bad about accepting the offer?'

Stuart waited for Joan to answer. He knew he was putting pressure on her again, but he wasn't entirely sure what the resistance was. He had an inkling it was to do with Sam and him, but was oblivious to her actual heartfelt feelings.

'Stuart, it's...' Joan managed to say, and then she paused and her lips quivered

William returned and plonked down their drinks. 'One Cinzano and lemonade for the beautiful fair maiden, and a pint of Old Peculiar for silly bullocks. Does anyone fancy some nibbles?' said William, like a naughty child with the key to the school tuck shop. Joan and Stuart both gawped as he dropped crisps, peanuts, pork scratchings, Mini Cheddars and scampi fries of varying flavours all over the table.

'I absolutely love bar snacks, I do!' said William.

Joan said, 'I can see,' and Stuart laughed.

William waited until Joan left for the toilet again and then asked Stuart about his feelings for Joan. Stuart insisted his feelings were irrelevant as she was in a relationship.

'You truly are a gentleman, Stuart Maskell,' said William, raising his glass.

Stuart clinked his glass against William's. 'There's no other way I'd rather be,' said Stuart.

'So what about this other fellow?' asked William, edging closer and lowering his voice.

'He really is a piece of work' said Stuart.

'How so?'

'He used to be our teacher at school,' said Stuart, shaking his head in disbelief.

'Go on, there must be more to him than that?' said William, wanting Stuart to open up.

'It's not fair on Joan to talk like this. She'll be back any moment. Let's just say I don't think he's good for Joan, not in the slightest.'

William looked at his friend and saw his expression had gone from jovial to deadly serious – almost angry. He had rarely seen Stuart like this. Normally, he was a calm, happy gentleman who rarely got cross or looked upset. Now, though, William could see his whole aura had changed.

'You… you don't think this Sam chap hurts our lovely Joan, do you?' said William, prodding the spot one last time.

A forlorn Stuart said, 'I don't know,' and raised his beer, drinking a few guilty gulps.

William thought Stuart's eyes were on the brink of welling up. 'Don't know' possibly meant yes, and the thought alone rocked William in his seat.

'But she's so lovely,' he said quietly. He too looked emotional. William was the type to wear his heart on his sleeve. He was highly sentimental.

Stuart looked pained, like he was suddenly aware he might be responsible. He stood up, cleared his throat and said, 'Same again?'

Still shocked and a little upset after the conversation, William watched as the toilet door swung open and Joan walked out with a big smile emblazoned on her face. He wondered what sort of person could ever want to upset such a fine, lovely lady. She reminded him a bit of his mum.

'Goodness me,' said Joan, looking at Stuart at the bar. 'Are you two trying to get me drunk?'

Stuart replied defensively, 'Most certainly not!'

'I was just kidding with you. Don't be so sensitive,' said Joan, before looking at William and raising her eyebrows as he stood up to let her retake her seat between him and Stuart.

'However, I won't be able to stop going to the loo at this rate,' said Joan. 'It's okay for you two, though. You can tie a knot in it!'

The three of them laughed as Stuart retook his seat.

'It's not me wearing the kilt,' said Stuart. Then he added: 'Whatever you do, Joan, don't ever look under the table. I made the mistake once, whilst out with William, of bending down to do up my shoelaces.' Stuart shuddered at the thought.

Joan pretended to have a look under the table and William roared his disapproval, and the three of them laughed until they cried.

The afternoon continued in the same vein. Conversations within conversations. Stuart continually wanting to check Joan was back on board with the rush hour crush project, and Joan being noncommittal. William probing Stuart about his feelings for Joan and her past and home life, and Stuart being coy. And then the three of them poking fun at each other in the nicest possible fashion, whilst drinking and laughing and having a wonderful time.

In no time William decided he cared not a jot for this Sam fellow – any man who hit a woman deserved nothing. If there was a slight chance that Joan would be remotely interested in him, he'd be up there as quick as a rat up a drainpipe, so to speak. Not that he'd chance his hand had she been with Stuart, as he loved him like a brother and best friend. But then again, this eventuality would certainly test Williams resolve. He really was mad about Joan. What a fine filly. Love at first sight.

Chapter 14

Sir William Wallace was also known as Uilliam Uallas, Uilleam Uallas, or William le Waleys to the Norman French. He died on the twenty-third of August 1305. He was a Scottish landowner who became one of the main leaders during the Scottish wars of independence.

Along with Andrew Moray, Wallace defeated an English army at the Battle of Stirling Bridge in 1297, and he was guardian of Scotland, serving until his defeat at the battle of Falkirk in July 1298. In 1305, Wallace was captured in Robroyston near Glasgow and handed over to King Edward I of England, who had him hanged, drawn and quartered for high treason and crimes against English civilians.

Since his death, Wallace has obtained an iconic status far beyond his homeland. He is the protagonist of the fifteenth-century epic poem 'The Wallace', by blind Harry. Wallace is also the subject of literary works by Sir Walter Scott and Jane Porter, and of the 1995 Academy Award-winning epic film *Braveheart*.

Name: William Wallace (Colin Waverly)

Fond of the sayings: By the great caber of Kilmarnock; Holy Moses; Jesus, Mary and Joseph; for the love of God; Christ on a bike; cor-bleedin'-bloomin'-blimey; heaven forbid; Donald where's me trousers; Big Nessie; sugary shortbread; tartan dreams, Holy Haggis; eureka; Jesus wept; sweet Jesus.

William woke up, hearing the old-fashioned phone chime downstairs in the hallway. If he let it ring for long enough, surely his mum or dad would answer it. His eyes were crusty with sleep and his mouth a little wet on the pillow from where he'd been snoring and drooling. As he rubbed his eyes and scanned the room, he noticed that some of his toys from childhood were gone from their usual places. Perhaps his mum had moved them.

Then he realised he'd been dreaming. Lost somewhere between unconsciousness and reality. He wasn't a little boy any more, and his mum and dad were dead. It was the same room but different; it had more modern belongings. The old phone must have been a memory too, as only last week the people from BT had come round and installed a new phone line with fibre-optic cables and a flashy, glowing box that allowed him to surf the internet wirelessly. His mum and dad would have been totally against the idea. 'We don't want no one messing with our wires,' he could almost hear the old lady say. They wouldn't have liked computers. 'Wi-Fi. Radioactive waves floating about the house. It's like living inside a bleeding microwave oven.'

Neither of his parents had seemed to read much either. William's dad occasionally skimmed through historical battle books, but always thought they were embellished by the writer's imagination.

'Hollywoodised,' he'd call it. 'Never would have happened like that.' He was like that generally: always seemed to know better. He disliked other people's opinions and versions of events, and had no time for imagination. That might have been connected to William's life choices and the way he turned out; perhaps he was always hoping for some sort of seal of approval, or at least looking for a reaction from his father.

He twisted out of bed and pushed his feet into his giant fluffy white ogre-feet slippers, the sort a child would wear, or a middle-aged William Wallace obsessive. He tried to flatten his unruly locks with spit on his palm. In his mind, he saw himself as a macho Mel Gibson-like figure: chiselled, rough and ready. He was the polar opposite of anorexic, deluded even, half-naked from the kilt up and muddy from barbaric battles, pouring cold water pulled from an ice-cold well straight from the wooden bucket all over himself. William's tartan pyjamas were ruffled at the ankle from being too long in the leg and far too little around the middle. As he'd got older and his waistline had expanded, his trousers, which should have got shorter, had instead been pulled up and over his bulging belly. As a very young man he might have worn a 34 x 30, but now he wore a 42 x 32. If he'd looked for a good fit via a decent tailor, they'd have panicked.

He shuffled to his new computer, picking his nostrils hairs with a finger and thumb. An audible 'tut' sounded when a protruding follicle was yanked from the inner sanctum of his nasal cavity. Mr Tickles, his cat, watched nonchalantly from on top of the washing basket in the corner of the bedroom. He wouldn't move until he heard William preparing his Highland Oats. His big slippers scuffed on the swirly ruby-red and orange carpet, building a monstrous static charge waiting for William to make contact with something metal. 'Hadrian's Wall!' he yelped as he touched the side of the computer. A little while later he would phone PC World and report a fault, blaming dodgy electrics. Switching on his system he made his way to the kitchen whilst the software fired up.

William made himself a cup of tea and a bowl of porridge. Sorting through his cutlery he selected his favourite spoon with the thistle motif on the handle. Pausing for a moment to look at his reflection in the picture displayed above the kitchen table: the Highlands with a single stag silhouette. William struggled to see big Mel Gibson staring back at him, so he sucked in his belly and puffed out his chest and gave himself a big, warm smile as he patted his belly. His nostrils flared as he dished out a smelly turkey-beef mixture of food in a bowl for Mr Tickles, and took his breakfast and shuffled back to his computer.

His first port of call every day was eBay. He searched for anything resembling traditional Celtic Scottish Highland paraphernalia. Most important, though, was clothing. Be it kilts, sporrans, sgian-dubhs, garters, socks, brogues, dress coats, shirts, bowties, tartan ties, hats or waistcoats, he was always in the market.

His ringtone on his phone was the tune 'A Moose Loose aboot This Hoose'.

'Heavens above!' he exclaimed, mostly to himself but also to Mr Tickles. MadScot69 had bid on a sporran with no minimum purchase price. This was big news indeed. Massive news. Decent sporrans were quite hard to come by on eBay, and MadScot69 didn't bid on anything unless he thought it was kosher or top drawer or the dog's dangles. (Or so William thought. Little did he know that MadScot69 was actually Gladys from Braintree in Essex and she too had very little Scottish ancestry.)

His real name wasn't William Wallace; he had changed it by deed poll. His actual name was Colin Waverly, but his obsession meant that by the time he'd left school, he was already known as Hamish, Mactaffy, Jockey, Sweaty Mcbetty and lots of other silly names kids came up with.

He had applied to *Mastermind* several times with Wallace as his specialist subject. He had owned and had read virtually every written reference to the man.

He regularly patrolled the Wikipedia site, furiously deleting any fact that wasn't verified (usually by himself).

He'd been manoeuvred out of several Scottish Highlander re-enactment groups for being too overpowering. He was generally a jolly and polite man, but all rationalism went out the window when historical accuracy was in question. First he wouldn't be keen to join in all the physical activities, and then he'd pick holes in every minute detail of historical exactness. Possibly a negative trait picked up from his father. 'Do as I say, not as I do' was the general rule of thumb with William and these groups, hence the reason he wasn't generally welcome for very long.

He was English and had no known familial connection to Scotland. He had checked fastidiously, but he never gave up hope. Perhaps somewhere in his maternal line there was an illegitimate fling with a Scotsman.

He'd never left his family home. He'd lived with his parents until they died and continued living in their house once they were gone. Their bedroom remained the same. His mother's wigs still sat on the dressing table, even though she'd been buried for fifteen years. His dad's suits and kipper ties still weighed down their hangers, gathering dust in the cupboards and providing occasional meals for the moths. William barely ever went into their room. He felt like they were still in there, just sleeping or having a rest. They'd shout out sooner or later for him to put the kettle on – and occasionally he'd call out to them too. Sporadically, Mr Tickles would curl up on their bed, but William would go in there and tell him off before coaxing him out with some cat treats. He didn't have any other family. Well, none that he kept in regular contact with.

Mostly, he stayed in his room, which had changed very little since he left school. Redecorated twice. He spent a long time looking at himself in the mirrored cabinet his dad had made. Every day he would spend an age getting dressed in full Highland regalia, fastidiously preparing to look as perfect as possible. He'd brush his curly hair with a comb until the wax/Brylcreem scum build-up was completely even at the base of the teeth. Then he'd look deep into his eyes and whisper, 'Aye, William,' before going about his day. He wasn't an ugly man, just portly, stout and different.

He had recently come up with a plan to buy cheap die-cast soldiers in Highland outfits, hand-paint their kilts in the correct colours for the different clans, and sell them for a profit on eBay. He had purchased about fifty figures so far and almost completely painted four to an acceptable standard. Unfortunately, they were taking a whole day/evening to painstakingly produce. He didn't have the steady hand or artistic skills needed. They had cost him four pounds ninety-five each, and he hoped to sell them for at least twenty pounds. But his first eBay effort resulted in a no-sell and one bid of fifty pence. He realised he needed to target his market a little better. He was open to the option of cutting his losses and selling the remaining unpainted forty-six miniature figurines. Or perhaps continuing the project over the very, very long term. It was certainly not one of his most successful projects, but he felt that with a little advertising or luck perhaps some more interest could be generated.

'What do you mean, he won't give it back? Jesus Christ, man – it's hers! We're not paying for him to use her bloody phone, Stuart.'

The editor was, understandably, annoyed that the plan seemed to have fallen at the first hurdle.

'You have to appreciate we aren't talking about a simple situation here, or person. It's delicate. She can't just demand it back,' said Stuart, trying to remain pragmatic and understanding to all parties.

'Of course she bloody can – it's her sodding phone, not his. What do you suggest we do then? Bloody delicate! We're wasting time pissing about here. Can't we call the police or something? Block the phone? Buy a new one? No work is being done whilst this sodding man has her bloody phone.'

'You have to try to see it from Joan's point of view. She has to live with this arsehole.'

Stuart asked Joan as sensitively as possible if she'd had any joy getting the phone back.

'Have you actually asked for it back?' he said.

'It's really difficult, you see. I can't really explain. I don't know where he's put it. And he doesn't really know I've accepted your proposal, or the money, or any of the other bits.'

What Joan really wanted to say was that she was too scared to ask for it back, because if she did, Sam was likely to go mad again. She thought perhaps he had hidden it or thrown it away. As far as he was concerned it was cut off, so useless to him or Joan.

What Joan didn't know was that Sam had switched the phone off but then switched it back on, so he could read all her text messages. He was especially intrigued by those between her and Stuart – what exactly they had said, or more specifically, what Joan had been conspiring. Every time he read a message shared between Joan and Stuart, anger and spite boiled up within him. And then the phone buzzed while he was holding it. At first he thought somehow he had been discovered. Then his interest was piqued when the phone suddenly started receiving new messages. The first said the phone was now reactivated. Then there was one from Stuart: *Just checking you're receiving. See you later?* Then another one: *So lovely to see you today, and so pleased to have you back on board. Hope the money helps. ;) PS: William was rather taken by you too. See, it's not just me. S xxx*

Sam read the last message several times. He checked the calendar stuck to the fridge with magnets. Joan had gone to work on that day, or so she'd said. And she'd categorically told him she had no more holiday-time left, so how come she had met up with Stuart and this other man, William? And what was all this about being back on board, and money? Joan had definitely been lying.

Sam read the end again, and again: PS: *William was rather taken by you too. See, it's not just me. S xxx.* Three kisses. That wasn't usual for friends.

He went through all the messages and found passwords to access Joan's blog and emails He picked up a bottle of whisky, necked a few mouthfuls and thought, *Time to have some fun.*

Sam spent the rest of the day reading and replying to as many messages as he could on behalf of Joan. Only he didn't reply in the patient, interested, honest, heartfelt manner Joan usually reserved for the rush hour crushes. Instead, he was brutal, rude, shocking, smutty and outrageous.

It was about midday before the editor received a call from the IT department saying Joan's account had potentially been compromised, or perhaps she had gone mad and that was why she'd written lots of expletive laden messages. The editor had no choice but to close all the rush hour crush sites down immediately and demand Stuart come to see him as soon as he got into the office.

Stuart was due in later; he was supposed to be seeing the doctor first. But as soon as he heard something was wrong with the rush hour crush and Joan, he dropped everything and went straight to work. He understood the editor's decision. He said he'd speak to Joan and find out what on earth was happening, although he already had a good idea – Sam was happening.

Stuart managed to talk to Joan at work, and she explained she still hadn't managed to speak to Sam. Stuart lied, saying they were taking down the sites and social media pages as a temporary measure, but it was nothing to worry about as they would get her a new phone soon and get it all up and running again in no time. Joan smelt a rat and was, understandably, concerned, as Stuart went to great lengths trying to explain it was nothing to worry about and was simply site maintenance. Joan reiterated she was waiting for the right opportunity to talk to Sam, and that she just hadn't found the time.

'Don't worry,' said Stuart. 'It's quite all right.'

Joan knew he wasn't being straight with her. Sam was a very capable liar, and Roy was decent too, but Stuart wasn't. She couldn't help but worry about what Sam might have done.

Stuart explained to the editor the sabotage to the Rush Hour Crush sites must have been Sam. Stuart told the editor he'd try to get the old phone back and see if he could get the truth out of Sam. But the editor told him not to bother; they'd just order a new phone. Stuart said he wanted to go, though.

He went to Sam and Joan's house and knocked on the door. A slightly drunk Sam opened the door, looking very pleased with himself. The next thing Sam remembered was waking up. Stuart had punched him clean on the nose, knocking him unconscious, and walked away.

Stuart called the editor to say he was right, he couldn't get the old phone. He told his boss to order Joan a new phone and take it out of his wages if necessary, and to cancel the old line.

He headed to the library, feeling quite happy with himself. He was going to tell Joan not to bother asking for the phone as it was cancelled, presumed lost, and that he'd get her a brand-new one. She didn't need to tell Sam a thing.

However, they missed each other on the journey, and Joan headed home to confront Sam and ask him if he had been using her phone and computer, and if so, had he done anything to her precious project? Had he perhaps ruined her site? But before she got a chance to defend her baby, he went mad, throwing the phone at her and accusing her of lying and cheating. Then he beat her up again.

Stuart called Joan at her work, but was told she hadn't been in and was off sick. Again he made the trip to her house.

'Joan, Joan, I know you're in there. I've just seen you moving.' Stuart had been looking through the letterbox as he noticed the tail end of Joan's dressing gown nip behind a door. He didn't hear a word for a minute. 'Please, Joan, whatever it is, let me know. Please don't shut me out. I know you're in there and can hear me.'

As Stuart watched through the little gap in the door, his view became obscured by the approaching figure of Joan. He straightened up in preparation for seeing his old friend, a little bit excited, as always. But what he saw would cut him to the bone and stay with him for as long as he lived. Joan's eye was black and swollen, her lip was busted, one nostril was blocked with congealed blood, and she held one hand curled up like an injured dog.

'Oh, Joan,' said Stuart, reaching forward and gently embracing her.

They stood in the doorway, Joan numb, trying to protect her hand and not saying a word, whilst Stuart failed to hold back the tears. His body reverberated and shook as he was overcome with emotion. Joan was oblivious.

'Where's Sam?' asked Stuart quietly, unsure whether to beat him to a pulp before or after getting Joan to safety.

'On the settee,' whispered Joan, looking around as if saying his name would conjure him up, before adding, 'passed out.'

Stuart told Joan to get her things whilst he checked on Sam. 'Go on, just grab some bits. You aren't staying here a minute longer.'

Sam was lying flat-out on the settee, an empty bottle of whisky next to him and an open transparent, orange, vial of medication on the floor. He was out cold. Probably his own doing, but Stuart wouldn't have blamed Joan for poisoning Sam. That was very unlikely, though, as she wasn't really thinking and was just functioning on autopilot. The TV was on quietly and Stuart imagined Joan had been watching it in silence for some time without actually seeing it.

Joan packed a bag. She hadn't been on holiday for ages and had no idea where she was going or what she needed. She bundled several pairs of knickers, a couple of day outfits that she would usually wear to work, her makeup bag, a spare dressing gown and a pair of slippers into a big black bin liner (she didn't own a suitcase).

Stuart told her not to forget her shoes, and then remembered the phone and computer bits. He didn't want to leave them for Sam to abuse any more. The phone was smashed to bits, but Stuart asked, 'Where's the computer?'

Joan attempted to motion towards the corner of the sitting room with her busted hand. Instead of pointing at the chair, she pointed at her feet, where both the computer and phone were plugged into a multiple plug socket. Stuart pulling out the plugs, and for a moment, as he held the laptop aloft, watching Sam breathe, he thought about smashing it down onto his skull, killing him. Did he deserve to die in his sleep? Stuart pondered, deliberating for a second. It was a nice way to go. Privileged. The best way to go. Sam didn't deserve that. The computer remained delicately poised. Even if the plug fell now it might wake Sam, or if nothing else, hurt him a bit. Perhaps Stuart could get away with just hurting him a bit. If he killed Sam, he would surely go to prison and then he wouldn't see Joan again.

A thousand thoughts flashed through Stuart's mind. The computer suddenly weighed a thousand tonnes. The last memory that went through Stuart's mind was Sam questioning Stuart's masculinity whilst they argued in the doorway.

'Real men don't hit women.'

Stuart suggested Joan stay with him, but Joan didn't like that idea; she didn't feel comfortable, she wanted her own space and staying with Stuart just wouldn't seem right. So Stuart and the editor put her up in a hotel near the paper whilst she decided how to get her life back in order and what to do next.

Stuart said, 'Do you want me to call anyone? Is there anyone you want to see? Your sister or kids maybe?'

But Joan said no. They were the last people she wanted to see, especially in the mess she was in. In a way, they would be justified in their opinion of her and Sam's relationship. She just wanted to be alone and without any fuss.

When Sam woke up, he felt slightly groggier than usual, and terribly hungry and thirsty, like he could drink a puddle. He woke himself up, uncomfortable, sweating and snoring on the settee. He had no idea what the time was or where he should be. It could have been day or night.

'Joan,' he called, his usual response when waking up on the settee, whatever the time. She might have been a lot of useless things, but when it came to telling Sam whether it was night or day and where he should be, she was usually spot on. He was sure it was a meal time, as his stomach was cramping and rumbling angrily. He needed food and drink desperately.

He looked next to the settee and saw the empty bottle of whisky and the empty phial of pills. Nothing really out of the ordinary there.

'Joan!' he called, a little louder, thinking perhaps she was still asleep in bed. His nose whistled with congestion. He noticed the pile of bloodied tissues next to the settee and felt his nose, remembering something about it bleeding. He pulled out a crusty, bloody bogey. He felt his face. Although it felt sore, he had a feeling the bloodied tissues on the floor weren't his.

He sat up on the settee, his head feeling woozy, taking a little longer than normal to get stabilised. His hands and knuckles looked and felt sore, grazed and bruised.

'Joan!' Sam called again, trying to remember the evening before. Scratching his stubbly chin, he looked around the room and noticed the broken remains of the mobile phone and the unconnected cables from the computer. Slowly, Sam remembered getting cross with Joan.

The house felt empty, like she was there in spirit but not in person. He panicked for a second, thinking he might have killed her and that she *was* there in spirit, watching him. Her ghost. Perhaps she was observing him, listening to him, while tucked away safely in the afterlife, on a cloud in heaven, watching him on a secret TV. Sam looked at the lightbulbs – maybe they were mystical hidden cameras.

He felt angry and confused. Where was she, and why had she done what she had done, and what had he done?

Joan figured that when her hand felt a bit better in a day or two, she could get out and try to trace a few rush hour crushes. She was comfortable in town, and Stuart's work wasn't far away if she got bored or lonely. She could go shopping and spend a few quid buying any bits and bobs she had forgotten in the rush to leave her home. The thought of going shopping for herself was a little bit exciting.

Stuart offered to pop by during the day and in the evening, and he offered to take her for lunch, but Joan politely declined, saying, 'It's very sweet of you to show so much concern, Stuart, but really, I will be fine. Please give me a few days just to relax and get myself together, and I'll be right as rain again.'

Joan felt like she had dealt with these situations before, and it was all a bit embarrassing dealing with them with outsiders.

Stuart was upset and mad, both at himself and the whole situation. He thought he detected a hint of anger in Joan's voice, and he was petrified that she blamed him, but he didn't want to push the whole thing any further than it had already gone. He had to try to do things Joan's way.

'Have you thought any more about contacting the police?' Stuart's mouth had formed the question he had been thinking but promised himself he wouldn't ask.

'Erm, no, I haven't. In a way, I kind of feel like I deserved it. If I hadn't been carrying on with the project and talking with you...'

'Joan, this is madness. You can't blame yourself.'

'I don't,' Joan said, and the line went quiet for a while. She was going to ask if Stuart was still there, but she could faintly hear him breathing on the other end.

'Right, erm, I see. I'm very sorry. Please forgive me. Honestly, it's no problem. If you need anything at all, just say, erm, please just call,' said Stuart, suddenly rushing the conversation towards the finish.

'Okay,' said Joan, quite removed, almost cheerily. 'I'll call you in a couple of days.'

'Okay,' said Stuart, disappearing down the plughole into despair and doom.

They both hung up and Joan went back to organising her next few days. Stuart sat in his comfy leather chair and lit his rollup as the tears flowed down his cheeks.

Joan stayed in the hotel for a week. The first few days, she enjoyed doing mostly nothing. She felt like she slept more than she could ever remember. She had baths and showers even though she didn't need them. She watched TV and slept some more.

Then she started to get restless. She contacted James at the paper with a few ideas for some flyers, two A-frame metro-style newspaper stands and a new placard, all produced in the same font and style as the website and the paper. She had them printed up at the Quick Print franchise close to the hotel. She asked the printer to deliver the bits directly to the hotel, as she couldn't wait for them because she had some more shopping and mooching to do. She was the girl about town.

The editor told Joan to keep receipts for whatever she needed to survive in the short term and the paper would put them through as expenses. Joan was getting good at asking for receipts for things and not feeling guilty about paying with somebody else's money. Originally, she had felt awkward and slightly embarrassed. But not now. She felt she was entitled to being reimbursed and deserved it. For too long in her life she'd had to beg and scrimp and save to buy anything, and from now on she wouldn't look a gift horse in the mouth. She had changed. Things had now changed. This was the new Joan.

When she got back to the hotel, the concierge told her the prints had been delivered, as requested, and a separate package had also arrived for her. The new Joan was loving this. She knew what it was before opening it. Sure enough, it was a shiny new phone.

The next day Joan woke up especially early; it was still dark out. She spent half an hour working out how to hold all the gear; it was a hell of a lot bigger and more cumbersome than she had anticipated. In the end she opted to use a new rucksack she'd purchased to replace the bin bag to carry the leaflets, and with the placard placed under one arm and the A-frames in her good hand, she should be just about ready to set off.

She had far too much to get on a bus or on a train, and she wouldn't have fitted in a taxi, but the walk to King's Cross from where she was staying should only take about half an hour, she figured. She didn't have to rush. Joan liked London and felt quite comfortable walking the streets. Putting the flyers in her backpack, she adjusted the shoulder straps admiring herself in the mirror. Her face was looking much better and she had done a good job of concealing the bruises. Joan really liked her new bag; it could be used every day, not just in London, and it felt comfortable and made her look like a traveller. She felt like she was a tourist on holiday in the city, Joan thought it might be fun to pretend she was on a sightseeing vacation.

Flicking off the lights Joan picked up her placard and A-frames and headed out of her hotel room, looking like a tourist going to a demonstration. Before closing the door and in almost total darkness she wrote down her room number, and the name of the hotel and its address, and slid the note into a compartment within her purse, just in case.

The busy London streets, hustled and bustled as Joan made her way along with early-morning autumn commuters. It was still dark and chilly, and the wind was blowing up a storm. Had it not been so dark and early perhaps Joan might have been a little more prepared for the weather. She hadn't wanted to turn the TV on too early in case she disturbed the other guests. More or less as soon as she found her walking pace, the wind picked up and then it started to rain. Undeterred, Joan marched on. This was the new Joan, the cutting edge, determined version. She wouldn't be put off by a little changeable weather. She wanted to laugh at the thought that the wind and rain were trying to stop her in her tracks and force her home. Suddenly, she had become stronger, a force of nature capable of battling earth's fury.

Joan managed to get to the station using the placard as a makeshift umbrella. The weather was foul. She tried to shelter inside the station and warm her feet a little. The placard had mostly protected her head, but from her legs down to her toes she was cold and wet. Standing near the entrance everywhere already seemed too busy and she could barely get close. Nevertheless, she battled against the current and set out her A-frames either side of the continuous ebb and flow of people entering the station. She picked up her slightly weather-beaten placard and started handing out the smattering of flyers she'd grabbed from her bag, which she'd stored away by squeezing it between the legs of one of the A-frames.

'It's only wind and rain,' she repeated to herself, feeling positive.

Before long a few people said hello and smiled at her, and some even gave her a thumbs-up. Joan felt slightly famous. People seemed to be reading her placard and willingly accepting her flyers for the first time ever, and she didn't feel like some sort of religious nut on a crusade.

As the flyers began to deplete, she noticed the large puddle surrounding the A-frame on top of her bag. 'Shit,' she said, running over, not sure how to hold the placard, pick up her bag and move the frame. She must have placed it on top of some sort of a drain.

'Bloody shit,' she said as she picked up the bag. It was soaked through. She didn't need to look inside to know the leaflets at the bottom of the box would also be drenched. Feeling cross, she didn't dare think about how many were ruined.

The rain continued to dribble down the placard, which twisted and jostled between her legs, buffeted by the wind. The other A-frame shuffled along, as if pushed by supernatural forces, and then fell flat on its face drunk.

'Shitting shittery shit,' Joan said, struggling not to lose it.

But she didn't. This was the new Joan. She counted to five and then nearly laughed as she headed towards the entrance. She didn't give a hoot if she was in the way. Someone would have to tell her to move. She picked up the box from the soaking bag, left her placard resting against the A-frame and headed off to find a dry spot inside the station entrance in which to leave the flyers. Powerful Joan, destroyer of wind and rain.

But Mother Nature wasn't finished with Joan; she was simply toying with her. The wind and the rain grew steadily worse, until the rain lashed down torrentially and the wind gusted with umbrella-wrecking force, so much so that people ran into the station much faster. That was when Joan heard the curse, then watched the stumble, then saw the back of someone tripping over the box of leaflets, then the gust of wind sending hundreds of sheets of paper blowing into the station like confetti. Some only made it a few inches and feet from the bag and stuck to the ground; others raced free, like untethered kites, flying at pigeon-frightening speeds up into the atmosphere and across the Euston Road. The majority somehow disappeared down the mouth of King's Cross station, with a few getting stuck on the giant stairway teeth. They soon became slippery, like leaves on a path, and quickly the wet, tiled floor resembled a crap ice-skating rink, with suits and high heels carefully meandering around the slippery, A5-paper banana skins.

Then Joan noticed someone picking up her placard and inspecting an A-frame. 'No, no, no,' she said, setting off after whoever it was. She thought at first it was a policeman, but then she noticed his London Underground uniform.

'Excuse me, sir. Please don't touch that, it's private property,' she yelled, trying to sound authoritative. 'It's mine!'

Joan ran over to the station supervisor, who was pointing at the A-frame as if telling his colleague to take it away. Without thinking, Joan immediately became involved in a game of tug of war. New Joan was powerful and assertive.

'What do you think you're doing?' snapped the station supervisor.

'Get your hands off my property!' demanded Joan. She had already lost her flyers and wasn't about to give up her A-frame without a fight.

'You don't have permission to do this in the station. You're trespassing, breaking the law,' said the sweaty-browed, overweight Underground employee. His jellylike midriff had wobbled free below his shirt during the tussle.

'I'm not in the station and I won't let you have this. Let it go,' snapped Joan.

'I certainly will not. Look at the mess you've made of my station!' said the fat man.

'It's not your station and I didn't make the mess,' said Joan.

'Yes, you did. It's your responsibility.'

'No, it isn't.'

Without thinking, Joan lashed out with her sodden bag, a sweeping arc, a dazzling hook-come-uppercut, spraying dirty brown water, and knocked the station supervisor off balance. He staggered backwards, flailing over the A-frame.

This was when the new Joan disappeared and the old, broken one came back.

She couldn't believe what had just happened. She watched, in a blurry, semi-conscious daze, as the station supervisor was sent tumbling and he rolled around like a floored champ, pawing at his bloodied head. People in fluorescent jackets rushed to help him back to his feet. Members of the public flashed into her line of sight, pointing and staring at her like she was a caged animal. Then: flashing blue lights and serious-looking people in uniform.

All the while, the rain fell and the wind blew. The only person who didn't seem to notice was Joan.

Stuart called Janet, Joan's sister, who helped get her bailed after she was charged with actual bodily harm and given a date to appear in court. Joan regressed into her shell, not wanting to talk to anyone, especially Janet and Stuart.

Once back at the hotel and with Joan asleep in bed, Stuart explained to Janet that Joan had been staying in the hotel for the last week after he had found her beaten up by Sam.

Janet was instantly furious and went into one, hissing, 'That dirty creep. What sort of lowlife scum… Useless man. I always hated him. I knew she shouldn't have trusted him. I always knew he was a wrong'un. Only Joan could end up with a loser like him. Why couldn't she see it? It was a plain to see for everyone else. But not bloody Joan. It's madness.'

Not once did Janet stop to consider how Joan was feeling, mentally or physically. But she did consider talking to Nikki and the kids.

Stuart suggested, as diplomatically as possible, that Joan might not want that. He was feeling slightly wary of the ranting Janet. He'd forgotten quite how intimidating she could be. Her youthful looks had disappeared, and now she seemed more masculine. Perhaps it was the authority she carried now she was a policewoman.

'It's family business,' said Janet, 'not for you to worry about any more. I'll ensure the right course of action.' She added, 'Do you think Joan needs psychological help? Counselling perhaps? Sectioning even? Do you think Joan is capable of looking after herself?'

Stuart felt sorry for Janet and Joan as siblings. They had grown so far apart, and the pain of years of separation had now led to a loss of sympathy and compassion. For the first time in his life he was glad to have been an only child and free from the jealousy and superiority complexes, the unnecessary and continuous comparisons, the uncalled-for opinions. As far as he could tell, Joan just needed loving – but unfortunately, she seemed to have decided, not by him.

All the while Joan pretended to be asleep, but she was listening to Stuart and Janet discussing her life as if she were useless and incapable of looking after herself. She hoped Stuart would put Janet in her place, but he just seemed to be agreeing with her.

Finally, she fell asleep, feeling more hurt than she had after any beating she remembered receiving.

Joan woke up early in the morning and started packing her bags. 'I'm going home,' she said aloud to herself.

She was disillusioned and fed up with living alone in a hotel and being treated like a baby and patronised. She was used to feeling bashed up. Why did everyone all of a sudden seem to want to have a go? Where had they all been for the last however many years? She missed her old life, however bad it seemed to everyone else. She missed Sam, and the booze. She was desperate for a drink.

Maybe he had learnt his lesson. He might know now that she wouldn't stick around if he laid a finger on her again. She would tell him that too. She would give him another chance. He wasn't that bad, she was sure. She should know.

Although he would never admit it, Sam was really quite scared that Joan might actually have left him, whether for someone else or on her own – both notions that had once seemed quite ridiculous but were now terrifying to him. He wondered, what if he had been right all along and she was actually plotting to leave him? Who was the fool now? She would have the last laugh. What if some of the things he had said to her half in spite and half in jest were true? Maybe she wasn't quite as pathetic as he liked to think. This really bothered Sam. Maybe he wasn't able to read her like a book. Perhaps he had done her an injustice. When – or if – Joan ever came home, Sam wouldn't need to act pleased to see her. He would be genuinely delighted to have her tidy up the place and look after him once again.

From the outside, the house looked the same. Home. Horrid, Joan thought. Foreboding, like the houses they showed on the news that had sections of the garden covered in tarpaulin as forensic teams set about digging up decomposing bodies. She traipsed up the path, casting angry stares at the weeds that jutted up through the nooks and crannies and the overgrown lawn, boxed in but fingering out, sprawling next to a messy wall of neglected shrubbery and nettles. She would try to get a hanging basket or something. Perhaps she would sow some seeds in the lawn. She could get some cheaply, and she liked gardening. This could become her new project, she thought, casting aside the pang of self-pity and swallowing the bitter pill of regret.

The door lock was as stubborn as ever. Joan paused for a second, looking at her slightly bruised hand on the key in the lock, and remembered fleetingly turning the key to her first home. How long ago that was. How young her hands seemed in her memory compared to the tired, stiff, bony old hands she was staring at now.

She wiggled the key around in the lock until it gave a little and then turned it hard anticlockwise, before leaning on and kicking the base of the old red door. It was all part of the knack needed to gain entrance to the house. Only she and Sam had the knack. If nothing else, they had that in common. She had been asking Sam to take a look at the door for as long as she could remember. Perhaps she should try to mend it, she thought. She remembered thinking once that if she kicked the door hard enough it might split in two, and then they would have to replace it. The door gave a little and Joan used her weight to push it open the rest of the way. It seemed to open a little more easily than normal.

'Hello, anyone home?' Joan called, more out of habit than because she expected a response. If she had wanted a definite reply, she would have gone straight to the pub or the bookies.

Where the door had rubbed against the carpet it had created a clean arc. Possibly the only unspoiled bit of the whole house.

The house had a musty air to it. It smelt of dirty old man. She knew the smell well. She made straight for the living room and pulled open the curtains, fighting briefly with the net curtains underneath like a panicked fish, before opening a window to get some fresh air into the place. Opening the curtains let in the light – and, unfortunately, revealed the full extent of Sam's inability to look after himself. She looked at the settee, where she remembered last seeing him. Then at the mark on the wall where he'd thrown the phone. In a little over a week without her running around after him, tidying up, he'd turned their home into some sort of dosshouse, a hell hole. Without her, he was a tramp. It looked like a squat. 'Oh, Sam.' She thought he was pathetic.

She left her new travel bag by the door, nestled in the clean arc. She hadn't had anything to eat all day except a packet of Munchies on the train and her stomach was rumbling. She thought about the breakfast buffet she had been enjoying each day at the hotel. Perhaps she could go back there, her belly suggested.

She set about collecting the rubbish in bin bags and moving them to the front door, and shifting the cutlery, glasses, mugs, plates and bowls that littered the floor onto any available space near the sink. She felt like she was getting dizzy, walking around in circles. At every turn Joan found new bits to pick up or stuff to drop off. She figured Sam had had a cold, as an almighty number of tissues were strewn over the floor next to his favourite chair. Any other reason for them being there was too hideous to imagine, so she banished any such thoughts from her mind, whilst accepting that particular heap of rubbish could wait for as long as possible before being tidied.

Joan was trying to run through every potential conversation, or argument, she might have with Sam when he got home when she heard the tell-tale whack of the front door getting kicked open. She froze on the spot, her mind went blank and all the different rehearsed scenarios evaporated. She felt scared.

'Joan, love, are you home?' Sam called.

Love! *Love?* She struggled to comprehend. His voice even had a cheerful ring to it. Like he'd sounded once when he won ten pounds on a scratch card. Like when she was at school. It was how he would sound if she ever suggested a sexual favour, a promise of fellatio. 'Really?' he'd yelp, like a happy Jack Russell presented with a whole turkey at Christmas.

And there he was, standing in the doorway. Her other half. The tramp. Her very own slob. Holding her new bag. She briefly imagined running, screaming, at him with an axe and sticking it in his head.

'Oh, hello, love. I've really missed you,' said Sam.

The words rebounded off the back of Joan's head and ricocheted around in her brain.

'Sorry?' Joan said. Meaning 'excuse me' and not an apology, but Sam took it the other way.

'Oh, don't be silly, you don't need to be sorry. I'm just so pleased to have you back. How is everything, are you okay?' Sam said, still holding her bag like it contained a present for him, still using that sexually expectant tone.

Joan was stumped; she had no idea what was going on. This was a different Sam. A familiarly filthy Sam. She could only just grasp that perhaps he thought she was still planning on leaving him, and this was his attempt to get her to stay.

'I'll make you a nice cup of tea, eh? Look, I've got some milk.' He held up her bag. 'That's not the milk – ha ha ha, silly me. That's a nice new bag. Shall I just pop it down over here?' Sam swivelled, looking for a place to drop Joan's bag. 'Here's the milk,' he said, triumphantly holding up a blue plastic corner-shop bag like it was a round-the-world sailing trophy. Joan almost wanted to laugh.

'Look at the state of this place, Sam,' she said, thinking she'd rather shove a spoon up her bottom than have him make her a cup of tea with those grubby fingers touching the teabag. 'No, leave it to me. I'll do it. Just give me a moment to finish off in here,' said Joan.

She stood still, momentarily distracted by the mound of festering tissues. Sam almost looked spritely as he lurched forward with guilty self-loathing etched on his face. The dirty dog didn't expect immediate redemption; she was going to make him work a little for it.

'No, no, don't you lift another finger, old girl. I'll sort it out right away. Absolutely no problem. You sit down, take the weight off your feet, and tell me all about your week. Did everything go all right? I mean, with the paper and all?'

He emptied the contents of the plastic bag straight onto the settee. Joan watched, flabbergasted, as the contents of the milk container sloshed around before coming to rest as he scooped up his dirty tissues and rammed them into the plastic bag, before standing up and wiping his hands on his grubby, greasy trousers. Joan thought she was going to gag. Sam stood there, grinning like a small child excited about Christmas or a dog, tail wagging and desperate to go and piss up a tree. Joan wanted to remind him why she had left in the first place. How had he come to the conclusion it was all about work? Was this his way of denying responsibility? Was he burying his head in the sand?

Joan looked Sam in the eye, took a deep breath and said, 'You know what you did.' Her heart pounded, and where tears would usually have welled up, a steely stare and frozen eyes looked back at Sam.

A standoff. Who would break first? Would he attack her again, or was he sorry?

'I'm sorry, Joan. Please forgive me. You don't have to straight away. I understand. I'm just pleased to have you back. Why don't you put your feet up? I'll tidy up around you. You don't have to tell me if you don't want to. But if you do, you can tell me – how'd it go? Did you get done what you wanted to do?' he asked again.

Chapter 15

Rebecca was hell-bent on making a name for herself at the newspaper. Her half-brother, James, had already managed it, seemingly fairly easily. He had slotted in well in the IT department and, according to her dad, was looking sorted career-wise for the foreseeable future. Her dad proudly boasted that James could stay for as long as he liked. The IT department was his for the taking; he had proved himself more than competent. He was revered and considered almost gifted. It was very unusual for a young man with no previous employment history to waltz into a busy newspaper environment and not be put off or overwhelmed by the snobbish egos and hissy fits of computer-illiterate journalists who didn't know their Adobes from their arseholes.

Rebecca, on the other hand, was going to have to work very hard for her position. Nothing ever landed gift-wrapped in her lap – unlike Daddy's golden boy, James.

Rebecca would always harbour some resentment for her half-brother – and her stepmum, although she was long out of the picture now. Daddy had finally seen sense. Rebecca had become accustomed to acting like a bitch and a spoilt brat from the moment her biological parents split up and James and his mum first came on the scene. They had tried to do the happy family thing. It had never worked. Unfortunately, old habits were hard to quit, and Rebecca had forgotten how not to be a manipulative cow, so that didn't change at all when the stepmum left the scene. Perhaps the ill feelings wouldn't have developed had her dad not split up with her mum. Perhaps it was her fault, she sometimes thought. She would need serious amounts of alcohol or drugs or therapy before she ever admitted that to anyone, though.

Through subtle pressure from the Russian owners, the editor was advised to shoehorn Rebecca into the main team of writers, even though there really weren't any current vacancies. This didn't go down well with Stuart, who thought the whole situation stank. So did the editor, who gesticulated wildly his frustration whilst receiving definite instructions over the phone, making faces to Stuart and tapping his pen on his computer screen that showed a line of text from the powers-that-be, which arrived via email simultaneously saying to expect a girl to start and it was their job to accommodate her. There were no ifs or buts.

They both conceded that James had been a success, but slotting the girl into the team of writers they currently had was a different kettle of fish entirely.

'You'll have to let her shadow you,' said the editor bluntly to Stuart.

'Over my dead body,' replied Stuart, not willing to chaperone some rich bitch born with a silver spoon in her mouth.

The editor looked to Stuart for support and understanding. He knew Stuart was generally full of hot air, and given time would be the most likely person at the paper to take the girl under his wing and show her the ropes.

'Listen, Stuart, my old mucker, will you do this for me? A little favour. My hands are tied.' The editor held his wrists up together, pulling a sad face at Stuart, like a prisoner in handcuffs. 'I think this is the start of the end for me,' he said, thinking he was losing control of the paper.

Stuart, who was against the whole 'jobs for the boys' old-boys' network, said, 'It's probably not always about you. More likely it's not what you know but who you blow.'

'Bloody hell, old man, that's a bit strong from you,' said the editor.

'Well, how else do you explain it? You used to have to earn respect. And besides, she doesn't have the experience.'

Rebecca only barely had the qualifications, and she hadn't graduated with flying colours like the rest of the writers, all of whom had various writing published, ranging from poetry to novels and blogs. They all had outstanding literary credentials and qualifications, and she didn't.

The editor had noticed Stuart seemed less patient and a little more stressed recently. The developing rush hour crush project and his relationship with his old school friend Joan seemed to be having both a positive and negative effect on him. He was right to be annoyed by the situation with Rebecca, but in the past it would have been Stuart who was determined to make it work and did his best to include her. He would have been the first to give her a chance, but now he just seemed slightly distracted, more reluctant and inappreciably bitter, angry and resentful, which was quite unlike him.

The editor went to great lengths to explain that whilst Rebecca became familiar with the paper, and all the procedures and protocol and staff, she would have to make do with shadowing Stuart. They tried to make a joke of it, suggesting it was best to stand downwind. Stuart was a bit like a loveable old Labrador, but this attempt at humour was met with icy disdain. Rebecca didn't do scatological humour.

'Do you have trouble controlling your bowels or something?' Rebecca asked, as if talking to an aged, deaf granny. 'Oh, that was a joke, right? Absolutely hilarious!' She smiled like she'd just inhaled old Labrador gas.

Both the editor and Stuart looked at each other, equally wounded by the razor-sharp, barbed rebuke. They were left licking their lacerations whilst feeling slightly embarrassed. The office, meanwhile, prickled with interest as this new ice queen launched herself onto the scene with breath-taking mustard. That little outburst ensured they would include her in as much as possible. Everybody did. But both Stuart and the editor hoped Rebecca would soon drown in the mountain of mindless scraps they would feed her – and quit, hopefully. They really didn't warm to her. But unfortunately, Rebecca didn't see her career path panning out that way. She saw herself learning Stuart's role in order to replace him, unless one of the better, more exotic main sections had an opening. She didn't really want to wait, however. She felt she was better than that. Sooner or later, she wanted the editor's job too.

In the meantime, Rebecca wanted to get writing straight away and get her articles in the paper. She wanted to see her name in print. She didn't care what she had to write about – how hard could it be? Besides, why should she wait, especially as they kept that useless old duffer Stuart hanging around. She resented him. She didn't like the fact he had a central desk. She didn't like that he was popular in the office and people confided in him and listened to his council. She didn't like the way he had his own personal collection of junk in the cupboards out back. She didn't like the way the editor seemed to listen to him. She didn't like that he was respected and was some sort of legend around the paper. She wanted to get rid of him. He was a relic anyway. And she sensed Stuart didn't like her either. He had judged her. He'd seen something going on with her and the office stud (ex-footballer Paul from the sports team) in her first week. Stuart didn't know exactly what he'd seen – it might have been sexual or drug-related – but whatever he thought he'd seen, she didn't want him mentioning it or holding it against her. It left her feeling vulnerable.

Rebecca lived in the hipster part of London, in a converted warehouse near Shoreditch. She had a semi-partner, a fuck buddy, but because she was so carefree, she could, and regularly did, pick up a one-night stand. She would leave them after the deed was done in the middle of the night or the next morning, or she'd bring them home if her boyfriend was away – either way, without a worry in the world.

At the paper she was soon queen bee of the partygoers who frequented many bars in London, doing coke and champagne and gin. They held court whilst looking down their noses at any friends or colleagues who had to leave early, or who had less disposable income, or who didn't fit their idea of cool or good-looking – and especially those who'd had the misfortune to fall in love and get in a serious relationship. They were the losers who had lost the plot. It was all about the career – right here, right now, that was where it was at. Queen Bee had decreed that from now on any male or female in the office who didn't agree with her new world order was fair game. Her crew didn't have the courage to challenge her, and they also vaguely appreciated the ideology she peddled. Her team of Nazis didn't see themselves settling down for a very long time, if ever, and kids were disgusting things that did not even register on their radar – ironically, quite close to Stuart's thinking once upon a time.

Rebecca made it absolutely clear to her cohorts that she planned to oust Stuart, and when she did, she would become more powerful. The short term aim was to win the ear of the editor. She joked perhaps she would lead Stuart astray, if need be, to get her own way. Her minions joked she would 'take one for the team'. She was deadly serious, though, when she replied that she would. It was one of the many ideas she was happily formulating.

After boarding school, Daddy had paid for Rebecca to go to university; that she'd completed her degree was seen as something of a miracle. Her father was proud of himself for investing so much money in her. He wasn't such a failure. She was quite popular with at least two of her lecturers, so that probably helped as well. The social life had been quite good too. After graduation, Rebecca and a group of her friends had set off travelling around Asia all summer, and in the winter they planned to go and do chalet work in Avoriaz for the ski season. Her life was mapped out in the short term. After the ski season ended, she thought perhaps she could head to Ibiza for the summer.

Then she was invited to Daddy's party at the newspaper in New York; he was retiring or something boring, and it would mean a lot to him if she was there. She made out it was 'like, a really big deal, like, and really not convenient timing'. So he said he'd fly her business class and give her some spending money. Her stepbrother had agreed to be there, and she didn't want to be outdone or miss out on anything, especially not to James.

When she arrived, she acted like she was the first person to have suffered from jetlag. This was partly down to having dosed herself up on sleeping pills and slept for ten hours solid, which had completely screwed her body clock. She acted like her usual self around her father and brother at the party; her dad found her rather amusing, but her brother thought she was a drama queen. Everything was so dramatic with her. As far as James could tell, the world had nearly ended and everything was a total catastrophe because the plane was a little late, she was beyond tired, and she'd become distracted at the hotel and had only had an hour or so to get ready before the party. Total disaster. First World problems, huh?

'Nice to see you, sis,' he said sarcastically, clinking his bottle of Bud against her glass of bubbles. She tutted at him as if he had nearly smashed her glass. He skulked off, having decided to leave his dad in the charming company of his stepsister.

'What's that in his face?' Rebecca asked her dad, noticing the piercing for the first time.

'He's going through a phase,' said her dad, like a parent still adjusting to having babies.

The party in New York was a lavish affair. They certainly seemed to know how to party, which came as something of a surprise to Rebecca. The free bar, DJs, celebrities and beautiful people were a step up from some of the student shindigs she had been subjected to over the last few years. Her dad introduced her to Alexei the Russian owner of the paper. He looked like some sort of dodgy politician and was flanked by even more shady-looking security guys. The Russian owner then in turn introduced Rebecca to his sulky, miserable son, who looked like a villain from a Harry Potter film. Alexei, happy with his matchmaking attempts, took Rebecca's father to one side and joked, 'The kids make a fine couple.' Rebecca's dad was unsure whether he or the Russian should be the most concerned.

Rebecca – not overly familiar with liaising with billionaire- tycoon offspring – switched to her default setting, bragging that her life was one epic party of getting high and swimming with turtles in Thailand.

The young man, Artem was temporarily stunned by the girl's self-confidence and hair flicks and pouting lips and wandering eyes. She boasted that her foreseeable future would mainly consist of being a hedonistic party-girl all summer and then an ice-cool snowboard bum come the winter.

'Totally wiped out on the slopes, man. Doing vodka shots all night, and getting "sick" air or wasted in a car in a storm on the side of a mountain. Totally epic, man.'

Artem began to lose interest. He was all about the billions he was worth and what he could buy and how much a mountain would cost him should he wish to buy one. Then perhaps people could pay him to ski, eat and live on it. He couldn't comprehend working, being a chalet girl or boy and having to serve other people. That was so far down the food chain, almost like being a slave.

Rebecca then realised he was looking down his nose at her, albeit while being slightly charmed by her quaintness, the poor little slave girl. With this, she rapidly changed tack, suggesting that when she was good and ready she would probably get a normal job, doing boring things, getting boring money. That was probably what her life would end up being like, predictable and boring. And then she would get old and have a family.

Artem, smirking, suggested, 'You could always marry a wealthy billionaire, then you wouldn't need to work.'

She wasn't sure whether this was a chat-up line or a put-down, and replied, 'That sounds really boring, and being a kept woman is so backwards.'

But then something else stirred inside her. Would it really be that bad? She visualised herself walking through a palace, draped in a fine silk dress, on polished marbled flooring, diamonds and gold around her neck, on her fingers and through her ears, like a scene from a perfume advert – falling into a lavish indoor swimming pool, whilst outside there would be beautiful horses in the stables next to the tennis court, near the helipad, not far from the garage full of Ferraris and Bugattis and Range Rovers and Bentleys. This might be a golden opportunity, she realised. What was the worst that could happen? Being a billionaire's missus definitely wouldn't be that bad.

Slightly ruffled, Artem suggested he wasn't boring, and she joked that she thought he probably was. So he suggested the two of them sneak off for a joint in the loo. There, they talked about married life and work a little more, mostly about what his life would be like, meeting pointless celebrities and rich girls and royalty. His life was mapped out for him too. He felt like he couldn't really control his own destiny. This was when he demonstrated a touch of self-depreciation as he noted that most people he met were spoilt and vacuous like him. They knew no other way. They were all like him: shallow and plastic, restrained and fake, it was an idealistic fantasy, a fabricated monster, just some realised that was their lives and others simply didn't care. He liked common girls, like Rebecca, who were free to do what they wanted with whoever. He also liked her bitchy, catty nature. She was like someone from his world who had it all and yet didn't. It was like she was the billionaire, she owned the world. He wondered if he could buy her enough that she would never want for any more. Could he buy her?

Rebecca thought she might be able to get him to fall in love with her. Treat them mean and keep them keen.

He suggested he could easily get her a good job at either of his family's newspapers, in the UK or the American counterpart 'The New York Metro', whenever she wanted it. It was all going to be part of his media empire to look after, sooner or later. 'Maybe one day you could help me run it,' he said, picking up on the interest showing on Rebecca's face.

They were getting high. He was sitting on the toilet, his own little throne, and she was standing with her back to the door. As they got more stoned, Rebecca teased him about her being the boss and him telling her what to do. As they relaxed and giggled, she unexpectedly shimmied her knickers off and hoisted up her dress and straddled his legs. He was unsure how to react at first, stuck somewhere between feeling quite stoned and self-conscious, and also not sure he wanted to get his suit dirty.

Rebecca leant forward, gently biting his bottom lip, and then took a handful of his hair, pulled his head to one side and whispered lustily in his ear, 'You are the owner and I'm merely the boss. We need someone to take control of this situation and conduct things in an orderly fashion. Someone really needs to take the initiative. You've led by example before, haven't you?'

'Yes,' he said, remembering his friend Olaf's eighteenth birthday party and the high-class prostitutes his cousin had paid for. But this was entirely different, unpaid for and in a toilet. His dad would not approve. This turned him on.

Rebecca was desperate for a decent story to get a foothold in the dark world of tabloid journalism. She was young, hungry, determined, carefree and ruthless, and would do anything with anyone to get to the top and get the job done. She knew all too well of the blog Joan had created – with a lot of help from her amazing brother James, according to her father – and had learnt the history behind Stuart's articles and the rush hour crush section. She had read Joan's blog and had watched with pity and scorn how the sad lady from a small town had struggled with her feeble quest. All the while, whilst she thought it was utterly ridiculous and pathetic, something kept clawing her back. It was like she loved to hate the daily feature. A scab she couldn't help picking. A guilty pleasure.

Rebecca had heard, through office gossip and from her darling little brother, that this Joan woman was connected to someone far more on Rebecca's wavelength. She'd even seen some of the stuff he'd written on her site before it got taken down, and the rumour that he was behind all the shouting she'd heard between the editor and old Stuart made her even more interested in meeting this Sam fellow. If he hated the rush hour crushes and Stuart as much as her, he must be okay, thought Rebecca. She wouldn't think twice about crushing the whole rush hour crush thing. It was nonsense, rubbish, a waste of paper, and she wouldn't mind ridiculing all those connected with it en route to its total destruction. She had already been blocked and kicked off the blog for poking fun. James had called her a troll; he was very cross with her and warned her he would tell the editor and Stuart if he ever caught her doing that again.

No one had ever got together because of the paper. The whole thing was a failure, a desperate, heartfelt, emotional failure. She spent hours getting drunk and pouring scorn on any colleague who showed even the slightest whiff of interest or sympathy with the rush hour crushes.

Then, one evening, she devised a clever stitch-up. Rebecca knew of the village nutter who dressed up like a Highlander, and thought the whole thing was laughable. She decided to pretend someone had actually seen and taken a liking to this William Wallace – when in reality it was just going to be her fabricating a story and playing a game. It was a wicked trick. If it got too serious or heavy, she could pull the plug. But if it went well and all played out just right, perhaps it might help her get her name in print, and maybe make Stuart, William, the editor, Joan and even her brother look foolish. Either way, they were now innocent bystanders added to Rebecca's spite list of people to try to take for a ride. If she could dupe them then possibly the readers would be fooled too. All of them would be caught up in her journalistic web of lies.

He must have collapsed out the back of the office in one of the storerooms where the servers and his old computers were. She heard the crash and went to investigate and see what the commotion was. No one else was up that end of the office at the time, just her. Rebecca saw him slumped on the floor against an old grey filing cabinet. His face was sagging lopsided, his eyes panicked, classic heart attack symptoms.

She calmly felt for a pulse, taking her time, being careful and thorough; his flesh felt all bristly, warm and alive under her fingertips. She looked at him, knowing he was weak and vulnerable. He murmured something completely inaudible and incomprehensible. She wouldn't rush. She felt his pathetic wisps of breath on the back of her hand. She wouldn't do anything quickly at all. She wouldn't do anything. She should react. She should react much more quickly. The miniscule amount of compassion she once had as an innocent child threatened to awaken and overpower the malice and spite, but then she remembered his face and the way he'd looked at her ever since he met her, but especially since he'd seen her in the cupboard that time with Jamie. His judgemental eyes. He was looking at her the same way now. Searching. She tried to gently close his eyes, like they do with dead people in the movies, but he opened them again defiantly and tried to murmur something. She imagined him saying, 'Get help.' She wouldn't. She was quite aware that every second was vital if she was desperate to save him, but she wasn't. He was one step closer to becoming one less obstacle for her to deal with in her mental chess game.

And Stuart knew it. His life was in her hands, and every moment she wasted made it more likely he would die or at least be part destroyed. He knew it and so did she, and he knew that too. A tear rolled down his cheek.

Rebecca thought about peeing on him. Whoever came and found him would think he'd had an accident. His final action. She patted him on the cheek, looking at his slightly crooked tie. The old duffer always looked smart, she had to give him that. She stood up straight and, without looking back, stepped over his stricken form and slowly made her way back to her desk. Nobody seemed to have notice her leave her chair. No one knew she had been out the back and seen Stuart there. She hadn't heard the phones ring either.

She sat back down and twiddled a pen for a while and sketched a flowery, curly penis in her diary. Staring at a cupboard door, she contemplated what to do at the weekend. Annoyingly, her heartbeat began to become more pronounced as the adrenalin started to kick in. She wanted to enjoy the moment and relax for a few minutes longer, but the thought that at any second the door might swing open and Stuart would stagger out was making her excited. This game, how long could they play it?

She waited a while longer, trying to remain calm. Still not rushing. Still not doing anything. Should she just phone an ambulance and just not say anything listening to the call operator asking what the emergency was? Should she start shouting and making a song and dance, running around hysterically? She imagined a damsel in distress in an old black-and-white movie. She wasn't that good at acting, and besides, plenty of colleagues knew her real feelings for the old man. Should she do a general 'all floors' tannoy announcement, asking for help? She felt strangely euphoric as she looked at his desk, alone in the room. She clicked her mouse a few times and checked her emails. Then she leant forward and picked up her mobile phone, selecting a number she'd called a few days ago.

'Hi, Sam? It's Rebecca from the *Metro* newspaper. Listen, do you fancy meeting up for a beer? I've got some things I want to run past you.'

The editor made the long, lonely walk to the pulpit. No amount of practice and public-speaking experience can prepare someone for the walk at such an event. The butterflies, the legs turning from concrete to jelly. The knowledge that all eyes are on you. You are the centre of attention. You. They are all awaiting you. What are you going to say at the funeral of someone they held dear? What makes you so special?

The church stank of incense and the editor couldn't help thinking that his old friend would have hated such an occasion. Instead, he was the guest of honour. It was so black and sad. So stifled, stuffy and restrained. Finally, the editor was there. The church looked full. Briefly, he scanned the room, gulping some saliva to lubricate the vocal cords.

'I've had the absolute pleasure of calling Stuart not only a colleague but a friend for the best part of forty years. He was more like a brother or a partner to me, someone I'd hoped would be an essential cog in the clockwork of my life for a good while longer.'

As the editor spoke, his emotion resonated with the vast majority of the congregation. Tears streamed down Joan's cheeks. William, also weeping, searched his pockets for spare tissues to pass to Joan. The church was full, mostly with ex-colleagues from the paper, but also a few elderly relatives.

The editor carefully described joining the paper a little after Stuart as a young man. He was something of a wild child, whereas Stuart was the newspaper's shiny, new golden boy. His first few articles had been really well received; his attention to detail while presenting the full picture and his ability to immerse the reader in the feel of his writing really made him stand out.

Rebecca had switched off already. She was only there because the rest of the employees from the paper were and it promised to be a bit of a knees-up afterwards. 'You can't beat a good funeral for an excuse to get wasted,' she said.

The editor briefly described what he thought marked Stuart out from himself and almost all other writers in journalism. He reminisced that in his early days he wrote an article about a young man who was commonly seen walking about town in full tartan. It was a less-than-sympathetic article about the village nut case, and other antiheroes who stood out around the local area, like 'Don the tramp' and the 'black-white woman' who dressed all in white. The article didn't present the full facts. It took the mickey, and didn't give the full picture about what had caused these people to be seen the way they were, and that drove Stuart nuts.

'It was the first time anyone had told me off or put me straight,' said the editor, becoming animated. 'Stuart was a kind, gentle man – but a man of principle, and if something was wrong, he would let you know about it. That was the difference between Stuart and everyone else. "You have to stand up for what you once stood for" – that was one of his favourite mantras.

'He pulled rank on me and said he'd rewrite my article. He said I'd still be able to publish it under my name, but he wouldn't let me submit my original article. I didn't listen and submitted it anyway. The then editor ripped me a new arsehole. Sorry, vicar…' said the editor, remembering where he was as the congregation giggled and gasped.

'He threw it back at me, so Stuart took me to one side and laid it out straight for me. We went out together and met the young man and learnt the full facts, and then I saw the bigger picture. Stuart's article was well received, even though it was in my name. It was the start I needed and the most valuable of lessons. We went on to become very good friends with one of the targets of ridicule in my article. In fact…' said the editor, acknowledging William, 'him being here today is testament to the strength of friendship and the high regard those that met Stuart usually held him in. He was the opposite of gutter press.'

Sam really didn't mind Joan going to the funeral. He was the happiest he'd been for a long time. Seeing Joan so hurt and cut-up proved how much she had liked Stuart, and the writer no longer being around meant there was little to no chance of her leaving him again. He was over the moon. He even enjoyed displaying a little mock sympathy and crocodile comfort towards Joan. And to top it all off, his new friend at the paper was likely to inform him of any of the sycophantic ghastliness that prevailed in the lead up to Stuart's funeral. Finally, there was someone in his life who appreciated his cynicism.

Nikki, Sophie, Janet and William were all sitting around Joan and waiting to speak with the editor, who'd made a really lovely speech. It wouldn't be right to leave having not conveyed sympathy for the pain he too was suffering. He'd even mentioned the rush hour crush articles and how pleased he was his special old friend had found such happiness in one of his projects in what turned out to be the final days of his life.

Stuart had confided a lot in the editor, far more than the editor would ever reveal. He knew, for example, about Stuart's lifelong love for Joan. Stuart would have told him to tell Joan whilst he was alive had he wanted him to ever reveal his true feelings. Joan could tell the editor wanted to say more. It was written across his face, which was etched with grief. There was much he wanted tell her about what her old friend had confided. She wanted to know everything too, the way you do when you lose a loved one: you want to know everything. Even looking at their handwriting on old letters or remembering the peculiar way they held a cup of tea or brushed their teeth. Given the chance, you would re-watch the memory again and again, until you got bored and it vanished, and then you'd wish to see it all over again. Such is the fickleness of the lives we lead, constantly wishing time away and not appreciating the little things until they are gone. This thought made Joan's heart ache even more. What had she done?

Afterwards they all agreed to go back to the editor's house. It would be far easier to chat and relax away from the oppressive, pressing stares of religious relics hanging from the rafters and etched into walls or painted on glass.

As Joan made her way back from the toilet to her sister and William, who were waiting in the lounge with a nice cup of tea, she marvelled at the splendour of the house. It was perhaps the nicest, cleanest, most modern shoebox she had ever been in. Small, but amazingly high, like a little house that had been hollowed out. Light streamed in through large glass doors that opened the rear of the house up to the world. The garden was boxed in by clean, water-blasted brick walls and had a neatly manicured lawn with inviting garden furniture arranged thoughtfully, desperate for loungers and sunny weather to end their redundancy. Her eye was drawn to an old article in a fairly plain black frame on the wall. Joan looked at the date. She would have still been with Roy when it was written. She started to read.

What makes the child into the person we become?

Colin, the youngest of the two Waverley boys, was born a month premature which may explain his impatient nature. He repeatedly kicked the back of the driver's seat; relieving his boredom, as the car was packed for the family's expedition to Scotland. A clip round the ear interrupted the beat as his father barked "look at my bloody seat!" A dull scuff marked the spot ... the car was crammed with everything bar the kitchen sink... Colin's mum Iris sprung to his defence "don't be so hard on the boy" as she tried to stuff in even more essentials.

Patrick ran through his check list for the 100th time

1. Prepare a route map.

2. Pack the tent

3. Pack fishing rods.

4. Frisbee and footballs......

Had he already packed them into the boot? He couldn't remember! Iris then presented a wicker basket containing three meals to eat en route to be kept at her side. However these too were wedged in the back for the duration of the 10 hour journey; long enough for the egg sandwiches to form a lasting memory for all the family!

They arrived slightly later than expected, mostly due to Colin's frequent need to urinate. Unfortunately the campsite was poorly lit ... the weary travellers looked at Patrick and realised to erect a tent in darkness was not part of his plan. In fact they had neither torches nor camper gas lights. Iris was fuming she crossly watched them attempting to pitch the tent in the light of the cars headlights. They quickly fell asleep, waking early to feast on Iris's cold banquet. Patrick was soon busy scribbling a new list of essentials to buy commenting 'isn't it great to be so free. Whatever we need we can just go and buy," Iris was still in a mood and wasn't about to fall for his nonchalant attitude.

Colin and Ryan meanwhile went to find somewhere to wee not fazed by their feet being soaked by the morning dew in the early morning mist. Patrick consulted his itinerary, he had meticulously planned to visit many interesting places, not forgetting the need for toilet breaks and a little shopping! But like most best laid plans, the first day was spent driving, searching for parking spots and of course purchasing those essentials. This time it was Iris's fault spending forever in the shops ... she glared at Patrick this was never to be her idea of a holiday... they ate in stony silence... culminating in a blazing row...the boys meanwhile chatted about cowboys and Indians.

No one slept well that night. Iris grumbled that this was the worst holiday ever and why hadn't they gone to Majorca like their neighbours? Patrick was still in the doghouse.

Unfortunately they all knew the reasons "prickly heat ... do you remember Margate?" Patrick just knew he had not the right constitution he was too fair skinned and allergic to sun creams. So a *visit to the castle would have to suffice. After another prolonged journey (more toilet stops) the boys tumbled out the car like excited puppies awestruck by the monument they bounded off to explore. Their parents quickly returned to their row... when better than a family holiday to clear all those skeletons from the cupboard ...undeterred the boys tore off running around re-enacting titanic battles, having the time of their lives.*

Later that evening, as peace was returning to the family, Ryan mentioned feeling poorly. His parents thought it was probably just a bug, a bit of food poisoning or an allergy. No one noticed the rash. It was agreed to return home, cut short the holiday, the weather was awful anyway, and the long journey would probably help Ryan to 'sleep it off'. But then they would need to sort out who would drop Colin at school if Ryan was ill for a few days. By the time they hit the service station for a toilet break Ryan's condition had worsened to the degree that they knew something was very wrong. Ryan didn't make it back to school.... nor home.

Colin's family fell apart, the joy torn from their hearts, their little family was no more, a 1/4 had been snatched away and would always be missed. Colin's parents did their best to distract him, encouraging him to read more. However he lived in his memory, with Ryan, running around the castle like brave Scottish warriors, fighting off evil English invaders, young heroes if only they had not left so quickly ... Ryan may have been ok!

Colin was gradually changing, he emerged like a butterfly from a pupa until one day he became the hero William Wallace, to be mutilated by the English, not just killed. That was what should have happened ... he wished he had died not Ryan. He could have sacrificed himself for the good of the family. That's what William Wallace would have done. Colin believed no one would have suffered as much, his poor parents would have been spared the grief of losing their favourite son. He blamed the English doctors they should have saved Ryan. His brother was his first friend, his best friend, and, for some time probably his only friend. The fiend meningitis meant nothing to him.

He wanted to put on his armour, pick up his sword, gather an army and do battle with the English foe, against those 'men in giant tortoise shells'. Colin became engrossed in his history books, searching for the source of the 'giant tortoise shell' warriors. His parents, overwhelmed by their grief, barely noticed his obsession unaware that Ryan had been taken by the 'men in giant tortoise shells'!

Colin's behaviour became more and more bizarre. He started to imitate one of his teachers who had a strong Glaswegian accent, he tried on his mum's skirts and dad's checked shirts (anything that resembled tartan). The family became more insular, hiding their pain and embarrassment from the public. The changes peaked one Christmas; his best present was a Scottish dressing up outfit, his first kilt, this completely overshadowed the rush of emotion he'd felt unwrapping a toy tortoise. Patrick and Iris consoled themselves believing that it was just a stage Colin would grow out of. Instead it developed, he was possessed, he called himself William and liked nothing more than to dress up as a Scotsman.

William's hatred and bitterness faded over time, years past but the obsession remained. It was a habit that had evolved from his remembrance of Ryan. He would never forget his brother and would never change. Why should he? He collected clothing and items that fitted his adopted character, William Wallace. It was his purpose, his raison d'être, it was his reason for living.

So the next time you notice someone who doesn't conform to your idea of normal, it's worth reflecting, is their eccentricity just an expression of personality or the logical result of life's pain and heartbreak? Those of us with preconceptions are often the misfits...... "Judge not lest ye be judged" .... It's best to live.... and let live.

Joan read through cloudy, teary eyes, Stuart's voice resonating in her mind.

When she finished, she became aware that William and the editor were standing beside her, reading the piece as well.

William looked at her, his face a picture of heartfelt tenderness and sincerity, and he said, 'Come now, Joan, dry your eyes, dear – his writing really wasn't that bad. I mean, the article wasn't all that bad. I've certainly read worse. Not his writing. Oh God, what have I said?'

They both looked shocked and then laughed, the laugh people do at funerals with close friends and family, the sort of relieved, unhinged laugh that's slightly maniacal and hysterical.

Nikki and Sophie walked up to Joan.

'Are you okay, Mum?' Sophie asked.

'I'm not your mum,' said Joan.

Chapter 16

Rebecca sat nonchalantly reading through Stuart's old notes and emails. She didn't respond to friends asking how he was doing and ignored requests for dates for potential lunch meetings. Delete. Delete. Delete. Some of these people would probably never know what had happened to Stuart. Best case scenario was they'd presume he'd retired and was living the good life. Delete. She didn't care. 'How you doing, old man?' Delete. 'Two free tickets for the West Ham FA Cup game, if you're about, mate?' Delete. 'Been a long time, no hear…' she would read in some. *Dead,* she responded in her head, feeling impervious.

The last week had been a real eye-opener for Rebecca. The editor was away on extended compassionate leave, and the majority of the office were still moping around like the world had been soiled. This had led to Rebecca realising just how little input was needed in the day-to-day running of the paper. The bulk was taken care of by people just doing their jobs. It was a well-oiled machine. *They've had it easy,* she thought. She would write an email to her Russian friend, telling him they were all lazy and asking why exactly they ran the show and when they were going to discuss 'rises and mutual benefit packages' and their possible world domination again.

Rebecca's finger froze. She was snapped out of her mindless email cleansing when she stumbled across a little pot of gold in the form of an email Stuart had sent himself with an unpublished article and an unused 'good to print' code. This was a system put in place to ensure manuscripts were double-checked before going to print. Whilst the editor was away, nothing could go to press without a GTP (good to print) code, which this unpublished article by Stuart had proudly emblazoned across the top. *Jackpot,* Rebecca thought. She could write an article, any article, attach the code and theoretically it would go straight to print with no questions asked, as it had the allotted code signed off by a department head. She was over the moon. Finally, she could write a piece, and if all went well she'd be properly announced onto the journalistic scene. No more playing second fiddle. She'd have proven herself.

Rebecca read through Stuart's intended article, the last piece he had ever written, a testament to all his years of practice and experience. It was as heartfelt an article as he had ever written, his swansong.

Rubbish, boring, gushing, she decided. Just another pointless, self-serving update on the trials and tribulations of Joan and the poxy rush hour crushes.

Rebecca printed out the composition and then started writing notes and putting harsh red lines through sections. She sat at her desk, referencing scribbled notes from her little black Moleskine diary. Her sprawling handwriting danced a leggy spider's walk across the pages. She wrote open questions to herself, suggesting she could write about Joan's past. There was some sort of marriage break-up to explore. Did Joan lose interest, rather than her husband leaving her?

When she was finished, Rebecca looked at her draft article and smiled. She'd successful stripped back the existing article and rewritten it completely, changing both the mood and direction of Stuart's work. In her mind, it really wasn't that bad – a bit of padding out and *voilà*. A hatchet job. A few calls and a couple of interviews later and she would be all set, more or less ready to go.

She called Sam and asked if he would like to meet up. Sam couldn't believe his luck. He was all ready for his usual day moving between the settee, bookies and boozer, but this would be so much more fun. He'd have a shower especially. They arranged to meet at a pub quite near Sam and Joan's house, one of the nicer pubs where he wasn't always made entirely welcome. Today would be different, though. With a smart young lady by his side, he'd get preferential treatment.

Sam offered to buy Rebecca a drink, but she said, 'No, no, no, don't be silly, the paper will pay,' handing her bank card to the barman. 'We'll start a tab,' said Rebecca assertively.

Sam couldn't help but think he had won the lottery. The landlord, meanwhile, looked quizzically at the pair of them, wondering why a nice young lady like her would want to be involved with a weirdo like him. This young lady obviously didn't know Sam like he did.

They moved to the side of the pub, next to a big redundant fire. Had it been winter, it would have been nice and cosy, listening to the wood crackling and spitting in the warm yellow flames. But it wasn't particularly cold and the open space just felt a little bit draughty. The settees were large and dark red, soft, deep leather types – the staff often had to check behind the squashed pillows due to patrons losing phones, wallets and other valuables. They took a seat opposite each other, settling in, peeling off layers until they felt comfortable.

Rebecca rooted about in her soft, quilted, chequered shoulder bag, pulling out a fancy A4 leather portfolio. In the bag was also an extra-thin laptop computer. The portfolio was strong and slim, to protect printed articles. Sam noticed the bag and its contents were all designer, very expensive; she looked the part. They probably cost what Joan earnt over several months.

Rebecca started off by saying she had written a piece that was going to print shortly and had hoped to pick his brains.

'Oh, very well done, you,' said Sam, jumping on the opportunity to pay her a compliment.

'Thanks,' Rebecca said, as if genuinely appreciative that someone in the world had recognised her achievements. She didn't need Sam's approval, but accepted it as some sort of offer of mutual, self-serving gratification.

Sam offered to read it, making a song and dance of it being 'his upmost pleasure and an honour'. He said he was more than happy to offer a careful critique, making a mountain of his English qualifications. He was, after all, 'Joan and Stuart's English master'. He smiled a wicked, twisted grin, saying 'good' and 'aha' as he ticked and slashed his way through the article, adding green lines, correcting grammar and highlighting commas and hyphens. He wanted to add some notes too.

'May I?' he asked.

Rebecca duly obliged. 'Go ahead,' she said, thinking she could always delete them again later, along with some of his more flowery terms.

As he talked, read her piece, drank his beer in large gulps and hoovered up fistfuls of peanuts, Rebecca scrutinised him. The semi-liquefied mulch of bitter ale and remnants of dry-roasted peanut powder swirling in his concrete mixer lipped tub under his greasy, manky moustache. What was it about him that Joan was ever attracted to? Rebecca wondered if he'd ever been an attractive man. He was certainly tall, and perhaps dark at some point. She switched off listening to his appraisal of her article and watched his skinny white ankles bobbing up and down, bursting free from his mustard-coloured socks, making way like a strand of wire up his thick woollen trouser legs towards his unimaginable nether regions. Perhaps he was massively endowed, Rebecca thought, smirking to herself.

Sam stopped talking and looked up, aware that Rebecca was looking at him. He smiled, as if flattered by the attention. Perhaps he had read the signs correctly for once and he was actually in here. Straight away he thought about getting her home and having sex with her. It was probably what she wanted, he thought, an experienced older man. Some of these high-powered city girls liked that sort of thing. He had never heard anyone say it to him, but it was entirely plausible in his mind.

Rebecca had an inkling of what Sam was thinking and wanted to laugh. *As if!* But she thought perhaps for once she should just go with the flow. Nothing wrong with building a bit of a relationship. He might prove a good ally, and it would make a nice change not having to add someone to her 'get list'. He always looked and smelt like he had used half a can of Lynx deodorant before their meetings, and his hair was slicked with some sort of hair product. He was disgusting, but he always made an effort on her behalf. The daft, silly old fool – there was no way he would think a younger lady like her would ever be interested in an old man like him. She was being an idiot thinking he thought that. She was wrong.

Rebecca told Sam about her plan to interview Joan. He thought it was a great idea. He praised the work she had already done, but really went to town saying how much he thought Rebecca should ask Joan about her children, health and money, all things she was very sensitive about. He also mentioned the past allegations made against him, which he denied totally, suggesting they were fabricated by Joan's sister as she wanted to control Joan's life. Rebecca agreed his story was entirely plausible – maybe she could interview the bitter lesbian policewoman too. She sounded like an interesting character. Maybe she could use these allegations and suggest Joan was involved.

Sam also relayed a story Joan had told him about a time she had been invited to a squash game and a friend of her ex-husband and his new girlfriend, Nikki, had tried it on with her. It all sounded very swingy. Rebecca thought the conversation was beginning to veer towards old ladies' gossiping. She would humour him for a little longer, but she thought it best to be careful around him going forward, as undoubtedly he had a vindictive side. Maybe the allegations of abuse were true.

'So, you never told me how you and Joan got together?' asked Rebecca.

'Well, my dear, it was an affair of the heart. She was infatuated. It ruined my marriage and career, but these are the mistakes we live for, wouldn't you say?'

Rebecca wasn't sure she could answer his question. 'If you say,' she said, noting his question.

'Are you saying your heart has never led you a merry dance? I mean to say, haven't you ever acted and regretted it later?' asked Sam.

It was his turn to ask the probing questions. Subtly, he caught the barman's eye, who in turn called over, 'Same again?'

Rebecca looked up from her notes and realised Sam was looking from his empty glass to her and back, like a hungry puppy. 'Yes, please,' she said to the barman, before replying to Sam. 'What were we saying?'

Sam smiled. 'You were about to tell me all about the naughty things your heart wanted you to do but your brain wouldn't let you.'

'Mr Hothouse, I'm really not that kind of girl. I do exactly what I want.'

Sam roared with laughter, leaning back in his chair and slapping his drain-pipe legs.

Slightly embarrassed by his seal-like laughter and the attention he was attracting, Rebecca raised her eyebrows, hoping he might tone it down a little. She wanted to find out why he was so nasty to the woman he had known virtually all her life. Was it just a male/female thing, a relationship born out of convenience? Why did they bother? Why not be with someone you liked? She couldn't get her head around it. Rebecca felt amazed to have met someone seemingly more twisted and more corrupt than her. Whilst thinking about how deplorable Sam was, she had a glimmer of self-realisation. Guilt, even. The second time it had threatened to show itself. Weakness, like the stirring she'd felt when she saw Stuart dying and did nothing. She snapped herself out of it. *Must get a grip,* she thought.

'Do you fancy a shot?' she said, trying to break the weak insanity that had crept into her mind. She got up and made her way to the bar. 'Four jägerbombs, please.'

The barman checked the time on the old cuckoo clock on the wall, as if her request wasn't allowed before a certain hour. Rebecca looked at Sam, who was leaning back in the chair with his long arms and hands crossed behind his head, like he was trying to look cool, calm and collected, but really he looked like he was at the top of a very slow and painful sit-up exercise. She couldn't help but laugh at him. *It's probably the booze,* she thought. However stupid and disgusting he was, he was kind of funny. She found herself laughing at him rather than with him. He didn't seem to mind either way and just chuckled along with her.

Rebecca thought she was somehow immune from his advances. Safe, even. Protected by the paper and her own sense of self appreciation. He was old and she was young. He wouldn't be interested in her. But then she thought perhaps he could be an opportunistic predator.

Then events became blurry. She remembered paying the bill and the barman sharing a strange sort of 'in the know' joke or suggestion with Sam, saying, 'Maybe I'll see you later.' Rebecca presumed that meant Sam was planning on going back to the pub after showing her whatever it was he had to show her at his home. She giggled like a schoolgirl at how rude that sounded, not realising she was fast becoming entangled in the web and that the barman had been giving her heavy measures on Sam's advice. A secret code shared between fellow conspirators. She was oblivious seeing him later meant he hoped she wouldn't be conscious. That was his preference, not Sam's. Sam didn't mind his prey awake. He was beyond caring. Pickings had been slim of late. Beggars couldn't be choosers.

Almost immediately after leaving the pub, Rebecca found herself in the back of a car being driven back to Joan's house. She didn't remember ordering a cab; the driver just seemed to be waiting for them. If she had known that was the plan, she'd have ordered one from the firm the newspaper had an account with. She would have received a receipt, making it easy to claim it as an expense.

'You should have said,' said Rebecca, slurring, thinking Sam would understand what she was thinking.

'Said what?' he responded, looking at her, in a quite tipsy state in the back of the car.

'You should have said we were getting a cab.'

The driver was a large, stern-looking Asian man with a very big nose and sprouts of jet-black hair protruding from his ears like thick-bristled paintbrushes. Beads of varying colours hung from the rear-view mirror, there was some sort of laminated photo of a person who looked completely different to him attached to an air vent, and a strong smell of feet was coming from his general direction. Rebecca thought it a little strange she was riding in the back alone, after Sam had got into the front of the taxi rather than sit behind with her. It almost seemed like he and the driver knew each other. The driver and Sam talked in hushed voices, with Sam occasionally swivelling around in the passenger seat to check on Rebecca with a fixed, slightly false smile. The driver seemed to watch her continuously in the mirror rather than watching the road.

Once they slowed to arrive outside Sam's house, Rebecca thought she heard Sam say, 'See you later?' – more like a question than a comment or a goodbye. The driver didn't seem as keen. (This girl was too old and quite aggressive for his liking.) She laughed as the taxi driver rustled around in the door compartments and glovebox as if he had no idea where the receipts were kept. The fact he struggled to pen a receipt and his writing was barely legible caused a great deal of hilarity for Rebecca, much to the driver's bemusement. The receipt had barely any information on it. She wasn't even sure it was in English. Without realising this simple request was possibly enough to have saved her life as one would-be attacker decided to try his luck elsewhere.

Walking towards the house, Sam said they could look at the bits he'd got to show her and perhaps have a coffee, if she was feeling woozy. Then, he suggested, they could call another cab from there when she was done to take her back to her work or home or wherever she wanted to go.

'Are you trying to get rid of me already?' Rebecca joked.

'God no, not at all, my dear,' he replied. 'On the contrary, you are most welcome to stay or Far-Coffee whenever you like,' he added, trying to be funny, making out he had something other than instant gold blend in store, shaking his hands like he was holding coffee beans. She saw this as some kind of old man's joke, a playful innuendo, suggestive flirting. He meant nothing of the sort, obviously.

Sam said he wanted to show Rebecca some pictures of Joan when she was younger. 'She really wasn't that bad back then,' he said. 'And the kids, it will be interesting for you to see them, I'm sure, for research purposes.'

He had an old slide projector he'd borrowed and never returned to school. He had masses of slides he had gathered from his time teaching. He wouldn't show her those, though. Rebecca wasn't the right audience for them. Perhaps just Joan's wedding pictures. He suggested she could use them in the piece.

'I'm sure Joan won't mind me giving you any that you might think could be beneficial. You could scan them, no doubt. She would get them back eventually, right? She's sentimentally attached, I'm sure, but she'd be honoured, you know, if you used them.

'You'll have to excuse the mess. We really don't have much time to do a lot around the place, and well… money is quite tight at the moment and I've not been well. And Joan's not the most domesticated,' said Sam.

'Oh, don't be daft. I'm sure I'll have seen a lot worse,' said Rebecca.

She couldn't remember seeing many. The house was dark, dingy and decrepit, like a student house that had just been tidied up following a massive party. Rebecca didn't fancy drinking coffee out of any of the variety of chipped mugs that sat festering in the sink, half-filled with cold coffee and ashtray water; and the clean ones drying upturned on the discoloured old tea towel wouldn't have been much better, she thought, looking at the manky sponge on the sink and nearly redundant budget washing-up liquid bottle. Someone obviously shopped at one of those ghastly Pound Stretcher places, Rebecca thought. Alcohol would probably be the safest option. Neutralise as many germs as possible, and then go home and drink some bleach.

Sam took full advantage of Rebecca suggesting booze, pouring very generous measures immediately. He debated with himself whether to make a move right there on the settee whilst she was still compos mentis or trying to get her into the bedroom where it was far more comfortable. It depended how pliant she was, he decided. He could bide his time; Joan wouldn't be back for hours.

He said, 'I'll get the old slide projector,' thinking he could shut the curtains and get it nice and dark in the lounge. He went off to the hall to fetch the stick that opened the loft in the hallway, the place where he hid his most incriminating belongings, amongst the bright-yellow fibre-glass insulation.

Rebecca checked out the picture on top of the TV of Joan and the kids. 'That photo was taken a few years ago,' called Rebecca; she was judging it by the clothes Joan and the kids were wearing.

'Sure was,' said Sam.

Rebecca guessed the twins were a similar age to her now. They were nice-looking kids. The sister looked a bit creepy, but she could have been friends with them or gone to school with them in another life. Rebecca couldn't help recognising the slightly detached expression on all of their faces. She could almost hear the photographer shouting, 'Say cheese.'

Sam returned to the lounge carrying a box he'd pulled from the loft. They sat down on the settee in the lounge, Sam scooping up the papers and magazines and whatever else he'd been reading and dropping them by the side of the settee, making a space next to

Rebecca. She'd kind of expected him to pull up a chair next to her or opposite, as the settee was quite snug, and as he sat back she immediately felt he was invading her personal space. Rebecca sat forward on the settee and swivelled slightly, side on, as Sam unfolded his long arms along the back of the settee. Had she stayed sitting back he'd virtually have had his arm around her.

'Why don't you relax a little,' he said, leaning forward and testing the water by patting her leg with his hand. 'There's no need to rush.'

Feeling slightly awkward, Rebecca edged a little further away, moving her leg fractionally out of his reach. 'Actually, I'm here to sort out this article, so is it okay if I just jump straight in and see what you have in the box?'

'Of course, help yourself, my dear,' said Sam, leaning forward and picking up both of their glasses. *A little refill,* he thought.

'Your article is looking really very, very good,' he said, walking back to the kitchen with a swagger.

He paid her another compliment, but she was still sober enough and quick/strong enough to dodge his advances.

He returned with the drinks whilst Rebecca was busying herself looking through the box. It was full of strange pictures. She had the feeling most people get when forced to look at someone else's holiday photos. Pictures in dusty old frames of people she didn't know. They all had slightly sad and twisted faces that coldly, blankly stared back at her. Who were these people? Were they dead? Should she be writing notes? What was the question again?

Suddenly, she felt helpless. She realised she had been really stupid and that she was incredibly vulnerable. No one knew she was there. She isn't even sure where she was. She felt woozy. Tired, even. If she closed her eyes, just for a second, she felt Sam edging closer, almost every time she blinked. She looked at her drink, wondering if drinking the last bit would be enough to send her over the edge. How did she get so drunk? The drink was quite nice, whatever it was. Certainly, it hit the spot.

Rebecca tried to remain calm and flirty and business like as she formulated an exit strategy. She didn't want to raise Sam's suspicions; he must continue to think he had a chance.

She finished her drink and suggested he make her something a bit different. 'Surprise me,' she said. 'I'm just going to the loo. To freshen up.'

'I'll show you where it is.' He reached up to take her hands, hoping to pull her down onto the settee, but she pulled away just in time, their fingertips brushing.

'No need – I've seen it right there in the hallway,' she said, pointing in the direction of the toilet, and with a little suggestive wiggle she trotted off.

Sam got to his feet and immediately she felt his presence bearing down on her, like a massive growing shadow, as she dived into the bathroom, feeling chased. She locked the door.

Sam called out, 'I'll just be in the kitchen making some more drinks.' He thought about what he might have stored away to 'surprise' her with. A concoction of drugs perhaps. Sleeping tablets should do the job. He flicked a couple loose onto the kitchen side and got a spoon to crush them down into a powder.

Rebecca checked her mobile. She had a small amount of battery and some signal. She dialled 999 but stopped short of pressing 'call'. She checked the locked door. Through the frosted glass panels in the door she saw the shadow of Sam fade away. Even the realisation he must have been hovering right outside the toilet, possibly just listening to her in the loo, freaked her out. She was really scared. Her knees were shaking. What could she do? How could she get out of there? Should she call the police straight away? No crime had been committed. Could she phone someone at the paper? Blag her way out? Pretend she was on the phone and just walk straight out? Would he attack her, thinking she was on the phone? She didn't know.

Sam called to her, telling her not to take too long. 'The ice will melt…'

He felt still in the hunt following her suggestive dance. Rebecca wondered how she could have been so stupid. She looked at the bathroom window. It was quite big; she could perhaps fit out of it. Slowly and quietly, she lifted the latches and opened the window wide open. She took off her high-heeled shoes and threw them, one by one, out of the window. She had thought about using them as a weapon to defend herself, but that wasn't an option now. She needed to climb up onto the windowsill. Just as she was about to climb up, thought, she remembered her bag. Her notes, her article and her laptop. 'Shit fuck shit.' She couldn't just leave her bag here; she needed it to work on her article. And she'd just thrown her shoes out of the window. 'Shit,' Rebecca hissed again.

She looked at the lock that moments earlier she had closed as quickly as she could manage. Now she was going to open it again as slowly and silently as possible, as if her life depended on it. She felt an uncontrollable urge to wet herself. The latch gave ever so slightly in millimetre nudges. Slowly, it gave way, until the door was unlocked again and there was nothing stopping Sam coming into the loo. Rebecca pulled the door open a tiny amount, praying there would be no sudden scream of metal on metal, no ear-piercing creak, her heart pounding like never before. As a tiny gap appeared, she imagined Sam's big face suddenly appearing in the crack and she felt a little bit of wee escape and she wanted to cry.

She could see shadows moving in the kitchen and hear cupboard doors being bashed and glasses being arranged and contents being stirred. Rebecca opened the door a little further, until there was just room for her to squeeze out, and silently she tiptoed as quickly as possible into the lounge to retrieve her bag. She picked it up swiftly, hardly breathing for fear of alerting Sam, sneakily creeping like a seasoned burglar through the house. Once she was holding her bag, the buckles chimed and clinked and rattled, and the floorboards creaked and her legs stopped working, and her knees turned to concrete, getting impossibly heavy with every step. She got back to the toilet, shimmied through the gap and quickly locked the door again.

Sam heard something and peeked his head out of the kitchen into the hallway, watching the shadows through the frosted glass in the toilet door. It was his turn to think he must have been hearing things. 'Are you okay in there?'

On the windowsill there was a dusty old blue bowl with scented sticks protruding with long dried out essence faintly emitting. Rebecca moved it quietly along, watching the dust slowly form up like snow on the edges of a well-groomed mountain piste. The paint and fluff build-up felt slightly sticky underhand. She also moved a picture of Joan with Adam and Sophie from when they were slightly older. For the briefest of fleeting moments Rebecca wondered what on earth had happened in Joan's life wishing she was a fly on the wall. The boy was very good looking, she noticed.

She tried to reach the windowsill from the toilet, but it was a bit too low. Not for the first time, Rebecca hitched up her skirt in a toilet, but this time it was out of desperation and self-preservation. Normally, she would take one for the team if it served her purpose, but this was different. It wasn't on her terms. She reached one foot out to the sink, spread her arms out like a spider monkey and managed to step up to the window ledge – knocking an empty soap dispenser into the sink. Rebecca cursed.

'Are you sure you're okay in there?' she heard Sam call, getting closer.

'Yes, fine, thank you,' she replied. 'Maybe turn on the projector, some slides would be good to see now,' she added, hoping she might manage to stall Sam.

She had to go from being a spider stretched out to Alice in Wonderland stepping through a tiny doorway. She estimated there was at least a six-foot drop to the ground outside the window. She sat on the wooden window frame, her legs hanging out of the window, the nylon of her tights on her heels catching against the brickwork side of the house. Microscopic Velcro. She dropped down and landed slightly awkwardly on the gravel path, which was a sobering realisation to the soles of her feet. She walked, bent double, with trepidation along the side of the house, feeling woozy and frightened. At the end of the pathway she felt trapped once again and claustrophobic as the fence seemed to grow higher and higher, the gravel underfoot sharper and more jagged, and the house darker and more foreboding. All the while she could hear Sam shouting and banging on the bathroom door, demanding that she come out of the toilet.

She noticed an old, rusty wheelbarrow and managed to prop it up in the corner where the fence met the house. Desperately, she clambered up, and she had enough height to hook a leg over and scramble over the divide, scratching the inside of her leg on an old wooden splinter on the way down.

Out in the open in front of the house where people could see her, she felt a little braver and safer. She stooped down, running past the front window and up the garden path and then out of the gate and away from the house. Still she could just about hear Sam calling out her name, thinking she was still in the toilet.

She checked the map on her phone as the battery entered the final one per cent. 'Just send me a fucking car,' was the last thing she managed to say as the battery finally ran out of juice.

Rebecca was determined not to make a big thing of the near-encounter, as Sam would be an integral part of her immediate plans. She reminded herself over and over again that nothing had happened. But she couldn't shake the feeling that something bad would have happened had she not escaped. She sent Sam a text explaining she'd had to rush off as she had something of an accident (ladies' problems) and was drunk and embarrassed – hence leaving in such a peculiar fashion.

Sam didn't question it or mind particularly. Women were very strange creatures. Nothing had happened, so there was no need for him to worry. He ended up having quite a good sleep, once he'd climbed into the toilet from the outside and unlocked the door.

In the short term, Rebecca was adamant she would not be seeing Sam again. Especially alone. In the longer term, she would deal with him. She would fucking destroy him. But first she needed to talk to Joan.

'Hi, Joan, thanks for coming to the paper and agreeing to meet and speak with me. It must be quite strange coming back here? God, I feel like I've known you forever. I've heard such a lot about you and am, like, literally your biggest fan.'

'It's quite all right,' said Joan, feeling like she was a celebrity.

'Listen, Joan – is it okay to call you Joan, or is it Mrs Hothouse?'

'Oh God, please just call me Joan.'

'Okay, Joan,' said Rebecca, writing in her diary, 'definitely not Mrs Hothouse.'

'Sam and I have never been married. It just never seemed appropriate really,' said Joan, drifting off as she remembered all the nasty rows and broken promises.

Rebecca watched as Joan seemed to wrestle with the here and now.

'Sam mentioned you stopped by to look at the photos.'

'I did. Thank you for those – I'll return them all to you as soon as the article is finished,' replied Rebecca.

'It's quite all right,' said Joan. 'They're mostly just gathering dust.' She didn't seem to have any emotional attachment to the photos at all.

'I know how hard the last few weeks must have been for you, and to be honest I still don't think I'm really over Stuart leaving us the way he did either. It was just so awfully sad for everyone. But especially you. No one knew him longer, did they? The paper just won't be the same,' Rebecca said tenderly, reaching out a hand to hold Joan's cold, papery skin covered bones in hers, and looking her in the eye for a moment, hoping somewhere in the recesses of her black, wretched heart an emotion would stir and somehow pump a tear from her dried-up, famished ducts.

Joan thought Rebecca seemed quite sincere. She hadn't really considered Stuart's death much from his work colleagues' point of view. She said softly, 'He must have been quite a big figure around the place,' trying to reciprocate the look of compassion Rebecca was giving her.

Again Rebecca reached out. She put a gentle hand on Joan's knee, looking like she wasn't far from losing control of her emotions. 'We all miss him terribly,' she lied.

Joan put her own hand on Rebecca's, smiling sympathetically, and said, 'I know, dear.'

They were now emotionally tied. The touchy-feely emotional foreplay had broken down their barriers.

Rebecca had set up the meeting as a backup plan, just to cover her own back. The idea was to get Joan to sign the permission to print. (Nestled somewhere in the small-print of the form was an agreement that no recompense would be due should Joan find insult or falsehood in the article.) Because Joan thought they were now friends and that they got on so well, she would sign off her permission, thinking the article was going to be kind to her and Stuart – sort of like an obituary and passing of the reigns from the old writer to the new.

Rebecca scribbled in her notes: *Perhaps suggest Joan had an open marriage*. Then came the relationship with Sam. Always hounded by Joan's ex-relationships – especially with Stuart, where there was a suggestion they were more than just friends. Poor Sam. Perhaps that was part of the reason he turned out the way he did? Rebecca wondered whether she should paint Sam as an almost-victim, whilst Joan was the swinging oddball.

Rebecca moved things on slowly and as diplomatically as possible, lying continuously, all the time reinforcing her questions with gentle hands and soft touches and crocodile tears, if only she could force them to rain down her cheeks.

'I wanted to talk to you about the rush hour crushes. I'm a massive fan, and the last thing we want to happen is that all the hard work and progress that's been made by you guys just falls to the wayside and is forgotten in these sad times.'

Joan hadn't really thought about the project much since Stuart had died. All she'd thought was that it was his baby and so perhaps it should be laid to rest with him.

'I'd not really given it much thought,' said Joan.

Rebecca grimaced like she'd tasted something foul, but then empathetically suggested that Joan had to continue. 'You mustn't let all your hard work be for nothing.

'I've started writing a piece, and with your permission I'd like to go over some old ground. You know, sometimes with a fresh set of eyes hidden gems can be found, you can turn over some new stones.'

Even Rebecca was unsure what she meant. She was just determined to build some sort of trust and agreement between her and Joan. She had to make her think they were friends and singing from the same hymn sheet.

Rebecca looked up from her notes and checked the clock on the wall. 'Joan, can I get you a coffee or a bite to eat at all? I can really recommend the almond croissants – they're delicious.'

Joan smiled. 'Oh, that's very kind of you, but please don't worry on my account. I don't want to take up too much of your time.'

Daft cow, Rebecca thought. *She thinks she's doing me favour.*

'Not at all, I have plenty of time and am feeling peckish.' Rebecca gave Joan a cheeky smile.

'Oh, okay then, if you insist,' said Joan, trying to replicate the cheeky grin.

As Rebecca went off to buy the pastries, Joan clicked her heels and looked around the busy floors, watching the glass lift carrying people from floor to floor. She imagined her old friend travelling in the elevator and a lump formed in her throat. How many times had Stuart taken that lift? Perhaps he'd even sat on that very chair in that canteen. Joan wondered what he would have ordered and whom his friends were. She felt the tears well in her eyes. Perhaps he'd liked Rebecca. She seemed really nice and said kind words and certainly seemed to miss Stuart. *Poor girl,* thought Joan.

Two guys got out of the lift, chatting. One of them was talking loudly and animatedly about imagining his phone vibrating in his pocket.

'But it wasn't, it was just my phone trying to communicate with me subliminally or some shit. God knows, crazy shit – probably getting bored or lonely or something. Sniffing my balls all day. "Hey, I'm here in your pocket. Play with me. Check the time or something." What's even stranger is it wasn't even in that pocket. So I still had to look for it and check to see if it had vibrated or was maybe communicating with my inner leg. Maybe my inner leg was missing my phone and sent messages to my brain, saying, "Check my phone." No one had called either. Still, I checked my emails, messages, phone, Facebook, favourite website. Anyone would think my inner leg was taking control of my body. Maybe it was a beetle in my trousers or... Joan! What are you doing here?'

Joan was snapped from her melancholy. 'Adam!' she said, immediately thinking of her son.

'Er no, not Adam, but you can call me Adam if you like. Are you all right?' said James, Rebecca's brother with the facial piercing and tattoos, as he held out his arms, looking for a cuddle.

He'd always liked Joan and had a genuine interest in the rush hour crushes. Plus, he felt the loss of Stuart and was also missing the editor.

'I'm here with your sister,' said Joan, as if it was quite a big meeting to be proud of.

'Oh my God, poor you! Why on earth are you with her?'

'James!' said Joan, shocked by his comments. He was always such a nice boy. He seemed to have grown and come out of his shell since their first meeting, but he'd never said anything negative about anyone. When she first met him, he'd looked a little surly and perhaps moody, but this impression was soon overcome.

Before he got a chance to say any more, Rebecca hastily appeared, carrying a tray of drinks and food.

'Brother darling, what a lovely surprise. They've let you out your dungeon.'

Rebecca always referred to the IT department as the dungeon, as it was in the basement and had no natural light. Plus it contained her brother, on whom she was far from keen; she felt he deserved locking up and leaving in a dungeon.

Joan noticed the slightly prickly atmosphere and dynamic between the siblings, and straight away was reminded of her own offspring's frosty relationship. They both seemed so nice; it was all very familiar and confusing to Joan.

James sensed his sister's growing resentment towards him for being there, and not wanting to alarm Joan, he said, 'Lovely to see you. We really should have a catch-up soon. Maybe have a chat about your website and stuff?'

Joan really liked the idea. As she'd said to Rebecca, she hadn't thought about the rush hour crush project much since Stuart had died, but just being around the paper and chatting about it with the kids had made her feel so much better – and, in a strange kind of way, a little bit closer to Stuart. She missed him and regretted not having had more time with him and not having been honest with him. But somehow this visit to the newspaper was reconnecting them again.

James fired his sister a glare as his mate from the IT department admired the food being brought out of the canteen by some female guests of the fashion editor. 'We've got to go. I'll catch up with you soon, sister.'

Rebecca didn't respond. She was slightly interested in Adam's geeky IT friend. Maybe she should visit the dungeon sometime.

Rebecca managed to get Joan to reveal all sorts of stuff 'off the record'. There was no 'off the record' as far as Rebecca was concerned. Joan suggested she had enjoyed a very intimate physical relationship with Roy when they were younger. (Rebecca translated that into Joan having quite an insatiable sexual appetite almost that of a nymphomaniac, and when this need for intimacy wasn't being satisfied by Roy Joan knew something wrong with their union.) Joan went to great lengths trying to explain that she understood the pressures on a young man, with a busy job, working long hours, and the arrival of kids, but had maybe become despondent with the lack of affection. Maybe she had wanted more children? Then Nikki came on the scene. But all the time Joan had never stopped loving Roy.

Joan also revealed her childhood crush on Mr Hothouse and all the details of their steamy affair. So Rebecca painted Joan as a marriage-wrecker.

'If you don't mind me asking, I couldn't help noticing… well, he was your school teacher, after all… Does being with an older man hold you back at all now? I mean, would you say you're happy and satisfied, or would you rather be with a slightly younger man?' Rebecca asked.

Joan felt a line had been crossed; she was uncomfortable answering those types of questions. Still, she confided in Rebecca, 'off the record', that as much as the idea of a younger man was appealing, she had changed since being ill. Perhaps Sam was the only man who could appreciate her now.

Rebecca wrote down that Joan was still looking for love, for Mr Right. The rush hour crush project was a convenient tool for Joan to scour the market in her personal search for a man. Cruelly and clumsily, even by Rebecca's standards, she'd missed the most crucial point: that Joan felt Sam was the only fish in the sea who would be interested in her. Yet she still summarised that Joan had failed to see what was obvious to the whole world: that Stuart had been that man, her rush hour crush.

The following day, James went to confront his sister. Rebecca saw him approaching and could tell by his expression that he was intent on causing a scene. Rebecca calmly stood up and walked to the cupboard near which Stuart had died, where the shrine to him was being built.

'I don't know what sort of sick game you're playing, but you need to stop it right now. Joan's a really good person and she doesn't deserve your nasty meddling.'

'Brother darling, so pleased you're taking an interest in my career, but just so you know… fuck off. It has nothing to do with you.'

James wanted Rebecca to know he was watching her. He didn't know what she had planned, but knowing his sister, it would be self-serving in some way and to the detriment of someone else. In this case, Joan. He really didn't think it was fair in any way to pick on her. She absolutely didn't deserve it.

'Listen, whatever you're planning on doing… don't. I'm warning you, I'll tell the editor!' he threatened.

'Don't be so utterly pathetic. Do you think this is kindergarten, you little berk,' Rebecca snapped back.

'I'll tell him it was you who trolled her site,' said James.

'Oh, that's very clever, Einstein. Go right ahead. Then both of us will get the sack,' said Rebecca.

'What do you mean? Why would I get the sack?' said James, feeling confused.

'Because it was your job to stop me and you didn't. You just covered for me,' said Rebecca calmly.

'But… what? That's not true,' said James, like a poker player holding duff cards.

'Yes, it is. You helped me,' said Rebecca.

'No, I didn't,' said James.

'Prove it. Prove everything. Prove you didn't cover it up and prove it was me. You can't, can you? You had your chance and you didn't act. Therefore, you're as guilty as I am.'

She was right, he should have done something at the time rather than covering it up. He was just as guilty as her now. He regretted wiping the computer's history and all traces of her handiwork. It would be her word against his and she would simply deny everything. What was worse was that she was a much better liar and actor than him; she would easily outmanoeuvre him.

James walked away, lost for words, whilst Rebecca returned to her desk to look at the finished article. She pressed 'submit' and watched as the article disappeared from her screen. The next time she read it, it would be on printed paper. She opened her little black notepad and added James's name to her list.

Chapter 17

Joan sat at her kitchen table, chasing a spoonful of cereal around a pool of milk. She was eating and not thinking, for a moment just consuming absent-mindedly, at peace, having breakfast and happily running on autopilot.

Then, typically, Sam entered the room, shattering her tranquillity. Triumphantly, he flung a newspaper onto the table with a nonchalant smirk.

'Well, what you think of that?' said Sam, hands on hips like the worst-dressed Chippendale in history.

Joan picked up the newspaper, hoping his vindictive glee had nothing to do with her. But with every page she turned, getting closer to the rush hour crushes section, she knew it would be, and in her heart she became aware that something ghastly was in store. Had Rebecca revealed something Joan had told her off the record? She already knew the answer. Of course she had. Perhaps that was why Sam was looking menacing and yet chipper. Maybe Rebecca had written something revealing about their relationship. Was Joan about to get beaten for something she'd said about them? She wasn't about to sit around and let that happen, not again. She barely had the will and desire to turn the last few pages, but she was done with playing Sam's games.

'What is it, Sam?' asked Joan, resigned to the fact it was going to be something bad, hence Sam's apparently jubilant grin.

'Open it. You'll see,' said Sam, determined to carry on his pathetic torture.

The phone rang, buzzing on the kitchen table next to her. It was William Wallace, his fleshy, rosy cheeks and smile photographed at the pub the afternoon they'd shared with Stuart before he died. She had forgotten they'd saved his picture to her phone so it flashed up whenever he called.

'Aren't you going to get that?' said Sam, switching his attention from the paper to then wanting to get a glimpse at Joan's phone. 'Whose that?' he questioned.

'It's just work,' she said, rejecting the call.

William would leave a message. *'Och, Joan. Please give me a call. Please don't be too upset, hen, but I need to speak to you urgently. Please give me a call when you get this message. It's about the paper. Stuart's paper. Well, he wouldn't have had any part of this, I can assure you. There must have been some mistake. Anyway, I'll try ye again later. All the best, my love. Please phone me.'*

Joan read the piece slowly, digesting every word, every truth and every allegation. It was a mixture of hateful gossip and spiteful revelation, like someone had printed her diary but added fabricated 'facts', like how she felt after certain events, slanderously using her name, thoughts and feelings. Like being wrongfully accused of a crime she hadn't committed. A made-up alibi.

'Well, fame at last, eh? You got what you wanted, did you?' Sam barked.

But Joan wasn't scared or intimidated – there was an almost playful tone to his aggression. Like a father pretending to be cross with a child, only his jibes were laced with malice. He was genuinely delighted at Joan's life being torn apart in print.

Joan stood up to walk away. She wanted to go and lie down on her bed.

'Well, where the hell are you going? Aren't you going to say something?' snapped Sam, as Joan went to walkout of the kitchen. But she wouldn't give him the pleasure of a confrontation.

'What's to say?' said Joan. She would have dearly liked to say 'Go fuck yourself' to Sam at that very moment, but she felt numb. Like a dagger had been sunk into her heart and twisted, and then twisted again for good measure. An unrepairable hole flooding with blood, a sandcastle moat breached by the returning tide.

Joan made her way to her room. All the while, the only face she could picture was Rebecca's. She saw Rebecca leaning across to her in the canteen and taking her hand in hers and looking into her eyes. Joan had trusted her. She'd reminded Joan a little bit of her Sophie. But for all her faults, Sophie had never done such a nasty thing as this. Sophie had caused Joan a lifetime of pain by choosing Nikki over Joan, but she had never been directly spiteful like this. She'd never attacked. This was as painful as any beating Sam had ever dished out, as any bereavement Joan had suffered – losing her mum, her dad, Nellie, Roy, Stuart, even her kids. This hurt as much as Nikki taking Roy. But why had it happened? It had taken her a lifetime to come to terms with what had happened before. She would never get over this.

A black cloud descended. A static charge built in Joan's head. She got to her bed and flopped down on the pillow. Joan desperately wanted to cry, but she couldn't. Absolutely angry and frustrated. She wanted to go back to sleep and never wake up. Going back to work was certainly far from her mind.

When she closed her eyes, she wanted to see her boy, but all she could see was Rebecca, looking back at her, tender and sensitively, before slowly laughing wickedly. Joan felt herself stiffen up and go rigid, before a volcano erupted deep inside her and she kicked her bed and bit the pillow, screaming into it, feeling her saliva on the covers wet against her cheeks. She threw a full-on childlike paddy, punching, clawing and kicking the bed in utter frustration. Years of pent-up pain and anger were released in an avalanche of uncontrollable angst.

Sam stood in the doorway silently, trying not to laugh.

Joan gave up looking at the paper; she dismissed it from her daily routine. She wanted nothing more to do with the newspaper and the rush hour crushes, the blog, any of it any more. She felt depressed and humiliated and totally let down by everyone connected with it. She'd thought she had some friends there. How could the editor and James have let this happen? Sod it. She didn't care anymore. She was done with it. If that was what Stuart's memory meant to them, she would rather not be involved. She felt betrayed, shafted and disgusted.

Unfortunately, the editor was completely unaware of the article that had gone to print, and of the complaints – of which there were plenty. They were dismissed, brushed under the carpet, deleted, destroyed. Rebecca and her minions were now in control.

William was still struggling to come to terms with the loss of his friend. The two of them had regularly sat in their favourite pub, just off the Strand. It had an ornate, hand-painted ceiling, gargoyles and Corinthian columns, and a warren of secret bars and cubby holes divided into sections – marbled and frosted glassed windows secured in heavily varnished wooden-beamed divides. A fine selection of real ales. It was slightly off the beaten track, so was lost to the majority of tourists, but still accessible enough to allow for the occasional wayward wayfarer. William and Stuart would both welcome the chance to chat up any friendly passers-by or groups of ladies wanting to interact with the funny old boys at the bar. 'Oh my God, your accent is just so cute,' an older, blue-rinse American lady once said to Stuart, whilst her travelling companion eyed up William's strong-looking knees, revealed by his kilt, with a look of lust.

Now it would just be William, and he didn't enjoy that thought. Stuart would have been comfortable sitting alone at a bar, but not William. His outfit was enough to draw the wrong type of curiosity, and without Stuart's presence it left him feeling vulnerable and open to ridicule.

He tried to keep busy, but found he missed not having Stuart's counsel whenever he had a story to tell about some silly scheme that had backfired or his latest confrontation with the re-enactment crowds. He had taken for granted how often they had communicated, usually with William telling tales of his adventures and Stuart laughing, and then Stuart telling William all about Joan. Recently, they had spent countless evenings talking about the complexities of the heart and the riddles of fair maidens' minds. 'They are a law unto themselves,' they agreed. To a certain extent, they were somewhat akin to an old married couple, often repeating themselves and telling the same stories again, but always happily and without arguing. They really were an ideal pairing. Best mates.

William remembered Stuart laughing until he cried and then fell off his stool in the pub when William told the story of being asked to leave a re-enactment meeting by a pompous old fool dressed in full Napoleonic uniform. He'd threatened William with his bayonet and William had swung his sporran in self-defence.

'They were wearing things that weren't available. I mean, eighteenth-century soldiers with digital wristwatches and bloody black sneakers. Heavens above, have you heard of anything quite so ridiculous? What's the point of dressing up at all if you aren't going to go the full distance? It's bloody madness.'

That was also the first time William had seen Stuart have a funny turn. How he wished now he had been more insistent on Stuart seeing a doctor.

William couldn't bear the thought of 'that bloody article' hurting Joan. He adopted Stuart's care for her, as if only he now knew the hard life she had endured and was possibly still suffering. William had been the victim of ridicule before. But this, coming so soon after Stuart's untimely death, was just not on. If it had been about him, he wouldn't have cared so much. But this was about Joan, and Stuart had cared for her ever so much – just like she had cared for Stuart, and as much as he had for the pair of them. They were all members of the same mutual appreciation society. Stuart would have been very angry about what had transpired. Something, anything would have to be done.

Joan had tried to go back to work quietly, but she was now the talk of the town. Everywhere she went, she felt eyes on her and she heard gossiping. It was like when she first got together with Sam – the playground whispers and catty stares. She gave up reading or thinking about the rush hour crush project, and the fight was gone from her in standing up to Sam. She slumped back into her mouse-like form, which ran round after him twenty-four/seven, putting up with his every demand. Whenever she went out in public, she would wear a headscarf and dark glasses and put up her hood. She hid herself away as much as possible.

William, meanwhile, hadn't given up on Joan, but he felt the loss of his friend and was struggling to come to terms with his death. As the days, and then weeks, passed, he became more irritable and lonely. He imagined Joan wouldn't be interested in being his friend any more, as it was the three of them who had clicked initially and he really wasn't sure she would give him the time of day. In truth, he hardly knew her. He knew of her more than he knew her. He was slightly nervous that he wouldn't know what to say to her, without Stuart acting as a buffer. She hadn't returned his calls and he felt somehow responsible for her pain. He hadn't eased it, which was just as bad as causing it. He wanted to be the solution, not part of the problem. He became aware he was making excuses. This wasn't part of the plan.

He also knew he'd fallen in love with Joan the very first moment he'd met her. Possibly earlier – he thought back to evenings just listening to Stuart wax lyrical about her. He remembered thinking she was everything Stuart had made her out to be and more. And those eyes... they looked into his soul and made him feel warm and cosy. And her laugh... he felt the whole world would laugh too when she laughed.

The problem was Sam. He'd proven a big enough obstacle to thwart Stuart. William had to tread carefully. But he would not be bested. Sam was his 'meningitis '. He was the enemy, and he would be defeated.

William decided that Joan being with Sam was the ultimate problem. Get her away from him and the rest would fall into place. A task, for sure, but certainly not insurmountable. William was wired differently to Stuart, cut from a different cloth, and had a different setting on his moral compass. As he'd said to Stuart: 'One whiff of an opportunity to be with Joan and I'd be in there, like a rat up a drainpipe.' William winced at the crudeness of his expression. He wondered what Stuart must have thought when he heard William say that. As he remembered it, Stuart had just laughed at the time.

William could see clearly that Joan was trapped. Black and white, none of the grey area that had always bothered and hindered Stuart. She had no choice, William knew; whereas Stuart had always believed she had, and respected that. William felt Stuart gave Joan too many choices to make and options to consider and that was his downfall. He should have seized the moment. He was too much of a gentleman. Was that possible? Stuart felt Joan could stay with Sam, or leave and be alone, or leave and be with him. They were all her choices. It was always left to her to decide. William saw it differently. He'd tell her straight: 'I want you with me.' No options, no confusion, no pussy-footing around. He'd take her by the hand and lead her astray. When the time was right, but as soon as possible. Maybe.

But all this presumptuous talk was jumping the gun. For all William's gusto, it was easier said than done. Especially as he hadn't even had a conversation with Joan since the funeral. For all he knew, she didn't care much for him.

Joan slipped back into Groundhog Day, continuously working every hour of the day and tidying up after Sam – who was typically insensitive and acted like it was about time Joan got back on top of running the household. He said she should stop moping about after 'that flowery twat she'd become infatuated with', as he was fond of describing Stuart. In her head, Joan briefly pictured smashing Sam around the face with a wok. She also imagined screaming the rudest words imaginable as he lay on the floor, spluttering for breath through his busted, blood-filled nose and mouth, spitting jagged, broken teeth, whilst looking up at the stars.

Then, one day, as she waited for her bus as per usual, she noticed a familiar face at the window. She had no idea William had taken the bus on purpose just so that he could speak to her; she didn't even consider the bus route wasn't in the general direction of his house. If she'd asked, he'd have just fibbed and said he was visiting friends, or collecting a package, or making the most of his freedom pass. Or something. He'd have lied.

Truth was, he'd spent days nervously trying to work out the logistics, checking timetables and stalking Joan – which really wasn't an easy thing to do for a man dressed in a kilt. He'd decided to catch her bus a few stops before she got on. He woke up early and parked in a quiet cul-de-sac not far from her house, before making his way over to the stop and waiting patiently. It then occurred to him he could have just as easily stopped at her bus stop in his car and offered her a lift. This way seemed more fun, though, and a little more charming. Thoughtful. He hoped Joan might feel a little more relaxed in a public place, and quite possibly free to ignore him if she didn't want to speak.

So there he was, sitting on the strange bus, travelling along unfamiliar roads with a childlike anxiety growing in his stomach. 'Och, come now, William,' he said to himself as his knee did a jig and his hands felt clammy.

All he needed to do was chat with her until she got to her stop and then, all going well, see if she would like to meet sometime for lunch perhaps, or go out one evening or at the weekend. He was sure she wouldn't think it too inappropriate. Well, she would, but he didn't care. 'Faint heart never won fair maiden,' he said, almost screaming with excitement as the bus approached the stop and he could make out Joan's silhouette.

'William, what on earth are you doing here?' said Joan, sitting down next to him, quite close, in her long, puffer-style coat.

William was so delighted he wanted to hug her. He'd had premonitions she might ignore him. 'I'm here to see you,' he proclaimed, completely forgetting his pre-planned fibs. He felt like he simply couldn't lie to her. It was impossible.

'Eh, what do you mean?'

'Well, I read the article in the paper and I was desperate to talk to you, and I tried calling and kept missing you, and... well, I don't know, I thought you might have been avoiding me or something.'

'Oh my God,' said Joan.

'I know this all must seem a little bit drastic. Please don't be alarmed. I promise you it's not my usual behaviour. Not that I have anything against taking buses or anything you see.'

'It's still a little bit drastic,' said Joan, trying to come to terms with William appearing on her bus.

'Well, you know, you do this trip every day, and I thought it might be nice. That is, if you don't mind the company.'

'Oh, William, it is really lovely to see you. It's just a bit of a surprise really. What on earth... I mean, what time did you get up to see me.? It's all a little bit...'

'I'm really sorry. The last thing I wanted to do was freak you out.'

'Don't be daft William, it's quite all right. What a lovely surprise.'

'It is a bit weird, though, isn't it?' replied William.

'It is,' said Joan, and they both laughed as William looked embarrassed and put his head on Joan's shoulder.

Joan patted his face. They were already comfortable in each other's space. They said how they felt without any need for diplomacy or tact. William felt comfortable laying his cards on the table, and Joan took William at his word. There was no awkwardness. It was what it was.

'Joan, that article was terrible. I don't know how it happened. Stuart would never have allowed it.'

'I know,' said Joan, 'but it still happened, it was still written, and everyone saw. I can't... I don't want to have anything to do with it, with them, any more.'

'I understand,' said William. As far as he was concerned, if that was what she wanted then the case was closed. They would move on and not mention it again.

'Joan, I have a function this weekend I'd like to go to. It's a re-enactment weekend at Wilburn Fort, not far from here. I'm sure you would find it frightfully boring, but I thought... well, if you weren't busy, would you like to come with me? I'll buy you lunch.'

'Erm, I really, well... erm, you see, obviously Sam wouldn't approve,' said Joan.

'I understand,' said William. He added, 'The offer is there. If you can get away, it would be lovely to see you. It would be great to have the company. If not, perhaps we could do lunch sometime. I'll meet you at work. There must be somewhere close by that's nice?'

Joan was feeling slightly flustered. 'I'm really busy with work and home.'

'Okay. Sorry, my dear, I'm acting awfully presumptuous. Please forgive me. No pressure. The offer is there.'

Joan already knew she wanted to go. She liked William. Being with him was fun. He made her feel happy.

'I can't promise anything,' said Joan, already trying to work out what she could say to Sam to get away and spend some time with William.

'Oh, William,' she said, patting his hand and lifting her arm so they sat with their arms locked.

'That's not the only reason I came to see you,' said William, putting his free hand into his jacket pocket. 'I've brought you a present.'

Joan looked at William, searching his face for clues.

'Here you go, for you.'

William passed Joan a thin, fabric-covered box. It was ornately decorated in red, black and gold, with some Chinese art depicting a dragon breathing fire and lots of swirling patterns. Inside it was Joan's grandfather's pen, which William had rescued from the Pawn shop on Stuart's command. He wasn't sure when the right time to give it to Joan would be. Stuart had never said. He just said, 'Keep it safe.'

But the gift resulted in Joan cuddling William and crying happy tears. Perhaps old Stuart knew what he was doing all along, and that was why he'd asked William to collect the pen and keep it safe.

The tears shed reinvigorated Joan. They washed away her heartbreak. They also galvanised William. He felt the joy flow through Joan, and at that moment he realised nothing else in his life mattered.

William woke up especially early. His finest outfit was hanging on the wardrobe and his favourite shoes were polished and his pheasant-feathered hat was ready to be put on. He'd arranged to meet Joan at her bus stop and then they'd drive from there.

When they arrived at the fort, the organisers met William, dressed in his usual regalia, and thought he was part of the entertainment. They had fun walking around whilst William asked the soldiers serious questions as if they were genuine recruits from that specific time. What was the food like? Pay? Weapons? How much action had they seen? What was the life expectancy? Were there any Scots in the regiment, and if not, could he join? Joan thought it was really quite fun.

After exhausting all the questions, an elated William proudly escorted Joan back to his car. He'd drained his lengthy list of memorised questions. These soldiers had fared better than usual, and almost all left without feeling rebuked or condescended to.

William's car was an old red Volvo estate. Quite why he needed such a big car was a mystery to Joan. Picking up on her quizzical look, William said sinisterly, 'There's enough room for a body or two in the boot.' They both laughed. 'It's ideal for carrying bits and bobs from the sales,' he said with a wink.

They got into the car and got comfortable. William was just thinking about where they could go for some lunch when he put the key in the ignition and the engine made a spluttering effort to come to life but then just stalled. 'Oh dear,' said William. He gave it a few moments and tried again. Still the engine threatened to start but just wouldn't. 'This doesn't sound good at all,' he said.

'What do you think the problem might be?' asked Joan.

'Well, I'm not exactly an expert on mechanical sorts of things, but I have a terrible feeling I've run out of petrol.'

'Oh dear,' said Joan.

'It's okay, I know a trick,' said William.

He got out of the car and put all his weight on the bonnet, making the car and Joan bounce up and down, before jumping back in and trying the ignition again. As before, it ticked but showed no interest in firing to life.

'Dear oh dear,' said Joan, trying not to laugh. Just watching William get in and out of the car in his kilt was amusing enough, let alone seeing him bounce up and down on the bonnet. 'What can we do?' she asked.

'I'm so sorry, this is so embarrassing. I've got a jerry can in the boot. I'll walk to the petrol station and fill it up, and then come back and get you. Will you be okay to wait here on your own? I'll be as quick as I can.'

Joan looked at the old fort and the rapidly emptying car park. She really didn't like the idea of waiting here alone.

'I'll come with you. It might be a nice walk, and the weather is okay.'

It had been sunny in the morning, but had actually become overcast and was positively cloudy and gloomy as Joan made her comment. Yet both Joan and William felt happy.

They grabbed the can and headed off, walking back up the road the way they had driven in.

'Do you remember seeing a garage at all?' asked Joan.

William wasn't sure, but he looked across some fields into the distance, thinking. He was positive they could cut through, making their walk considerably shorter. 'I think we could go cross-country for a bit – what do you reckon?'

'Come on, we'll scoot across there. It'll be an adventure.'

Joan laughed as William boyishly climbed the old wooden fence. His cocking his leg over the highest panel was a sight only slightly less revealing than his entering and exiting his car. She wondered if men were incapable of wearing skirts in a feminine, dignified fashion (watching him scoop his tackle and rearrange his kilt was a memory that would last a lifetime). She was baffled that he seemed incapable of certain actions, despite having been a skirt-wearer for many years. Perhaps it really was just a male/female thing.

He hadn't considered their footwear; neither of them were wearing decent walking shoes. His fine leather brogues and Joan's comfy plimsoll-type footwear both absorbed water as soon as they set foot on the wet grass. Apart from being soggy, it was quite a pleasant walk, until they encountered some frisky-looking horses. Joan wasn't at all keen to cross the field as the horses jostled for a better view of

William, thinking his jerrycan could contain sugar lumps, apples or some other horsey hors d'oeuvre.

'Shoo! Scram! Goddamn it, be off with you, you cursed beasts.'

Even this Joan found hysterical, watching William get flustered and yet still not lose his temper as he valiantly tried to flap the horses away. They, in turn, shook their manes and tails, stamping their feet defiantly.

'Bloody stubborn beasts, aren't they?'

They decided to take a slight detour. 'Perhaps we should head that way,' said Joan, pointing further down the field towards what looked like some cattle drinking troughs and a path heading up and away.

They intended to cross the wooden barrier that skirted alongside the edge of the field, but they ended up getting totally bogged down in a really muddy patch. William tried desperately to act the gentleman, whipping off his beautiful black jacket with polished silver buttons and shiny lapels and offering to lay it on the mud for Joan to walk across, in a dramatic, romantic gesture.

But she told him not to be absurd. 'You'll get it ruined, you daft apeth.'

William then said, 'If you're sure,' and with a practised move he swung his coat over his shoulders. But unfortunately, this momentum led to him losing his footing, as his slick leather brogues slid, with little resistance. He ended up in a kneeling position, facing Joan, as if he was about to propose.

Time stood still for a second. William felt powerless as Joan stood before him. Some unknown force held him where he was, looking up at his queen, waiting to be knighted or beheaded.

Eventually, Joan offered him her hand, breaking the spell. He went to accept her hand, but it was covered in mud. He then offered to give her a piggyback, because her lack of movement had meant she too was now stuck fast and she was worried that if she tried to move she would fall over.

'Hold on, I'll help you.'

But all William did was slip over again in the muck. Joan had the uncontrollable giggles; her cheeks were hurting and wet with tears, and she was worried she was going to wet herself as she was laughing so much.

William couldn't help but make it worse every time he moved. His shoes would come off and he'd curse harmlessly, but then slip and slide like a bad ice skater. He never got angry, just really, really red in the face, and he was totally covered in mud.

If it weren't for the repulsive smell, Joan would have highly recommended the experience. 'You could sell tickets,' she quipped.

'Hey, at least one of us can be seen in public,' said William, flicking the mud from his hands and scraping fingertips full of grime that had found its way onto his eyelid.

'How about I give you a piggyback out of here, then I'll be your Saint Christopher?'

Joan snorted as the swamp creature removed his jacket again, revealing a bright, clean, unblemished shirt for her to climb on board. William wrapped his shoes up in his jacket and crouched down, so it would be easy for Joan to clamber on. Joan was a little taller than William, so his crouching down didn't really help, and she found herself bending onto his back. Immediately, she was aware of the size of his body, the feel of his skin under his shirt and the heat he was emitting. Then she became aware that her feet were still on the ground, even though he was standing up. She found herself more or less hugging him from behind. Before he even tried to lift her up, she was giggling uncontrollably again.

Finally, William set off, managing a few triumphant footsteps. He imagined Joan sitting proudly on his back, riding aloft, thinking, *Why, William, aren't you strong*. Instead, she realised her plimsoll had been sucked clean off by the mud and she kicked out her legs in front of William so he could see the footwear was missing.

'Oh, good gracious,' he said, turning around to look down at her shoeless foot – before losing his balance and slipping over. Both of them ended up in a jumbled heap, totally covered in mud.

William was devastated, trying desperately to help Joan up from the sticky, writhing, muddy mess and upset that he had soiled his unblemished fair maiden. Previously resplendent in his full Highland dress, he was now completely filthy, slipping and sliding uncontrollably as he tried to help Joan to her feet. He fell over again, helpless, like an upturned turtle, his kilt up around his midriff, revealing his tackle.

Joan, blushing and not sure where to look, offered a hand to help him up, but William succeeded in pulling Joan over again, and they both fell down onto the muddy field. As they tumbled back, Joan fell onto William and ended up lying on his chest, looking him in the face. They stopped laughing and examined each other's face in close detail. Tenderly, gently, William wiped away some mud from Joan's face, brushing her hair from her eyes before tapping her nose with his muddy finger, giving her a little spot right at the tip of her nose. Joan tried to focus on it, going cross-eyed for a moment, before looking back at William, into his beaming, deep pools of blue just gazing back at her. Then, gradually at first, the distance between them shrank very slowly, until she could feel the heat of his face on hers, and then their lips touched.

This time they didn't try to get up, they just held each other closely, laughing, still flat out on the ground. They laughed till they stopped and just looked into each other's eyes, trying to read each other's mind. It was like they were silently communicating, like a million fireworks were being released, like they'd known each other forever, like they'd been waiting for each other for as long as they could remember. And then they kissed again and time stood still. Holding each other on the ground, covered in mud, tenderly, gently, they laughed and kissed some more – and then it started to rain.

Eventually, they got to their feet, holding hands, and walked on gingerly. Joan was overwhelmed by how bad William felt for having got her muddy; not, seemingly, for kissing a lady in a long-term relationship. He really cared about how muddy he'd made her, like it mattered over everything else.

William felt awful. But he felt amazing too. He wouldn't have changed a thing, and he didn't want to let go of her hand.

Joan felt like she had taken some sort of strange drug, or was drunk without having drunk anything, or in a parallel universe where this sort of thing happened. What was happening? She didn't know. And whilst it was happening, she didn't care. She felt perfectly muddled, muddy but muddled.

'My God,' Joan said.

'What is it, my dear?' asked William, worried Joan was already regretting their actions. She was sure to feel guilty sooner or later; it was natural.

'What on earth would Stuart be thinking if he were watching?'

William chuckled and squeezed Joan's hand. He wasn't a religious man, but this sort of sentiment he enjoyed greatly.

'Oh, Joan, he would be truly jealous.'

Joan was a little taken aback. 'Why would you think that?' she asked, feeling naïve but already suspecting the answer.

'Because, my dear, quite like me, he was utterly mad about you. Always was.'

Joan felt a wave of happy/sad melancholy sweep over her. 'What a strange situation and thought,' she said, feeling slightly confused and awkward.

William replied, 'Well, he knew from the moment we met his number was up,' and then he laughed his laugh, which Joan was rapidly becoming very fond of indeed.

She smacked him on the arm. 'I did love him, you know,' she said, looking at William earnestly.

'I believe you did,' said William, before adding, 'but not like that, eh? You loved him like a brother or another family member. He was good to you, supportive, a rock. Right?'

William was right. Joan had loved him exactly like William had described, but not physically. She had linked arms with Stuart and they'd walked and talked and she'd felt safe and unchallenged, supported and loved. But here she was, barely knowing William that long, and already they were sharing intimate feelings and holding hands. She lifted their hands, looking at William's slightly larger, muddy hands holding hers and their fingers intertwined like they fitted. She felt comfortable.

'Oh, William, this is a mess.'

'Not really, my dear.'

They walked to the petrol station, looking like they had been mud-wrestling. They filled the petrol can and made it back to the car. They didn't talk much on the drive back to Joan's, but they both agreed they definitely wanted to see each other again soon and they hadn't regretted a thing that had happened. Joan needed to work out what was what. She had lots to sort out in her head.

William said he had time and he would wait for her, but not forever.

Joan said, 'Thank you, William, for my pen and everything. I really have had the most amazing day.

Chapter 18

Joan and William spent more and more time together. Some days William would meet Joan for lunch at her work; he'd be waiting for her with a picnic on a bench in the local park – sandwiches with peanut butter and, Joan's favourite, ham and piccalilli. Other days, he'd surprise her again by sitting on her bus or escorting her home. The majority of the time they just talked, like they had a lifetime of memories and feelings and thoughts that needed to be shared before time ran out. They enjoyed cinema visits, meals and countryside walks.

Sometimes Joan would say she was working late or meeting people from work, but generally she decided to be upfront with Sam and pretend she had nothing to hide. 'I'm seeing William today,' she'd say. Sam acted like he didn't hear or care, and he didn't at first. Then he noticed she was making a bit more of an effort with her appearance and seemed more full of herself – jolly, even. Traces of the old Joan were returning, and she was avoiding him and ignoring him in a way he wasn't used to, like she didn't need or care about him all of a sudden. The house seemed lighter and tidier and less repressive; everything seemed slightly different... shifted.

Joan hadn't done anything really wrong, not yet anyway. She would, though. She was quite sure of it. But at the moment she was content with stolen kisses and holding hands. So she hadn't any need to feel guilty just yet. Premeditated cheating. Fantasising. *Can you cheat on a cheater or abuse an abuser?* she wondered. Was thinking about doing something really as bad as doing it? She'd imagined killing Sam plenty of times but never had. Did that make her a potential murderer? Or just normal? A real murderer would just do it, whereas a normal person would go no further than just thinking about it. A sane person knows when to act on crazy thoughts. Would having a physical relationship, or ever considering one, with William make her a cheater? Should she even care? Why couldn't and shouldn't she just enjoy it for a while, she decided.

Sam hadn't asked outright, 'Is anything going on?' So Joan hadn't had to lie. Had he asked, perhaps things would have been different. Instead, she had told William she was keen to see him, but to take things slowly at first whilst she assessed the situation with Sam and considered all the other permutations and fall out that would come should their relationship be made public. Sam and Joan had been together a long time. There would be so much to sort out. Goodness knew how he would react. Lots was going on and she needed to get her head straight – but unfortunately it seemed to get more muddled every time she met up with William. That's not to say she wasn't enjoying seeing him. It was quite the opposite. She was quite sure she was falling in love with him.

Sam became increasingly anxious about losing control of Joan, unsure what she was up to and also worried about confronting her and losing his temper. In reality, never had Joan been better placed to pack her bags and leave him. He had no idea or plan formulated. He was unsure whether to act nice to her and tidy up his act a little, or beat the resistance and truth out of her.

He sent a message to Rebecca, asking: *Do you know anything about this William chap, an old friend of Stuart's? Maybe something to do with the paper. Can you get him to clear off for me?*

Rebecca read the message several times. Her skin had crawled when she noticed Sam's name flash up on her screen, but there was something in this text. She recalled seeing the kilt-wearing man in the office with Stuart and the editor, and seeing him and Joan together at the funeral. From memory, they seemed quite close even then. What was Joan up to? Surely she couldn't be having an affair, Rebecca thought, intrigued.

William came down the stairs towards his front door after hearing the letterbox clatter. He figured he had received some mail. Perhaps it was the limited-edition, kilt-wearing, vintage, eagle-eyed Highland Action Man he'd discovered on eBay. He got to the door to see a *Metro* newspaper folded in half and sticking partway into the cage (at some point in time someone had decided the letterbox needed protecting by a cage, or at least that bending over was too much of an effort so they created a wire bird's nest to remedy the problem). He delved into the black metal cage, unhinging the thin budgie door.

'A newspaper?' he said aloud to himself. 'Curious.' He opened the front door and looked out into the street, half-expecting to see naughty scamps running away, giggling, playing knock-down ginger, but he couldn't see anyone. Just as he was about to bin the newspaper he noticed a blatant red line marked out with felt-tip around a post in the rush hour crush section. He read it carefully, becoming peculiarly self-aware and strangely embarrassed, as one would if hearing a group of people talking about oneself. He felt a little taken back. It was Stuart's section, Stuart and Joan's more recently.

He went back to the front door and opened it again, wondering who had been posted the paper through his door and why. He felt like he had received a Valentine's Day card. He would have dearly liked to have called his old friend Stuart at that very moment, but all he had for company was Mr Tickles the cat.

'It seems I have an admirer,' he said, puffing out his chest proudly. 'If I didn't know better, old man, I'd think this was your handiwork,' William said, talking into the heavens.

Who had highlighted the section and who had posted it through his door? Who even knew where he lived? Only Joan, and perhaps the editor, but he was sure they would have called or left a note at least. They wouldn't have posted it and hid. It was all very strange.

William decided to phone Joan. He was due to see her later in the day, but in his excitement he got a little carried away. Whilst strangely euphoric at first, he soon realized his unexpected admirer might actually be seen as competition or a love rival by Joan.

'Och hello, Joan, my sweet. Can you talk, and how are you today?'

'Good morning, William. I'm good, thanks. Yes, I can talk. *He* is still dead to the world, snoring. Did you have a good night's sleep?'

'Dreaming of rescuing fair maidens,' said William, the charmer.

'I'm seeing you for lunch, right?' Joan sounded bright and happy, but this would soon change as she was flooded with a range of emotions.

'Well, Joan, my dear, it's like this: I couldn't wait till later. I just needed to talk to someone. Well, not just anyone, you know, someone who'd listen. I'm not quite sure what to make of it all really, and, well, I mean, it's all so strange.'

'What is, William, what's happened? Are you okay?'

'Oh, I'm quite all right. Well, better then all right, it would seem. Apparently, I'm quite the catch.' William laughed out loud but Joan's silence soon stifled his feel-good factor.

'William, I'm not sure I understand what on earth you're talking about. Is everything okay?'

'Sorry, Joan, my dear. Listen, I'm taking this as proof that indeed you know nothing about the paper and didn't post it through my letterbox this morning.'

'What paper, letterbox, this morning? Do you know what time it is?'

'No, right, I see, curiouser and curiouser.'

'William, would you kindly tell me what on earth you're going on about?'

'A paper, your paper, Stuart's and yours, with a rush hour crush about me, circled in red pen.'

At first William felt slightly embarrassed explaining what he'd found and awkward as he clumsily asked for advice on how best to deal with the situation. It became apparent quickly that Joan's answers were slightly prickly and guarded, almost aloof. She was equally intrigued, yet incapable of acting impartial. For as long as she could remember Rush Hour Crushes had been her raison d'être, and despite her best intentions, she couldn't help acting defensive, flippant almost, as if she were a jealous child or lovesick teenager. No matter what she said or how she said it, unintentionally it came out wrong and she had one foot deeply entrenched someway down her gullet. This was all frustrating and absurd, even more so because Joan was already in a relationship with Sam. No matter how lousy it was, it was real; she had the scars to prove it. Whereas William was still free and single and well within his rights to pursue whatever love interest presented itself, even if she felt slightly hurt and jealous.

William, in turn, felt awkward and confused. *Women are like bloody buses,* he thought, *like the first bud of spring breaking free of the frozen, muddy ground, only to be trodden on before its flower gets to bloom and show the world all its beauty.*

Joan and William's relationship was being derailed. William was aware that even being slightly intrigued was an act of betrayal, of cheating on Joan – however minutely. But there was still a chance he was wasting his time pursuing Joan, whereas here was an unknown

Texan beauty who had approached him. She was after him. He was a man.

The conversation on the phone became very awkward, almost pathetic.

'Why should I care what you do? Of course I think it's exciting,' said Joan, realising she was talking defensively and communicating like she would usually do with Sam.

For William, the stone, cold reality that Joan was in a relationship became undeniable. . Now both Joan and William had people influencing their every action.

The longer the conversation continued, the more confusing it became. William was in a terrible quandary. He wished he'd never called Joan and he wished he'd never seen the newspaper. He wanted to turn back the clock, forgetting he'd seen it.

At the end of the conversation, Joan felt terribly frustrated that she hadn't been straight with William about the way she felt.

'So shall I still see you at lunch?'

'Erm, actually, I'm not so sure. I'm really rather busy at the moment,' she lied.

'Okay, fine.'

'Fine.'

'Bye then.'

'Right, errr, bye.'

'Bye then.'

They both hung up.

Joan felt bitterly hurt; there was a burning in her chest like she'd been knifed through the heart.

William just stared at the phone, totally unsure what had just happened.

'Bloody bollocks,' he finally shouted.

But despite everything, he still couldn't help but feel slightly intrigued by the Texan.

Joan got herself a copy of the paper, and from that moment on she read it again almost obsessively. She'd broken her abstinence and fallen off the rush hour crush wagon. She couldn't help but be slightly interested in William's admirer, but also, because she hadn't been paying any attention to the paper, she was intrigued to see how the column had developed and continued without her or Stuart's guidance. It certainly looked different – not awful by any stretch of the imagination, just more modern. James had updated it, making it seem flasher, not as busy, with black and neon colours.

Joan checked her blog and found that it too had been updated. Badly, she decided. It looked like a Soho tattoo saloon bar or, worse still, a pornographic website. It was probably just a more modern design than she was used to, but it was really not her cup of tea. She had quite liked the original simple black-and-white cherubs, and the fonts and layouts that looked similar to the paper's. But unfortunately, Rebecca had been changing and destroying as much of the old style as possible, along with choosing the racier and wackier crushes to feature, so the content was a lot more risqué and, if possible, absurd.

To the delightful, well-dressed, mature Braveheart: I watched you from afar, meandering through the busy crowds of Euston Station, your resplendent feathered hat standing erect upon your fine, majestic head. Your Texan princess wonders if you'd share what's hidden in or under your sporran?

Joan laughed, but then felt a pang of jealous anger.

Rebecca had created the Texan. She was the lady who had noticed the charming man in a kilt. She had set it all up. Rebecca had sent a team of minions to keep an eye on William as much as possible over the space of a week, documenting his every movement. They even fitted a GPS tracker to his car. They knew where he went and when. They needed to find her a time when he was regularly in a public place, where it was possible he'd come to someone's attention. As regular as clockwork, he'd been taking the trip across town to see Joan, and on this trip he nearly always passed through London Euston. The meetings with Joan hadn't gone unnoticed by Rebecca and her team – they had been documented and photographed and filmed.

The editor, back from his extended leave, made it clear to the staff at the newspaper that he was planning on retiring and the process of handing over the reins would start immediately. The news was met with a mixture of shock and sadness – and, from Rebecca, pure elation. Another foe bested. Losing his old friend Stuart had forced the editor to reappraise what was important in his life, and how best he should spend the rest of his days. After careful consideration, he had decided his work no longer had the same gravitas, especially now his right-hand man had left the building. He never thought for a second it would have had such a profound effect. The editor had loved his job, ever moment of it, and rightfully felt very proud of all he had achieved and the wonderful team he'd assembled.

He made a point of saying he would spend some time with all the departments, carefully seeking his successor, and would ensure it was a full and thorough process. 'You never know, it might be someone from within the organization, one of you, promoted from within. That maybe the route that the powers-that-be will opt to follow.' (Rebecca's sphincter twitched.) 'New and fresh ideas. Jazz things up a little.' But everyone should rest assured, he said, that his leaving wouldn't affect anything. The foundations were laid. The paper was in a strong place.

On the contrary, it might be a good thing, Rebecca wholeheartedly believed. She thought the soppy old bastard was taking the piss. *Good riddance,* she thought.

He gave himself a few months, perhaps even half a year, to get himself straight and ready… the long goodbye.

The editor called James and Rebecca to his office. 'Nothing to worry about,' he assured them. 'Just wanted to chat things through and get up to speed with a few bits.'

He was a little shocked by the rush hour crush site's dramatic new styling. Initially, he'd thought that Rebecca and James must have collaborated and worked quite hard updating everything, and he didn't want to seem overly negative. Especially with Rebecca – she was such a prickly, nasty character, and he really didn't want to deal with any potential flare-ups with her. Besides which, he liked James and wouldn't want to hurt his feelings. Especially with them being siblings, he didn't went to come between them. He was baffled by how they could be related. He was totally unaware of the hostility between them and preferred to tread carefully. Had it been James's handiwork in the main, he certainly wouldn't want to upset him. James was a valued member of the team, a jewel.

The editor asked, as sensitively and gently as possible, whether they'd been in touch with Joan and consulted her. Rebecca insisted she had and that they had met up and had a good talk, but that Joan really didn't want to be involved in the section or newspaper any more. The editor was unsure what Joan really thought about it all, as Rebecca flippantly said everything had been agreed. She was adamant Joan really didn't want to speak to anyone at the paper, as she was still far too hurt, and had told Rebecca to just go ahead and change whatever she liked. Rebecca lied, and the editor considered giving her the benefit of doubt. It was possible they had got on and were amicable – stranger things had happened. Joan certainly seemed like the sort of person who could befriend anyone. The way Stuart had portrayed her, the editor thought she was a bloody saint. But he was a little suspicious, as Rebecca seemed eager to move on and brush the conversation under the carpet. Something didn't add up. It was entirely plausible, but it felt wrong. Forced, even. And he didn't trust Rebecca at all. She was a wasp in mosquito's clothing.

Perhaps it was in good hands now – maybe he'd been wrong about Rebecca. He congratulated them both on the good job they had been doing with the site and section. He noticed Rebecca seemed to think it was funny that he should be pleased. Her strange attitude was back: like she had done something and got away with it; like she hadn't done anything at all and it was all James's hard work. James certainly didn't look as pleased, more like he was winning the booby prize or had been handed the soggy biscuit.

The editor brushed his teeth and shuffled to bed. His beautiful trophy wife was all curled up, already softly snoring, as he went to turn off the side light. He leant over to drink a swig of water, and – more out of habit than because he thought anything might have been received – he checked his phone. A new email sat unopened in his inbox. A finished article. He clicked it open, thinking it was probably a random bit of mail that had been lost in cyberspace, the way some emails with massive attachments occasionally disappear into the ether, only to reappear randomly months later. But instead it was a backed-up copy of Stuart's last article, which had been found hidden away on Rebecca's computer.

James had sneakily retraced her steps. He'd found the article stored away, backed up in the temp files, like a shadow hidden away in the recesses of the computer's dusty old hard-drive.

The editor had no idea who had sent the article to him, only that it had a code suggesting it was good to go to print and was from the paper's main production email address. It had been forwarded on to him anonymously. The good-to-print (GTP) file number was the subject header. The editor read the article with tears welling in his eyes as his old friend's voice spoke to him from beyond. Why hadn't this article gone to print?

The very next day at work, he looked up the article in the archives and read the version that had gone into print circulation with the good-to-print code. He nearly had a heart attack himself. His knuckles turned white and his blood boiled as he became so angry he smashed his own computer, kicking it to the floor. 'Fuck!' he spat as he stamped on the large chunks of plastic and the shattered screen. He wanted to go out into the office and grab the little witch by the hair and drag her physically out of the building himself. Forget that, he wanted to throw her out of the fucking window and watch her flailing body hit the pavement in a fleshy crimson splash. He was unsure whom to talk to, but had quickly worked out that Rebecca had rewritten the article and the anonymous email had probably come from James. To say the editor was utterly furious would be an understatement.

Because the code on the article Rebecca had used wasn't given to her, it was meant for Stuart's article, her actions were clearly gross misconduct. The article itself was libellous. Everything about it was cause for instant dismissal. The editor would usually have gone to the HR department, who would have sorted out the situation very quickly and easily. But because Rebecca was friends with the owner, he thought perhaps he should let them deal with it. It was a clear-cut case, as far as the editor was concerned, and he felt sure the owner would take his side and dismiss Rebecca immediately.

The owner's personal assistant thanked him for raising the issue and said to leave it with them and they would look into it. At first the editor thought that they were probably making arrangements, sorting out the paperwork, perhaps looking into moving her to another business interest. He was wrong. He tried calling them, leaving messages for them to call him back when they had a chance. They didn't. He wrote more emails and left more messages, asking them to get in touch, but they didn't. They were busy trying to work out how best to deal with him.

In the end, the editor took a call from a Russian lady he'd never heard of or spoken to before, who bluntly told him she was calling on behalf of the owner. She said they felt Rebecca had acted with intuition and foresight, and that had Stuart still been alive then the code would have been in use, but as it wasn't, Rebecca was free to use it. As far as they could tell, the article hadn't been badly received at all, and if anything, the aesthetics of the paper under her guidance seemed to have moved considerably in the direction the management team wanted, in keeping with their vision for the future model.

The editor couldn't believe what he was hearing. To make matters worse, she went on to suggest the owner felt perhaps the editor might want to consider bringing forward his retirement plans and leave a little earlier.

He sat down at his desk, barely bothering to say 'right' and 'I see', just staring at the pile of broken computer parts wedged into his bin in the corner of his office. Rather than being angry and planning on disciplining Rebecca, they were considering promoting her to a newly created 'assistant editor' position. She would most probably work alongside whoever replaced him.

The slightly threatening Russian voice said, 'It is probably for the best. You don't want us rocking the boat for you. After all, you must be looking forward to the lovely pension package we are offering you, yes? It would be a terrible shame if upon retiring you suddenly found you were receiving a greatly reduced pension, right? We are sure your lovely young wife wouldn't like that, right? We've been good to you, right, we've looked after you, right?'

The editor felt like he'd been working for the mafia all his life and had never realised – not until now, and it was too late. He felt himself being placed over the barrel, his trousers tugged down by a vodka-swilling gangster. It was probably best he kept his mouth shut for the time being. He wasn't sure what else he could do.

The editor surprised Joan at work. The same geeky, harassed student girl who had once thought Stuart had taken a funny turn on the uncomfortable-looking chairs felt a sense of déjà-vu as she was sent off to find Joan. Again, she was relieved to be seeking human interaction rather than a literary reference. How much longer could this square peg waste a lifetime in this round hellhole? She found Joan with a shopping basket of books, looking up at a wall of dusty novels, and told her there was a gentleman waiting downstairs to see her.

Joan automatically thought it was William. 'Oh, is he wearing a kilt?'

The girl looked at Joan as if she was on drugs.

'You know, like a Scottish tartan skirt?'

'I know what a kilt is,' snapped the girl. She was just about fed up with working there and everyone thinking that this was the pinnacle of her intellect, worth and skillset. 'If you must know, kilts are not and were not solely worn by the Scots, in fact.' The girl went to dish out both barrels of a fashion history lesson, but decided against it. 'You know what – who cares. He wasn't wearing a kilt, okay. He was dressed like a traditional, well-paid Englishman, probably close to retirement having worked in a long and rewarding career, unlike me!'

And with that the girl spun on the spot and trundled off, leaving Joan a little taken aback.

'I only asked if he was wearing a kilt, dear,' called Joan after her, not completely sure what she'd done to warrant such a response, and also because she wanted to reply something rather than just stand there, open-mouthed, like a lemon.

Joan was surprised to see the editor.

'Hello, Joan, it's nice to see you again. Can you spare me five minutes?'

Joan put down her basket and looked at the clock. She hadn't forgiven him for the article, but would at least allow him to explain himself.

'Joan, my dear, I only just returned to work this week, and I found out about that article last night.'

Joan looked the editor in the eye and could tell he was telling her the truth. His eyes were fixed on hers. His voice crackled with anger and remorse as he spoke.

'I'm so sorry. I can't believe what has happened. I felt sick to the stomach reading that abomination of an article.'

Again Joan read his face, but this time reached out a hand and rubbed his arm.

'Here, let's take a seat,' she suggested, and they both sat down next to each other on the chairs.

He carefully explained all he knew to Joan, stressing that Stuart's article had been very different. He promised to send her a copy, but insisted that for the time being she shouldn't show anyone if at all possible. He wasn't entirely sure who was involved, but it was his wish to see them face the consequences before he left.

Joan asked why he was leaving, and he explained that losing Stuart had broken his heart and that this debacle was the icing on the cake. His final mission would be to try to rectify this situation as best as he could. He was sure the paper was now rotten to the core.

He then suggested perhaps it might come to the point where Joan might consider suing the paper.

Joan said, 'I think it was Rebecca.'

The editor admitted he was sure of the same, but unsure about James's involvement.

She said she had always liked James and would be surprised if he was involved. But then, she'd also thought Rebecca had seemed nice and sincere, so she no longer trusted her own judgement of people's characters.

The editor said, 'It's well worth you keeping your distance. Don't get involved in anything, even if they try to contact you with some blog award or something.'

Joan then remembered William. 'William!' she gasped, looking worried.

'I wouldn't worry about old William,' chuckled the editor. 'He wouldn't be on Rebecca's radar unless he was involved with you or…' The editor watched Joan's cheeks flush. 'Oh, Joan, really?'

Joan didn't know what to say. At first everything had seemed so trivial and innocent but naughty. Then, all of a sudden, she'd felt exposed and in massive trouble.

'What's going on, Joan?'

'Nothing, well… I'm not sure it's any of your business.'

'Oh, Joan, please don't be like that. I know you don't really know me, but I feel like I know you. I spent countless evenings chatting with Stuart about you. I know an awful lot, perhaps more than you know I know. And William and I go way back too. As much as you feel it might not be anything to do with me, I assure you it is. I'm very much involved. Now, please, what about William?'

Joan liked the way the editor spoke to her: very matter-of-fact, to the point and succinct.

'Well, we have become kind of close.'

Joan waited for the school teacher-like rebuke, but on the contrary, a little misty tear seemed to well in the editor's eye and the corners of his mouth curled ever so slightly.

'That's really just perfect, absolutely lovely,' he said sincerely, blinking glistening eyes.

'Mysteriously, early one morning, William received a paper, your paper, with a rush hour crush circled. And it was about him.'

They both sat there, trying to come to terms with everything that was happening. Finally, the editor broke the silence.

'It's that little bitch again. Mark my words, she's out to get him.'

Without having to think too hard, Joan had read the editor's mind and worked out whom he was thinking of and had come to the same conclusion.

'Do you think she knows about me and William?' asked Joan.

'God, I hope not, for your sake,' said the editor. 'You'll have to warn him, tell him not to get involved. Whatever she's up to, both of you steer well clear whilst I'll try to think of how best to deal with the situation.'

'I've already tried,' said Joan, looking forlorn. 'He didn't seem to believe me. Or at least, it all seemed to come out wrong when I tried to talk to him.'

'What did?' asked the editor, intrigued.

'Well, I guess he thought I was jealous, which in a way I was. But now I don't know. I guess I feel sort of vindicated. And also sorry for him, and bloody furious that this girl seems to think messing with our lives is okay.'

'We're going to have to get William to see sense. I think what I'll do, if it's okay with you, is print off Stuart's last article and give a copy to William with instructions not to show anyone, but to ring me or you once he's read it.'

Joan looked at the editor quizzically. 'Why should I mind if you forward Stuart's article to William?'

Again the editor's eyes glistened. 'I think perhaps there was a reason the article never went to print. I think perhaps he wanted to show you, or even William, first. . I'll email it to you a little later, and things might be a little clearer.'

The editor stood up and said, 'I shan't keep you a moment longer.' He tugged his shirt sleeves a little so they looked equidistant each side of his cuffs.

'Very smart,' Joan said instinctively, and she was rewarded with a smile from the editor, along with a warm embrace and a kiss on each cheek. He smelt of expensive aftershave.

'I'll be in touch,' he said, and with that he turned and left the library, his smart Oxford shoes sounding like a slow applause as he walked away.

Joan went home. She was desperate to speak with William, but unsure how to go about approaching the matter. The editor had said he'd try to track him down and talk some sense into him.

Joan cooked dinner, and hoped to check her emails once Sam either hit the bottle or disappeared down the pub. But he seemed to sense she was eager for him to go out, and was hanging around like a bad smell. He ate his dinner and made a song and dance about what she wanted to watch on the television.

'I don't care,' said Joan irritably.

'I was only asking what you wanted to watch. Good God, woman, what's got into you?'

'Nothing,' said Joan defensively. 'Watch what you like. I think I might just go and run a bath.'

Sam watched as she picked up her phone and walked up the stairs.

She was acting strangely, he was convinced. Why did she need her phone to go for a bath?

Joan turned on the taps and sat on the loo, opening her email program. One from the editor sat unopened in her inbox. This was it, she thought. Her last ever communication with Stuart. The bathroom filled with steam and the trickle of the water cascading down into the bath replicated in a minute scale on the cheeks of her face. Her chest heaved as his voice once again spoke directly to her subconscious, one to one with her soul, a chat like he was in another room. Rivers of tears clouded her eyes, before being set free to flow unabated.

So there it was, set out in black and white for all the world to see, the brains behind the rush hour crush revealing their true inspiration. She sat on the toilet till the bath nearly overflowed, reading and rereading each line. Stuart had truly loved Joan, that much was clear, and he wrote that should he not be the man for her then his biggest wish was that perhaps his best friend would be. For what greater love could a man bestow upon a woman than his blessing that another might be a better option? It was not only a message from the grave, but also the ultimate rush hour crush.

Joan then realised William was right when he said Stuart had loved her all his life. Only then did she understand that he'd wondered about her on every journey, wherever he had been. Joan was his rush hour crush. But Stuart was right: she had fallen in love with William. Stuart had seen it from the very first moment they met. He recognised the look in her eye from when they were kids; it was how she had looked at Roy. She had never looked at Stuart like that. He was the brother she'd never had, the father figure, even. They had a meeting of minds, but their love was as true as it was different. It was his crush, not hers.

Chapter 19

Rebecca took out her electronic notepad and practised a few headlines. It was the way she had become accustomed to formulating her articles: she thought of the headline first and then wrote the story to complement it.

Secret sordid love affair revealed

Twisted love rats

Rush hour crush star in jealous love triangle – ménage a trios?

She set about writing the piece that would go with her revelations about a Z-list celebrity, famous from the rush hour crushes. *Local celebrity Joan caught out in steamy love tryst romps with local oddball/village idiot, kilt-wearing William Wallace fanatic.*

Through basic searches, Rebecca had learnt that William Wallace had changed his name by deed poll. She decided to use that as an angle in her article. It was his big secret, after all. A dark secret, Rebecca suggested, casting accusations that he had been trying to hide something from his past. Maybe he was responsible for something truly terrible, maybe he had been convicted of something ghastly – she suggested he could be a paedophile or rapist or murderer and had changed his identity for that very reason. (However blatant and stupid that would seem: the opposite of incognito, a man in hiding dressed in a kilt.)

At the same time, the editor also started to write a piece, using the permission-to-print code that Rebecca was going to be allocated. His would be very different. He was planning to describe Rebecca and her plot to destroy William and Joan and Stuart's legacy. His article would show that Rebecca had planned to allude to Joan as some sort of nymphomaniac, a sex addict in an open relationship who was some kind of wife-swapper type. The editor would completely rebuff the allegations on her behalf, writing that they were made without any proof or substance and were totally made-up, figments of Rebecca's twisted imagination. To suggest Sam was the heartbroken partner left out by William and Joan was also utterly absurd. The editor was unsure how he could deny this, but somehow he would endeavour to debunk such an outlandish suggestion. Rebecca would once again insinuate that Joan had used her involvement with the rush hour crush section as a vehicle to meet men. The editor would thoroughly refute the claim, which had no proof or substance.

According to Rebecca, William Wallace, in particular, was looking for hassle-free sexual liaisons. And that was where Rebecca first started formulating the sting idea, inspired by Sam's revelation of a possible affair between Joan and William. Her plan was to lure William and Joan to a hotel room and take photos of them together to prove her story. She'd tempt William to the hotel by setting up a liaison with the Texan, and Joan would go along too, probably rushing to his rescue. Rebecca hoped Joan might catch William in the act with the Texan. That would be the best possible outcome. Joan would probably be tempted to go along to try to warn William; he had become incapable of doing anything without consulting her first. Even though Joan didn't think the Texan or Ruby as she had come to be known was real, she'd go along as well, with the intention of proving herself right and also to pick up the pieces of William's broken heart and ego. But she would be totally unaware that Rebecca had also invited Sam.

Rebecca painstakingly arranged for hidden cameras and a host of her most trusty minions to watch out for when the protagonists entered the fray. But she only told them about William, Ruby and Joan. Sam was all her doing, her special secret ingredient.

Rebecca didn't know she was also being watched by the editor and his team. They had been tipped off by James, but he too didn't know anything about the Sam surprise.

Sam would arrive at the hotel thinking Rebecca wanted to meet him for some sort of sexual liaison. He'd bathed himself in aftershave and slicked his hair with gel and put on his favourite moth-eaten corduroy jacket; he'd even trimmed his pubes and talcumed his Y-fronts in the hope of making a good impression. He had no idea Rebecca had set this hotel meeting up to trap Joan and William and him. The fake Texan thing was little more than a side dish to the main course.

Rebecca was desperate to expose Joan and William. Setting them up together in the hotel room and then having an angry Sam turn up. She could just sit back and record the fallout. If Sam didn't turn up,

Rebecca could even bribe William and Joan if she had to. She would get more photos and records of them together.

Joan and the editor knew that Ruby wasn't real, but they were oblivious to Rebecca's blackmail plan and Sam's involvement, all they knew was what James had managed to pass on.

As Rebecca began fine-tuning her next article and setting up Joan and William as best she could, she conspired, with a little help from Sam – albeit mostly without his knowledge. Sam, in his naivety, was only too eager to tell Rebecca all about how he and Joan had got together. He embellished the details, letting his warped imagination run away with him. Apparently, Joan enjoyed making love whilst reading Keats. Listening to him recite Chaucer drove her wild. Like some ladies fancy for a foreign accent, she seemed potty about hearing old English. Rebecca noted down that Joan probably liked to hear William speak in a broad Scottish accent whilst in full costume at the same time calling herself Maid Marian.

Sam also suggested to Rebecca that Joan was the type to go off with other couples rather than stay with just him, and she was interested in swinging parties and keys in pots and making love in the open air, and had shown a real interest in dogging recently. Sam suggested that might be Joan's next project, after the rush hour crush blog: doggers who fell in love or top dogging sites or something along those lines.

Rebecca was clearly just using Sam. But occasionally he provided gems, like the dogging suggestion, and this was gold dust to Rebecca.

She was pandering to his sick and twisted mind, manipulating him into position, massaging his ego, and from time to time it proved worth it.

She told Sam she had heard a rumour about an event. Completely top secret, off the radar, friends of friends, that sort of thing, very hush hush, but by the sounds of it 'right up his alley'. Sam wasn't a hundred per cent sure she knew what his alley was, but nevertheless he was intrigued. Rebecca suggested he might find the event very interesting. As far as she currently knew, it was due to happen at a hotel, on a day as yet undisclosed – but her sources would endeavour to tell her and he should rest assured that she would make sure he would be the first to find out the details. Without doubt, it would be a happening he'd not want to miss.

Sam being Sam – blessed with a one-track mind and also deluded – thought she was suggesting a sexual liaison of some sort. Maybe she really did know him. Rebecca had reopened the lines of communication and Sam was as willing as ever to jump in head first, providing Rebecca with any information or inspiration she might need.

Joan smelt a rat from the moment William first suggested the existence of Ruby the Texan. She had her suspicions it was Rebecca's handiwork in action once again; the editor had also learnt it was all part of Rebecca's elaborate plot. But they struggled to persuade William to see sense. It seemed he couldn't accept the truth, or had an element of pride that stopped him comprehending that he was being made a fool of and set up.

The editor managed to get James to break cover and join forces with Joan to warn William he was being used. But he still remained unconvinced. 'Why would anyone go to all this trouble? What purpose would it serve?' He decided not to give up hope of meeting his crush, just in case the Texan was waiting for him and he could prove his doubters wrong.

This was when Joan, James and the editor formulated a plan to turn the tables on Rebecca and basically play her at her own game. James explained that Rebecca wanted to catch William at a hotel with Ruby, and they decided to record her in the act of producing the set-up. But to do so they needed to keep the rouse going, so they all played along as if totally unaware.

The editor pretended he was going about the process of leaving the paper, giving the impression he really didn't care so much any more about what went on at work.

Joan carried on doing her job and seeing William here and there, albeit slightly less than before. She was a little hurt by his interest in another woman and also his pig-headed pride, but also interested in how the whole charade would play out.

James, meanwhile, acted as a double agent. He was his sister's reluctant confidant. She was certain he wouldn't betray her, and she thought she'd be able to manipulate his involvement, to keep him in line. So he acted himself, slightly nervous and warning her not to do certain things (which she ignored), saying she wouldn't get away with her plan, but going along with her. All the while, he was setting up the infrastructure, getting phones and recording kit so Rebecca could carry out her plan. He was the mole, reporting regularly and secretly to the editor. So although Rebecca believed she was catching William and Joan in her spider web, the hunter had become the hunted and she was being given enough rope to hang herself.

The editor called in lots of old favours and made sure a few well-placed friends in the media were fully aware of what Rebecca was up to. He had been in the trade long enough to have made some strong and powerful friendships and allegiances. He arranged for some of the best old-school hacks in the land to set up cameras and recording devices around the hotel so they could record all of Rebecca's antics. They would have people watching her and her people wherever they were and whatever they were doing, and also listening to her every comment – all on the proviso they understood the backstory and that it had nothing to do with Joan and Sam. When the time came, they would tell a story of Rebecca trying to destroy William's life in a cruel vendetta inspired by her continual dislike of the rush hour crush legacy. Should Joan be mentioned or involved, it would only be in the capacity of previous victim and friend trying to warn William away.

The editor, James and Joan planned on making sure Joan would only say to William exactly what they had written in a script, rather than give Rebecca any potential material from any situation that might develop. The editor would pen a basic scenario.

'Keep it simple,' he said. 'See if we can't bore Rebecca out of her hiding place.'

He was also putting the finishing touches to his own article, a fitting tribute to his old friend. He'd be proud to publish it once this whole mess was put to bed. The truth behind the sabotage of the Rush Hour Crush section and his report on the terrible bint who was supposed to be taking over the reins at his beloved newspaper. *His* bloody paper. A piece on the rogue reporter, Rebecca, that described how, in a secret sting operation, they were able to record her in the act of trying to set up, besmirch, ridicule and harass poor William and Joan.

William was sitting at a table in the bar. He'd been shown to the table by an overly friendly member of the hotel staff who treated him like he was some sort of celebrity, as if he'd been waiting for his arrival. William felt like everyone in the lobby bar was waiting for his arrival and giving him funny looks. He felt slightly paranoid.

'What's he doing now?' Rebecca barked into her headset. She was watching William on her telephone screen and he just seemed to be sitting there doing nothing much at all.

'Nothing, Jen,' said the chief minion. 'He's just sitting there twiddling his thumbs.'

'Tell the barman to deliver the envelope,' snapped Rebecca impatiently.

In the little brown envelope was a note: *Room 112. Come up and see me. Let's get acquainted – Ruby*

If anything, this made William even more hesitant. What sort of woman would invite him straight to her room? It seemed very improper. He wasn't sure how these things usually occurred, but normally, he presumed, one met in a public place. Going to a hotel room seemed very forward. Perhaps it was an American thing. He was sure Joan would never arrange to meet a complete stranger in a hotel room.

He sat there, pondering his situation. Maybe this was a bad idea after all. Perhaps he ought to just head home and forget it ever happened. He wondered whether, if he sat there long enough, Ruby would come and find him. How had he got into this situation? And why did he feel so strange about it? Perhaps he should stop dithering and head upstairs right away. Goodness knew what he might find. But that was it, which was the problem. It wouldn't be Joan. What on earth was he doing there?

As he sat spinning the note between his fingers and thumbs, Joan walked in and calmly sat down opposite him, like an apparition.

'Jesus fucking Christ!' he said. 'Oh my God! I mean, erm, what a surprise!'

Joan just smiled at him and patted him on the hand, looking at the note he was twiddling with his fingers. He passed it to her and she read the message.

'You can still go if you like,' she said suggestively, raising her eyebrows, immediately going off script.

'Oh, Joan, I don't even know what I'm doing here. How did you know where to find me?'

'It's not important, William,' she replied.

'I was just intrigued, I suppose. Vanity perhaps. I guess I was afraid to chase what I maybe couldn't have and –'

'It really doesn't matter,' said Joan. Given time, putting herself in his shoes, she had decided she'd have been equally intrigued.

Rebecca sat twitching in the hotel room. Things weren't exactly going as she had hoped.

'Send in Ruby,' she snapped at the minion in the cupboard.

'Send in Ruby,' came the muffled relay from within the cheap Ikea-made cupboard.

Rebecca was still totally unaware that Joan and co. had been tipped off about her plans to tempt William to the hotel under the pretence that he was meeting the fabricated character Ruby. She was also unaware the other side were expecting to see his friend Joan join proceedings. Rebecca hoped this might cause fireworks, but nothing of the sort had happened. So she then hoped her other ingredients, Sam and Ruby, might bring the situation to the boil once she added them into the equation. These were the only parts of the scheme the editor, James and Joan had failed to foresee, because they hadn't been privet to all her plans. No one had been.

So it was that Sam now stood, next to the concierge desk, looking at the contents of his envelope, whilst all the hotel staff and guests buzzed around him like bees in a hive. The envelope contained photos of Joan and William: walking hand in hand through a park, sitting on a bench and eating sandwiches, sharing a romantic, scenic kiss. As he looked at the photos, a violent rage grew inside his soul. His knuckles burnt and he felt like his head would explode with jealousy. If he saw Joan right then he wasn't sure he'd be able to contain his anger. He'd punch her right in the face.

Then he noticed the note on the back of the envelope: *See me in the bar*. Did the note mean Rebecca or Joan? He couldn't be sure. He was feeling a little hurt and confused, and very angry. He didn't like the notion of being out of control, and already he was of the opinion he was being slightly manipulated – Rebecca's speciality. What was going on? It must have all been Rebecca's doing; she was playing games with him. Why did she want him there? Why show him those photos? It could only be because she wanted to make him jealous. She wanted some sort of reaction. But what was in it for her? Sam wondered. She either wanted him or was planning on blackmailing them, Joan and this other chap – by his clothes Sam deduced it was William. That was the only logical explanation he could come up with. He would need to decide whose side he wanted to be on.

He picked up the photos and made his way around to the bar, where he saw Joan and William sitting at a cosy-looking side table together, looking at each other earnestly. William seemed to be saying he was sorry to Joan. Sam walked up without saying a word and dropped the envelope on the table. The photos of the pair of them splayed out, looking back at them.

A horrified, guilty-schoolgirl look spread rapidly across Joan's face, and she gulped nervously.

Watching the scene on a monitor in the hotel room, Rebecca yelped a little triumphant 'yes' with glee.

Watching on a large-screened laptop wired into the hotel's own CCTV, in the car park out the back in a big silver SUV, the editor mouthed, 'Who the fuck is that?' to James, who looked blankly back at him, shrugging his shoulders.

William worked out from Joan's face and Sam's scowl exactly who had just joined them sitting at the table. He quite quickly accompanied her on the naughty step, feeling very awkward indeed – and feeling Sam's bony knees knocking into his own, encroaching on his personal space, his long leg levers needling up into his own thick-set, puffy knees.

'Well, this is all very cosy, isn't it?' said Sam, swivelling around in his seat to take in the décor.

Unsure what to say, William said, 'We don't want any trouble…'

'Who's we?' Sam shot back, leaning forward across the table and laying his hands down flat, before balling his fists.

William fidgeted slightly in his seat, trying to make himself seem marginally taller.

'Who's we?' Sam said again, switching his burning, beady-eyed stare to Joan – the stare she'd seen a thousand times before at home but never out in public.

'Sam, I don't know what you're talking about.'

'Don't think I'm stupid, woman. Look at the photos,' Sam hissed.

'Excuse me, don't you bloody talk to her like that,' said William, feeling his heart start to pound with adrenalin.

'Oh look, the Scotty dog's got a little bark,' sneered Sam.

'Sam, not here, not like this,' said Joan, trying to calm the situation.

'I think we will do this here and I think I will speak to you exactly how want,' said Sam, standing his ground.

Joan was pinned in by Sam, so even if she wanted to get away, she couldn't until Sam decided to move – unless she clambered over or around him.

Rebecca was loving every second of this and was desperate for it to escalate.

The editor, thinking quickly, said to James, 'You stay here. I'm going in. If you go in, your sister will know you've double-crossed her. I can explain to the three of them. It might be the only way to stop this escalating and turning violent.'

The editor jumped out of the car and ran through the car park and into the foyer. You could hear audible gasps of shock and see eyes fixing him as members of his staff realised who he was. A few onlookers made to get up and leave straight away, but the editor swivelled his head and waved at them, like he knew exactly what they were thinking and where they were going, like he had eyes in the back of his head.

One of Rebecca's minions hissed, 'Shit, the editor's here.'

They just watched as he entered the fray like an American wrestler.

The editor slid in next to William, saying, 'Fancy seeing you here.' He caught both William and Sam by surprise, but also Joan, as she realised this was totally off-script.

Rebecca sat frozen, watching her plans suddenly start to unravel.

'Who the hell are you?' questioned Sam, feeling annoyed he'd lost his impetus.

'How terribly rude of me,' said the editor. 'I'm the editor of the *Metro* newspaper. I was friends with your old pupil Stuart, and I like to think of myself as a friend to both William and the lovely Joan here. From your appearance and demeanour I'd guess your name is Sam. Am I correct?'

The editor reached out a hand and unleashed the vicelike grip that had been his secret weapon and the key to his success for the last twenty-five years. He wasn't a particularly big man, but he had that in his armoury. Not many men had felt the force and forgotten it. You ask any man and they'll tell you they remember a very firm handshake and a wet one. The editor's was without question one of the firmest many men had ever felt.

'Now, I believe we have a little situation here, and if I'm not terribly mistaken… actually, forget that, I *know* we're still being listened to right now. Come out, come out wherever you are, Rebecca. You can make this a lot easier to explain. Or perhaps I'll just continue and you can fill in the gaps later. It's what you specialise in, isn't it, dear – fabricating nonsense or, for want of a better word, bullshit. Excuse me, Joan.'

For the first and last time, William and Sam shared a look of mutual feeling: abject confusion. What on earth was the editor talking about? They wondered. It was as if he was talking to hidden fairies or was seeing ghosts.

'Sorry, let me explain a little better. You're all being set up. You're being watched and listened to at this very moment.'

'Why are you watching us?' said William.

'Oh, my dear William, I'm not watching you. I'm watching *her*.'

'Who's her?' asked Sam whilst looking at William like they were the only two not currently supposed to be residents of the funny farm.

'Rebecca,' said Joan.

'Exactly,' said the editor.

'Oh,' said Sam.

'Do you hear that, Rebecca? We are watching you. We are watching all of you.'

The editor then stood up and started pointing at his newspapers employees, who suddenly looked up, like rabbits in the headlights, realising they'd been rumbled. Some tried to hide behind menus or shrank into their seats, and others tried to discreetly slip away hoping to disappear through the car park.

'Some of the staff here are even in on it.' The editor tapped his nose, looking at the concierge. 'But we know something Rebecca doesn't. Are you coming out, Rebecca?'

The editor leant across and picked up a plastic flower sitting on the table. He tapped the flower head, smirking, before picking it up and shouting 'Coooooooeeeeeeeeee' loudly into its petals like it was a microphone. 'Crude but effective,' said the editor like a Bond villain, turning the pot upside down, removing the inner pot and revealing the batteries and inner workings.

Joan, William and Sam sat staring at the editor, somewhere between aghast and in spellbound awe. He was really good.

'To be honest, I think you've probably all been watched for some time now.'

'Shit,' said Rebecca, still trying to stop the ringing in her ears after the editor's 'cooooooeeeee'. She was desperate to hear exactly how much the editor really knew, and hoping he was bluffing.

Then Ruby turned up. 'Well, hello there, cowboy.'

It was without doubt one of the worst American accents any of them had ever heard. They all looked at each other and back at the very large-breasted lady whose brassiere looked on the verge of spilling her very full bosom all over the gobsmacked assemblage. They were stunned by her appearance: the cheap nylon dress and imitation fur, finished off with a tacky-looking cowboy hat, the type popular with ladies on rowdy hen parties.

'Hells bells,' said William.

Ruby's invitation for him to accompany her to the hotel room, coupled with a suggestive eyebrow raise, was met with an audible gulp, gasp and spluttering.

'No way. I mean, certainly not. Erm, no, thank you… erm, not at all,' said a visibly disturbed William.

Ruby looked like an adult entertainer or prostitute with some sort of addiction to cakes or alcohol – probably both. William couldn't be certain, but either way she had a capacity for lots of it. William was horrified, and he wasn't interested. Which was a view shared by the editor, and even Sam was looking at her like she was slightly more of a challenge than he'd fancy.

Joan piped up: 'Excuse me, dear. I won't call you Ruby, as we all know that's not your name, but who sent you here?'

'Listen, sweetheart,' Ruby said, keeping in character. 'You can call me what you like, but unless I get matey boy here up to room 112, I'm not getting paid my money.'

William put his head in his hands. All this was his fault.

The editor watched William become engulfed by self-pity and guilt, and felt his heckles start to rise again.

'Listen, darling, if you can give us a little more detail about who hired you, we shall make sure you're fully reimbursed,' said the editor.

'I can't,' said Ruby, dropping the phony accent.

'Can't or won't?' said the editor.

Sam looked on, thinking perhaps he could offer his services for the team, but he didn't think Joan would appreciate or understand that. Or maybe she would. He toyed with the idea of offering the suggestion.

'Can't,' said Ruby. 'I work for an agency. It's all very discreet. We have to look after our clients' confidentiality.'

'I see,' said the editor.

Sam wiggled as if desperate to say something but unable to get the words out of his mouth. Joan watched him, bemused. She sat there surrounded by William and Sam and the editor and now Ruby, with Rebecca listening in somewhere else.

'Room 112, you said?' Joan commented, looking at Ruby, then William and the editor.

'Yes,' they both agreed.

'That's where we'll find Rebecca,' said Joan.

At that moment Rebecca said, 'Shit shit shit.' Jumping up, she knocked her cup of coffee off the side of the bath, from where she'd been listening and watching the events unfold. She had been perched on the edge of the tub for so long her butt cheeks had gone numb. She flung her laptop onto the floor, knocking the shower hose off the bath mixer, which then wriggled around, biting her feet like a metallic snake, spitting coffee around her drenched feet and ankles.

'We've got to get out of here, right now,' she said, leaving caffeine-covered footprints as she climbed out of the bath.

Ruby was supposed to have led William straight to the bedroom, and then Rebecca and her assistant would get photos or a video of him in the act. Even half in bed or just in the hotel room getting undressed would have done it. Ideally, then Joan would have turned up and it would have all gone to bedlam, cumulating in a final crescendo of carnage when Sam rocked up. It had pretty much all gone wrong, and now everyone was onto Rebecca and on the way up to confront her.

Rebecca fell out of the bathroom, trying to grab any evidence of them having been in the room. Her mate in the cupboard rolled out, momentarily dazed by the light after having sat in near-total darkness for the best part of two hours with his head between his knees, his only source of light the green LED signalling the camera's standby mode was still active and the crack in the cupboard door. He'd been squashed into that coffin in the main room, holding the camera, ready to pounce.

'Quick! Grab the card,' Rebecca screamed.

They pulled the plastic card from the wall socket and the room was plunged into darkness.

'We'll take the fire escape,' she said, running out of the room and up the corridor.

Joan, the editor and William had hastily made their way to the lifts, with Sam skulking behind, a bit of a spare part. He wasn't sure he wanted to find Rebecca, just in case she started accusing him of being part of the plot to set up Joan and William. He was perhaps the only person to have figured out that she was planning on blackmailing them with the photos. She was going to either write a really shitty article or extort them for all she could, he figured.

As Rebecca and her co-conspirator ran down the stairs, heading for the fire escape, they flew unchallenged, down several flights until they reached the basement. They thought they would be clear to sneak away through the underground car park, that they'd escaped without anyone noticing them. But as they pushed the final door open, they were dazzled by a cacophony of flashing cameras, illuminating the dark, artificially lit subterranean landscape – light-blue painted concrete walls throbbing with pulsing strobes.

A team of photographers in pig masks called Rebecca's name, whilst she and her counterpart looked like pilled-up ravers, gobsmacked and confused by the crescendo of noise and barrage of pyrotechnics.

The fallout provided the editor with the opportunity to work out who exactly had taken up with Rebecca, who was in her team, who was a bad egg and who was being blackmailed. It was clear she'd infiltrated the finance department and was using Joan's money to pay off some people. One by one, the editor clipped wings and was able to cure the cancer eating away at the paper.

James was again called in to see the editor. The other staff were unsure of his involvement, but seeing as his sister was in it up to her neck, they understood his repeated trips to see the boss. James explained to anyone that would listen that his dad would disown him if he thought he'd gone against his sister.

The editor explained to James that when he was younger, his relationship with Stuart had been a little different. Stuart had taken the editor under his wing when he was 'wet behind the ears'. He too had been volatile and slightly reckless, he reminisced. The editor explained he'd thought he knew better than those around him. He'd had the idea to write a particularly clumsy piece, similar to what Rebecca had planned, but with the guidance of Stuart he'd changed direction. Maybe that was part of the reason the editor had felt Rebecca deserved another chance and had given her the benefit of doubt, but she seemed too far gone to be helped now. She was malicious and twisted, a career criminal of the tabloid journalist kind.

The editor explained that he had seen all sorts whilst in the job. The previous editor from whom he'd taken over had left due to some sort of phone-hacking scandal. Others had been involved with dodgy politicians and crooked celebrities, gangsters and all sorts of lowlifes. He'd dealt with rapists, murderers and child molesters. He'd seen and heard it all: members of staff caught in other stings, drink and drug problems, all manner of substance abuse, self-harming, bullies…

But Rebecca was something different. The editor thought it was probably only a matter of time before she started alleging improper conduct or God knew what else, just to further her career and protect her interests. She was a nightmare. Working under her would be a terrible and dangerous existence, as she was ruthless and didn't care for anyone. The editor joked, 'Perhaps she would make a very good boss after all?' She was the polar opposite to him.

A muted hush came over the floor as Rebecca made her way to the editor's office. She'd not been seen for a few weeks and most presumed they'd never see her again. This was totally unexpected. Surely she wasn't about to receive another reprieve.

Her body language was different, though. She didn't seem to be scanning the room and sharing nonchalant looks with fellow conspirators. All her friends had deserted her. They'd had their court martials. Only her victims and those who refused to join her gang defiantly looked up at her now as she did the walk of shame, like a child sent to the headmaster's office. Her demeanour suggested she knew the writing was on the wall. The editor had been given the green light to fire her. Those who mattered no longer cared about her heritage.

She tapped meekly on the editor's door before popping her head around it.

'Give me a moment, please,' the editor snapped angrily.

So Rebecca let the door go and hovered around outside his office, feeling the eyes of the entire room boring a hole in the back of her head. She didn't dare turn around and face them. But every second she was made to stand outside his office like a naughty schoolgirl, the embarrassment and humiliation grew tenfold. She wanted to just walk away there and then, save a little bit of pride. She looked at her watch. Perhaps one more minute. Still the eyes of her colleagues stared into her soul. The burgeoning hubbub signalling the growing appetite of those desperate for the next instalment. The second hand on Rebecca's Rolex watch seemed to be moving more slowly than she ever remembered.

Finally, she heard a muffled 'Come' and she entered the editor's office, ready to face the music.

As the door shut, a few of the braver members of staff got up from their desks to edge a little closer to the editor's office. They weren't looking glum or nervous – they were positively excited by the imminent dressing-down. The bitch had it coming.

The editor carried on tapping away on his laptop, absorbed by something far more important than the bit of trash standing before him. He was happy to prolong the torture indefinitely.

As he seemingly ignored her, Rebecca just stood in front of his desk, unsure whether to say something or take a seat.

Finally, he stopped what he was doing and closed his laptop and just stared at her for a moment.

'Well, I'm not entirely sure what you were trying to achieve, but you certainly achieved something. Your demise, thankfully,' said the editor. 'What would you like to happen now? I'm curious,' he continued.

Rebecca finally spoke. 'I'm sorry,' she said in a feeble voice.

'Excuse me?' said the editor.

'I made a mistake. I'm sorry. Can I have another chance?' Rebecca croaked, before theatrically turning on the waterworks in a final roll of the dice. It was predictable and calculated, as always.

'Have you gone out of your bleeding mind? What is it with you and this poxy rush hour crush vendetta nonsense you've had?' shouted the editor. 'I gave you a chance and you fucked it up, and now you've fucked it up some fucking more for good measure? It's one thing writing a shit, poxy article that gets under the reader's skin. It's a whole different ball game making up shit just because you've got some sort of issue with some entirely innocent people. You are a nasty fucking cow.'

Spit flew across the table as the editor lost his rag, smashing his hand down on the lid of his computer.

Relief poured out of his mouth, body, skin and every sinew as he finally told Rebecca what he thought of her and her actions. He realised he wasn't being very professional, but he no longer cared. He was shouting for Stuart, Joan, William and all the other members of staff she'd intimidated and manipulated.

'Believe me, you are well and truly finished now. Get your stuff and get out of my sight. You fucking repulse me. I don't want to see you around here ever again. Go, go, just go.'

As she walked away, wiping away her crocodile tears, the editor sat back down at his desk, shaking with emotion and adrenalin. He wanted to cry real tears of pent-up emotion. He wanted to get drunk, raise a toast or two to his old mate Stuart. But first he needed to check whether he'd broken his computer again.

James asked the editor, 'What's going to happen to Rebecca now?'

The editor revealed that, on his say-so, several rival papers were planning on running an explosive story about the next potential editor of the *Metro* being involved in a blackmail/extortion plot involving some of the readers and partners of the paper. Rebecca had successfully plunged the paper into a scandal and made it a laughing stock. The editor had laboured that point to the Russian owner who in turn hoped his son had learnt a valuable lesson, that the whole newspaper industry was mocking them. This, he had known, wouldn't do their egos any good at all. He'd sent them his article, which he'd written in response. They'd finally agreed that Rebecca's actions had made her position untenable, and had said they were forced to either let her go completely or move her to a different role, out of the public spotlight, perhaps in another part of their organisation. 'Maybe coal mining in Siberia,' the editor joked.

'I appreciate it's important that Rebecca never knows about your involvement in helping us uncover what she was up to,' the editor said to James. 'But I'm sure she will be looked after nevertheless. She has made some very powerful friends already. No doubt she'll be back one day, but I'll be long gone by then hopefully.'

The editor shook James's hand. 'You're a good lad,' he said earnestly. 'I find it near-impossible to believe you two were cut from the same cloth. I want you to know I'm very grateful, and I know Joan is as well, and we'll be forever indebted to you for your intervention. Should you ever need anything, please don't be afraid to ask.'

James blushed – he'd never really been given both barrels by a superior, and here he was being afforded the full red-carpet treatment from the editor.

'Also, James, I've recommended you for the assistant editor's role, and I'd be quite willing to act as your mentor and assist you in any way, should you be interested?'

In the aftermath, Joan found herself back at home with a stewing Sam. At first, he gave her the silent treatment, like he still hadn't had a chance to work out what had happened to their relationship and how best to deal with the potential threat to their living arrangements. Sam didn't dare ask if Joan still loved him. He already knew the answer. Besides, that was not the sort of conversation they had. Theirs had become a relationship of convenience, based on little more than companionship. Sam was savvy enough to know he hadn't been much of a partner for a very long time. But his pride was still hurt. Even if Joan was planning on leaving him, he didn't need to be happy about it. He didn't need to make it easy for her to leave him – he could still throw a few spanners in the works.

Theoretically, Joan could leave him, and then he would be in serious trouble. Where would he go? He could beat her up again and intimidate her so she would be too scared to leave him, but that approach hadn't worked fairly recently, and she'd said she wouldn't stick around if he ever did it again. So they had reached an impasse.

Joan couldn't bear the silence anymore. She hadn't made the decision to leave Sam, as she had been slightly alarmed by William's pig-headedness in seeking Ruby and was wondering if it might prove a question of 'better the devil you know' or even 'out of the frying pan and into the fire'. Perhaps all men were idiots. Joan was quite sure she already knew the answer to this.

So as they sat down for dinner one evening, after Sam grunted a thanks of appreciation for the perfect fry-up Joan had cooked, she simply said, 'Nothing happened, you know. Those photos. Everything. We were just talking. Nothing more. We're just good friends.'

She didn't know why she'd said that; perhaps to give herself some thinking time, or maybe just to give herself some peace. In the back of her mind, she felt like she didn't owe Sam anything. She never would. She would do whatever was right for her from now on. But Sam was on borrowed time and skating on very thin ice.

'I think you should make it up to me,' said Sam suggestively.

Joan wanted to be sick.

'Not tonight, Sam, maybe at the weekend,' she lied.

William was as fed up as he'd ever been. He'd have to persuade Joan he was truly sorry and that he really wasn't as bad as Sam.

'Whatever must she think of me?' said a morose William, stroking Mr Tickles. He was drunk from finishing off a particularly expensive bottle of brandy. Mr Tickles wasn't one for understanding human emotions, but he appreciated the cuddles as William unloaded his self-pity and loathing.

'I've been such a fool,' he sobbed.

Before the incident at the hotel William had first conceived the idea of contacting Joan's son whilst sitting with her during her lunch break, eating sandwiches. The mother–son relationship was one William envied, having not had children himself, and the thought of having children and yet not enjoying a healthy relationship with them filled William with terrible sadness on behalf of Joan.

Joan's sandwiches were somehow the best he'd ever tasted. He heard himself making contented 'nom nom nom' noises as he ate. She seemed to find the best bread-and-butter combination, always so fresh, delicious, soft white dough and crisp, poppy-seed crust. So sitting there that day, listening to Joan talking earnestly and heartfelt about the troubled relationships she had with her children – but especially her son, who had been with her for so long, when times were really tough, when she felt so much younger and he was just a little boy. Joan reminisced that perhaps it was the happiest but loneliest time of her life.

It was clear to William just how much she missed her boy. It was an incredibly presumptuous, strange and risky idea, but what if he managed to contact Adam and persuade him to come home and visit his mum? If the lad was anything like Joan but didn't like Sam, then just maybe they might get along too should they ever get the opportunity to meet.

William sent Adam a brief message via Facebook.

Dear Adam,

I hope you don't mind this approach out of the blue?

Nice to e-meet you. I just wanted to get in touch as I thought perhaps I might be able to persuade you to visit your mum. I know it would make her terrifically happy, and I couldn't think of a better present for her.

I appreciate you don't know me from Adam (excuse the pun), but I have become very good friends with your mother, and I was also good friends with your godfather, Stuart, who in turn was good friends with your father. So in a bit of a morbid kind of way, we are already connected.

Anyway, I won't beat round the bush. I also wanted to let you know I don't very much care for Sam. I appreciate this is exceedingly rude, risky and forthright of me, but I gather from your mum you might share the same feelings. I like your mum very much, and I just wanted to let you know there would be another friendly face here should you ever decide to return.

I hope you don't mind this direct approach. I believe it is more in keeping with how your generation operates.

Hope you are enjoying your travels.

Yours, William

Iamwillwallace@gmail.com

PS: I am happy to pay any airfare you should incur, and will gladly pay for a return ticket so you needn't feel trapped and could leave whenever you wanted.

William met Joan from work and offered to drive her home. At first they sat in silence, and then he finally revealed what was on his mind.

'I know it's forward, and recently I've been a terrible idiot, but I want you to know all that has changed. I've changed. I know I was stupid. I thought perhaps there was someone else out there who wanted me, just me – no complications. I know I want you, but I was afraid I couldn't have you. But I believe I can now. I don't think you're happy or want to be with Sam. I think we could be very happy together.'

Joan understood what William was suggesting. He had pulled up a little way from where she lived, so they were sitting not far from her house, with its spectre looming large in the car window. She knew Sam was milling around inside. She pondered saying, 'Fine, let's go, let's start a new life, right here and now.' But what would happen to her previous existence within those walls? She felt like a budgie afraid to leave her cage. The door opened onto the real world, and that was scary and unpredictable. She was like an inmate, institutionalised by a life with Sam. And there was a lifetime of memories. It was her home. It was shit, but it was her shit. If she just left then she'd probably lose the lot. She imagined a drunk, angry Sam, completely naked, laughing as the house and all her memories (however bad) burnt and perished to dust in the ground…

Perhaps it wasn't a bad idea. A clean slate, she thought. Perhaps Sam would disappear too.

William watched as Joan was wracked with difficult emotions.

'I'm sorry, my dearest Joan. I promise I didn't mean to cause you any further grief. I've been a fool and hurt you enough already. But you must know, it's vitally important – you don't need to stay there a moment longer. Joan, I love you. I promise you, I love you. I will be here, there, wherever and whenever you need me. I know I've made a terrible mess of things. But I promise for as long as I live it will never happen again. Should you choose to join me, we could be happy. I'm so sorry for letting you down.'

William broke down, overcome with self-pity. Joan didn't find it attractive much, even if it was slightly refreshing.

Joan leant across and kissed the blubbering William. It was a strangely passionate kiss, more designed to shut William up than anything else, but it worked perfectly. He sat in his seat like he'd been whacked with a frying pan.

'Good grief!' he said.

'I'm going to stay with Sam for the time being, William,' said Joan, watching as William's bottom lip started to wobble again.

'Oh, Joan, you really don't have to.'

'I know, but I just need a little longer to get myself straight. Thank you, though, William, for your patience. I honestly do think we will be together soon.'

William was truly worried about Joan and didn't want to leave her with Sam a moment longer. The thought of her sleeping with – or being beaten by – Sam tore him apart inside.

As Joan went to leave William's car, he leant down, pulling an ancient sgian-dubh from below his knee. It was a treasured decorative piece that was supposed to sit ornately in his gartered hose. It looked more like a fancy letter opener than a dagger. 'Here, take this. It'll give you good luck and might keep you safe.'

Joan looked at the ruby in the hilt and chuckled. She'd seen more grisly and threatening butter knives and nail files.

'Thank you, William,' she said, climbing out of his car.

'Please go home and have a good night's sleep.'

William waited as Joan walked away towards her house. He couldn't help but feel frustrated and useless.

Joan couldn't help stifle a little laugh at William's tears of indignant rage. She had waited a lifetime for someone to love her, and now he'd arrived, she already wanted him to be slightly different. More like a manly, silver-screen movie legend, she decided. When she had told William she was staying with Sam, she'd have preferred William to have replied, 'Frankly, my dear, I don't give a damn.'

One last night. She really wanted to be with William. He genuinely was a lovely, kind man and they got on so well. He might be quirky, but she had come to love him.

In the morning, she'd tell Sam they were over.

Chapter 20

Sam woke up with a start. Was that bang in his dream or real? Joan lay next to him, curled up asleep, quietly snuffling and snoring, obviously oblivious to any bump in the night. He rubbed his crusty eyes and tried to get comfortable again. Probably just some kids horsing around outside or a neighbour slamming a car door, he decided.

He watched as lights slashed the darkness, tracing the walls and ceiling with flame-like fluidity, thinking they were probably in his imagination, the start of a dream or from passing cars.

Then a moment's realisation… His heart stopped beating. His brain questioned the lights. Those lights in the room and hallway weren't from any car. Cars lights didn't usually light up their room like that. A car would have to be driving around inside the house and have an incredibly narrow beam. Tick-tock, tick-tock: the ticking clock in the hallway got increasingly louder as his senses tuned in to every sound. He held his breath. The choking compression of his heart in his mouth and his pulse pounded ever louder in his head. No, these weren't car lights. A concrete lava flowed through his veins, setting him rigid, like a petrified statue, in his bed. The light was from a torch. The shuffling noises were from someone in his house. An intruder. His brain was lit up by a flash of lightning. Blind panic.

The concrete splintered and shattered as the covers on the bed were torn aside. A voice summoned up from deep within him unleashed with primeval force, demanding immediate action and attention.

'Get out of my house!' he bellowed as deeply and powerfully as he could. His vocal cords, rudely snapped from silence, sounded like an air-raid siren before the first words were audible. Sam wanted the intruder to think he'd woken an ogre of massive proportion, not a scared old man.

The peace was certainly shattered. The intruder was certainly aware that his presence had been noted, even though it came as little surprise – he hadn't expected a warm welcome.

Sam jumped out of bed quickly, grabbing the wooden broom handle he kept nearby for security, never believing it would be needed in self-defence – at least hoping it would never be needed. No, the club was usually the last thing he touched when having a tidy-up or changing the house around. Broadly, it stayed where it was, a pointless wooden pole, ignored, by and large just gathering a small amount of dust, hidden away in the cupboard or under the bed. Joan hated thinking he might use it on her one day, but was too scared to hide it or throw it away.

Sam was a bully, but like most bullies he only picked on those who were smaller and weaker than him. He had never really been a very physically fit type; he was no alpha male. He saw sportsmen as intellectually weak, hence the need to utilise their brawn. He was resentful of healthy, good-looking men, especially if they seemed to have some sort of business acumen. He'd never regularly got up and exercised – he didn't see the point – and he wasn't into any sports (except those of the sexual kind). He was a vindictive, cruel beanpole, nearly the opposite of a gentle giant. His height made him seem an imposing man, but he was just nasty and malicious, more inclined to use mental torture on Joan or anyone else unfortunate enough to get close, rather than physical aggression. He saved that solely for Joan; he'd struggled to break her mentally, so he controlled her physically. He was the lord of bringing those around him down. Bitchy comments and spiteful snipes were second nature to him. He'd be nice when out in public or with old colleagues or his peculiar friends, but behind closed doors he was a different master. Generally, he ruled his house with a wicked tongue rather than an iron fist. He was a smart man and had been reasonably good-looking once upon a time, perhaps a little before Joan was a schoolgirl.

'Joan, get up, for God's sake – we are being burglarized!'

Joan pulled the covers close to her, not having had the benefit of the precious few seconds he'd had to work out what on earth was happening. She ran his words through her mind again, registered the anxiety in his voice – and flew out of the bed, much more quickly than Sam. Her mind was sharp, like a razor. This was her house. She loved this house. Her house. Her home. Her babies' home. They'd had good times and bad times here – her and the babies, that was. More bad than good, but that was due to Sam. When he was drunk and asleep or out, it wasn't so bad. Who was this person trying to take what little they had away from them? It might be bad, but it was their bad. They had so little anyway. How dare they try to take it?

If Sam was an ogre, Joan was going to go banshee, crazed witch. Like a mother goose defending her chicks, she crackled and cackled and hissed with pent-up fury behind Sam.

'Get out, get out, get out!' she screamed.

It had probably been nearly twenty years since they'd last acted together but now she willingly followed him into action, a united front against a common enemy.

As Sam disappeared down the stairs, Joan stopped to put on her slippers. Sam got down the stairs in a few steps and found the front door ajar. He bashed it aside, still making the strange air-raid siren wail as he ran up the path and out into the street, looking left and right, panting. Where had the bastard gone? He looked up and down the road; he couldn't see the intruder anywhere.

'Stay away from my house!' he shouted into the night.

His voice seemed to disappear, sucked up by the orange globes hanging in the night sky buoyed up by the lampposts. A black, damp stillness hung in the air. There were no footsteps running off into the distance. All was silent, like when you wake up having sleepwalked naked into the street in the middle of the night. The neighbours didn't stir.

Perhaps the intruder was hiding in the bushes. A moment's thought that someone was watching him made Sam swing round, clutching the wooden stick. A cricketer's air shot. No one was there so far as he could see.

Then, for the first time in many years, and only fleetingly, he worried about Joan. Was she watching him from inside the house? Laughing at him looking absurd, no doubt. She would probably think he'd dreamt it all in the first place. She'd be smirking as she watched him, standing there with his stripy pyjama bottoms flapping around his ankles; she'd think he looked a fool. He imagined her being repulsed by his long, cracked grey-yellow toenails integrating with the filth, worms and slugs stranded on the cold, damp tarmac; his toes curled. No doubt she'd be chuckling, thinking about his skinny chest and the smattering of white hairs on his shoulders as he waved a stick and tried to look manly. She was laughing at him, sneering, 'Who's he kidding, pot belly and all?' She'd probably left the front door open in the first place. All this was her doing somehow. The lazy cow was probably still in bed, not putting the kettle on and making a nice cup of tea to calm his nerves, like any decent woman would do. How had he ended up with such a useless wench?

Perhaps it had all been a dream. Why weren't the lights coming on? Had Joan even got out of bed? Absentmindedly, Sam tugged on one of the long hairs protruding from his earlobe. He felt puzzled and lousy as the adrenalin rush started to subside and his general feeling deteriorated into a muzzy stress head. His feet felt cold and wet. 'I'm bound to get a bloody chill now,' he mused aloud, imagining all the dog's muck and maggots squirming and crawling around between his toes. He gingerly picked his way along the path like he was treading on egg shells. Maybe Joan was right about him, he decided. He walked back to the house, checking over his shoulder and behind bushes and under neighbours' cars as he went.

He'd have to check the house to see what, if anything, was missing. Maybe call the police. Sod's law Janet would probably turn up. No doubt it would all become Sam's fault somehow. 'Old iron drawers,' he cursed.

First, he'd wake Joan up and tell her what had happened. Not that she would be any help or believe him, the useless cow. There was that bitterness again that she always made him feel. Nothing he did was ever good enough for her – for any of them really. Why wasn't he happy? He'd protected her and their home – he should feel good. He'd been a man.

Where was she? He couldn't believe none of the neighbours had stirred either. And what was the time?

Perhaps his headache was down to the red wine from earlier in the evening. Budgen's had a special offer: three bottles of Merlot for a tenner. He'd drunk two to Joan's one. They had briefly argued before falling asleep. Maybe that's why she'd slept through the bang. He fancied another glass of red wine if Joan hadn't finished her bottle, or perhaps a cup of tea would be better. Hopefully, she had put the kettle on.

He scanned the path all along, flicking his lighter briefly to illuminate the way. His head pounded as the tension seeped through his tobacco-smoked, alcohol-rinsed arteries, and his body and brain argued that he should still be tucked up warm in bed. He scrunched up his face and clawed at his thick, greasy matt of dandruff-flaked, unruly hair as he saw that the old stones in front of the door had been disturbed. Scratching the stubble on his chin, he caught the old, bloodied wart he'd snagged many times whilst shaving, this time his fingernail was responsible for flooding his pain receptors with multiple flashbacks to times he'd accidentally cut himself, a life time of bleeding warts.

He paused. He'd almost forgotten to look in the key's old secret hiding place, he wasn't sure if there'd still be a set of keys present. It had been so long since anyone had checked or even been locked out. The only people who knew the spare set of keys was kept there for emergencies were Joan's sister and the kids.

He gently ran his hand down the length of the front door and inspected the handle. No damage was immediately obvious. It was the same door with the peeling paint that had repelled Stuart a year or so ago.

Sam pushed it open slowly, sensing someone on the other side. The parted curtain revealed a figure dressed in a white nightie standing over a body slumped on the hallway floor. Holding what looked like a knife. Expressionless.

For the second time that night, Sam's heart stopped still as he struggled to comprehend the scene. He traced the outline of the body, trying to work out who the stranger was and feeling slightly euphoric that Joan had defeated them.

Joan's shoulders were shaking, her head was bowed and snot, tears and dribble waterfalled down from her face.

'Oh, Joan, what on earth have you done?'

'I... I... It was dark, I didn't see him, it was so fast, I didn't mean to...'

'Oh, don't be silly, Joan, it's fantastic. Rather him than you, eh? You were only defending our home, old girl,' said Sam.

'It wasn't like that. We collided. I bumped into him, knocking him over, and he fell down with such a bang. And I think I accidently stabbed him too. What if I've killed him?'

'Oh, Joan, I'm sure the authorities won't care about some scummy druggy burglar.'

Sam crouched down to take a closer look, squinting his eyes before standing up and turning on the hall light to illuminate the gruesome scene.

Then Joan collapsed to her knees over the crumpled form.

'My boy, my darling boy!' she said, gently touching his face, pushing back his hair to reveal his ghost-white face. 'We collided on the stairs and you fell. I didn't mean to. I'd never hurt you – it just happened. It was an accident.'

For a second Adam looked like Roy, like he was just asleep, and she tenderly caressed his ashen cheek.

Sam quickly reassessed the situation. 'You know, you'll probably get into terrible trouble for this. It's all your fault. Nothing to do with me. You shouldn't have stabbed him. Why on earth did you do that? I always said you were a little bit crazy. Now look what you've done. You've killed your son, and everyone will see what a nutter you are and what I've had to put up with, living with you all these years.'

Joan didn't look up. She just continued to gently caress the side of Adam's face with the side of her hand. Her beautiful boy. She was oblivious to Sam's taunts and words.

'I know what everyone thinks of me. Your sister, your colleagues and all your snooty, know-it-all friends from the paper – I know you were all having a good old laugh at me. I could easily have written for that paper or done the pathetic blog that you wrote. I never really got the accolades my skills warranted. I know you all look down your noses at me. I know you've told them some wicked, evil stuff about me that's blatantly not true. Well, here you go, it's plain to see for everyone: you're a bloody psycho.'

'Mum…' The weak voice shivered out from Joan's lap, stopping Sam in his tracks. Adam wasn't dead, but his life was seeping away.

'Adam. Oh, Adam, you're alive! I'm so sorry. Quick, Sam, dial 999. He's still alive!'

Joan pleaded, but Sam didn't do a thing. He just looked at her, reviewing the situation, recalculating possible outcomes, sequences of events, actions and reactions – every action would have a positive and negative reaction.

'Sam, he's dying. Quick! Please!'

'Erm… no, Joan, I don't think I will get the phone actually. I think I'll just let this little scenario play out, tragically and charmingly, as it is. After all, at the moment is it me with blood on my hands?'

Joan froze, looking at her hands. Was Sam really doing this? Playing a sick game with her son's life, right then and there?

'Sam, please!' she screamed, feeling a little ripple of pain come from her son's stricken form.

'What if we call the ambulance and he gets better? What then, Joan? Is he going to move home and we'll just start living like a happy little family again? What if I want to continue like normal, eh? What about what I want? No, he being here changes all that. First you and your new mate William and now him. Right now. It's all too convenient. All too perfect.'

Joan looked at the phone in the hallway, sitting on its little charge point. She went to gently put Adam's head down on the floor and call the ambulance herself, but Sam read her thoughts and picked the phone up off its receiver before threatening to throw it at the wall.

'I'll just say it was smashed in the commotion,' he said.

Joan was virtually in the 'get set' position already. Sam's last words were met with her leaping up and launching herself into a running head-butt into his midriff. It sent him staggering back into the front door. The wind was temporarily knocked out of him, but he grinned at Joan as she tried to work out her next plan of attack. She was desperate for the phone, and he tormented her by holding it just out of her reach. She didn't want to play, so she grabbed at his outstretched arm, using all her weight and her nails to claw at his arm.

'Ouch, you little cat!' he said, punching her clean in the side of the head.

As she recoiled for a second time, shaking off the effects from the blow to her head, she looked at her son, lying wounded on the floor.

'Sam, he needs to go to hospital right now. Please, for God's sake…'

'No. You need to go to jail. You are a bad woman.'

'Sam, please.'

He grabbed the phone unit and pulled at the telephone cable twice as if he was starting the petrol lawnmower. His evil intent grew stronger as the connector shot from the wall. He threw the phone and cradle down, smashing them on the wooden side table, dashing that chance of rescue. He looked at her with a face that suggested victory.

Then Joan remembered her mobile. It was still on her bed, charging. She jumped over Adam and scrambled up the stairs, but when she got halfway he grabbed her ankle, making her fall down onto her chest. As she tried to pull herself away, up the stairs, he dragged her forcefully down, carpet burns ripping at the underside of her arms and scorching her belly, until she was between his legs. He then put his weight on her back, half-sitting on her, crushing her into the stairs, and grabbed a handful of her hair, pushing her head down and to the side so he could see half her face. She was trapped as he leant in towards her face.

'You must have known I wouldn't just let it go,' he sneered. 'You must have known that at some point I'd get even for all the embarrassment you've caused me.'

Joan didn't say anything; she couldn't if she'd tried. He was squashing her chest, so even breathing was hard, and his hand was pushing more of his weight onto her face. She felt the pressure shift from her cheeks to her jowls as he muttered his hatred into her face.

'I'm just going to keep you here a little while longer. Shouldn't take too much time now. Just long enough for us to be doing it at the moment your son dies.'

There had been many times in Joan's life she'd felt like she had reached the final straw or the straw that broke the camel's back. There had been times when she'd just given in, thinking life would be far easier if she just went with the flow. Those times she seemed like a different person, like someone who simply survived in a self-preservation society. In her own little bubble. Ignored by the majority. But that wasn't this Joan. This Joan no longer cared about her life at all. Sam couldn't hurt her now. She wasn't prepared to give up this time. She would not lose this fight.

She was going to wait until Sam became distracted as he tried to humiliate her. He'd probably lean close to her face again, and then she'd twist with all her strength in that direction, hopefully catching him unaware. He presumed, like always, that she would just accept her despoilment subserviently. He was wrong. She was gathering her strength. It was all or nothing now. She was going to fight back.

Sam leant in close whilst trying to force his way between her legs. He pulled her hair between his grubby fingers towards the side of her mouth. He went to use his finger to fish-hook her mouth. Big mistake.

Joan bit his finger like her son's life depended on it, like a starving animal offered a sausage. She was the secateurs cutting a rose-less thorn bush.

Sam howled as she wriggled around, teeth latched on to his finger, still between his legs but now facing him. She tried to kick him in the nuts, but he put his knees together and fell down towards her, so they were lying face to face, only separated by their flailing arms and fingers.

Joan was more angry, focused and desperate than at any time in her life. She aimed her fingers at his eyes, determined to inflict as much damage as possible.

'Damn you to hell, Joan!' Sam said.

'I'm here already!' Joan screamed, releasing his bloody finger from her jaws.

She jolted wildly like a rugby player, one hand reaching for his ear, hoping to rip it clean off. Sam fought back, pushing that arm back with both hands. Blood from his finger splattered up the wall and across their desperate faces.

Joan sent her free right hand up like a rocket, swinging it through the air, its trajectory a perfect arc. At the end of her arm, clenched in her balled fist, was the sgian dubh. Its beautiful jewel glimmered slightly as it continued its journey, until it came to an instant halt, having reached its destination with a satisfying 'flup': straight into the side of Sam's neck.

Rebecca arrived home to find her on/off boyfriend had moved on. Her bags were packed and waiting for her by the front door, whilst the happy couple sat nonchalantly eating dinner and watching TV. It was another highly embarrassing moment in her life. Anastasia had arrived and displaced her, and she felt like a ghost looking on at her previous life, like a person gawping at a fish tank in which her former self was swimming about.

Part of her wanted to rush around the apartment, checking for any valuables that she'd paid for, but the shame made standing there a moment longer almost unbearable. Her life had been packed away into three big travel bags, just like when she went skiing after university when she was little more than a student happily spending Daddy's money. She wasn't even sure how she could get the luggage, her life, her belongings, downstairs. She hadn't packed. Perhaps stuff would break. Carrying baggage was the sort of thing she would usually expect *him* to do for her. It was his job, like emptying the bins. Her bags were at the front door where she used to leave the rubbish for him to remove. She was being chucked out like rubbish.

'Can you at least carry the bags downstairs for me?' Rebecca called out, trying to sound a little bit helpless.

Her ex-boyfriend looked like he was about to offer some assistance, but then Anastasia calmly replied on his behalf.

'No.'

Nothing else. They just carried on ignoring her, leaving Rebecca feeling even more cut out and isolated.

She would have to call a cab and go straight to a hotel. She could try the old taxi firm the paper used. The account number was probably still the same. They knew her anyway, and she was sure they'd do her a favour.

She was mistaken: they declined to help her out. She offered to pay, which they appreciated, but they insisted on cash up front. She checked her wallet, sure she still had rolled-up notes from her session with chief minion Jamie from the sports desk. (It had all got a little bit kinky with him. He'd snorted cocaine off various parts of her anatomy whilst promising he wasn't giving Rebecca a sympathy seeing-to. *Oh, how the mighty have fallen,* he'd thought whilst degrading her in ways he never would have risked a few weeks earlier.)

Rebecca would have to get some cash from a cashpoint. She didn't know whether to run downstairs and grab some money whilst leaving her bags there, or just leave right then and try to drag them all by herself… one by one, down the full five flights of concrete stairs, clattering on every step, announcing to all the neighbours, 'The bitch is leaving.' She had never made friends with anyone else in the block. She felt they were all beneath her. They were all silly hipsters, whereas she saw herself as a high flier, slightly more home counties; she was more Chelsea or Surrey than Hoxton.

She didn't know what she was any more. Neither did she know where to go. She thought Jamie might be an option, but his fiancée was due back any moment, and she wouldn't really appreciate Rebecca gate-crashing their happy reunion. Plus, she'd think it strangely suspicious that some old work colleague had turned up and there was a change of bed linen. Jamie had never changed the bed.

Her daddy was abroad. Perhaps... *Oh God, the shame!* she thought. Her only immediate option appeared to be her brother.

Any journeys or expenses would have to go on her plastic. Rebecca had no idea what her overdraft limit was or how long she could keep spending on credit cards. This was all new territory for her. She would have to try to call Daddy and ask for another emergency loan. He'd sounded pretty adamant the last time she'd tried. She would have to tell him she was virtually living on the streets.

Perhaps she should contact the council or something. Maybe they'd give her a house. Maybe she would need to sign on. Was she entitled to any benefits? Rebecca had no idea. Outside on the street she looked at a bedraggled-looking Eastern European selling *The Big Issue*. She wasn't far off that situation. Surely her dad wouldn't allow her to sleep on a park bench? She could put on several layers of clothes to keep warm.

Rebecca's dad wouldn't give her any money. He'd heard through his contacts what had happened at the paper and was ashamed. She had humiliated him. He'd even had a row with James, asking why he hadn't informed him about Rebecca's predicament.

James had told him the truth: 'Dad, you've always sided with Rebecca. You think the sun shines out of her arse. She reminds you of her mum or something, but I bet she wasn't like Rebecca. She's not a nice person. You never listened to me. Until it came from your old work pals, you never considered anything I said. Well, now you know. I tried to tell you. I've been trying to tell you for years, but you never listened.'

Rebecca pulled up in the taxi looking a little like a tramp. James and his other half watched from the front window. 'Good luck,' said his boyfriend as James made his way outside.

He dug out the cash from his wallet to pay for Rebecca's taxi, and grabbed the two bags from the boot and the one on the passenger seat. James thanked the driver on Rebecca's behalf. She managed to forget to say 'please' or 'thank you' to both the driver and James for their help and service. She just stood staring at the house.

James prepared himself for another catty comment. He kept reminding himself that no matter how desperate and disgusting she was, she was still his sister, so he would take her in – he would do what was right. He was cooking before she had arrived, whilst his boyfriend, the good-looking one from the IT department, sat on the sofa watching rubbish TV and stroking a King Charles spaniel called Vashti.

James left one bag by the front door and took one, and Rebecca took the other. He showed her to the spare room in the house, which

Rebecca had never seen. She had never visited. She had no idea he had such a cute little home. It was warm, light and very tidy. Old, heavily lacquered wooden floorboards creaked slightly underfoot. All the rooms were painted in very light pastel colours. The house felt cosy and loved and grown-up. On the wall of her room were various photos of family and friends with James and his partner, and even their dad. There was also a canvas on the wall of his real mum, looking beautiful and young. The house was very homely and it left her feeling very inadequate.

James stood in the doorway and said, 'Can I get you anything? We're cooking dinner. There'll be plenty for you as well.'

Rebecca wasn't sure what to say; she was feeling slightly humbled. 'Is he your boyfriend?' she said, struggling to repay his generosity.

'Nearly three years now,' said James proudly.

'Nice,' said Rebecca.

That would do for one day, James thought.

'Quite the little homemaker, aren't we?' said Rebecca, the old bitch side of her threatening to bite the hand…

'It's home, we like it and we're happy,' said James defensively.

'I mean, it's really grown-up. You've surprised me, that's all,' said Rebecca, trying to soften her previous comment. 'Actually, have you got any pain relief or alcohol? I've got a splitting headache,' she lied.

Rebecca was standing outside the hospital having had her stomach pumped, feeling empty, lonely and useless. She sucked on a cigarette as an ambulance pulled into the hospital and she noticed her sorry reflection: dressed in a hospital gown, she looked white and dishevelled.

As the vehicle pulled to a halt and the rear doors opened, the driver and doctors appeared, flanking a trolley that emerged from within. Following the nurses was Joan, covered in blood. The ambulance staff pushed the gurney into the hospital, with a terrified, grief-stricken Joan following straight after.

Rebecca tried to see if it was Sam on the barrow, straight away thinking Joan had probably hurt him. But instead she saw a young man she recognised, as if she'd had seen somewhere before, in a movie or in another life. He looked like an angel. His face was a pale but he was conscious. He looked at Rebecca, and she at him.

Suddenly, she felt responsible, responsible for everything. It was all her fault. Perhaps she should go and help Joan. She felt overwhelmed. Everyone, including her dad and brother, would probably hate her now. What had she done? She had ruined Joan and Sam and William's life, and pretty much killed Stuart.

Still the man stared at her, like he knew everything. He stared into her world, and then blinked, as if he knew and understood. And at that moment Rebecca felt her knees go weak and she dry-retched. She couldn't help but smile back as he was whisked away and the sliding doors shut. Rebecca wasn't sure, but it felt like he couldn't take his eyes off her, like he didn't want to lose sight of her.

Adam tried to lift his head as he entered the building, but he couldn't. He wanted to wave his hands or wiggle his fingers, but the pain was too much. He didn't want to die – he wanted to see her again. She looked vulnerable and he felt sorry for her.

As the ambulance staff and Joan had whisked Adam into the hospital through the sliding doors, a piece of paper had fallen off the trolley. Rebecca walked back into the hospital, picking up the paper as she went. There was a splodge of blood, almost like a circle, covering one of the rush hour crushes.

23751512R00282

Printed in Poland
by Amazon Fulfillment
Poland Sp. z o.o., Wrocław